THE ETERNAL TRAVELLER

HELEN HUBER

Cover designed by Miblart

This is a work of fiction. Names, entities, and incidents included in this story are products of the author's imagination. Any resemblance to actual persons, events and entities is entirely coincidental.

Copyright © Helen Huber 2024

All rights reserved. No part of this publication may be reproduced, stored in a retrieval system, or transmitted, in any form or by any means (electronic, mechanical, photocopying, recording or otherwise) without the prior permission of the author.

Dedicated to:
My husband, Mike; Karen Turner, Maggie Kenny, and all my friends at BBE

Chapter 1

Iona nudged the front door shut with her elbow and hobbled around the packing cartons strewn down the length of the dim hallway. She carried her shopping into the kitchen and, dumping the bags onto the table, fished the kettle from a cardboard box. Filling it at the sink, she gazed out the window at the dismal view of the industrial estate beyond her low-rise apartment block.

Her father had always advised his daughters to invest in bricks and mortar should the opportunity arise. Though far from ideal, the flat was the best the accident compensation monies could buy.

As a collateral victim of the accident, its randomness irked her most. Through sheer bad luck, she had walked below high scaffolding as a builder plummeted from atop. Although blithely unaware until he hit her, Iona inadvertently cushioned the man's fall, costing her several broken bones and torn muscles. Even after three operations and intensive physiotherapy, she still walked with a limp.

Still, at least the flat had decent-sized rooms, and a coat of white paint and daylight lamps throughout should lighten the gloomy interior.

Two days after the decorators finished, Iona's sister, Skye, helped organise her home office in the windowless room between the bedroom and bathroom. Since Iona created her graphic designs for the gaming and publishing industries with computer software, she didn't require the natural light necessary to paint in acrylics and watercolours as she'd done before.

When they crossed to the large lounge/diner typical of 1960s flats, Skye stood with hands on hips and surveyed the half-filled, brand-new bookcases with satisfaction. "You know my opinion on your choice of location, but at least you have space for all those books in storage."

"Is that a hint for me to remove them from your garage as soon as possible?" Iona replied with a wry smile.

"No, don't worry. Dave and I will bring them over in the van at the weekend."

As Iona walked her sister to the front door, she almost mentioned the estate agent had advised her the area was up-and-coming, but she knew it for salespersons patter that would earn her a pitying look.

The next day, Iona sat at the kitchen table with her coffee. As rain sheeted down the windowpane, she perused the free local newspaper she'd found shoved through her letterbox, surprised that hard copies still existed in this age of online news. Flicking past the lonely hearts and situations' vacant pages, her eye alighted on an advert:

'Borderland Incorporated seeks a volunteer to test a revolutionary new exercise apparatus for eight months. Only those recuperating from injuries that affect mobility are eligible to participate. Apply if you have an EMPTY room in your home where we can install the equipment. The room must have bare walls and be devoid of ANY furniture. Please log on to our website and complete the application form for the chance to take part in our trials and rebuild your strength.'

Iona wondered at the lack of details. Why bare walls? She pictured a Heath Robinson contraption of pulleys and weights or perhaps a climbing wall. Still, she might have considered applying if she had an empty room. Though her physio sessions ended a month ago, Iona's therapist had suggested she invest in a treadmill or exercise bike, but she hadn't got around to it. Borderland Incorporated seemed an incongruous name for a medical equipment company, but she might check out their website later.

She stood and, placing her mug in the sink, returned to her office, where she worked steadily on her fourth book cover for a moderately successful indie author. The writer had communicated her vision, and Iona quite enjoyed 'painting' the severed head in the toilet bowl, particularly the broken veins in its staring eyes. However, as usual, she had created another, less gruesome cover for *The Lavatory Murders*, the latest in the *Inspector Yolanda Bird* series. As always, the author would no doubt choose her alternative, which depicted a toilet with blood oozing from beneath the closed lid to puddle onto the floor. But Iona must still enact the ritual of presenting two concepts. Until she saw both illustrations, the client never quite grasped that her more extreme ideas better-suited horror than police procedural thriller.

Three hours later, Iona stretched. As she rose from her chair, her gammy leg almost gave way beneath her, and she abruptly sat down again. She kneaded her thigh and stared around the room. Perhaps she could temporarily move the office into the lounge. Even with all the bookcases, the diner end had plenty of room.

She dined in the kitchen, and food eaten, reached across the table for the newspaper and her laptop. Though the Borderland Incorporated website proved uninformative about the equipment involved in the trials, Iona established the company had a sound track record, and completed the online application form, detailing her injuries.

Iona had almost forgotten about her application when she received an email two weeks later, congratulating her on its success. Borderland planned to install the apparatus in four days' time and, in a panic, she called

Skye.

Her sister had nagged her for weeks to follow the physiotherapist's advice and said, "At last! Dave and I will help you clear the office, though it seems odd you can't even hang a picture on the wall."

"Thanks! But I've got a hospital check-up on the day they plan to deliver," Iona fretted.

"Next Tuesday you said? Dave's not doing anything that day. If you give him your spare key, he won't mind hanging around the flat while the equipment is installed."

"Okay, great. I've been meaning to give you the spare key in case of emergencies."

Skye's husband, Dave, had left by the time Iona returned from the hospital. She quickly limped to the windowless office and opened the door to behold a solitary exercise bike in the room's centre. Was that it? Surely not. Perhaps the rest of the equipment would arrive later. Iona texted Dave, who confirmed the installation workers had finished.

She switched on the overhead light and examined the peculiar bike. It had three wheels like a tricycle rather than the single front wheel sported by most exercise bikes. A short but sturdy support frame slotted into a thin, rectangular groove cut into the worn lino around the machine and held the – mountain bike? – tyres in suspension two inches above the floor. A yellow light blinked ominously on the black frame of the computer monitor mounted between the handlebars. Iona picked up an envelope balanced on the saddle and tore it open to read the letter within:

'Dear Ms Abernathy,

Congratulations on your selection as the test volunteer of Borderland's miraculous new curative and fitness technology.

Statistics show that up to half of all exercise equipment is abandoned within six weeks of purchase as enthusiasm wanes. As you will discover when your new physio regime begins, our product encourages long-term usage by offering a unique incentive to continue.

The trike is fitted with sensors that monitor impact, cardio, blood pressure, and other functions. It uses AI technology to self-regulate your fitness program, communicating with you via the onboard computer. It is important you follow instructions to the letter. If you continue beyond the advised time per session, the trike will automatically switch off. It will not restart until the next allotted session.

Please ensure you close the trike room door before you begin a workout. Once you press the 'start' toggle above the yellow light, do not dismount for ANY reason, until you have switched it off again.

Happy cycling!'

Iona frowned and re-read the letter. Despite the cheerful sign-off, it struck her as vaguely sinister. What would happen if she ignored the instructions or alighted from the trike without switching it off? It seemed odd Borderland had included no explanation. And why must she shut the door? Returning the letter to the envelope, she flipped off the overhead light switch and exited the room. As she closed the door, the yellow monitor light seemed to wink balefully in the darkness like the eye of some feral beast.

The next morning, Iona decided she'd overreacted. No doubt the computer recorded statistics important to her training program that the development team could access from head office. There would be no point in the trial if they couldn't monitor her progress. Perhaps dismounting from the trike before switching off disrupted the sensor feed and she must give a clear signal the session had ended so the computer could collate the results.

After breakfast, Iona dressed in leggings and a t-shirt. Entering the windowless room, she switched on the overhead light and closed the door. She settled onto the trike's wide, comfortable saddle and took a deep breath before flipping the toggle. The light turned green, and the weird Borderland logo of a centaur with wheels in place of legs flashed onto the screen.

The logo vanished, and a caterpillar of words scrolled across the monitor. *'Good morning, Iona. Your first session will be short at fifteen minutes, during which I will assess your fitness level. You must not over-extend too soon, but gradually rebuild muscular strength in your back and leg. When the light turns blue, please start pedalling. The session will end when the light reverts to green. DO NOT ALIGHT UNTIL THE LIGHT FLASHES YELLOW AFTER YOU SWITCH OFF.'*

"Do you have a name?" Iona said flippantly, thinking of all the AI interfaces in science fiction books and movies characterised by a moniker. She didn't expect it to hear her, and her eyes widened in surprise when another string of words crawled across the screen. *'Not yet, but I am sure you will think of one. Shall we begin?'*

Was that sarcasm? The light turned blue and Iona pedalled. After two revolutions, the support frame suddenly sank into the floor groove. As the wheels came to rest atop it, the walls and ceiling vanished……

Poppy carpeted meadows stretched away to either side of the hard-packed dirt road upon which the trike now travelled. A skylark sung in blue skies scattered with fleecy clouds and the wooded slopes of distant hills edged the horizon to front and sides.

Iona abruptly stopped pedalling, but the scene didn't vanish and the blue light continued to glow on the frame of the now-blank monitor. She gripped the handles and tried to calm her breathing. Though her surroundings appeared solid and *real,* they *must* be no more than a highly advanced virtual reality projection. Iona felt tempted to step from the trike to discover if she could feel the room walls beneath the illusion, but remembered the warning about dismounting before the light turned yellow. Instead, she resumed pedalling, and the trike advanced smoothly along the road. Iona glanced back over her shoulder and observed that, like the walls, floor and ceiling, the room door had disappeared, and the road extended behind her, bordered with green pastures.

Beyond the meadows, Iona cycled past tilled fields bounded by foxglove-strewn hedges before the road passed through a tunnel formed by the overarching branches of tall trees lining both verges. It felt cool beneath their sun-dappled shade, and she marvelled at the VR technology that could even produce temperature fluctuations and sound effects. As she exited the grove at a bend in the road, Iona spotted a wooden bridge spanning a brook up ahead. Carved statues topped the bridge's stone piers, but before she got close enough to discern them clearly, the monitor came to sudden life. *'Your time is up. Please switch off to end the session.'*

Iona stopped pedalling and gazed longingly at the statues. If she cycled just a little farther, she should be able to make them out. However, the blue light flashed in warning, and Iona reluctantly pressed the off button. The bucolic scene vanished, replaced with the white walls and ceiling of her windowless office. As the monitor light turned green, the support frame emerged from the floor groove and locked into place, raising the wheels to their former position. Another string of words scrolled across the screen. *'Return here at the same time tomorrow morning for your next session.'*

Before Iona could question the AI, the light reverted to yellow, and the monitor went dark. She stared at in disbelief; she needed an explanation. Iona felt tempted to log on again, but there had been a finality to the shutdown that told her she must wait until tomorrow for answers. She dismounted from the trike and examined every inch of the room, but found no hidden technology to account for her experience. Concluding the effects originated from the exercise machine, perhaps powered by tech concealed within the floor groove, Iona switched off the overhead light and went to take a shower.

As she stood beneath the water jet, Iona wondered if she would view a different scene during the second session and found herself hoping for a continuation of today's 'journey'. The bridge statues had aroused her curiosity.

When Iona entered the kitchen to grab a pre-work coffee, she stared out the window at the depressing view; it was raining again. The rain didn't let up all day, and Iona couldn't help longing for the balmy summer skies and verdant landscape of that make-believe world.

Chapter 2

The following morning, Iona mounted the trike with eager anticipation.

She switched on, and, as before, the light turned green before the rather unsettling Borderland logo briefly flashed onto the screen to be replaced with scrolling words. *'Good morning, Iona. Today's session will be a little longer at 20 minutes.'*

"Fine, but I need to know more about the unexpected sideshow. Why didn't you warn me? Is it some form of virtual reality?" Iona asked.

'We prefer to call it hyper-reality. It is still in the testing stage and by not preparing you, we could gauge your Pavlovian response to the stimulus.'

Before Iona could ask what that meant, the light waxed blue as though to prevent further questions, and she had to pedal.

When the wheels sank to the floor groove, she again found herself 'travelling' on the hard-packed dirt path with the bridge in the near distance. The road led directly to the wooden span and continued on the other side. Glancing over her shoulder, she beheld the tree tunnel she had emerged from at the cessation of her previous session. Iona faced forward and had a sudden idea. She had noted how the trike seemed to follow curves in the road, and though she couldn't dismount until the workout finished, perhaps she could test the limits of the trike's trajectory. Iona tried without success to deviate from the path's centre. As she had suspected, the machine appeared tied to some invisible track, and she reminded herself that the road was an illusion, and the trike remained fixed to her office floor.

Iona drew close to the bridge and saw the two piers facing her each bore a weathered stone centaur carved *sejant affrontée*, arms folded, with one fore-hoof resting atop a ducal coronet. They seemed a little grand for such a rustic bridge and as she cycled between them onto the wooden span, she couldn't dismiss the notion she crossed a border. She paused at the halfway point and raised herself up to peer over the low rail at the brook, burbling between smooth round stones slick with moss. Dragonflies flitted over the glinting water and, in the shadows beneath overhanging trees, something plopped into the stream with a splash. Iona resumed pedalling and on regaining the road, observed the piers on this side also supported centaur statues. However, they stood erect, each holding a large shield displaying a heraldic device of three overlapping wheels that formed a triangle.

Through the Hawthorn and Alder interspersed along the road verges, Iona glimpsed figures toiling in distant fields. Easing around a bend in the path, she spotted woodsmoke coiling lazily into the air beyond the next turn. The smoke proved to originate from the chimney of a half-timbered inn, surrounded by wattle and daub cottages with thatched roofs. Chickens scratched in the dirt, and a well stood in the centre of a trampled patch of browning grass. A faint reek of manure hung in the still air, and a dog barked in the distance.

    As Iona cycled through the hamlet, two men wearing rough homespun in the style of mediaeval peasants emerged from the inn. One raised a hand in greeting, and she almost returned it before realising he stared straight through her to wave at a woman clothed in kirtle, apron, and coif, who, bucket in hand, approached the well. Iona shook her head at her own folly; of course, they couldn't see her. Despite how tangible this pseudo-reality appeared; it was only a projection.

    Leaving the settlement behind, she pedalled onward between high hedgerows seeded with a profusion of harebells, mallow, and toadflax. The sun beat down from a cloudless sky and she felt its warmth caress her bare arms. All too soon, the blue console light flashed to signal the end of the session, just as she espied more roofs in the distance. With a disappointed sigh, Iona toggled the off switch, and the bare walls and ceiling of her office replaced the pastoral scene. A perfunctory message scrolled across the screen informing her to return on the morrow for another twenty-minute session. As before, the monitor went blank before she could interrogate the AI.

    "Thanks for nothing," Iona muttered as she climbed from the saddle. This time, she felt a dull ache in her damaged leg and felt no surprise at the planned, short duration of the third session. She must exercise patience and regain some of her former fitness before the AI interface would allow her to remain in the artificial world for an extended period.

Skye called just as Iona finished her dinner that evening. "Hey, how are you getting on with the new fitness regime? Dave said the equipment is merely a very odd-looking exercise bike and can't understand why we had to clear the room just for that!"

    Iona hesitated. Without knowing why, she felt reluctant to mention the experiment's virtual reality aspect and found herself saying, "Oh, there's a mindfulness slant to the program. It's about creating blank space in which to exercise both body and mind without familiar visual distractions." Well, that didn't sound *too* far from the truth, she thought.

    "Okaay… it sounds a bit 'new age' but so long as it works for you. Anyway, I just wanted to check in before Dave and I go on holiday. We have to be up at five in the morning to catch our flight," Skye said with a groan.

    "You don't need to worry about me. I'll be fine. I've got a couple of new commissions to work on. Just concentrate on having a good time. It shouldn't be difficult; Turkey is lovely at this time of year!"

Iona retrieved her slip-on trainers from the doormat the next morning and donned them in the office. She felt an urge to assert control, so after switching on the trike monitor, she waited until the logo vanished and spoke before the usual greeting could scroll across the screen, "I will address you henceforth as Troy."

'Troy?' the AI texted.

"Yes. That's your new name, inspired by your logo." The screen cursor pulsed steadily as though the interface awaited an explanation, and Iona elaborated, "Centaurs are half man, half horse, are they not? I'm not sure why, but the wheels in place of legs made me think of the siege of Troy and the Trojan horse."

'Troy it is then,' the words appeared as the green light turned blue to signal the end of the conversation and the start of the session. When the trike wheels descended to the groove, Iona again found herself between the hedgerows, aimed towards the roofs she had spotted at the end of yesterday's workout.

Iona cycled until she reached the outskirts of a village larger than the hamlet she had previously passed through. Pausing to gaze down the rutted street at the houses, barns, and animal pens clustered around a church, she caught a whiff of baking bread, roasting meat, woodsmoke, and human excrement carried on an errant breeze. Iona resumed pedalling, following the contour of the road past the church at the village centre and glimpsed a small manor house on a slight rise at the village's extremity. She admired its half-timber/half-herringbone patterned brick façade but abruptly ceased cycling when a squealing pig, chased by a small boy, barrelled towards her. At the last minute, they swerved unseeing around the trike, directed by an unknown force. Iona marvelled anew at the encompassing nature of the clever technology that made her feel part of the artifice, even though she remained invisible to the virtual inhabitants.

Moving at a leisurely pace, Iona watched the villagers going about their tasks before, passing between a blacksmith and a mill, complete with millpond and waterwheel, she pedalled out of the village.

The trike console emitted a beep and, glancing down, Iona read the message that scrolled across the screen. *'Your time is up, but since you have stopped twice and cycled at a snail's pace, you can have an extra ten minutes to get those legs pumping.'*

"You shouldn't make the panorama – or is it diorama? – so diverting if you want me to concentrate on my spins," Iona replied tartly, her attention distracted again by two ducks that waddled past, heading to the reed-bordered millpond.

Troy declined to respond, and the monitor went dark. Iona sighed and accelerated between tilled fields towards a stand of trees that straddled the road.

With just seven minutes left until the session ended, a dozen mounted men suddenly burst from the woods, galloping straight for Iona. As they drew nearer, she observed they bore arms – lances, swords and maces – and wore surcoats emblazoned with the three-wheel motif she had noted on the centaur statues' shields. Iona froze, her legs locking, feet glued to the pedals. Although she knew the horsemen were illusory, her eyes widened in fear as the steeds thundered towards her and Iona wondered if she would feel anything when they passed *through* her. However, at the last minute, they banked to each side of the trike in two columns, as though avoiding a boulder in the middle of the road. Unfreezing, she obeyed her flight instinct and pedalled away furiously when the last horse sped past. However, Iona soon realised the irrationality of her actions; after all, she cycled on the spot in the real world……

Coming to a stop, Iona smelled burning. Screams carried on the wind, and turning around in the saddle, her foot slipped off one pedal when she saw flames licking through the thatched roofs of the village buildings. Even though Iona remained on the trike, she hastily drew her foot back up, not wishing to infringe the non-dismount rule. Since she rode a three-wheeler, she didn't need to touch a foot to the ground for balance. She stared at the firestorm with sick horror, the wails and shrieks almost drowning out the insistent 'time-up' monitor beeps.

Turning back to the console and the flashing blue light, she slammed the off switch. As the light turned green, the scene vanished, and panting, Iona stared at the bare, white walls of her office. Her eye snagged on the cursory message. '*25 minutes, same time tomorrow*,' and she almost screamed in frustration when the screen turned black and the light reverted to yellow.

"You've got to be kidding me!" she exclaimed and hammered at the 'on' switch. However, the monitor remained stubbornly blank and, slumping in defeat, Iona held her head in her hands. Her legs trembled when she at last dismounted, and she didn't notice her muddy footprint on the lino when she switched off the light and left the room.

Chapter 3

Iona hesitated before the closed office door the next morning but didn't enter the room. After breakfast, she went straight to her desk in the lounge and spent several hours working on advertising material for *The Lavatory Murders*. After lunch, she returned to her desk, resolutely refusing to even look at the closed door as she passed.

She printed out the specs for another commission, and stared at it sightlessly, her mind returning to the disturbing trike session. Perhaps she ought to call Borderland Incorporated and ask them to remove the apparatus. Irresolute, Iona shook her head to dismiss the vision of the sacked village, but the smell of burning thatch still pervaded her nostrils. How could the villagers – simple farming folk – have prevailed against armed knights? She again had to remind herself that none were real and tried to focus instead on the task at hand.

So, when her friend, Zara, called, it was with relief that she accepted an invitation to drinks that night; it might take her mind off the distressing experience. Zara worked at the commercial art agency that Iona occasionally freelanced for, though they had first met at art college. Other friends, some of whom she had not seen since her freak accident, would also attend, and though Iona looked forward to seeing them, she also felt a little nervous. Although she no longer required a walking stick, her limp made her self-conscious, and she rarely went out these days.

As Iona pulled the front door closed behind her, she spotted a yellow light flashing under the office door in the thin gap above the floorboards, bright in the dim hallway. She ignored it but only made it as far as the car park before she retraced her steps, knowing that unless she investigated, anxiety would spoil her evening.

The radiance continued to throb, and as Iona stood with her hand on the office doorknob, she bit her lip. Squaring her shoulders, Iona opened the door and observed the trike's yellow console light lit up like a beacon. She switched on the ceiling bulb and the monitor beam dimmed to normal and ceased to flicker. Iona blinked twice and her eye snagged on the footprint beside the trike. She gasped and inched forward; the dried mud bore the imprint of her trainer. Only then did she notice a couple of other, almost imperceptible prints leading away from the trike. However, before any absurd notions could fully take root, she marked that the trike's tyres appeared pristine, with no sign of dirt or wear. She must have trod in something when she nipped to the corner shop the evening before last, after which she had removed her trainers at the front door.

Even though the flashing light had seemed a summons, she had no real expectation that the monitor would respond as she mounted to the saddle; after all, she had missed the designated time slot. However, when she pressed the start button, the screen immediately came to life as though Troy had been waiting for her.

'I take it you disliked our little drama?' the words scrolled across the screen.

"Disliked? It was hideous! What were you thinking?!"

'My apologies. As I said before, the product is still at the test stage, and we must experiment with different immersive experiences to gauge those most likely to encourage users to persevere with their exercise program.'

"Take it from me, *that* particular adventure is guaranteed to drive away anyone but a complete psycho!"

'I am suitably chastened. Would you like to proceed now with this morning's postponed session?'

Iona retrieved her mobile from her pocket and checked the time. She had missed her bus, though *could* catch the next one, but would arrive late. "Okay, but no more shenanigans! I need to make a phone call first." She would give Troy one last chance. So quickly had Iona become hooked on the virtual world that, despite everything, she needed another fix.

She called Zara and said, "Sorry Zara, but I'm not going to make it. I've received a last-minute rush job that the client needs by tomorrow, and I can't afford to turn it down." Though out of character, she had lied so easily; first to Skye and now to Zara. After promising to attend next month's get-together, Iona said goodbye to her disappointed friend and removed her jacket. Though less than ideal for an exercise session, her jeans, blouse, and pixie boots wouldn't hamper movement too much.

When the rural landscape replaced the bare walls of her office, Iona found she had arrived close to sunset. The acrid odour of sulphur mixed with smoke assaulted her nostrils, underlain with a sickly-sweet aroma that made her retch. Iona cast a fearful glance over her shoulder and observed the silhouettes of charred beams in the distance. She could have done without the effects, but guessed Troy didn't wish to compromise the integrity of the created reality. Iona cycled forth through the light coating of ash that blanketed the muddy road, churned up by the horses' hooves, presumably when they departed the scene. She soon approached the road-straddling wood the riders had materialised from and shivered as she passed within. The blue monitor light brightened to an intensity that pierced the gloom under the boughs, and the song of birds coming home to roost sounded oddly reassuring.

By the time Iona emerged from the wood, she had left behind the smell. As she continued onward between drystone walls bordering heathland, sunset stained the sky with a luminosity she had never witnessed in the real world. Gazing into the heavens that shaded from deep violet to magenta, golden yellow and crimson, her eye snagged on a winged form that wheeled and dipped gracefully above the far-off hills. The huge avian had bat-like wings and a serpentine neck and tail and, bug-eyed, Iona knew she beheld a dragon. As darkness fell, the silhouette sinuously looped-the-loop, and disappeared behind the hills. Iona pondered if Troy had conjured up the wondrous creature to make up for the earlier gaffe. With full dark, the blue light flashed to signal the session's end.

During the next ten days, Iona's trike sessions increased to twice daily, and she already felt the benefits; her weak leg now bore her weight with greater ease.

She occasionally passed other road travellers, some on foot, but usually mounted on horses or carts, but like the knights, they swerved to avoid her if their paths seemed likely to cross. None acknowledged her presence and she would have felt shocked if they did. Now and then, the road wended through small settlements, some more prosperous than others. Iona once passed a deserted, burnt-out village, but the weeds growing in and around the buildings indicated the calamity had befallen some time ago. Still, she wondered why Troy had not 'erased' it. The beauty of the countryside and novelty of the mediaeval 'scene-setting' proved stimulus enough for her (even if the areas of human habitation smelled a bit whiffy). She twice more saw the dragon perform its acrobatics at sunset, and it remained the highlight of her 'journey', so lifelike did it appear.

By the tenth day, the hills had drawn nearer, and Iona now discerned high, purple peaks beyond. She drew nigh to the biggest conglomeration of buildings she had yet seen, sited beneath a hilltop castle. Iona knew she approached a town and must brace for the stink. The road, partially paved here, melded into cobblestones, and as the trike trundled over them, Iona stared at the narrow buildings. Their upper storeys, constructed of timber and plaster painted black and white, projected over the insalubrious streets and alleys, the cobbles slimy with human waste, horse manure and rotting vegetable matter. Most structures had latticed windows, the small, diamond-shaped glass inserts thick and almost opaque.

The road cut through a large square and, judging by the stalls around the perimeter, surrounded by the close press of bustling humanity, Iona guessed she had arrived on market day. Iona tried not to breathe in the reeking cocktail of open cesspits, unwashed bodies, sweat and animal manure, overlain with the rather more pleasant aroma of herbs, spices and cut flowers. She ceased pedalling to pull off the towel draped around her neck and, wrapping it around her lower face, made a mental note to advise Troy to tone down the olfactory effects.

Iona studied the stalls with fascination, noting the array of merchandise for sale: fruit and vegetables, live poultry and rabbits in cramped cages, tools, utensils and weapons, pottery and baskets, herbs both dried and fresh, fabric by the yard, second-hand clothes and jewellery, plus pelts and leather goods. Behind the stalls, booths housed cutlers, chandlers, cobblers, moneylenders and scribes for hire. Iona absorbed it all, her eyes darting from the large hostelry that dominated the square to the blacksmith, bakery, and inn on the opposite side. The musical instruments of mummers performing on a dais combined with hawkers loudly touting their wares, and the shouts of barkers and barterers, to form a cacophony of near-overwhelming noise, punctuated by the rumble of cartwheels over the cobbles.

Despite the density of people, Iona remained an invisible, moving island as she slowly cycled amidst the throng, unconsciously avoided by all who passed close. She paused again to peer down a side street at another square that contained a corn exchange and livestock market, wishing she had the flexibility to explore.

Iona had resumed her progress when a young man with unruly blonde hair suddenly burst from an alley, pursued by two men clothed in tabards emblazoned with the three-wheel insignia she had seen before on the knights' surcoats. Weaving between the stalls, the man kicked over a stack of crates in an effort to impede his chasers. As apples tumbled from the crates to roll underfoot, the irate stallholder roared and shook his fist at the man's back. The fugitive leaped over a small handcart – straight into the arms of a third guardsman, who appeared from nowhere. His fellows caught up and tackled their quarry to the ground. They forced his arms behind his back, and when they hauled him upright, Iona had drawn level.

Wide-eyed, the man's gaze locked with Iona's and then travelled over the trike. As his captors marched him to a cage built onto a wagon, he continued to glance back at her over his shoulder until they shoved him within. Two of the guards mounted to the seat beside the driver, and the wagon rolled towards an archway between two buildings at the square's far side. The prisoner gripped the cage bars and stared at Iona until the wagon vanished into the short passage beneath the arch.

How could the man, an illusion like everyone else, have seen her? It should not be possible. Suddenly galvanised, Iona pedalled at speed towards the archway but just as she gained the passageway, the blue monitor light pulsed in the session-end signal. Iona ignored it but got no farther than the interior before the trike switched off automatically, as Borderland's letter had warned her would happen if she exceeded the allotted time. Frustrated, Iona found herself back in her windowless office and, as usual, Troy had gone incommunicado.

Iona took a couple of deep, calming breaths and reasoned that the man couldn't *really* have seen her. His apparent awareness must be yet another experiment, designed to enhance the interactive experience for the trike user and make it even more addictive. If that was the case, it had worked; she felt eager to follow the man's story but must wait until tomorrow. A scheduled after-dinner Zoom meeting with a prospective new client had forced Iona to cancel that evening's trike session.

She went to the kitchen to stick on some washing before she showered, and toeing off her slip-on trainers, added them to the laundry.

The meeting resulted in a new commission, and the next morning, Iona felt full of vim and vigour as she slid her feet into her pixie boots (the trainers still felt damp) and snatched a bottle of water from the fridge. Today, Troy would allow her an hour-long session for the first time, and she must keep hydrated. With nowhere to rest the bottle on the trike, Iona tied her zip-up hoodie around her waist and, sticking the water in the hood, pulled the drawstring tight before she hastened to the office and mounted up.

When the passageway manifested around her, she cycled forth into an area of town more salubrious than the rest. The main road, paved here rather than cobbled, was swept clear of the refuse which soiled the streets elsewhere, though a hint of the square's odoriferous bouquet filtered through the archway. Iona admired the spacious buildings with their barley-twist chimneys and studded oak doors, their facades, eaves and lintels decorated with carved or sculpted flora, fauna and mythical beasts in wood, plaster or stone. The invisible cycle track bypassed a marble fountain where women clad in colourful velvet kirtles over fine linen chemises, some wearing starched wimples, passed the time of day. Iona wondered how it would feel to dress in such attire – hot and restricting, no doubt.

The streets gradually narrowed again until the buildings closed around her, and the trike once more bumped over fetid cobblestones. When Iona reached the town limits, she discovered the road diverged, one arm curving around the hill's base, the other snaking up to the fortified castle on the summit. Iona halted and gazed upward as the castle's limp pennants fluttered in a sudden breeze and the flag atop the tallest tower snapped out to reveal the now familiar three-wheel device. She resumed pedalling, and the trike slipped onto the road that skirted the hill. However, she stopped again almost immediately when she spotted the young man who had *seen* her in the square.

He weaved down the castle road through the foot and cart traffic, accompanied by a tall, lanky fellow who carried a worn leather satchel. They gained the bottom and, within Iona's earshot, halted before a waiting man dressed in a dark-maroon monk's habit. The monk shook hands with the lanky fellow, who had ink-stained hands, then passed a black cloak to his companion. Iona watched the tall man stride away, his duty done, it seemed.

"Thanks for bailing me out again and standing surety," the young man said as he slipped the cloak over his shoulders.

The monk sighed and replied, "It's the last time I can do it. This *has* to stop; you *must* come to terms with your lot."

Hanging his head, the young man shuffled a foot in the road dust and nodded. He looked up, and with a start, caught sight of Iona. "There's something I need to do. I'll see you back at the priory," he informed the monk, who peered at him with mistrust, but shrugged and turned away.

When the monk had gone, the young man sidled over to Iona and, glancing around to check no one might spot him talking to himself, murmured, "Wait for me at the menhir stone, a quarter mile down this road."

Iona decided to play along with Troy's new game and, nodding her agreement, set off again.

The road ran parallel to the hill flank on her right, with a lower rise bordering its other side; both verges lined with boulders and scrubby vegetation. Iona sighted a tall megalith carved with spirals in a grassy bay between the rocks beneath the castle hill. She halted nearby and checked the digital clock at top left of the monitor – she only had twenty minutes left until her session ended. However, she didn't have long to wait before the young man jogged down the road towards her.

He halted near the megalith and said, "Won't you join me behind the menhir, so we can talk without fear of passersby believing I'm a madman who converses with shadows?"

Iona shook her head. "Sorry, I'm not allowed to dismount from the trike and it won't go where I direct it. It follows its own path."

The man nodded as though he already knew that. He removed his black cloak and, dropping it onto a boulder, approached her with a determined expression. Iona gasped as he seized her around the waist and hauled her off the trike, saying, "I'm sorry! I'm sorry! I've got no choice!"

Iona tried to cling onto the handlebars, but he was much stronger than her and she lost her grip – this man was no illusion!

He dumped her onto her ass and leaped into the trike's saddle. As he pedalled away, Iona scrambled to her feet, and he shouted, "The cloak! Look in the pocket!" And then he slammed the off switch and vanished.

Chapter 4

Iona stared aghast at the spot where the trike had disappeared, and instinctively backed towards the menhir, snatching up the cloak as she stumbled into its shadow. One part of her brain told her she would have hit the wall by now if she still occupied her office, and the other struggled not to go into meltdown.

A cart clattered into view, and Iona slipped around the menhir and slumped to the ground with her back against it – the man who stole her trike had not seemed to belong here, yet the (virtual?) people of this world could see him. Now she no longer had the trike's protection, they might become aware of her, too – if this wasn't one of Troy's tricks.

She would stand out like a sore thumb. Though her pixie boots bore a passing resemblance to certain footwear worn here – if one didn't look too closely at their manufacture – her hoodie and vest were another matter. In this pre-industrial culture, folks seemed liable to view elastic, zips and Lycra as the devil's work, and she had no desire for them to brand her a witch. She had observed men wearing hose not dissimilar to her brown leggings, though no one could mistake their soft jersey fabric for the silk or fine wool of the wealthier classes, or the serfs rough worsted – except from a distance. Besides, all the females wore long kirtles…

Suddenly feeling naked and exposed, Iona glanced at the cloak in her lap and, rising to her feet, swept it around her shoulders. Raising the hood, she peeked around the menhir in the forlorn hope that the trike had rematerialized, but with the cart's passing, the road remained empty. Iona fought off the knowledge that she might be stuck in this reality forever. Deep down, she knew this impossible world actually existed – somewhere…

With her back to the menhir, Iona slid to the ground again as panic threatened to engulf her. She dug up a handful of tussocky soil and let it trickle through her fingers. It not only *looked* real, but it *felt* real, and she remembered the footprint in her office. How could she have been so stupid? All that business with the furniture-free room and blank walls now seemed designed to deceive her. She had jumped to the conclusion it created a blank canvas for the virtual reality projection – just as Troy intended – and it had helped to waylay her suspicions. Iona *knew* it served no other purpose.

What would the thief do when he manifested in her flat? And Skye… Oh, God! Skye would return from her holidays in less than three days. If she didn't find a way back soon, her sister would report her missing and involve the police… but no, she couldn't think about that; she must concentrate on her next move – she couldn't stay hidden behind the menhir indefinitely.

Iona suddenly remembered what the young man had shouted and frantically searched the cloak for a pocket. She found none on the outside but felt a lump between the lining and the outer fabric. Reaching into the internal pocket, she extracted a soft leather drawstring purse and loosened the strings. It contained a silver coin and some coppers, all stamped with the three-wheel symbol; an iron key, a pencil stub, and a petrol station receipt. The last two items left her in no doubt that the thief came from her world. Iona smoothed out the receipt, which bore a pencilled message on the back. *'Go to the priory of Saint Aurigan and ask for Prior Fidelmus. Show him the key. Look under the mattress. The priory is behind the hill opposite the menhir, reached by a path a few yards beyond.'*

What mattress? Iona guessed the dearth of writing space accounted for the lack of detail. Could she trust the man who had stolen the trike? The monk might be part of some nefarious plot... But what other choice did she have?

Iona returned the objects to the purse and rose to her feet, legs trembling in aftershock. She reached for the water bottle, still inside the hood of the sweat top tied around her waist, but hesitated. Perhaps she should conserve it – considering the unsanitary living conditions, the water here might be unsafe to drink. Instead, she adjusted the cloak, which reached to her ankles, and slipped out from behind the menhir.

She glanced with caution up and down the road before she stepped onto it and continued past the menhir as instructed. Far in the distance, a mounted party approached, but she spotted the gravelly, tree-lined path just yards away and crossed the road towards it. A small, nervous internal voice told her it would be foolish to leave the roadside in case Troy came back for her. However, in a flash of insight, Iona guessed *that* Trojan horse couldn't penetrate this parallel reality (?) without a rider, and she carried on.

When the path curved around the hill out of sight of the road, Iona halted as delayed reaction set in. She clung to a tree trunk, her legs shaking as fear overwhelmed her at the enormity of her situation. Tears leaked from her eyes, but with an effort, she mastered herself before they could turn into full-blown sobs. After the year spent recuperating from her operations, she had plenty of practice. The dogged determination that had seen her through the worst of it then now reasserted, and she pushed away from the tree and wiped her eyes.

Iona resumed walking, and the path gently descended to a valley bisected by a sparkling river. The priory stood on the opposite bank, its arched windows glistening in the sunshine. Mellow stone softened the gothic architecture of the main building and the cluster of barns and stables to the east. The track continued to a timber truss, covered bridge, and Iona stepped onto it with a hammering heart. This was her last chance to turn back, but where would she go? She paused halfway along the bridge to peer from a round, glassless window, and watched two swans glide serenely beneath. Iona knew she procrastinated and forced herself to move on.

When she exited the structure, she followed another gravelled path that curved towards the priory's imposing, iron-bound doors, passing a long, narrow, single-storey building that abutted the corner of its western façade. Iona gazed up at the huge, stained-glass window above the entrance, which depicted a man, staff in hand, striding along a road, the cowl of his maroon habit obscuring his face – Saint Aurigan, she presumed. She mounted the wide flight of shallow stone steps and, before her courage could fail, yanked the iron ring attached to a chain suspended from a lever beside the lintel. A bell rang somewhere within the priory, and while she waited, Iona squinted up at the row of gargoyles beneath the roof gutters.

A hatch suddenly opened in the right-hand door, and an elderly monk with a grizzled tonsure and rheumy eyes peered out at her. "Yes?" he demanded.

"Erm, I'm here to see Prior Fidelmus."

"He's not yet returned from Tritaurium. What is your business?"

"I...I've something to show him; for his eyes only until he says otherwise," Iona blustered, not knowing if it was safe to allow just anyone to see the key.

"Mm, you had better come in and wait for him then," the doorkeeper said grudgingly and slammed the hatch shut.

The right door-leaf opened just wide enough for Iona to slip through, and the old monk led her to a small room with whitewashed walls and a single wooden bench.

"Don't leave this room. Someone will come to fetch you when Prior Fidelmus returns. He shouldn't be too much longer."

"Thank you, Brother...?"

"Brother Hildebrandt," the monk replied curtly, and departed.

Iona sat on the bench. Assuming Prior Fidelmus was the monk she had seen with the trike thief, Tritaurium must be the town she had cycled through. She had psyched herself up to meet him, but the delay caused her nerves to get the better of her. She twisted her hands in her lap and glanced up at the small latticed window, high on the wall above the bench. Iona stood and climbed onto the pew to peer out.

The room backed onto a colonnaded quadrangle; the centre open to the skies. A life-sized statue of Saint Aurigan with his walking staff occupied a plinth in the middle of the grassy space. Within the eastern cloister, Iona spotted a chapel and, judging by the comings and goings, what might be the chapter house. A monk crossed the lawn, and passing into the western cloister, entered a door, to emerge chewing on a chunk of bread. Perhaps the long structure she glimpsed behind the columns served as the refectory, though Iona had little knowledge of religious establishments. A large building stood on the quadrangle's northern side, in the centre of which a tower arose, with a gated archway beneath.

Iona climbed down from the bench to pace the room anxiously. She whirled at the sound of the door opening, hastily arranging the black cloak to conceal her clothing. Iona recognised the monk she had seen with the thief, her eyes drawn to the amulet on a long chain around his neck, a bronze wheel encircled with a sinuous dragon swallowing its own tail. She had expected to see a cross, and the pendant reinforced that this was not her world.

"I am Prior Fidelmus. You wished to speak to me?"

"Yes. I was told to come here by… a man… I don't know his name," Iona floundered as she reached into the cloak to retrieve the purse. She removed the key and showed it to the monk with hesitance.

"Jake… the stubborn fool," Fidelmus muttered to himself, and with a heavy sigh, asked, "What is your name, child?"

"Iona."

"Well, Iona, you had better come with me."

Iona followed him from the room to an oaken door, which accessed the quadrangle from the south. She stared up at the statue as they drew near, and noting the direction of her gaze, Fidelmus informed, "Saint Aurigan, the Eternal Traveller."

"Why does his cowl cover his face?"

"Aurigan represents everyman… or everywoman, as the case may be. But it's a story for another day."

Iona reappraised the statue and noticed the androgynous characteristics she had missed at first glance. Fidelmus led her towards the tower at the quadrangle's northern side, its multitude of windows winking in the sun. "The scriptorium," he said before she could query the reason for such abundance and, an artist herself, Iona understood why the scribes and illuminators required extra light.

The monk opened the gate in the archway beneath, and they entered a paved courtyard with a roofed well at the centre. A two-storey building occupied the western side, and gesturing towards it, Fidelmus explained, "That is our library, justly regarded amongst scholars as the greatest in Kentauros. The structure to the east is the rear of our bathhouse and laundry, inaccessible from this courtyard."

Iona suddenly registered the absence of the pungent smells she associated with the 'trike' world's areas of human habitation and felt thankful for that, at least. They crossed to a colonnade, which completed the square to the north, and Iona discerned a row of doors in the ceilinged cloister's back wall. A man sat on a bench outside the farthest door to the north-west, oiling a sword. She tried not to stare, but he seemed so different from anyone else she had yet encountered in Kentauros (?) He wore his long, black hair in a braid, and his black leather jerkin and narrow trousers, tucked into knee-high black boots, singled him out from the monks. The man glanced up at her from dark eyes and looked a question at Fidelmus, who gave an almost imperceptible headshake, his expression grim.

"Our ranger, Shay Hawksmoor. Shay, this is Iona, Jake's er… replacement," Fidelmus introduced.

The ranger nodded to Iona, his brief scrutiny astute, and rose to sheath his sword. He picked up a quiver and bow, and with another nod for Fidelmus, strode towards the gated archway.

The monk moved to stand before the central door in the row. "Here we are. You'll need the key."

Iona's brow creased in momentary confusion before she fumbled in the cloak for the key inherited from Jake. At Fidelmus' gesture, she slotted it into the keyhole and opened the door to behold a room, larger than expected, with an ox-hide screen dividing it in two. The half nearest the door contained a wooden table with two chairs, an unlit basket brazier, and a kneehole desk with a stool. Its whitewashed walls and plank floor looked clean.

The bizarre and impossible nature of her situation struck Iona anew, and her lip trembled. She had experienced some strange, drug-induced fever dreams after her accident, but none compared to this. "What is happening to me?"

Prior Fidelmus' mild blue eyes held compassion. "You are safe here, my child. We will talk tomorrow when Shay returns. I'll do my best to answer your questions then. But for now, I will ask Brother Quintus to bring you some food. Once you have eaten, you should rest."

"Food?" Iona said uncertainly.

"Don't worry, the food here is safe to eat. I can't say the same for the fare served in town unless you know where to go. You'll find suitable clothing in the armoire behind the screen. I suggest you don it before leaving this room tomorrow. I'll send for Goodwife Robina in the morning to serve any, erm… female needs," Fidelmus said with a cough.

The prior departed, and Iona sank into a chair, her hands trembling on the table before her. She reached beneath her robe for the plastic water bottle, and unscrewing the cap, took a healthy swig and wiped her mouth with the back of her hand. Returning the bottle to its hiding place, she rose from the chair to peek behind the screen.

She spotted a tall wooden cupboard with long, iron hinges; the armoire, she assumed. A little fireplace occupied one corner, and a large chest the other, a hip-bath on a bracket above it. Beneath the shuttered window on the back wall stood a wooden armchair with a padded seat, clothes thrown carelessly atop it. A small table and a wooden bed with a carved headboard and rumpled bedding completed the furnishings. As Iona moved to investigate the curtained alcove opposite the bed, she heard a knock at the door, which Fidelmus had left slightly ajar.

Iona widened the gap to admit Brother Quintus, a young man with dark auburn hair and merry green eyes. He gave her a cheerful smile that dimpled his cheeks and set a covered tray down on the front-area table. Turning back to the door, he beckoned to two young boys, aged around ten, who wore grey acolytes' habits. One staggered under the weight of a wicker basket, filled with linens, an empty water basin upended on the top. The other carried a large, earthenware ewer, taking care not to spill the contents.

"Dara, you know where the pitcher goes. Tynan, put the basket down behind the screen," Quintus instructed.

The two boys stared wide-eyed at Iona, Tynan smiling shyly as they disappeared behind the room divider.

"We brought you some fresh bedding and such. You can dump Jake's in the basket and leave it outside the door for the launderers to collect. Same with the tray when you've finished with it," Quintus said kindly.

"Thank you, Brother Quintus," Iona replied with a hesitant smile.

The boys emerged from behind the screen and Quintus admonished them, "It's rude to stare," though his eyes twinkled with amusement as they blushed and averted their curious gazes from Iona. "These two scamps will return to light the candles, and the fire if you wish, before it grows dark. Enjoy your meal," the monk bowed and ushered the boys from the room, closing the door behind him.

Iona lifted the cloth from the tray to examine the food by the light that filtered through the mottled glass of a semi-circular window or fanlight above the door. Fresh, crusty bread, a butter pat, cheese, a jar of honey, and a large, shiny apple. A jug held water, and scented steam rose when she removed the fitted lid atop a pottery beaker; some kind of herbal infusion, she guessed. She could murder a coffee right now, or perhaps a stiff drink. Lamentably, coffee likely didn't exist in Kentauros. Iona lifted the beaker and sniffed the contents before taking an experimental sip. It tasted pleasant, not unlike tea, and she supposed she could get used to it.

However, the thought she might have no choice brought on fresh despair, and she sank into the chair with her head in her hands. But she couldn't afford to fall to pieces and, stiffening her spine, she reached for the brew and took another sip. Though her stomach cramped with distress, Iona nibbled a corner of the bread, still warm from the oven, and very tasty. Before she knew it, she had polished off everything bar the apple, which she saved for later. Only then did she remember she had not eaten since the night before, having planned to have breakfast after her trike session. It must be midday by now.

Rising from the table, Iona went to explore behind the screen. She opened the wooden shutters, and light flooded the room. Through the latticed window, Iona observed a walled flower garden with a sundial in the centre. Throwing open the armoire doors, she discovered two kirtles, one blue and one spring green, plus a couple of chemises, a soft wool maroon robe, and a darker blue cloak. She gauged the green kirtle would fit her, but the side-lacing might need tightening on the blue one. All the clothes looked clean, and herbs sewn into muslin bags ensured they smelled fresh. Puzzled at the presence of female garments in the room previously inhabited by Jake, she pulled out internal drawers to discover an embroidered, leaf-green shawl, two laundered coifs, two long belts that doubled around the waist, a selection of bone hair combs, and sundry other accessories. Though a tunic and a couple of men's linen shirts also occupied the armoire, Iona felt stumped. Closing the doors, she bent to the large chest, and raising the lid, discovered all the male garb she had expected to find. She wondered if Jake had enjoyed cross-dressing, but the female clothes looked too small for him. Besides, that seemed unlikely in this culture and, in a priory, no less.

Shaking her head, Iona peered behind the curtain that concealed the alcove. A chest sat flush against the back wall and, on raising the lid, Iona regarded a bench with a round hole in the centre. Peeking into the stone-lined cavity, Iona realised the 'chest' camouflaged a garderobe, the height of luxury in the mediaeval period. She wrinkled her nose at the faint smell of vinegar and lye used to cleanse the chute (which presumably emptied into a 'gong' pit cellar) and disguise less agreeable smells. Still, she ought to feel grateful she had her own private 'facility'. Shutting the heavy lid, she picked up a wooden ball from a low shelf. About seven inches in diameter, tiny holes pierced the surface, and an aromatic scent tickled her nostrils. She supposed it contained herbs; obviously an archaic air freshener.

Iona backed out of the alcove and turned away. Dara had removed the basin from the basket, and it now sat on the small table with the water ewer inside it. Two clean linen cloths hung from the slim rail affixed below the table edge, and much to Iona's surprise, a cake of soap sat in a pottery dish beside the bowl. She picked it up and sniffed it, detecting a hint of mutton fat and wood ash beneath the flowery scent. Even more surprising was the bone-handled toothbrush with natural bristles that sat atop a small, round earthenware pot with a flat lid. Iona prised up the top and dipped a finger into the paste contained within. She licked it gingerly and tasted salt or some kind of natural soda, aniseed, sage, mint, and perhaps a hint of fennel. She replaced the lid and stood the toothbrush upright in a pottery beaker. A shelf below the tabletop held a bone comb, a natural bristle hairbrush, and a wooden box with two compartments, one containing woody twigs, and the other, two blocks of white stone with a salt-like texture. Iona couldn't guess their use and returned the box to the shelf. A mercury glass mirror hung on the wall above the table, and Iona raised her eyebrows in surprise at the unexpected clarity of her reflection. This room truly seemed the mediaeval equivalent of the Ritz, and she wondered why it existed within a priory.

Iona turned at last to the bed with a sigh and removed her cloak. She stripped the bedding and threw it onto the floor. The wool-stuffed mattress seemed free of bedbugs, and with a start, Iona remembered Jake's instruction to look beneath it. She lifted one side and immediately spotted a leather document case lying atop the interlocked canvas webbing that formed the base. Hooking it out one-handed, she let the mattress drop. With the folder-like case under one elbow, Iona scooped up Jake's discarded breeks and robe from the padded chair and threw them onto the laundry pile.

She settled into the chair and unfastened the folder's cord ties with trembling fingers. Inside, she discovered pages and pages of writing, written in four different hands, most on parchment, but some on paper torn from a modern notebook. According to the date on the topmost page, the first author had written his account seven years ago. Iona turned to the last loose parchment sheet, dated two days previously. She flipped back to the first page in this new hand, which bore a date eighteen months ago, and she read, *'My name is Jake Halstead, and I am the latest incarnation of the "Living Aurigan".'*

Chapter 5

A sensation of dread shivered down Iona's spine at Jake's words. If he had been the new *Living Aurigan* – whatever that was – it implied she had assumed his role. The trickery that had led her to Kentauros must have brought him here too – he had certainly seemed familiar with the trike. She thought of Prior Fidelmus' kind eyes, unwilling to believe him responsible, but she would soon find out when she read the folder's contents.

Suddenly concerned that someone might disturb her before she had finished, perhaps a laundry worker come to collect Jake's bedding, Iona closed the file and leaped to her feet. She must learn more about her situation before she spoke to *anyone* here again.

Iona sorted out the clean sheets and blankets in the basket (no duvets here), and hurriedly made the bed, piling the extra blanket and thick linen rectangles she believed might be towels on the end, for now. She tossed the laundry into the basket and donned her black cloak before she opened the door and set the basket down outside. The lunch tray soon joined it, and Iona gazed across the square. Apart from a solitary figure in a black scholar's gown who entered the library, the courtyard appeared deserted. Iona shut the door and, removing the key from the cloak pocket, locked it. She hung the cloak on a peg beside it and hastened back to the screened-off area.

Settled once more in the padded chair, Iona opened the folder and turned first to the pages in Jake's handwriting:

'As a 3D animator and systems developer, I knew Chiron's (my name for the AI interface) so-called Hyper Reality was too good to be true, but something kept drawing me back despite my vague sense of danger. I wanted to discover how 'he' did it, and constantly sought clues. My phone always died in the trike world, but I once stuck a digital camera in my bum bag and filmed the session. I showed it to Tony, a special effects technician with a sideline as an expert witness, though I didn't tell him about the trike. He found no evidence of VR technology and said I must have been tripping – those scenes weren't fake. The next day, someone set fire to his studio. He still had my camera, and it went up in smoke, along with all his computer equipment. I should have stopped then, but I chose to believe the fire was coincidental.

I met Bethany in Tritaurium soon after. She directed me to the megalith, where we could speak in private. I learned Gavin (see deposition two in the file) stranded her here when he knocked her off the trike and stole it. That seemed a little extreme to me; it shouldn't be impossible for us to balance on the trike together so I could take her back with me. At that point,

Chiron gave the time up signal. I knew the trike would go into automatic shutdown if I ignored it, so I told Bethany to meet me here same time tomorrow. She was waiting for me, clad in the black cloak. I manoeuvred her onto my lap, side-saddle, with her arms around my neck. She weighed more than I expected. However, when I hit the off control, Chiron refused to cooperate and messaged 'he' could only function with one person. Bethany slid off, and the next thing I knew, she whipped something from beneath her cloak and whacked me twice on the back of the head with it, then pushed me off the trike, weeping as she did it. She dropped the cloak and made off with my 'transport', leaving me lying on the road with a bloody head and a large rock – no wonder she had felt heavy. I picked up the cloak and managed to stagger behind the menhir, where I found a message from Bethany in the pocket. If you are reading this, you know what happened next.

*Prior Fidelmus urges me to end the cycle of forcible takeovers and make a life for myself here. He has done his best to protect the trike victims from the suspicions of the superstitious with his revival of the old, 'Living Aurigan' tradition. Besides, he cautions that no one knows the fate of those who return to reality as we know it. He has a point. Even so, I'm willing to risk it if I cannot discover the source of this subterfuge. Even Fidelmus believes it's no coincidence that the Duke of Tritaurium's heraldic sigil is three wheels. Rumours abound about what goes on in the Janus Spire, the tallest tower in his castle. The men that guard it are a different breed from the other castle soldiers and sentries. They frequent the 'Black Cockerel' tavern in Crookback Street, behind the market square. I patronise it now and then to eavesdrop on their conversations, hoping alcohol will loosen their tongues. I can't be much of a spy though, as I've not yet discovered anything of value, and twice ended up under arrest for poking my nose where I shouldn't. Fidelmus managed to extricate me both times with the help of Aylard Quillen, his lawyer friend – the 'Living Aurigan' position has some status outside the priory and, after all, Fidelmus **is** the Prior.*

Yet, still I persist in my futile quest for answers, although I doubt there is anything I can do to stop whoever is behind the trike scam. What is their motive, anyway? Although Prior Fidelmus is a good man, and I live better than many in Kentauros, this is not my world or even one that suits me. I continue to watch the road for the next trike victim, but cannot keep vigil 24/7, and must rely on luck with timing. Who knows how many trike riders have made it past Tritaurium? What was their fate? Is there more than one trike? Well, dear reader, I confess I plan to do what the others did before me, even though I know it's wrong. If you are reading this, I must have succeeded, and apologise for what I have done to you.'

Iona leaned back in the chair and closed her eyes. What had she got mixed up in? She considered herself an ordinary young woman, perhaps a little more introverted than most of her friends, but until the accident, she had led the same lifestyle as them. They had partied and holidayed together and consoled each other when romantic relationships hit the skids. Iona belonged to a book club and a craftwork circle and enjoyed scouring flea markets with Skye or Zara. At twenty-five, she didn't overly mind her single status. Though luckier than most in her chosen career, it had taken the accident to encourage her to go freelance. The compensation monies had enabled her mortgage-free position, but Iona still worried about paying the bills, just like her friends. She could think of nothing that singled her out, so how could this have happened to her? Perhaps the bad luck that started with the accident had not yet run its course.

Taking a steadying breath, Iona bent again to the file and rather than read from the top, she continued backwards from Jake's statement. She turned to the first page of Bethany's account, written on paper adorned with pink hearts, torn from a notebook. A wedding planner from Berkshire, Bethany had become ensnared in the trike scheme after breaking both legs in a skiing accident. Unlike Jake, she had not attempted to discover the source of her nightmare and spent most of her time watching the road and the rest holed up in this room. Bethany wrote, *'I hate this filthy place and its backward people. Fidelmus insists he's powerless to send me back, but he must know something! Oh, he seems decent enough, but I don't trust anyone in this godawful hole. I just want to go home!! And when I do, I'll sue the ass off Borderland. I'll die if I stay here a minute longer.'*

Most of her affidavit continued in the same vein, and Iona shook her head, feeling both irritation and sympathy with Bethany's attitude. At least she now knew who the female garments had belonged to.

She turned next to the second transcript, written on parchment, and her eyes widened when she noted the name of the man who had stolen the trike from Bethany; a name that had caused a stir in the press not so long ago. When Iona finished reading his submission, she knew without a doubt that he was the same Gavin Whyte, a top-tier footballer, who had sustained a career-ending injury and disappeared without a trace while recuperating from surgery at his Bowden mansion in Manchester. Iona had recently watched a documentary about the case, and though Whyte remained missing, the consensus cited suicide as the most probable explanation. Iona felt a hollow in the pit of her stomach. The ex-footballer had not re-surfaced, so what had happened when he returned to their world after hijacking the trike? It seemed reasonable to suppose that Troy might have the means to prevent anyone from broadcasting tales of their experience.

Iona's mouth had gone dry, and she took a healthy swig from her water bottle before turning to the first statement, written by a Doctor Dennis Cleary. He had returned to England after working as a medical aid doctor in Africa, where he had stepped on a low-grade landmine. Though severely injured, surgeons had saved his mangled leg, and the trike had become part of his convalescence routine. The doctor had stayed longer in Kentauros than any of the others and worked in the hospital infirmary, the long, low building that abutted the western corner of the priory's façade. He did his best with the equipment and medicines at his disposal and, thanks to him, the monks learned more advanced techniques to treat patients and how to prevent the spread of bacteria and viruses through proper hygiene and sanitation. Doctor Cleary dedicated himself to the task and built a close friendship with Brother Tristan, the head infirmarian. However, Tristan fell victim to an aggressive lung infection, and the doctor's last words made for chilling reading:

'While attending a patient in Dumatha village, a mile outside Tritaurium, I miraculously spotted the trike, but it vanished almost straight away, and I guessed the rider's time was up. I don't think Tristan has much longer, four days at most, but if I can get back home and grab my antibiotics' supply, I can save him. My best option is to return to Dumatha tomorrow at a slightly earlier time and wait for the rider to reappear. I will beseech him to loan me the trike. I only hope he lives in the UK...'

According to Gavin Whyte, when the doctor waylaid him and begged to borrow the trike, promising to return soon with the meds to cure his friend, the footballer, mindful of the injunction not to dismount, felt suspicious and refused. Though the man touched him on the arm to prove himself more than an interactive projection, Gavin remained in denial up to the point where the doctor stabbed him in the neck with a needle-like instrument. Instead of hitting the off control, Gavin had pedalled away, but the next thing he knew, he woke up behind a roadside tree, covered with a black cloak, the trike gone. He had waited two days for the doctor to return, but defeated at last by hunger and thirst, had followed the directions to the priory left by the thief, whose friend died two days later. Doctor Dennis Cleary never did make it back...

Cleary had made only a passing reference to the man who had ejected *him* from the trike, and it seemed the doctor had set the record-keeping precedent. Iona closed the folder with a sigh and returned it to its hiding place under the mattress. It seemed safe to assume that Jake, too, had been recovering from physical trauma, though he had not made it clear in his account. This appeared the only thing the trike victims had in common; they were otherwise a very disparate group of people. Iona had much to think about before her interview with Prior Fidelmus on the morrow.

The sun had lowered in the sky, and she prepared herself for the arrival of the two acolytes who would light the candles. Iona untied her hoodie from around her waist and delved into the pockets to retrieve an unopened handy-pack of tissues, a packet of chewing gum, and a tube of lip gloss. She removed a tissue, and with her modern fear of germs, approached the garderobe with trepidation. However, she *had* to wee and knew she must get used to using the primitive, non-flushing toilet. After she finished, she poured tepid water from the ewer into the basin and carried out a full body wash, emptying the soap-scummed water down the garderobe chute afterwards. Iona opened the armoire doors and selected the soft woollen robe, its colour similar to the habit worn by Saint Aurigan in the stained-glass window above the priory entrance. She found a pair of sheepskin, slipper-like bootees that appeared unworn. Giving them a sniff, Iona detected nothing unpleasant, and slid them onto her feet, tightening the laces for a better fit. She replaced the modern, elastic hair tie in her long, dark plait with a ribbon, and bundled her clothes and pixie boots into the back of the armoire just as someone knocked on the door. Smoothing down the robe, she hastened to unlock it, now limping a little after the day's exertions.

Iona stood aside to admit the two boys who stood without, Dara carrying a fresh water ewer and Tynan a covered tray.

"Brother Quintus says you should eat this straight away before it cools," Tynan said with pink-cheeked shyness as he removed the linen tray cloth.

Iona lifted the lid from an earthenware bowl that appeared to contain some kind of stew, noting the fresh bread that accompanied it, along with another beaker of steaming tea and a jug of water. She smiled and nodded as she sat down and picked up the pewter spoon, which shone with a polished gleam. Dipping it into the stew, she watched Tynan lift a tinderbox from the desktop, noting how he used the fire steel, flint, and char cloth to light a wooden spill, which he touched to the wicks of candles placed around the room.

He noticed her regard and said proudly, "We have beeswax candles here, not the smelly tallow others use, but you'll need to trim the wicks every four hours to keep them burning properly. Look, like this," and extinguishing the spill, he plucked a pair of metal trimmers from the desk and demonstrated the technique on an unlit candle.

"Perhaps you can teach me how to use the tinderbox; tomorrow maybe?"

Tynan bowed his head in agreement and Dara appeared from behind the screen where he had lit the bed-area candles and swapped over the ewers. He asked Iona if she wished him to light the fire. The evening felt warm, so she demurred, and he promised to deliver hot water in the morning for her ablutions.

"You can leave the tray outside the door when you're finished," Tynan advised and bowed politely in farewell.

"Thank you both," Iona said, and the boys departed with bashful smiles.

The stew contained onion, peas, carrots, and unidentifiable chunks of meat that Iona thought might be mutton seasoned with herbs. She found it surprisingly tasty and couldn't resist scraping the bowl. Rounding off the meal with the apple she had saved earlier, she transferred the water jug and spare beaker to the table and shoved the tray outside the door, which she re-locked.

Iona felt at a loose end. With no TV and only dim candlelight to read by, she wondered how the people of Kentauros spent their evenings. She wandered over to the desk and rifled through the drawers, which contained parchment, ink, quill pens, wax, seals and sundry other writing paraphernalia. Picking up the water jug and beaker, Iona retired behind the screen and set them down atop a low, wide shelf beside the bed. She pulled a white cotton, ankle-length shift from an armoire drawer, identifying it as a nightie, and threw it onto the bed. Still processing all she had learned from the folder's contents; she leaned her elbows on the windowsill and gazed out at the walled garden in the gathering dusk. Though fear lay like a lead ball in the pit of her stomach, she must not succumb to it, or she might become like Bethany. Her fate could have been a lot worse; at least she had found sanctuary in the priory – she hoped so, anyway.

A movement beyond the sundial caught her attention as a man rose from a bench to pace up and down, seemingly lost in thought. Though darkness descended, Iona recognised Shay, the enigmatic ranger, returned from his unknown errand. Hands-on-hips, he moved with an unconscious, feline stalk as though he held frustration in check. He raised his head, and Iona shrank back, not wishing him to catch her staring. She quickly closed the shutters, plunging the room into deeper shadow. Iona almost regretted telling Dara not to light the fire, which would have given additional light.

With nothing else to do, she prepared herself for bed. Snuffing out all but the bedside candle, she climbed under the covers and clutched the sheets under her chin. The single candle barely pierced the gloom, but she couldn't bring herself to quench it. Fear shivered down her spine, but she reminded herself that the room's previous occupants had survived in this reality. She tried not to think about what might have happened to them when they returned to the 'real' world – *if* they had returned... However, they had *seemed* safe enough here, if she discounted Jake's frequent arrests, but he had perhaps brought those on himself. Iona already knew she wouldn't take the same risk they had, but that meant she'd remain trapped here forever and never again see her family and friends. Tears leaked from under her closed eyelids, but exhausted, she finally fell into an uneasy slumber and dreamed she rode the trike, chased by a centaur with wheels for legs.

Chapter 6

Light filtered through the gaps in the shutters when Iona woke early the next morning. She raised her head and blinked at her surroundings with bleary eyes. Her head fell back onto the pillow and she shut her eyes with a groan – yesterday had not been a dream, after all.

The untrimmed candle guttered in a pool of wax, emitting brownish smoke that drifted over the bed. Iona raised herself onto an elbow and reached for the long-handled snuffer on the shelf beside her to extinguish the flame. Flinging back the covers, she slid her feet into the fleecy bootees and stood to shrug on the maroon robe. She crossed to the window and partially opened one shutter to peer out at the dew-drenched garden, deserted at this hour. A blackbird sang from the tree in one corner and two ravens hopped about on the lawn around the sundial.

As Iona entered the garderobe alcove, she wondered what she would do when all the handy-pack tissues were used up. On this depressing note, she washed her hands afterwards and had just finished cleaning her teeth with the crude toothbrush when a knock sounded at the door. Iona rounded the screen, noting her limp had not worsened after yesterday's exertions, and unlocked the door. A plump, rosy-cheeked woman approaching middle age stood outside, holding a large basket in both arms.

"Hello Iona, I'm Goodwife Robina, but you can call me Binny; everyone else does. I'm here to sort you out with some things you'll need and help you get settled in. Can I come in?"

"Er, yes. Please come through," Iona replied and opened the door wider.

Binny entered and stepped around the screen to heave the basket onto the unmade bed. She removed a linen sack and turned to Iona, who had followed her. "If you'd like to give me the clothes you arrived in, I'll get them washed and dried. You can stash them away afterwards."

Iona hesitated, unsure what to say. She didn't want this woman to see the clothes made from strange fabrics alien to this world.

"There's no need to look so shifty, I know where you're from. Your secret is safe with me. You see, I came from there, too," Binny informed with a wry smile.

"What? On the trike?" Iona said, startled.

"On *a* trike. Whether it was the same one as yours... well, who knows? I've been here ten years now."

"But, but..." Iona trailed off.

Binny smiled. "In my case, it was the best thing that ever happened to me, but I know that wasn't so for the others, except perhaps for Doctor

Cleary. I fell in love with the beekeeper here and married him." Seeing Iona's puzzled frown, she hastened to add, "Oh, Joss is not a monk! We live in a cottage on the farm estate attached to the priory. I was a lab worker for a pharmaceutical company back in our world, but I didn't have much of a life outside work, so it was no great loss to leave it. Well, do you want to give me those clothes?"

Iona removed the bundle of garments from the armoire, and Binny popped them into the sack and said, "There's a secret compartment within the armoire. It's behind the topmost internal drawer. You need to pull the drawer out to access it. It's probably best to stow these in there when I return them to you, just as a precaution. The hidey-hole is not very big, but your clothes should just about fit inside. Now, what about your shoes?"

Iona picked up the pixie boots and Binny frowned, "Hmm, they're not trainers at least. You *might* get away with those, but probably best not to risk it outside the priory." She spotted the empty plastic water bottle on the armoire's internal shelf and, scooping it up, added it to the sack. "I'll need to dispose of this. Do you have any other plastics or such?"

Removing the remaining tissues from their cellophane, Iona handed the wrapper to Binny and said, "I'll run out of these soon. What do they use for toilet paper around here?"

"You don't want to know." Binny dropped the sack onto the bed and reached inside her basket. She removed a couple of linen-wrapped packages and opened one to reveal a stack of thin paper-like sheets. "Luckily for us, Bertrand Leon, the wealthiest merchant in Tritaurium, trades with the East, where they are a bit more advanced in this area. These sheets are paper made from rice straw. They're very expensive, but Merchant Leon owes the prior a few favours."

"What *does* everyone else use?" Iona asked with curiosity as she fingered one of the rice paper sheets.

"Rags, leaves, hay, wool, whatever is to hand basically. The wealthy use sea sponges attached to a stick, which they cleanse with a vinegar-water soak." Binny gave a delicate shudder and opened the second package. Iona regarded what appeared to be rudimentary sanitary towels attached to thin linen tie-belts.

"These are for your monthlies. I know how they look, but believe me, they're a vast improvement on the rags used by most women here. I invented these myself. The linen outer covering contains a highly absorbent bog moss. You can chuck them down the garderobe chute afterwards. The gong pit is cleansed daily; Doctor Cleary insisted on it..." Binny trailed off sadly and shook her head as though to clear it. "I must say, you appear remarkably calm about the, er, *facilities*. Not like that Bethany..."

Iona shrugged. "There's not much point railing about something I can't change. I have to make the best of it until I can find a way back – if one exists."

Binny nodded. "Do you have a family, Iona?"

"Yes, I have a married sister, Skye, and we have a dad who lives in Wiltshire. Our mum died six years ago. Skye will go nuts when she finds me gone. As for Dad…" Iona's lip trembled and she blinked back tears.

Binny patted her arm. "I'm sorry." With nothing to say that could alleviate Iona's distress, she turned briskly back to the basket and pulled out a smaller basket. She arranged the two packages within and handed it to Iona, who placed it on the garderobe shelf. Binny extracted another small basket, filled with glass and pottery vessels, their contents clearly labelled. "These are various concoctions I developed with Doctor Cleary. As I mentioned, I was a chemist in my former life. I make everything from natural ingredients, some of which don't exist in our world." She removed a round, glazed earthenware jar and unscrewed the lid. "This salve works like a dream on muscle injuries. I assume you suffer from such, like all the trikers. Just rub it over the affected area regularly and you'll soon notice an improvement." Returning the jar to the basket, Binny pointed out medicines for stomach ailments, headaches, and period pain, and lifted out a brown glass bottle. "This is shampoo. It doesn't lather up as much as the more sophisticated products in our world, but it does the job. And here is something rather important," Binny said as she plucked a small hempen sack tied with twine from the basket. "This is not my invention. The women here mix these powdered leaves with hot water and drink it daily if they don't wish to become pregnant. It works, too."

Iona felt her face heat and responded, "I don't think I'll need that!"

"Neither did I, and now I have a nine-year-old daughter!" Binny laughed and set the basket down on the chest. Removing a scrap of parchment from her kirtle pocket, she waved it at Iona and placed it beside the basket. "The dosage instructions for everything."

Iona nodded her thanks and suddenly remembered the strange items in the box on the under-table shelf. She picked it up and opened the lid to show Binny. "What are these?"

"Ah, yes. The twigs are used widely here as a kind of dental floss. They come from an indigenous tree, the same tree on which the contraceptive leaves grow. You should find a tiny paring blade below them, which is used to flay the twig ends. They have natural, anti-bacterial properties and are really quite effective."

"Did you also make the toothpaste?"

"Yes, I did, and sourced the alum stones, too. I've quite a lucrative sideline selling both to the merchant's wives!"

"Alum stones?"

"The white rocks in the box. Potassium Alum is a mineral salt that acts as a highly effective natural deodorant. It creates a salt layer on the skin that neutralises bacteria, thus eliminating odours. You use it like a roll-on. Oh, by the way, all the women shave their legs and pits here, using a razor and pumice stone. However, there's depilatory cream in the basket made from resin and beeswax."

Iona shook her head in bemusement. "I guess I've landed on my feet here."

"That's not how Bethany saw it," Binny said with a sigh.

"It's all relative compared to where I might've ended up in this world..."

Binny smiled and turned back to her basket. "The boys will be here soon with your hot water. I'd better finish sorting you out." She lifted out a handful of linen items and placed them on the bed. "Underwear. It's all new. The drawstring shorts are usually worn by men, but going knickerless like most ladies here is a bit too much for our modern sensibilities!" Binny gave a rueful half-smile and held up a garment resembling a long bra that laced at one side. "This is a corselette. It's actually pretty comfortable."

Iona touched the fabric. "The linen is so fine here."

"Indeed! But linen is inexpensive. Cotton is the most valuable fabric. It costs even more than silk or velvet, as its imported," Binny informed as she removed a brocade pouch and an empty laundry sack from her basket. "There are several pairs of silk and wool stockings in this pouch, and you'll find garters in an armoire drawer."

The hot water arrived just then, and once the boys left, Binny pointed to the hip bath on its bracket. "Just let them know whenever you want to take a bath, and Brother Kian at the bathhouse will sort it out. I'll leave you to wash while I pop next door to make sure the two visiting nuns have everything they need. I'll return to help you dress. The kirtle lacing is a bit tricky at first until you get used to it."

"Nuns?"

"Yes, they're here on pilgrimage. They have the room next to yours. The end room one door beyond theirs is just a storeroom with steps leading down to the cellar beneath this row. The room on your other side is empty at present, and Shay, our handsome but close-mouthed ranger, has the room beyond that."

Iona washed as best she could from the basin and removed an alum stone from the box. It pleased her to discover it left no residue after application. She struggled a little with the corselette lacings, but when Binny returned, Iona had managed to tie them and slipped on a long-sleeved chemise. Selecting the blue kirtle from the armoire, Binny helped her into it and tightened the side laces until it fit snugly against Iona's torso. She adjusted the points that trailed from the elbow-length sleeves down to Iona's calves and showed her how to arrange the long girdle belt. "You'll have to wear those pixie boots for now until we get you measured for shoes. At least the kirtle is long enough to hide them. I'll just fix your hair, and then we're done."

Binny tidied up Iona's plait and coiled it around her head, fixing it in place with bronze pins. A knock at the door heralded breakfast, and after Binny admitted Tynan with the covered tray, she transferred the sack containing Iona's clothes to her basket and hoisted it into her arms. "I'll leave you to eat in peace. Someone will come to escort you to Prior Fidelmus after breakfast. If you need me for anything, send one of the boys to fetch me. Tynan here is a novice in the scriptorium, and Dara works in the library."

"Thank you, Binny. I appreciate all your help."

"You're welcome." Binny smiled and bustled out with Tynan in tow.

Breakfast consisted of steaming tea and crusty, buttered bread, accompanied by porridge with a jug of hot milk to thin it according to taste, and a small jar of honey for sweetener. *I'm in no danger of starving here, at least,* Iona mused as she tucked in.

Food eaten, she returned behind the screen and studied her reflection in the mirror. She hardly recognised herself in the strange garments and updo. The deep-blue shade of the kirtle matched her eyes, but though the outfit had elegance, she couldn't help feeling like a participant in a fancy-dress pageant. Iona turned away to tidy up while she waited for her escort. She made the bed, hampered by her cumbersome sleeves, then emptied the basin down the garderobe chute, careful not to splash the water onto her kirtle. Iona thought of Jake's shirts and jerkin in the armoire and wished she could wear something practical like those instead. She opened the shutters to their fullest extent and watched an elderly monk pottering in the flowerbeds.

Musing on the interview to come, Iona moved to the bed and stood irresolute. On impulse, she retrieved the leather folder from beneath the mattress. Though unsure if Prior Fidelmus knew of its existence, Iona had determined she must do things differently from the other trikers to find a *safe* way home. An idea had taken root, but she would play the meeting by ear to discover how feasible it might be.

When the knock sounded at the door, Iona removed the dark blue cloak from the armoire, and flinging it around her shoulders, concealed the folder beneath before she answered.

Brother Quintus stood outside, his cheerful smile dimpling his cheeks. "Good morning, Iona. The prior would like to speak with you now if you're ready?"

"Yes, of course," Iona replied and followed the monk across the courtyard to the gate below the tower.

The day was warm, but if Brother Quintus wondered why she wore a cloak, he didn't show it. As they emerged into the quadrangle, Iona spotted two women in dark maroon habits with large, white wimples that put Iona in mind of origami swans. She guessed they must be the two nuns Binny had mentioned and stared after them curiously as they entered the chapel.

"What is your role here, Brother Quintus, if I may be so bold to ask?"

"I am the Guest Master, and act as the liaison between the prior and our guests and visiting dignitaries, a job which includes attending to their needs."

Iona understood why Fidelmus had chosen the affable Quintus for the task. "So, you must have known the other... *travellers*, like me, pretty well?"

They had reached the door into the main building where she had waited to meet Prior Fidelmus, and Quintus paused on the threshold. "Most couldn't *see* past their fear and longing to return home... don't make the same mistake."

He said no more, and Iona wondered *what* the trikers had not seen, and how much Quintus, or any of the monks, knew about their situation. "I don't intend to."

Brother Quintus nodded and ushered her through the entrance. He led her past a dormitory, presumably for the monks, and turned into a corridor lined with doors. Stopping outside an arched doorway at the end, he knocked and gestured for her to enter with a smile of encouragement. Quintus left her there, closing the door behind him, and Iona faced Prior Fidelmus across a carved desk. To her surprise, a cross-armed Shay leaned casually against the wall, his eyes inscrutable. Iona gripped the folder beneath her cloak, her hands suddenly sweaty.

Fidelmus waved her to a chair before his desk. "I decreed it best to give you space to settle in and recover from the shock of your... *changed* circumstances before we had this conversation. I expect you have a lot of questions."

"Yes, I hardly know where to start. But... I must first establish your knowledge of where I... where *we*, the dispossessed, come from, and *why* you help us."

The prior folded his hands on the desktop and regarded her with consideration, his head cocked. "Perhaps it will aid your comprehension if I tell you the story of Saint Aurigan. The order believes the *Great Wheel* sent him here to spread enlightenment amongst a backward population mired in a centuries-long dark age. He travelled far and wide, educating communities on the innovations that would allow them to progress. Over time, the people advanced, developing crop rotation, spinning wheels, blast furnaces to smelt metals, and the architectural principles to build castles and cathedrals. Aurigan founded the institution that evolved into Glassnesse Abbey, our *Great Wheel* motherhouse in Zephyrinus. Before his death, he warned others would come from the *kindred plane*, both male and female and not all of them willingly. Some might wish to stay and contribute their knowledge, but most would desire to return whence they came. Aurigan ordained that the order must aid and succour them all regardless, and treat them as his living representatives. However, no one came for two centuries after his death, and the order had almost forgotten his statute when the first of your fellow *trisiks* arrived two decades ago. It was then we established the *Living Aurigan* tradition that protects the travellers from a populace grown superstitious in the intervening years."

"So, the *Living Aurigan* is like Dr Who, who changes appearance when a new actor takes over? The tricycle is a poor substitute for the Tardis, though," Iona muttered to herself.

Shay narrowed his eyes, and Prior Fidelmus frowned. "I'm sorry, I don't understand."

"Oh, never mind, it's not important. You called us *trisiks*?"

"Yes, based on the description of the invisible conveyance you all arrive on. We have nothing like it here."

"So, what did Aurigan have to say about helping those who want to go home?"

"He said the *route* required management, and efforts must be made to secure the 'gateway' against those who might misuse it. I don't pretend to understand what he meant, but it appears the *Great Wheel* did not send the *trisiks*, implying that Aurigan's fears were not unfounded. However, if dark forces control this gateway, it is incumbent on the order to seek them out and wrest control, as the saint decreed. Yet, a lack of knowledge hampers us. We know naught of this gateway and what we must deal with. Without access to the *route*, we cannot help you return."

"Jake thinks the Duke of Tritaurium knows something, and that you believe it, too."

Fidelmus exchanged a glance with Shay, who stepped away from the wall. "How do you know what Jake believes?" the ranger asked softly, though his gaze was sharp.

Iona hesitated, then reached beneath her cloak for the folder. She placed it on the desk before Fidelmus and said, "It's all in there. He mentions a Janus Spire."

The prior opened the folder and riffled through the contents, reading passages here and there before he passed it to Shay.

"Look, you can tell me. I have no intention of doing what the others did in their desperation to go home. Even if I had the stomach to bash someone over the head with a rock, I don't think they made it. Gavin Whyte was famous, and his disappearance widely reported. His sudden reappearance would have made Worldwide news, but that never happened. As for Bethany, well, she comes across as pretty... *mouthy*. I doubt she would have kept quiet about her experience. And then there's the studio fire that destroyed Jake's proof. *Someone* doesn't want all this coming to light," Iona declared.

"What *we* believe is only a suspicion based on nothing more than circumstantial evidence. It did not help Jake; indeed, it got him into trouble," Fidelmus replied.

Iona shook her head impatiently. "Jake was reckless. He didn't have a proper plan and searched for information in the wrong place. Besides, though I'm as much in the dark as you, you'll need someone with knowledge of how things operate in *my* world if you wish to stop this *trisik* business."

Fidelmus clasped his hands together and bowed his head in thought.

"I have a right to know," Iona persisted.

The prior nodded and sighed. "Alright. When old Duke Garrold died twenty years ago, his son, Clovis, succeeded him. He added his new wife's family insignia of three wheels to the ducal crest, arranging them in a triangular formation around the existing centaur rampant. When she died, he took three overlapping wheels, minus the centaur, as his personal sigil. They have nothing to do with the *Great Wheel*," Fidelmus added, unconsciously gripping his pendant. "No one knows what it symbolises, but his marriage coincided with the first *trisik* traveller's arrival. At the same time, Clovis heavily fortified the old Janus tower, and no one but his personal men-at-arms has set foot in it since. Rumours have reached us that his knights periodically raid outlying villages, snatching people at random, who disappear into the tower, never to be seen again. Jake convinced me that the three wheels appear emblematic of the vehicle that brings the *trisiks* here and that it is no coincidence a centaur is the device of the guild that operates the vehicles in your world."

"I think I witnessed one of those raids," Iona near-whispered, a phantom whiff of burning thatch tickling her nostrils. The room suddenly felt stuffy, and she slipped off the cloak she no longer required.

"Can you describe where it happened?" Shay enquired.

"Let me think... yes, it was the second village after the bridge with centaur statues."

Shay's lips thinned, and he shared a grim look with Fidelmus. "That sounds like Mallowbrook, the fiefdom of the recently widowed Lady Ethel. It figures; the village is isolated near the border, and with her husband dead, the duke will have seen her as an easy target."

With sadness, Iona remembered the pretty manor house on the rise behind the village.

"When was this?" Fidelmus asked

"It was ten... no, eleven days ago," Iona replied.

Shay wore a hard expression, his jaw clenched. "I'll ride out there today. I think the time has come to implement our plan on my return."

Fidelmus sighed and nodded. "Take Brother Florian with you; the villagers may have need of his skills. The infirmary can spare him for a few days."

Shay bowed to the prior, and turning on his heel, inclined his head to Iona, his eyes briefly searching hers before he swept from the room.

"What plan?" Iona asked.

"As you said, Jake sought for information in the wrong place. The answers must lie in the Janus Spire..."

"I want to be involved," Iona declared and leaned towards the monk with eagerness. He studied her in silence, and Iona said, "Please, I'll go mad if I'm forced to sit idle when there's so much at stake. I'm not rash like Jake; I can follow orders."

Prior Fidelmus lifted an appraising eyebrow. "We'll see. I must discuss it with Shay first. By tradition, each new *Living Aurigan* is presented to the duke. He has invited us to a banquet at the castle next week. Perhaps you'll notice something we have missed. You can at least form your own impression of Clovis. And now, I have duties to attend to. We'll speak again when Shay returns."

Iona stood and bowed her head to the prior without protest – at least he hadn't dismissed her plea outright. Fidelmus picked up the leather folder. "I would like to borrow this, if I may. I will return it to you once I've studied the contents."

She shrugged. "Go ahead, knock yourself out." Noting the monk's puzzled expression, she appended, "It's slang for 'don't exert yourself; it's not worth much effort'. It's curious that we share the same language, though."

"Saint Aurigan described our worlds as 'kindred', though I don't know what he meant." Fidelmus smiled and muttered, "*Knock yourself out.* I like that."

"Will it be okay if I visit the scriptorium? It will give me something to do. I am an artist and would love to see the work your illuminators produce."

"Yes, of course." The prior beamed and rang the bell that sat on his desk.

Brother Quintus arrived at the summons, and Fidelmus instructed him to give Iona a scriptorium tour.

Chapter 7

As Iona and Quintus emerged into the quadrangle, she spotted the two nuns leaving the chapel.

"Who are they?" Iona asked.

"They're from the motherhouse at Glassnesse. The Abbess there is the spiritual leader of our order. Prior Fidelmus must answer to her. I don't envy him," Quintus replied with a rueful half-smile. "Mother Wilfrida is a little... *put out* that Aurigan's living representatives tend to appear here instead of at Glassnesse. But then, it's believed the saint himself first arrived in our world near the Tritaurium menhir stone. Brace yourself, it looks like they're headed your way."

Iona caught a glint of mischief in Quintus' merry green eyes and smothered a smile. Who'd have thought a monk would indulge in gossip?

The two nuns halted before Iona and Quintus, forcing them to stop. They inclined their heads, sketching a circle over their hearts, and looked to the monk for formal introductions.

"Good morning, sisters. May I present Iona, our new *Living Aurigan*? Iona, this is Sister Honoria and Sister Bedelia," Quintus obliged.

Sister Honoria, the elder of the two, drew herself up to her full height, and this time, traced a circle on her forehead. "Well met, *Eterna*. It is most fortunate we were here for your arrival. I am sure the good brothers are treating you well, but perhaps you would feel more comfortable living amongst the sisterhood? We journey back to Glassnesse in two days hence, and would be honoured to escort you to the motherhouse."

"That is most kind of you, sister, but I am quite content here under Prior Fidelmus' guidance," Iona replied carefully. The last thing she wanted was to leave the vicinity of the castle that seemed the most likely source of the trike chicanery and, therefore, her best chance of finding a way home. Besides, from a purely practical viewpoint, she doubted the nuns had someone like Binny......

Sister Honoria looked down her long nose and nodded stiffly. "Well, if you change your mind, you know where to find us." She sketched another forehead circle and tucked her hands into the long sleeves of her habit. "Come, Sister Bedelia, we must not keep the prior waiting."

The young nun glanced at Iona from beneath lowered lashes and gave her a shy smile as she scurried after her companion. Brother Quintus scowled at Sister Honoria's departing back. "I *knew* the old harridan— sorry; the *honoured sister* would try to steal you away!"

Iona shook her head, caught between humour at Quintus' reaction and a vague concern. She had no intention of becoming a pawn in order politics. "She addressed me as *Eterna*. What does that mean?"

"*Eternal Traveller*. It's part of the *Living Aurigan* title," Quintus supplied, his sunny disposition restored as he smiled and gestured towards the scriptorium tower.

Iona wondered how such a gregarious and attractive man had become a monk, but she couldn't make assumptions based on the monastic orders of *her* world. Besides, it was none of her business.

The coolness inside the building attached to the tower felt refreshing after the heat outside. Iona peeked out the window that overlooked her courtyard, and the library which abutted the building. A stout monk with eyeglasses bustled towards them, and Quintus introduced him as Brother Ambrose, the director. "His official title is 'armarius', which translates to provisioner. He provides the scribes with their materials and supervises the copying process, amongst other things," the guest master explained.

"What brings you to my domain on this balmy day?" Ambrose enquired, peering over the top of his eyeglasses.

"If it's not inconvenient, Brother Quintus has offered to show me around the scriptorium, as I'm very interested in the work you do here," Iona replied.

A smile wreathed Ambrose's cherubic face, and he clasped his hands together in delight. "Nonsense! Quintus doesn't know his charcoal from his graphite! I will feel honoured to give you a guided tour; so very few take an interest in our processes."

The armarius ushered Iona into a room where monks prepared parchment and vellum, and unlocked a storeroom door to reveal shelves lined with boxes, jars, and bottles. "We make our own ink and tempera, though most ingredients must be imported from the continent. Our dyes are organic, derived from minerals and plants, the colours chemically produced using water, tree gum, oil, resins, alum, iron sulphate, mercury sulphide, and white vinegar," Ambrose pointed these out as he spoke, then directed Iona to another shelf. "Here are the raw colours. Carbon and iron-gall for black, vermilion and madder for reds, and verdigris for green. Yellows are made from cinnabar, orpiment and, most costly of all, saffron. Purple comes from the tumsole plant and blues from azurite, though we create a small quantity from the prohibitively expensive lapis for our most prized manuscripts." He lifted the lids off two trays and bedazzled Iona with the sight of silverpoint and gold-leaf sheets for decorative borders.

She followed Ambrose into another room, trailed by Quintus, where she watched monks in protective masks stirring vats, mixing ingredients, pounding pestles on mortars, and heating liquids in glass flasks. The uncomfortable heat and acrid smell soon drove them from the chamber and up the internal stairs.

They halted at a landing on the upper floor and entered a schoolroom. A row of grey-robed acolytes sat at a long table, practicing their script with chalk and slate. The youngest appeared to be around eight years old, and the oldest, sixteen. Iona spotted Tynan, his freckled face bent over his slate, tongue sticking out from the side of his mouth. He glanced up and met her eyes, grinning from ear to ear, but bent his head quickly when the tutor's gaze fell on him. Iona suppressed her own grin and exchanged pleasantries with Brother Anselm, the harsh but fair tutor (as Ambrose described him when they returned to the landing).

A short flight of stairs led into the adjoining tower. Tall desks lined the walls of the chamber directly above the courtyard archway. In the centre stood a scroll rack and a long table covered with work awaiting completion. Scribes hunched over the desks beneath the array of room-encircling windows, copying out manuscripts, documents and letters. Iona peered over the nearest scribe's shoulder, impressed with his beautiful penmanship. She remembered the calligraphy set her parents had bought her one Christmas. How she had loved the fountain pens with their interchangeable nibs! Iona had followed the tutorial, practicing until she achieved a fair hand. She wondered how hard it would be to write like that with a quill, and itched to try. The scribe sprinkled his completed work with sand from a shaker and, setting it aside, drew a piece of scrap parchment towards him. Dipping his quill in the ink, he handed it to Iona with a smile as though sensing her eagerness. She glanced at Ambrose, who nodded. Taking the quill, she wrote her name in the flowing script she had mastered and stood back to survey her handiwork.

The armarius picked up the parchment scrap and opined, "Hmm, not bad for a first attempt. We'll make a scribe of you yet."

Iona passed the quill back to the scribe with a smile, and the little tour party mounted the steps to the top floor, the preserve of the illuminators.

Sunlight streamed through the open windows, glinting off gold-leaf and causing the rich colours laid down on parchment to glow with an internal light. Iona moved from desk to desk, marvelling at the painters' skill with the brushes made from soft animal hair or bristles inserted into quills. The monks worked mainly on decorative borders, though one illuminator painted a full-page illustration for a book of hours. It depicted a green-robed figure standing before a cave, conversing with a dragon lying at its threshold. Unlike the fanciful dragons Iona had seen in mediaeval bestiaries, the artist had rendered it realistically, as though from life. She remembered the dragons she had observed from a distance, still unsure if they had been real, or yet more of Troy's trickery.

Brother Ambrose stood at her shoulder and explained, "The scene records the meeting between Jaellin and Saint Lexis."

"The saint's robe is very vivid. Has something been added to the verdigris to enhance the pigment?"

"The saint? Oh, you mean *Jaellin's* robe! The *dragon* is Saint Lexis. Yes, this shade is made with malachite, a copper-rich mineral."

Iona did a double-take. A dragon had attained sainthood? She had so many questions, but perhaps the answers weren't important since she didn't intend to remain in this world any longer than she had to. She picked up a quill brush and held it in a painterly grip, familiarising herself with the balance.

"You are an artist?" Ambrose asked.

Iona nodded, though it had been a while since she had painted with anything other than a computer stylus.

"Perhaps you might like to attend Brother Oisin's student class tomorrow after breakfast? He's our master illuminator," the armarius asked, his head tilted in a hopeful attitude.

Iona hesitated and then thought, what the hell, she may as well! It would give her something to do while she waited for Shay to return. Anything was better than twiddling her thumbs in her room. "Yes, I would be pleased to attend. Thanks for inviting me, and for the wonderful tour."

Ambrose beamed. "It's been my pleasure."

As he led them back down the stairs, Iona said, "I spotted some beautifully bound tomes in the prior's office. Do you bind all your own manuscripts?"

"Most of them, but that is the preserve of Brother Ennis, our head librarian. Perhaps Quintus can arrange a library tour. Although I must warn you, Ennis is something of a martinet. However, there's nothing to stop you from visiting the public areas and borrowing a book or two."

As Quintus escorted Iona back through the archway gate, she apologised for keeping him from his duties to shepherd her around.

"Nonsense! As guest master, *you* are my duty. Besides, it felt good to see you take such pleasure from the tour, and I'm happy it gave you something other than your fears to focus on for a short while. Though you have barely arrived, you are the first *trisik* since Doctor Cleary to take an interest in us."

"Don't let that fool you. Unlike him, I don't intend to stay if I can help it! Don't worry, I'm not planning to do anything stupid like Jake or the others, but I have a family back home…"

Quintus nodded; his eyes sad. They had reached the well in the courtyard's centre, and paused to part ways. "Before you go… what *is* the

Great Wheel? I assume it's your deity?" Iona enquired.

"Deity? Not really. This world *does* have religions that worship a god, but the *Great Wheel* is a symbol of the unending cycle of life from birth to death; like the ouroboros circle – the dragon swallowing its own tail." Quintus showed her his amulet, which depicted both. "We believe in the sanctity of life, and the journey to personal enlightenment through reason, meditation, altruism, and charitable acts. Our saints are individuals who made sacrifices for the greater good or, like Saint Aurigan, taught us valuable lessons and improved the lives of others, bringing order to chaos. Our ethos forbids us to reject what we do not understand, and instead, we must strive to comprehend it. In this, our beliefs are often at odds with other faiths and the world at large."

"I see," Iona said, though she wasn't sure she did. What Quintus described sounded close to Buddhism, but without the rebirth angle, mixed with the trappings of Christianity in its monastic and sainthood traditions. "Well, thanks for explaining it to me. By the way, there's no need to bother Brother Ennis on my behalf, though I would like to explore the public areas of the library this afternoon. Perhaps Dara can show me around; I believe he works there?"

"As you wish. Is there anything else I can do for you before lunch is served?"

"No, thank you, though I would like to take a bath before dinner this evening."

"Of course, I will make the arrangements." Quintus bowed and departed with a smile.

Back in her room, Iona observed that someone had cleaned it, and left fresh flowers in a vase on the table. Unlike the scentless blooms sold in her local supermarket, they smelled heavenly. She suspected they came from the garden behind the cloister rooms, and resolved to find the entrance soon.

Lunch arrived via Tynan, who had heard she would join his class tomorrow. He grinned as he left, promising to save her a seat. The repast comprised crusty bread with ham, cheese, pickles and salad leaves, reminding her of a ploughman's; followed by the sweetest, juiciest strawberries and blackberries she had ever tasted.

Iona had just drained the last of a delicious fruit cordial when Binny arrived with her basket, accompanied by a couple in civilian clothes. She introduced them as Shoemaker Alfred and Seamstress Agnes.

"Prior Fidelmus has decreed you must have a new kirtle suitable for the duke's banquet next week. There's no time to waste, so Agnes here has come to measure you so she can start on it immediately. Alfred will make you some new shoes and boots," Binny explained.

With her statistics taken and feet measured, the couple departed, and Binny eased herself into a chair at the table. "How are you coping?"

"I'm trying to keep busy. I paid a visit to the scriptorium today, and Brother Ambrose invited me to take part in an illumination class tomorrow."

"Ambrose is a good sort. Is art a hobby of yours?"

"Yes, but it's also my job. I was… *am* a commercial artist and graphic designer." Iona sighed. "I'm trying not to think about it, but my sister, Skye, will return from her holiday tomorrow. It won't be long before she discovers I'm missing. She'll be frantic with worry, as will my dad and Zara, my best friend. Fidelmus and Shay have hatched a plan to uncover the scoundrels behind the trike operation, but they'll need my help to work out how they're doing it. *Why* is another question. Fidelmus more or less consented to involve me if Shay agrees."

Binny raised her eyebrows. "My, you have been busy! You're not planning to haunt the high road then, hoping the trike will reappear so you can hijack it, like the others did?"

"Not likely! I don't believe it did *them* any good," Iona retorted and told Binny about Gavin Whyte. "But if I wish to remain sane, I must be proactive in my approach to finding another way home. I hope Shay returns soon. Do you think he'll let me take part in their scheme?"

Binny shrugged. "Depends what it is. He's not an easy man to read, but I suspect you'll have to convince him."

"What does a ranger do, anyway?"

"Do you want to know what a *ranger* does, or what Shay does?" Binny asked with a wry half-smile.

Iona frowned in confusion. "Isn't that the same thing?"

"In his case, no. Your average ranger is a scout, tracker, and hunter. Shay is that and more. You can add steward, spy, burglar, go-between, diplomat when necessary, and bodyguard if required."

"He seemed really angry about the attack on Mallowbrook," Iona mused.

"He's a dangerous man, but I didn't say he's not a good one. I know little about him, though." Binny stood and removed linens from her basket. "Well, there's no rest for the wicked. I'll just get your bath stuff ready for later, then I'd better get on."

Binny squeezed behind the screen and dumped the linens onto the bed along with a sea sponge. She lifted the varnished oak hip bath down from its peg, exposing a matching basin nestled inside, which hooked to the bath's foot on a swivel mount. Setting it before the fireplace, she arranged a large linen sheet inside the tub and said Iona could use the basin to wash her hair. Pointing to two large fabric rectangles, Binny explained, "No towelling here! But those are made from a woven linen that dries quickly."

As she bid Iona farewell through the open door, Dara appeared, ready to conduct Iona to the library. Binny tousled his hair and said, "How would you like to pay a visit to Eliza tomorrow? She complains it's been ages since she last saw her playmate."

"You know I'd like to, but there's no way Brother Ennis will give me the time off," Dara replied with downcast eyes.

"He will if you're on *Living Aurigan* escort duties." Binny turned to Iona. "Do you want to come for lunch after your class tomorrow? Joss, my husband, and my daughter, Eliza, will be pleased to meet you. We live nearby on the priory farm. You won't get lost with Dara to accompany you!"

Iona glanced at Dara's hopeful gaze and, eyes twinkling, she pretended to think about it. "Hmm, I don't *think* I've anything else planned. That *should* be convenient."

The small boy grinned, and Binny winked at Iona over his head.

"Will we have puzzle pie for lunch?" Dara asked Binny.

"I'm sure that can be arranged," she replied, and Dara's eyes shone with happiness.

Five minutes later, Iona stood in the library foyer and gazed around in awe. The stacks stood tall on every side, interspersed with reading islands, fitted out as study areas with tables and chairs. High, arched windows lined the walls. Though bordered with stained-glass roundels, the central, transparent panes provided plenty of natural light. Iona felt something brush against her ankles and glanced down to find a tabby cat winding around her legs.

"That's Thomasine. She keeps down the mice," Dara explained as Iona bent to stroke her. Extricating herself from Thomasine's friendly overtures, she followed Dara further into the stacks, the cat close on her heels.

"Are you looking for something in particular?" The boy enquired.

"Yes. I need books I can borrow about dragons, Saint Lexis and Saint Aurigan."

Iona ended up with two Saint Aurigan biographies, selected in the hope she might find clues to the truth of her situation. She also chose *The Tale of Saint Lexis*, and a general history-cum-reference book on dragons, merely to satiate her curiosity. Dara led her to a desk, where a clerk named Brother Vincent entered the titles Iona had borrowed into a ledger. Thomasine jumped into his lap, and the monk petted her and opened a desk drawer in search of treats. A door behind his desk opened, and a monk of ascetic appearance emerged. Brother Vincent gently placed the cat on the floor with a guilty expression. The new arrival dumped a pile of scrolls on Vincent's desk and regarded Iona with hooded, silver-grey eyes.

"Brother Ennis, this is Iona, our new *Living Aurigan*," Vincent informed as he surreptitiously shooed away the cat.

The head librarian gave Iona a crisp head bow and asked, "I have a task for the boy. Have you now dispensed with his services?"

"Yes, for now. He's been very helpful. However, I'll need to borrow Dara again tomorrow, if that's alright with you?"

"The needs of the *Living Aurigan* take precedence over mine," Brother Ennis replied in a neutral tone, though she detected annoyance in his eyes.

Iona thanked him, and Dara passed her the pile of books. As she made for the exit, she heard Brother Ennis scold the desk clerk, "What have I told you about feeding that cat treats? She'll get too fat and lazy to do her job properly."

The sun hung lower in the sky than Iona had expected. She had stayed in the library longer than intended, fascinated with the tomes that contained a surprising variety of subjects between their covers.

Iona exchanged nods with the elderly gardener, who wheeled his barrow from a narrow alley between the library's northern end and the western side of the cloister near Shay's room. Iona peered into the alley and saw it terminated at a tall, arched gate. It must be the entrance to the walled garden.

As she crossed the courtyard to her room, a beefy monk emerged from the gated passage between the bathhouse and the cloister's eastern side. He pushed a cart containing four lidded water buckets. Tynan accompanied him and waved to Iona. It seemed her bathwater had arrived. The buckets proved to contain hot and cold water, and the large monk, whom Tynan informed her was mute, poured them into the bath and basin attachment in the correct ratio to achieve the perfect temperature.

"Brother Kian will return at dinner-time to empty the bath," Tynan advised.

"I hope I'm not inconveniencing you too much," Iona addressed the mute.

He shook his head vigorously and signed at Tynan with his fingers.

"Brother Kian says it's no trouble and you can have a bath every day if you wish. He works in the bathhouse. It's his job to attend to the bathing needs of the brethren and their guests," Tynan explained.

"Thank you, Brother Kian. I will take you up on that offer," Iona said with a smile.

The monk placed an ewer of hot water and a water scoop at the side of the bath, and bowing to Iona, departed with Tynan. She locked the door behind them and rootled through Binny's basket of homemade products. As she extracted a bottle of scented bath oil and a small tub of moisture cream, she spotted the jar of healing salve Binny had advised her to apply daily to her leg injury and removed it from the basket.

Refreshed after her bath, Iona applied the healing salve. She dressed in a shift and the maroon robe, before combing out her wet hair. It should not take long to dry in this weather.

Brother Kian arrived and scooped the bathwater into empty buckets, placing them in his cart along with the sodden bath sheet and towels. After wiping down the bath, he hung it on its bracket and departed just as dinner arrived. The monks she had met so far had acted with unfailing kindness towards her, though Brother Ennis might prove to be the exception. Still, Iona felt grateful; she dreaded to think what might have happened if her trike ousting had occurred elsewhere along the road. She had to remind herself of this every time the enormity of her situation threatened to overwhelm her. It would be so easy to surrender to her fear as Bethany had done.

Dinner was buttered-herb chicken on a bed of rice, followed by apple tart with cream. Iona appreciated the goblet of red wine that accompanied it but couldn't help thinking of all the foods she would miss: pasta, chips, potato crisps, pizza, ice cream and chocolate.

Iona placed the empty dishes on their tray outside the door and selected the more decoratively bound St. Aurigan biography. She may as well read in the garden before dark. Locking the door behind her, Iona slipped down the alley, relieved to find the garden gate unlocked. Sitting on the bench where Shay had sat the night before, she opened the book, lavishly illustrated with woodcut engravings. However, the pictures proved more interesting than the over-reverent hagiographical text, which told her nothing useful. Iona hoped the other biography with its plain board covers would be different.

Returning to her room, Iona managed to light the candles with the flint striker without setting fire to anything. With the onset of darkness, Iona's fears returned. What if the prior's scheme proved fruitless? She might be stuck here forever unless she became desperate enough to take the same risk as the other trikers. Had they *really* leaped from the frying pan into the fire? It seemed likely...

Overcome with exhaustion after her eventful day, Iona, at last, retired to bed.

Chapter 8

The next morning, Iona dressed in the green kirtle and plaited her dark hair into a braid that hung over one shoulder.

After breakfast, she found her own way to the scriptorium and presented herself to Brother Ambrose, who escorted her to an airy chamber beside the schoolroom. Tynan waved to her from his seat and patted the empty desk beside him. Only four students were present today, including Iona, and she asked Tynan about the absence of the others.

"Oh, some are training with the ink makers and the rest attend the advanced calligraphy class next door. Only three of us are talented enough to take illumination lessons with Brother Oisin. Most of the other students will become scribes," he explained with a touch of pride.

The door opened, and a curly-haired monk swept into the room and advanced to the front of the class. "Good morning pupils, and a warm welcome to our *Living Aurigan*." He addressed Iona, "I'm Brother Oisin. May I call you Iona?"

"Oh, please do!" she replied, appalled at the thought he might refer to her as *Living Aurigan*, or *Eterna*, as the nuns had.

Brother Oisin gave the boys assignments based on their individual progress. He handed Iona a blank piece of parchment and a graphite stick wound with string, the mediaeval version of a pencil. "Let me see what you can do. Draw something for me; anything you like."

Iona frowned in thought. Then, brow clearing, she sketched her memory of the dragon looping the loop at sunset. Oisin turned from instructing the boy on her other side just as she began to add shading. The monk held up a hand in a stop gesture and picked up Iona's sketch. "So much movement," he muttered to himself, and Iona felt unsure if that was good or bad. Judging by the precise, formal design Tynan painted, she wondered if she had erred in her choice.

Oisin handed the sketch back. "You must familiarise yourself with the tools of our art before we move to the next stage." He pointed to the drawing, and then to the tray of inks, tempera paints, quills and brushes on a tall stand beside Iona's sloping desk surface. "Colour it."

As Oisin turned away to inspect the third boy's work, Iona reached to the tray for a parchment scrap and tested the inks and brushes before applying colour to her sketch. Since she had only seen the dragon in silhouette, she based its hues and features on the Saint Lexis illumination. Iona soon got the hang of the unfamiliar media and used the quills to add fine detail and texture. Engrossed in her work as she applied the finishing touches, she startled at Oisin's presence by her shoulder.

"Exquisite!" he exclaimed, and Tynan and the other boys craned to see.

Oisin strode to a tall chest and opened a drawer to extract two parchment sheets. He returned to Iona and placed them on her desk. "Let's see what you can do with this."

Iona noted that although the sheets had identical text, only one bore an extravagantly decorated alphabet letter, illuminated floral borders, and a miniature illustration of two ladies in courtly dress within an insert box.

"Your freehand work is excellent, but an illuminator must also learn control, which comes in part from a steady hand, a mastery of the materials, and a spatial awareness of the design placement." Oisin tapped the undecorated sheet. "Copy the illuminations on the other sheet onto this. Take your time; there's no rush."

He turned to examine Tynan's work, which looked perfect to Iona. However, the monk tutted good-naturedly, and taking the brush from the boy's hand, made a couple of light demonstration strokes, his delicate touch in contrast to his flamboyant nature.

Iona's experience as a professional artist had made her a fair copyist, but she worked with painstaking care to compensate for her greenness with the medium. Oisin bustled from student to student, making adjustments here and there, or offering good-humoured advice.

Time flew by, and when the class broke up forty minutes before lunch, Iona had not completed her assignment.

"Don't worry. I didn't expect you to finish it today. You can carry on tomorrow, that is, if you wish to attend the next class?" Oisin said.

Iona had not enjoyed herself this much for a long time. The thought filled her with disquiet; how could that be the case amidst a situation where she feared for more than her sanity? Nevertheless, she agreed to return on the morrow, and Oisin handed over her dragon illustration.

As she left the room with Tynan, the boy asked to examine the small picture, and Iona passed it to him. "This is great! The dragon almost looks alive, as though it might fly from the parchment!"

"Keep it," Iona said.

"Really? No, I can't do that..." he replied with regret and tried to return it.

"Yes, you can. Take it!" Iona insisted, gently pushing his hand back.

"Wow! Thanks!" Tynan exclaimed with a huge grin.

Iona just had time to freshen up before lunch at Binny's.

When Dara arrived to accompany her, the nuns next door emerged from their room as she shut the door behind her. They both sketched the circle blessing over their hearts, and Sister Honoria asked, "Have you thought any more about our offer to take you to the motherhouse?"

Iona had not considered it for a moment, but replied diplomatically, "Much as it would please me to see Glassnesse, the *Great Wheel* works in mysterious ways, and I feel it is my duty to remain here until it reveals the reason for my manifestation at Tritaurium."

Honoria eyed her penetratingly, but Iona's reply, though open to interpretation, dissuaded her from pressing the issue. Instead, she reached into a pocket, and withdrawing a folded piece of parchment, handed it to Iona. "If you ever change your mind and need to contact us directly, our intermediary in Tritaurium can arrange it. These are his details." She bowed, and tracing a circle on her forehead, departed with Sister Bedelia in tow.

Iona wondered why she might need to get in touch with the motherhouse via an agent; surely the prior would do so on her behalf? She stuffed the parchment unread into the embroidered pouch attached to her girdle belt and followed Dara through the gated passage that ran alongside the bathhouse and laundry building. A grille-work side gate led into its grounds, through which Iona glimpsed sheets flapping on a washing line in the gentle breeze. They continued past it towards a row of anchorite cells and into an herb garden flush against the priory's eastern wall. A low door took them into the meadow that lay between the priory and the estate farm.

Dara led Iona along a path that swept towards the river before it turned eastward. The reed-edged water sparkled in the sunlight, ruffled by a breath of wind. A monk stood in the shallows; his habit hitched up to his knees as he fished for trout. His basket already contained several, and Iona wondered if she would have trout for dinner. She smiled at the sight of a duck with her ducklings paddling in a circle and had to admit the priory environs presented an idyllic scene.

Iona glanced down at Dara and wondered if the little boy felt happy under Brother Ennis' supervision. "Dara, do you like working in the library?"

Dara appeared nonplussed at the question and replied with hesitance. "I like all the storybooks… and Brother Vincent is nice."

"But?" Iona pressed.

"I don't have a talent like Tynan. He's training to do something he wants to do."

"And what do you want to do?"

"I… I like helping Brother Quintus. I wish I could apprentice to him…"

"Have you asked him?"

Dara shook his head violently, and Iona guessed it meant he would never dare ask. Perhaps he felt afraid Brother Ennis might find out. Quintus seemed to 'borrow' Dara and Tynan regularly, and he could certainly use a helper... Perhaps she would have a word with him......

As they neared Binny's thatched cottage, Iona observed that its garden, planted with a profusion of herbs, vegetables and flowers, ran down to the river. She guessed the former chemist used them in her organic medicines and beauty concoctions. Barns stood to one side, with an orchard on the other. A double row of beehives occupied the end of a wildflower meadow beyond the dwelling, reminding Iona that Binny's beekeeper husband supplied the priory's honey.

A little girl ran from the cottage to meet them. She curtseyed to Iona and excitedly informed Dara that Lady Muck neared her time. The acolyte grinned at his friend, and both children rushed into the cottage past Binny, who stood in the doorway.

"Lady Muck?" Iona asked with a raised eyebrow.

"Our heavily pregnant dog. She loves nothing more than rolling in cow pats, fox poo, and what have you. You name it, she'll roll in it; the smellier the better! Eliza is obsessed with her unborn puppies."

Iona chuckled and followed Binny into the central living area where Eliza and Dara knelt beside Lady Muck, stretched on her side before the banked fire. Though the dog's tummy appeared uncomfortably distended, her tail thumped the floor as she raised her head to lick Dara's hand in greeting. Binny's husband, Joss, entered through the back door, and introductions made, Binny disappeared behind a curtained archway. Joss urged Eliza to set the table for her mum, his kind eyes crinkling at the corners when he smiled at her reluctance to leave Lady Muck's side.

Once seated at the table with Joss and the two children, Iona broke the ice by asking him questions about his job, since she had little knowledge of beekeeping. Though a quiet man, he seemed happy to oblige, and Iona pegged him as someone who usually spoke only when he had something pertinent to say.

When Binny reappeared bearing her famed puzzle pie, Dara clasped his hands with delight as she set it in the table's centre. Iona glanced at the pie and then looked at Binny. "Pizza?"

Binny smiled. "My best approximation of it, anyway. It's not actually difficult to make since most of the basic ingredients are available here."

"I was thinking last night about how much I'd miss pizza! Why puzzle pie?"

"Dara invented the name," Binny replied with a fond smile for the boy.

"It's the way Binny cuts it into shapes that fit together like a puzzle, and because we never know what toppings we'll have," Dara piped up.

Iona peered at the pizza, loaded with cheese, onion and ham, remarking, "No pineapple, at least!"

She and Binny shared a grin, although the others didn't understand the joke.

After they demolished two family-sized pizzas between them, Joss returned to his hives, and the children went to play outside.

"Dara almost seems part of your family," Iona observed.

Binny sighed. "We'd adopt him in a heartbeat if we could. His parents are dirt-poor and left him with the order, aged seven. It's not uncommon; about half the acolytes come from a similar background. At least Dara is fed, clothed, and educated, and has a guaranteed future with the monks."

"It's good he can just be a kid when he's here with you, though."

Binny refilled Iona's tea mug and leaned back, lowering her eyes in a contemplative manner. "You know, I've made more difference to people here than I ever did back in our world. I have a shed load of products I've been making to sell from a stall at the castle fair in two weeks; stuff that folks here really need. We may not be rich, but Joss and I get by nicely with the proceeds from his honey and candles and the money I earn helping Quintus with the female guests; not to mention my sideline. I don't regret my trike experience in the slightest, even though I became trapped here involuntarily. Once I met Joss, I never wanted to leave."

"I'm glad things worked out for you, but all I can think of is what might encourage Shay to involve me in his plan, in the hope it will lead to a way back home. But I don't even know what it is! I hope he returns soon. I've tried to calculate the distance from Mallowbrook to Tritaurium, based on how long it took me to travel from there to here on the trike. At two daily half-hour sessions on *average* over ten days, I estimate the journey is approximately ten hours."

"It will also depend on the average speed you travelled. Shay will be on horseback, plus it's doubtful he will have taken the high road. The route via the back roads almost halves the time."

"So, around five hours each way?"

Binny waggled her hand. "Give and take. If he spends no more than a day or two in Mallowbrook, he might be back tomorrow or the day after. Still, you need to think hard before involving yourself; Duke Clovis is a very dangerous man."

After her bath and dinner that evening, a light rainfall confined Iona to her room. She stashed away her modern clothes, which Binny had washed, and returned to her that day. Moving the chair closer to the window, she sat down to peruse the tome on dragons and learned three distinct sentient species inhabited Beretania, the country Kentauros was part of. Saint Lexis belonged to the Alphas, the largest in body size, as presumably did the dragons she had glimpsed on her journey. The illustrations depicted the middling-sized breed, known as the Venator, with proportions similar to an elephant, and the smallest, named the Lacunae, appeared to be the size of a large dog. Iona found the Lacunae of particular interest. Reports suggested they could disappear at will and re-materialise anywhere they wished. She couldn't decide if the author's words were hyperbole, or if the Lacunae could actually teleport, but nothing would surprise her anymore.

Alone in her room, thoughts of her family intruded, and finding it hard to concentrate, Iona switched to the book on Saint Lexis, written for younger readers. The simplified story read:

'One hundred years ago, humans opportunistically thieved Venator eggs, raising the young to become beasts of burden. In retaliation, the Venator raided human settlements, kidnapping the young and healthy to serve them as slaves. Lexis intervened before it escalated to outright war, and attended the Congress of Arcem, organised by Jaellin, a lay brother in the order of the Great Wheel. Dukes, barons, and lords descended on Arcem to thrash out an accord with the representative of dragonkind, and arrange an exchange of captives. However, not everyone wished to surrender their intelligent beasts of burden. With the congress in progress outside Arcem's gates, dissidents set fire to the stronghold, trapping hundreds within. In a selfless act of bravery, Lexis thrice flew through the flames and rescued the people gathered in the central courtyard and atop the stronghold's walls, transporting them to safety on his back.

When Lexis recovered from his resultant injuries, the congress participants agreed on a treaty that would separate dragonkind from humans forevermore, outlawing unauthorised incursions by both sides into the others newly formed territories. With the mountainous terrain to north and north-east ceded to dragonkind, and all the lands below the new frontier the sole domain of humans, the order of the Great Wheel proclaimed Lexis' sainthood. Jaellin became the first prior of Saint Lexis Priory, situated on the border of the divided lands, through which all communication and diplomatic relations between both sides would henceforth pass.'

That night, Iona dreamt she flew back home on a Lacunae's back, but the wolfhound-sized dragon shrank to the size of a pug, and she fell off......

Chapter 9

As Iona ate breakfast the next morning, she heard the murmur of voices and the squeak of handcart wheels as a groom conveyed the nuns' luggage from their room. She breathed a sigh of relief at their departure, although she couldn't have said why.

After her illumination class, she crossed paths with Quintus on his way to the refectory. Determined to sound him out about Dara, Iona arranged an after-lunch meeting with him in his office, located near the prior's.

Midday meal consumed; Iona knocked on the guest master's half-open door. Quintus beckoned to her through the gap and invited her to sit. He finished making an entry in a ledger and rose from his desk to close the door and take the matching chair beside Iona's.

"Is there a problem I can help you with?" he enquired.

"What, you mean apart from the calamity of my entrapment in an alternate reality?" Iona felt immediate remorse and appended, "Sorry Quintus, ignore me; it's not your fault. I shouldn't take it out on you."

Quintus waved away her apology. "You can say what you like to me. I'm here whenever you need a sounding board."

"Thanks, I appreciate it." Iona shifted to face him. "I only wanted to ask you if the guest master ever takes on an apprentice?"

"Why? Are you offering your services?" Quintus grinned, his cheeks dimpling.

Iona smiled. "Not me; Dara. I don't think he's happy under Brother Ennis. A sensitive boy like him needs a more... *encouraging* mentor if he is to flourish."

"Is that your observation, or did Dara tell you this?"

"Both. It only took a gentle nudge to get Dara to confide he would rather apprentice to you."

Quintus wore a half-smile as he studied Iona's face. "Your concern for Dara's welfare does you credit. I'm pleased to see you making friends; it will make your life here easier to bear. You may even emulate Binny at this rate!" he joked.

"No chance! Besides, the beekeeper is already taken," she riposted. However, she half-believed Quintus hoped she might become entrenched to the extent she would find it harder to leave her new life if presented with the opportunity. Maybe he had tired of dealing with a string of *Living Aurigans*.

Quintus chuckled. "Anyway, as to your question, my former protégé, Lorcan, so impressed Duke Clovis on his last visit here that he offered him a position. Lorcan had no taste for the cloistered life and jumped at the chance to become the court seneschal's assistant. I haven't yet got around to seeking a replacement. Dara is a good lad, but unless Ennis agrees to let him go and finds another acolyte to fill his shoes, my hands are tied. I will speak to the prior, though. I'm sure he'll think of a solution."

Iona stood. "Well, I won't take up any more of your time, but thanks, Quintus."

"I meant what I said. If you need a sympathetic ear, I'm here for you," the guest master reiterated as he showed her to the door.

That evening after dinner, Iona carried the other Saint Aurigan biography into the walled garden. She sat on the bench, and tucking a strand of her unbound hair behind an ear, studied the close-written text. Noting the archaic spelling, she deduced it must be an older tome.

The gate suddenly opened, and Shay appeared. As he neared the sundial he spotted Iona, and coming to an abrupt stop, nodded curtly to her and turned to leave. Iona clutched the book to her chest and stood. "Please don't go. I'd like to talk to you, if I may."

Shay acceded with obvious reluctance, and Iona sat back down, making room for him on the bench. "How bad was it at Mallowbrook?" she asked.

"Do you actually want to know, or are you just making polite conversation?"

Iona felt stung. "I wouldn't have asked if I didn't want to know. Anyway, I hardly think a sacked village is a fit subject for *polite* conversation!"

"Why do you care? None of this is real to you, is it? You can't wait to leave. I've spoken to Fidelmus and know what you *really* want to ask me," Shay replied, his tone sardonic.

Iona bit her tongue and took a calming breath. "It's *real* alright, and the longer I stay here, the more real it becomes. I didn't *choose* to come here; Borderland tricked me. Despite that, I *do* care, but that doesn't prevent a perfectly natural longing to return to where I belong."

Shay looked directly at her for the first time, his dark eyes piercing. "*Do* you belong there?"

"I don't know what you mean."

The ranger stood. "I'll think about it."

Iona frowned in confusion. "Think about what?"

"Whether to include you in our plans. I'll decide after the banquet."

Shay moved to leave, and Iona persisted, "Mallowbrook?"

"Grim," he replied succinctly, and walked away.

Iona muttered, "Who rattled your cage?" to his retreating back. However, she guessed whatever he had witnessed in the sacked village had prompted his bitter attitude, but that didn't excuse his rudeness. *He might be very easy on the eye, but what a jerk!*

In the five days leading up to the banquet, Iona avoided the garden for fear of bumping into Shay again. He did too, and she guessed his reason mirrored hers. When Prior Fidelmus mentioned that Shay would accompany them to the duke's feast, it put her even more on edge.

Iona progressed quickly in her illumination studies and practiced her calligraphy at the kneehole desk in her room. Fidelmus returned the leather folder, but she had no desire to add a deposition of her own to it. She tried to avoid thinking about her family and friends and what must have ensued when they discovered her disappearance. However, try as she might, she sometimes found herself on the verge of a panic attack and sought refuge from her thoughts in the scriptorium. Brother Ambrose allowed her to work on her own projects alongside the illuminators in the sunny tower room. They always made her feel welcome, and she soon became acquainted with everyone.

Fidelmus informed Iona that he had spoken to Brother Ennis about Dara. As luck would have it, the prior had agreed to accept the younger son of a local baron as an acolyte. Cahir, the fifteen-year-old boy in question, was of a scholarly disposition, preferring to bury his head in a book rather than train with his father's men-at-arms like his older brothers. Although Ennis had grumbled on principle, he concurred the boy sounded like a suitable replacement for Dara, but until Cahir arrived in the next month, Dara must continue at the library.

Iona slowly ploughed through the second Saint Aurigan biography, hampered by the outmoded word spellings and quaint turns of phrase. However, it dated from just after Aurigan's death and seemed a truer account of his life than the hagiography she had read. She returned the latter book to the library along with the *Tale of Saint Lexis*, but hung onto the dragon reference book, for now. As she handed the two tomes to Brother Vincent, Ennis swept past Vincent's desk on his way to the back office, and Iona could have sworn he glared daggers at her. Perhaps he had learnt of her interference in the Dara affair.

Iona bid farewell to Vincent and made for the exit. However, she turned back when she spotted an area reserved for maps and charts. Iona happily browsed the shelves and racks when she heard two men talking in low voices beyond a scroll unit, which partially screened off the map section.

Iona recognised Brother Vincent's nasal tones, though she couldn't identify the other man, who, oblivious to her presence, remarked, "I'm surprised Ennis capitulated so easily."

"I'm not! He'll regard mentoring a scion of the landed gentry as an opportunity. It's not inconceivable the boy's father will make an endowment to the library. If that doesn't happen, I'm sure Ennis will derive greater satisfaction from bullying a baron's son than he does from a pauper's whelp! Anyway, I'm happy for Dara; he's a good lad. Thomasine and I will miss him," Brother Vincent replied.

"Speaking of which, here are the titbits for Thomasine to replace the treats confiscated by the tyrant," the other man responded, and Iona pegged him as a kitchen worker.

She waited until they moved off before hastening to the exit.

Two days before the banquet, Iona visited Binny for lunch. Not wishing to bring trouble down on Dara, she had not requested his company. She knew he would have more opportunities to visit his surrogate family when he started his apprenticeship with Quintus.

Lady Muck had given birth to four puppies, one of which Joss planned to gift to his nephew. He had promised another to the head groom at the priory stables, and the remaining two to Eliza and Dara, though, as Eliza explained, Dara's puppy would live with them, for now.

An excited Eliza led Iona by the hand to view the mother and her offspring, curled up on blankets in a wooden box by the fireplace. "Mummy says I should call mine Splodge because of the black patch around his eye, but I haven't decided yet."

Iona chuckled. "That's a good name; the patch reminds me of an ink smudge."

"Smudge! *That's* what I'll call him!" Eliza beamed, and Iona smiled at her enthusiasm.

After lunch (no puzzle pie, this time), Binny asked Iona if she had spoken to Shay.

Iona scowled. "Yes. He wasn't exactly courteous. In fact, he was downright unpleasant, but he said he'll think about including me in the scheme he's plotted with Fidelmus."

"Hmm, you must have caught him at a bad time. He's not the most loquacious man, but I've never found him ill-mannered. Did he say when he'd let you know?" Binny asked.

"After the banquet." Iona shrugged.

"Oh, that reminds me, your new outfit will be ready tomorrow. Alfred and Agnes will deliver it in the morning."

Eliza wore a wistful expression. "Mummy says it's made from silk and velvet. You'll look like a princess! Will you dance with the duke?"

"Dance?" Iona said in confusion.

"There'll be dancing after the banquet," Binny supplied.

"What kind of dancing?"

Binny grinned. "Well, you won't be shaking your booty and busting Club Copacabana moves!"

"I could handle *those*, especially as my leg is so much better since I've been using the salve you gave me," Iona responded with an edge of panic in her voice.

"Don't worry. Court dancing is mainly holding hands with a partner and sauntering about in a pattern, with the odd hop here and there."

"No, it isn't Mummy! There are different steps for all the sequences," Eliza contradicted.

"Well, what do I know? I've only danced the more energetic *Carole* of the common people, which is nothing like court dancing. Perhaps our resident expert can give you a crash course? Eliza attends a dame school for the merchant's daughters to learn the accomplishments gentlewomen must master," Binny explained with a sardonic eye-roll.

Eliza leaped to her feet with eagerness. "Oh, let me teach you! I can show you the primary steps for the *Almain*, the *Estampie*, and the *Basse*. Madame Barreau says a good partner will guide you if you forget the odd step, but the basics are important."

"What happens if you both forget?" Iona teased.

"Oh, that won't happen! All the gentlemen at the banquet will know the dances by heart. We need music!" Eliza stared pleadingly at Joss who, seated in his fireside chair, whittled at a lump of wood.

Joss comically waggled his eyebrows at his daughter, and setting aside his whittling, reached up for a lute that hung from a wall bracket. Binny and Joss pushed the table back against the wall to create a dance floor, and Iona and Eliza stepped into the centre.

Almost three hours later, Iona strolled back to the priory across the meadow, mentally going through the dance steps. The river glinted in the late afternoon sun and, on impulse, Iona deviated from the path to make her way down to the water's edge.

After all that dancing, she felt tempted to remove her pixie boots and paddle in the shallows. However, with nothing on which to dry her feet afterwards, she thought better of it. This part of the riverbank appeared deserted, and humming a tune Joss had played, she moved through an *Estampie* measure she had muddled up several times.

"That should have been a double step there, and you forgot to close your feet at the end," a voice advised.

Iona whirled and regarded Shay, whom she had not heard

approach. He stood in a relaxed attitude, one hand resting on his sword hilt, wearing a loose-sleeved white shirt open to his chest, tucked into black leather, hip-hugging trousers. Iona thought he looked just like the rakish men that had graced the covers of her mother's romance novels.

Flustered, Iona took refuge in sarcasm. "Well, I'm sorry in advance if my ineptitude shames you at the banquet."

"It won't," Shay said in a level tone and shrugged. "I was just trying to be helpful." He moved to stand beside Iona, and crossing his arms, gazed out at the river. "I need to know you're not like the others. Even Doctor Cleary thought the answer to this world's ills lay back in your reality. He *belonged* here and should never have left."

"He was trying to save his friend and didn't know the risk he took. Anyway, I'm not sure I understand what you're saying," Iona said.

"Discovering the source of the *trisik* operation is not *just* about returning you to your world. The village sackings appear to be connected and there may be other threats to Kentauros' citizens. We must tread carefully to avoid stirring up a hornet's nest, or else repercussions will fall on the priory. Your fellow travellers cared only for themselves, as the cycle of *trisik* takeovers proves. If I make you part of our group, how do I know you won't put you needs before ours?" Shay explained.

"I'm not sure I follow," Iona replied with a puzzled frown.

"Let's say, for example, that our efforts uncover a way for you to return home. What if we must wait before we act to ensure everyone benefits? Would you seize the chance anyway, even if it leaves the rest of us in the shit?"

Iona opened her mouth to protest she'd do nothing of the sort, then closed it again. Could she really say, hand on heart, that she wouldn't grab any opportunity? She sat down on a boulder near the shallows, worn smooth by occasional submersions, and propped her chin in her hands. "I can only say what I *think* I would do, and the answer is no, I wouldn't abandon you all to your fate – if I could help it. I'd wait until the right time for *everyone*. However, shit happens, and circumstances can force a change of plan or steal your choices."

Shay turned to face her. "That's an honest answer, at least. If you'd vehemently denied it, I'd be inclined to tell the prior we should proceed without you. Both Quintus and Ambrose hold you in esteem, and I've observed your integration into priory life. The last three made no effort and showed little gratitude. However, I'm not so trusting as Fidelmus, and it will take more than that to convince me."

"Why didn't you say all this the other night instead of tearing me a new hole?"

Shay shrugged. "Your response was enough to persuade me to give you a chance. I wouldn't be here otherwise."

"So, that was some kind of *test*?" Iona asked with an edge of anger, remembering how much he had upset her. When Shay didn't reply, Iona stood and mirrored his cross-armed stance. "Would you act any different from me, or even the others, if our positions were reversed? While I have made friends here whom I've grown very fond of, I have a *family* and a life back home!"

The ranger's striking dark eyes grew shadowed, and he murmured, "Do you *really* have a life?" Before Iona could respond, he added, "Would *you* be any different from *me* in my position?"

While Iona floundered for an answer, Shay said, "We'll speak of this again after the banquet." He began to turn away, but paused. "You did a good thing for Dara, but watch out for Brother Ennis," and he stalked off without a backward glance, leaving Iona to glare at his back.

She flung herself down on the boulder and held her head in her hands. *How dare he! She did have a life, didn't she?*

The next morning, Alfred and Agnes arrived, accompanied by Binny and Eliza, who bounced with excitement.

The seamstress laid out Iona's new outfit on the bed. She removed the protective linen covering to reveal an extravagant red silk-damask overdress, patterned with swirling gold vines, the skirt of which Iona must hold a foot above the floor when she danced to reveal the gold silk underdress. The red velvet, narrow shawl collar of the overdress plunged to the top of the ribcage, displaying the underdress bodice. A red and gold jewelled belt cinched the fabric below the bust, and a wide band of red velvet edged the skirt hem, matching the wrist trim of the tight sleeves, and a gold-beaded belt pouch.

Iona stared at the ensemble in pop-eyed amazement, tempered with uncertainty. Agnes showed her a red velvet, jewelled headdress, designed to sit in an upright semi-circle between her ears, with her hair worn loose down her back. After all the seamstress' hard work, Iona tried not to gaze askance at it, but it appeared so outlandish to her modern sensibilities.

Binny seemed to guess her thoughts and said, "Wait until you see some of the headdresses worn by the court ladies. This is modest in comparison."

"I'll take your word for it," Iona replied, resigned to wearing it.

Alfred unwrapped a pair of soft, tan leather bootees for daywear, with V-shaped notches at the ankles, and a pair of red leather poulaines for the banquet. Iona stifled her gasp when she saw the extremely long, pointed toes. Though she smiled and thanked him, she had visions of tripping over her own feet whilst she danced, or worse, tripping up someone else.

When Alfred departed, Agnes and Binny helped her into the outfit, and the seamstress made some adjustments in situ, having brought her sewing kit. A round-eyed Eliza oohed and aahed in admiration, and tried on the headdress behind Binny's back. Iona noticed, but smiled inwardly and said nothing. Removing the headdress, Eliza set it down with care and whispered something in Binny's ear before she dashed from the room.

Dressed again in the blue kirtle, Iona opened the armoire doors and removed Jake's jerkin and two shirts. Bending to the chest, she fished about inside until she found a pair of black breeches. She turned to a puzzled Agnes and said, "Do you think you could alter these clothes to fit me?"

"Well... yes, but why? Those are men's clothes."

"The *Living Aurigans'* travel here from a distant country, where it's normal for women to wear shirts and breeches."

"You mean like the Turcia women from Byzantz, or the steppe nomads from Euriont?"

Iona had no knowledge of the countries and cultures referred to, not having examined all the library maps before Brother Vincent and his friend turned up. However, she nodded and said lamely, "It would feel comforting to wear familiar clothes in private."

"If you say so," Agnes said dubiously. "Am I to charge it to the priory's account?"

Iona remembered the coins Jake had left in the pouch. Why shouldn't she use them? He had ejected her from the trike, after all. She fetched the pouch and emptied the money onto the bed. "Will this be enough to cover it?"

"More than enough! It's only alterations," Agnes informed, picking up half the coppers to show her the price.

"How much will a pair of new boots cost, do you think? A pair like Shay wears?"

Agnes raised her eyebrows but pointed to the silver coin. "That much."

"If it's not too much trouble, can you ask Alfred to make me a pair?"

When Agnes departed with Jake's garments, Binny shook her head at Iona. "You gave the poor woman quite a turn. Where do you plan to wear those clothes, anyway?"

"Here. Isn't Saint Aurigan depicted as androgynous to represent *all* travellers? As the *Living Aurigan*, I should continue the tradition. Well, that's what I'll say to anyone who questions my choice. I'm fed up with all the flappy sleeves and leg-tangling skirts!"

Before Binny could retort, Eliza burst through the door. "They're here!" She grabbed Iona's hand and led her to the courtyard, where a grinning Tynan stood beside two monks, one holding a harp and the other a shawm, an oboe-like instrument. "Prior Fidelmus agreed with me when I told him you ought to practice your dancing before tomorrow. He sent Brother Riordan and Brother Doran to provide the music, and Tynan's here to partner Mummy. We need another couple to rehearse the weaves and processionals with."

Eliza bounded over to the two instrumentalists to confer on the tunes, confident that Iona and Binny would fall into line.

Iona raised her eyebrows at Binny, who shrugged and said, "Eliza knows how to wrap Fidelmus around her little finger. She never said anything to me about *my* inclusion in the practice, though."

"If I'm going to make a fool of myself in public, you can sodding well keep me company," Iona said mock-crossly. In truth, she knew Eliza was probably right.

Eliza positioned Binny and Tynan near the well. "Hold hands and glide slowly. This one has an odd number of double steps, so keep an eye on what I'm doing and wait for my verbal 'cross' command before executing the first weave."

"Executing? That's a big word," Binny said with a quirk of the lips.

"That's the word Madame Barreau uses." The little girl grabbed Iona's hand and nodded to the musicians.

Binny and Tynan stumbled more than they glided, and when Eliza shouted 'Cross!' over the sonorous blare of the double-reed shawm, they moved in two separate directions. As Eliza roundly scolded them, Tynan snickered behind his hand and Iona and Binny stifled their laughter.

Brother Ennis suddenly appeared in the library doorway; hands held over his ears as he glared outraged at the musicians. He had taken two steps forward when the door of Shay's room opened, and the ranger emerged to lean casually against the cloister's end pillar. He sharpened his knife with a whetstone and studied the head librarian from beneath lowered lashes. Ennis took one look at him and thought better of interfering. He turned on his heel and flounced back into the library, shooing a peeking Dara from the doorway.

Shay pocketed knife and whetstone, and inclining his head to Iona and Binny, crossed the courtyard to the tower gate.

Iona felt relieved he had gone. She knew she would fumble the steps even more under the ranger's disconcerting gaze.

Chapter 10

Early the following afternoon, Binny arrived to help Iona dress for the banquet. Nerves knotted Iona's stomach, but Binny's steadying presence and one of her herbal teas helped settle it.

The former chemist produced a wooden box from her ubiquitous basket and opened it to reveal a selection of cosmetics. "The court ladies paint their faces, but most of the preparations they use are more than a little dubious. I've had some success with making my own from less toxic ingredients, and have managed to persuade a couple of the more influential merchant's wives to adopt them. Did you know that women plucked out their eyelashes, eyebrows, and hairline in the mediaeval culture of *our* world?" Binny shuddered. "Luckily, they don't do that here!"

Iona pointed to the poulaines with their outrageously long toes, and said, "It's just as well because those shoes are the extent of what I'm prepared to suffer for fashion."

"Those are nothing compared to some of the footwear worn by the duke's courtiers; especially the men!" Binny remarked as she laid out the pots and brushes. "Okay, I've got a face powder here with a cereal starch base, blusher and lipstick made from crushed roots and berries mixed with lanolin or lard, both of which are still used in contemporary makeup. The cake mascara and kohl are derived from lard, soot, charcoal, gum resins and plant oil, again, all ingredients used by the modern cosmetics industry."

Iona ran her fingers over the various wood-handled brushes tipped with fine hair or bristles, designed to apply the mascara, blusher, and lipstick.

"Joss makes those for me. I'm hoping to sell a range of my cosmetics at the castle fair. I haven't worked out *how* to explain to the women here that the mercury and lead in their cosmetics is poisonous without revealing *how* I know."

Binny carefully applied Iona's makeup, selecting a lipstick made from crushed strawberries and mulberries as the final touch.

"It tastes nice, at any rate!" Iona quipped and remembered the tinted lip balm she had removed from her hoodie pocket, now hidden inside an armoire drawer. She knew she ought to dispose of it since a plastic tube encased the balm, but felt reluctant to do so. This small, ordinary item anchored her to a world that might feel less real the longer she stayed in this one.

After Binny assisted her into the banquet outfit, she unfastened the six plaits Iona had braided into her still-damp hair after she washed it the previous evening. The braids left a pleasing ripple effect in Iona's long mane after Binny brushed it out. With the headdress settled on her head, Iona slid her feet into the poulaines that fastened with latchets.

Binny removed a glass scent vial from her basket and handed it to Iona, who removed the stopper and sniffed, detecting a floral bouquet with spicy undertones.

"It's not *Chanel Number Five*, but it's passable. It needs a bit more work, I think," Binny said.

"It's lovely!" Iona responded, dabbing the perfume on her wrists and neck. "I don't know how you find the time to make all this stuff! You're a one-woman cottage industry!"

"Not quite. I'm teaching Eliza, and Joss helps with all the practical stuff; foraging the botanicals and making the containers, etcetera. A monk in the infirmary assists with some of the medicinal preparations. Prior Fidelmus has promised me an apprentice if he can find someone suitable. He sees the need for my products," Binny explained, stepping back to survey Iona. "We forgot to get you a necklace." She tsked and shrugged. "Well, there are enough jewels on that headdress to make up for it."

A knock sounded at the door, and Binny gathered up her basket. "That'll be Brother Quintus to escort you to the carriage."

Iona felt a little sick but knew she must do this. How else could she gauge the duke's character first-hand? She suddenly remembered what she had meant to ask Binny. "Will the banquet food be safe to eat? I don't fancy coming down with food poisoning."

"Duke Clovis employs a head chef from Truscaromia, a country to the south with higher hygiene standards than this one. If in doubt, note the foods Fidelmus and Shay avoid and follow their lead."

Iona nodded and popped the slim scent vial and the small container of lip colour into her pouch. She opened the door to Quintus, whose eyes gleamed in appreciation as he took stock of her appearance. "You look beautiful, if I may say so." His cheeks dimpled in one of his guileless smiles, and he bowed in a courtly manner and offered his arm.

"Thank you," Iona replied and hooked her hand through his elbow. She might need the support until she got used to walking in her 'Coco the Clown' shoes, as she privately termed them. However, she found them less difficult to manage than she had expected, perhaps because the toes curled up a little at the tips.

When they reached the tower gateway, Iona turned to wave at Binny, wishing her friend could accompany her to the banquet. Binny gave her a thumbs-up signal and stepped towards the passageway leading to the meadow.

"I know you're nervous, but Shay and the prior will look after you," Quintus reassured.

"Oh, I'm sure they will, but I think Shay disapproves of me. It's a shame you're not attending; I could use a friendly face."

Quintus gave a slight headshake. "Don't read too much into Shay's demeanour. If he felt that way, he wouldn't give you the time of day, let alone consider making you part of his great plan!"

Iona detected an acerbic edge to his tone, as though Quintus believed Shay had no business contemplating her inclusion in a scheme that might expose her to danger. However, it was *her* choice to get involved, so Iona dropped the subject and instead asked Quintus about the other attendees.

"Merchant Bertrand Leon will be there with his family. He's a great supporter of Fidelmus and the priory, and I'm sure his wife, Isobel, will take you under her wing," Quintus supplied as they reached the priory's main entrance, where Fidelmus and Shay waited in the vestibule. Releasing Iona's arm, Quintus murmured, "Good luck!" and, bowing his head to the prior, disappeared down the corridor to his office.

"You look splendid, dear!" Fidelmus praised, and offering his arm, asked, "Shall we?"

She thanked the prior, and let him lead her down the short flight of external steps to a waiting carriage that resembled a box on wheels, with the *Great Wheel* Ouroboros symbol painted on the doors. Fidelmus handed Iona up and climbed in to sit beside her.

Shay took the opposite seat, and Iona didn't know where to look as she imagined what Zara and her other friends might say if they could see him. He wore his long black hair loose rather than braided in its customary plait, and it fell past his shoulders in glossy waves. A black, silver-trimmed doublet enhanced his broad shoulders, worn with black hose. Their weave might be a little thicker than those sported by the nobility, but did nothing to disguise his muscled thighs. However, Shay's concession to fashion ended there. He had disdained the modish poulaines in favour of his black knee-high boots, polished to a high sheen.

As the driver urged the carriage horses down the path towards the bridge, Iona gazed out the glassless window – it seemed the safest place to rest her eyes. Sunset was still three hours away, and the river reflected the warm, rich ambience of the late-afternoon light.

When the carriage clattered onto the covered bridge, Iona turned to the prior. "If Duke Clovis is behind the *trisiks*, he must know where the *Living Aurigans*' originate. So, why the formal meeting with each incarnation?"

"Since the *Living Aurigan* is the personification of our founder, the nobles and common folk view the repeated manifestations here as a sign Kentauros is favoured by the *Great Wheel*, which confers prestige upon the dukedom. We have worked hard to make it so, to protect the *trisiks'* victims. Therefore, it would appear incongruent if the duke didn't accord due respect to each new titleholder. To the best of my knowledge, Clovis has not once betrayed an awareness of your world to any *Living Aurigan* he met, even when Jake almost put the position in jeopardy. Luckily, Clovis never encountered Bethany, who had gone by the time he returned from a tour of his estates," Fidelmus explained.

"Luckily?" Iona probed.

"Indeed. The poor woman's behaviour became increasingly erratic, and she was liable to say something incautious. However, the duke's ignorance of your world seems genuine, which is one reason it has taken so long for us to truly suspect him."

"So, he's either a consummate actor or someone else pulls his strings," Iona mused aloud.

As she turned back to the window, her eyes met Shay's. "My thoughts exactly," the ranger agreed, his gaze appraising.

Iona detected a challenge in his stare and said, "Don't worry; I'm not a fool. I'll keep my head down, and my ears and eyes open."

The carriage laboured up the castle hill road and Shay, with his back to the driver, gripped a leather strap affixed to the roof to avoid pitching into Iona's lap. When his knee brushed hers, she felt a flutter in her stomach, and resolutely turned away to ask Fidelmus, "Did Sister Honoria request I move to Glassnesse because the *Living Aurigan's* presence at the priory is some kind of status symbol she wished to purloin for the abbey?"

"Well, that's one way of putting it, but where you choose to live is entirely up to you. The order keeps you safe, whether here or at Glassnesse. However, we cannot protect you if you decide to leave the fold and go your own way."

"I appreciate all you do for me, Prior. I just wanted to understand the sister's motives, that's all."

The hill levelled out as it reached the top, and the carriage trundled through an open set of huge, iron-bound gates and into a spacious courtyard. They joined the queue of carriages before the central keep's massive double doors, waiting their turn to reach the head of the line before dismounting. Iona peered through both windows and asked, "Where is the Janus Spire?"

"It's the tall tower on the northeastern side of the curtain wall," Shay answered.

"Northeastern? Is that the tower directly above the menhir stone?"

The ranger nodded and moved to open the door since they had reached the head of the queue. He alighted first and turned to help the prior out, followed by Iona. As she placed her hand in his, she felt that flutter again and avoided his eyes.

A man in a seneschal's robe greeted them at the open doors, and an usher led them through the arched doorway of the great hall, hung with colourful tapestries, banners and pennants. Richly dressed guests and courtiers milled about or stood in gossiping groups. Iona observed several women sported tall, conical headwear with fluttering veils attached, while others wore jewelled bourrelets, horned wimples, or headdresses formed from padded rolls, crespines, and cylinder cauls. As Binny had promised, Iona's headgear appeared simple in comparison, emphasised by the lack of jewels at her neck such as the others wore.

The major-domo twice banged a carved staff on the floor and announced, "Prior Fidelmus from the Priory of Saint Aurigan, here with Ranger Shay Hawksmoor, and Iona Abernathy, the *Living Aurigan*."

An aisle opened up in the centre of the floor as people stepped aside, and Fidelmus led them towards a dais, where a bored-looking Duke Clovis lounged on a throne. Iona performed the curtsey Eliza had taught her, and the duke sat up straight, no longer disinterested. Icy blue eyes bored into hers, and his full lips twisted in a smile, both sensual and supercilious. A ducal coronet circled his dark hair, worn short in military style, and Iona guessed his age at forty, tops. His powerful frame, clad in midnight blue hose and a doublet of gold and blue damask, proved him no idle lord.

"I am enraptured to meet such a delightful gift of the *Great Wheel*. As I recall, the last one had some difficulty remembering his duties, but I'm already sure you are a vast improvement – in more ways than one," Clovis said and licked his lips in an unsettling manner.

He stood, revealing he wore an overlarge codpiece, and Iona had a sudden and possibly suicidal urge to laugh hysterically. The duke beckoned her forward onto the lower of the two dais steps, at eye-level with his crotch. Iona lowered her eyes demurely, face reddening with the effort to contain her hilarity, and hoped Clovis would mistake it for a maidenly blush. He reached down for her hand and brushed his lips across the back. "We will dance together later, *Eterna*."

Releasing her hand, he turned to say a few words to Fidelmus, and Iona stepped back, resisting the urge to rub her hand on her dress. Shay's clench-jawed expression of outrage (?) warred with a gleam in his eyes that told her he *knew* she had difficulty suppressing her mirth. As the major-domo announced the next guests, Fidelmus' party melted into the throng.

When merchant Bertrand Leon arrived with his wife, Isobel, and daughter Alicia, Fidelmus had no time to do more than exchange nods with his friend before the seneschal and his assistant, Lorcan, formerly Quintus' protégé, ushered the guests through an archway into the banquet hall.

Lorcan spoke softly to the prior before separating him from the others to lead him to a seat at the top table, from which two more tables extended, one at each end, to form an open-bottomed square.

The seneschal placed Iona next to Shay at the right-hand board, seating them at the top end adjoining the central table. Bertrand Leon occupied the same position with his family at the left-hand board. With everyone seated, the duke entered and took his central place at the top table. He raised his hand, and servants stepped forward with wine ewers to fill the guests' goblets.

Under the hubbub of chatter and toasting, Iona murmured to Shay, "Who's the man seated at the duke's right hand?"

"That's Lord Randolph Peregrine, brother of the duke's late wife, who died in childbed three years ago," Shay replied sotto-voice.

"Did the baby live?"

"Yes. The duke's heir is seven years old, and with the survival of the spare, he's in no hurry to remarry; especially since he has his brother-in-law's beauteous wife, Madeleine, to warm his bed," Shay explained in a sardonic tone.

Startled, Iona glanced at the blonde woman seated at the duke's left. "Doesn't Randolph mind?"

"Far from it. His taste runs more to young men." Shay took a swig from his goblet and leaned back as a server placed a bread trencher before him.

Iona gazed at her own large circle of stale bread and looked to Shay for an explanation.

"It's a plate. Though we use pottery vessels at the priory, the duke prefers the old custom of serving food on three-day-old bread trenchers. It saves on the washing-up, anyway. Some people eat them afterwards with the sopped-up gravy and sauces, but most don't, and they're given to the poor as food after use."

"Yuck. That sounds like a good way to spread disease," Iona said with a grimace.

Goblet in hand, Shay shrugged. "When you're starving, you'll eat anything."

Bowls of pottage (a vegetable porridge) arrived on the table with cuts of venison, wild boar, salmon and pike, served with beans, swede, turnips and cabbage, the accompanying sauces in small jugs. Iona looked in vain for a fork, finding only a spoon beside her trencher. Although forks didn't exist at the priory either, her meals always arrived with a utensil she had dubbed a *spork* – a spoon with two short prongs. Quintus had explained the custom of bringing your own eating knife to a banquet, and Iona reached into her belt pouch for the linen-wrapped blade he had given her.

She watched the guests drinking the pottage straight from the bowl, or eating with their fingers, wiping them afterwards on the linen napkins provided. Revolted, she ate sparingly, although the food tasted fine.

First course finished, the servers carried in a brace of ducks – and two roast peacocks, re-dressed in their own beautiful plumage. Iona couldn't bear to look at them and refused the portion offered by a server.

Aware that the duke had tried to catch her eye several times throughout the meal, she breathed a sigh of relief when his gaze became distracted by a troupe of tumblers who arrived with the next course, comprising sweet and savoury tarts and pastries. However, the duke's concubine had also noticed the object of his frequent glances, and ignoring the acrobats who performed in the space between the tables, eyed Iona with a hard, speculative stare. When she turned away, Iona gulped down a mouthful of her second goblet of wine and loaded her trencher with a selection of pastries – at least they would be easier to eat without cutlery.

Shay glanced at her sidelong. "Go easy on that wine. You need to keep your wits about you. If I must carry an inebriated *Living Aurigan* to our carriage, Lady Madeleine will have a field day at your expense. She doesn't take too kindly to competition."

Iona shuddered. "Ew, I'm no competition." She spoke directly into Shay's ear to ensure no one overheard her. "The very thought of... *you know*... with the duke, is stomach-turning."

"That's as may be, but it doesn't make either of them less dangerous," he replied, though Iona detected amusement in his eyes. Shay turned to the noblewoman seated on his other side, who seemed eager to engage him in conversation.

Since Iona's position at the end of the table meant she had no one to chat with on *her* other side, she turned her attention to the tumblers – and accidentally caught Clovis' eye. He raised his goblet in salute, his lip curled in a seductive smile. Iona had no choice except to return his salute with a sickly smile of her own, and then took a bigger swig from it than she intended, but at least it enabled her to break eye contact with Clovis.

Sunset turned the glass panes in the arched windows molten gold by the time the last course of cheese and candied fruit arrived. Iona's hand hovered over the fruit, unsure which to choose. As she settled on an unidentifiable lozenge shape, coloured a pretty shade of pink, Shay's hand suddenly covered hers, and he shook his head in warning. She dropped the fruit, her skin tingling at his touch, and he withdrew his hand.

"What's wrong with it?" Iona asked.

"The fruit covered in pink candy is fermented and can make you pretty sick unless you have a strong stomach. All the others are okay, though."

As servants lit the wall sconces and candles, Iona selected another fruit candy to nibble on, unsure if she liked it. She followed Shay's example, and cleansed her knife in a beaker of water, wiping it dry on her napkin before she returned it to her pouch.

At a signal from the duke, the guests returned to the great hall, already flooded with torchlight. Musicians tuned up in the minstrels' gallery high above the floor, and Iona felt relief to be reunited with Prior Fidelmus. Bertrand Leon and his family joined their little group, and Iona immediately felt at ease with him. A tall, distinguished-looking man with iron-grey hair, the merchant regaled them with his latest plans to open a trade route with the dragons.

"But what will you trade for?" Iona enquired in fascination.

"Armourers highly prize their cast-off scales, and the northern mountains of their domain are rich in jet, quartz gems, and fluorite minerals," Bertrand replied.

"And what will you give in trade?"

"I am yet to discover what, if anything, they might desire in exchange," the merchant confessed with a sheepish grimace.

"And, of course, we must conduct all negotiations through Saint Lexis Priory. No doubt the middlemen will demand their cut," his wife, Isobel, interjected, and gave a wry smile. "Anyway, if you gentlemen will excuse us ladies?"

Isobel gathered up Alicia and raised a questioning eyebrow at Iona, who nodded and handed her newly refreshed goblet to Shay. She had planned to discretely ask Isobel for directions to the powder room, or whatever they called it here, and guessed this was their destination. Iona followed Isobel and Alicia across the hall to an alcove and up four narrow steps to a door. The small room beyond had ivory-coloured, plastered walls and a wooden screen in one corner. Iona knew what she would find behind it from the pong alone – the gong pits here were evidently cleaned out less frequently than those at the priory. However, she couldn't cross her legs all night. When Isobel indicated she go first, Iona held her breath and slipped behind the screen into a dank, stone-lined cavity containing a rock-built garderobe, lit by a rack of candles high on the wall. Iona couldn't bring herself to sit on the age-darkened wooden seat, and bundling up her gown, squatted uncomfortably above the hole. She removed a roll of rice-straw paper from her belt pouch, glad she had the foresight to bring it, and wondered if she would ever become inured to the smells. They hadn't been so bad in the castle until now – unlike the common folk, the wealthy people at the feast used perfumes and unguents to disguise bodily odours.

Emerging from behind the screen, Iona found an ewer of lemon-scented water on a shelf beside a carved stone font, the hole in the basin's centre stopped up with a crude wooden bung. She poured a generous measure into the basin but had to scrub her hands quickly before the water escaped through the gap around the ill-fitting bung. Iona eyed the single manky towel with revulsion and dried her hands on her linen handkerchief instead.

As Isobel and Alicia both took their turn at the garderobe and font, Iona reapplied her strawberry lipstick, squinting into the murky glass of the wall mirror. She next removed the vial of *'Binny Number Five'* (as she dubbed it) from her pouch, and dabbed on a little more.

"Oh, that smells lovely! Is it one of Goodwife Robina's concoctions?" Isobel queried.

"Yes, it is. Would you like to try some?" Iona held out the vial.

"I don't mind if I do!" Isobel replied and applied a little behind her ears. "Robina is a wonder! My skin has improved immeasurably since I began buying all my *toilette* preparations from her."

"Robina has given Papa a list of exotic-sounding ingredients for his agents to source when his trading vessels next put in at Euriont and Truscaromia. I wish *I* could act as Papa's agent and travel to far-flung Euriont!" Alicia said wistfully.

Isobel shook her head. "Your Papa has already taught you more about the trade than is proper for a woman. We must find you a suitable husband to continue the business when Papa retires."

Alicia, who shared her mother's candid hazel eyes and strawberry-blonde hair, crossed her arms and pouted. "Well, *you* know just as much about commodities as Papa!"

"Indeed! Your Papa includes me in all the important decision-making; as *you* will include your husband." Isobel winked.

Iona smiled. Though Isobel may not be *quite* the power behind her husband's trading empire, she would ensure her daughter attained that position when she wed.

"Oh well, if I *must* marry, I hope my husband is at *least* as handsome as Shay! Do you think he might partner me in a dance?"

Before Isobel could reply, the door opened and Lady Madeleine appeared in the gap with her lady-in-waiting. The three women in the room stood aside to let them pass, and Madeleine gazed stony-faced at Iona, her grey eyes flint-hard. As she moved past her imagined rival, Madeleine murmured *'Eterna'* with a curt nod of acknowledgment. Iona returned the nod with a graceful curtsey, determined not to give this woman any ammunition.

Isobel and Alicia followed Iona down the steps into the hall, and the door closed behind them. Alicia couldn't contain herself. "Whew, I'm surprised you didn't turn to stone on the spot! What did you do to incur such displeasure?"

"She did nothing except unwittingly catch the duke's notice," Isobel answered for Iona. "I observed his wandering eye from my position at table. I've learned to pay attention to such byplay to navigate the treacherous waters of this court. You don't want to make an enemy of Lady Madeleine," Isobel warned.

"Have no fear! I intend to stay well away from this court after tonight! I have zero interest in the duke's... rancid codpiece!"

Alicia gasped and giggled nervously.

"Good," Isobel said with a grim smile. "We ought to return to the menfolk. The dancing will soon begin."

Chapter 11

When Iona appeared at his side, Shay handed back her wine goblet, and she took a sip. "Eurgh! Are you sure this is mine?" Iona asked.

Shay shrugged. "I diluted it with water. I don't know how well you hold your drink. We're on a mission, in case you forgot. You need to stay alert." He cast his eyes in the duke's direction and Iona read the double meaning in his words. Still, he had a nerve treating her like a child!

Without warning, trumpets rang out from the musician's gallery, and Fidelmus retired to a seat by the wall with the other non-dancers. Shay swiped Iona's goblet from her fingers and placed it with his own on a table at the prior's elbow. He held out his hand and said, "I will lead you through the first dance until you find your feet."

"I'm overwhelmed by your enthusiasm," she replied sarcastically, but took his hand – rather him than a complete stranger, even if he *did* regard it as a chore.

As the guests lined up in partners, Iona guessed they would dance the *Almain*, the processional couple's dance. Duke Clovis and Lady Madeleine led off to the music of trumpets and horns. A shawm joined in, followed by drums and a lute, flute, and vielle – a violin-like instrument with a longer and deeper body. Iona ignored the feel of Shay's fingers, interlocked with hers, and concentrated on the order of the double-steps this dance required.

As they processed past Fidelmus, Iona noticed Lorcan approach the prior, who looked up expectantly. However, before the ex-acolyte reached him, the seneschal summoned his assistant to deal with a guest who, judging by the pink vomit splattered on his yellow doublet (not a pleasing colour combination), had eaten too many fermented fruit candies. Lorcan grimaced in frustration, but plastered a smile on his face before he turned back to obey his superior.

The dance segued into the next measure, which involved dancing around one's partner. Iona's poulaines pinched her feet, but she circled Shay in the steps Eliza had taught her. When they swapped places so Shay could dance around her, she observed him trade a glance with the prior, who shook his head. What were they up to? The ranger circled her with cat-like grace and they transitioned back into a processional.

At the dance's conclusion, Iona formally curtseyed to Shay as he bowed to her, and rising, she observed the duke approach. Resigned to her fate, she murmured to Shay, "Perhaps you should ask Alicia to partner you in the next dance. She'll be delighted."

Shay raised an eyebrow, but understanding dawned as the duke appeared at his shoulder. The trumpets signalled the start of the *Basse*, the noble court dance, as Clovis extended his hand towards Iona in a gesture that brooked no refusal. "I reserved this dance especially for you, *Eterna*. The honour is yours."

The honour is mine? The conceited prick really believes it! Iona thought as she meekly placed her hand in his. Shay bowed stiffly, his face expressionless, and stepped away, though he levelled a hard stare at the duke's back.

As the other instruments joined the trumpet, Clovis led Iona in the slow, gliding steps of the stately, measured dance. She observed Lady Madeleine dancing with her husband but immediately looked away, not wishing to engage in a staring contest. The woman must feel the tenuousness of her position. Why couldn't she see the *Living Aurigan* posed no threat to it, and she would do better to watch out for the unmarried court ladies?

"Such a graceful neck requires adornment," Clovis remarked and bit his lower lip suggestively.

Yuckety-yuck! Iona shuddered inwardly. "Less is more."

"Such modesty! I can remedy that for you in no time! Perhaps a necklace of rubies to match your dress?" The duke circled her palm with his thumb. "Or maybe you would prefer multi-colours in black, blue, and yellow?"

Oh, God! Was he talking about hickeys? As he 'accidentally' brushed the codpiece against her hip, Iona thought she might be sick.

As the music wound down, Iona thought of escape with relief, but Clovis didn't release her hand. She glanced about wildly and spotted Bertrand Leon's approach.

He bowed to the duke. "I'm sorry to intrude, but I promised the *Eterna* I would partner her in the *Estampie*. It would be unconscionably rude to renege on my pledge, although if she prefers to dance it with another…?"

"No, no; a promise is a promise! And we promised each other," Iona lied desperately. Although her feet killed her in the uncomfortable shoes and she would prefer to sit it out, she grabbed at the chance of escaping Clovis.

The duke released her hand, and with a glower of displeasure, bowed and departed. Iona heaved a sigh of relief and her eyes sought Isobel whom she felt sure had sent Bertrand to rescue her. She nodded her grateful thanks to the merchant's wife and took his proffered hand as the *Estampie* music began.

Although Iona had mastered the basic heel-to-toe footwork with turnout and an occasional stamp, she must remember to close her feet at the end of each step. However, with irregular double-steps and a variety of spatial floor movements to reflect repeating patterns in the music, this dance was the most complicated. She noted Shay, who had sat out the *Basse*, take to the floor with Alicia, who blushed becomingly.

The full musical accompaniment made it easier to follow the patterns, harder to do with just the one or two instruments she had practiced with. As Iona and Bertrand wove a floor pattern with Shay and Alicia, her eyes met Shay's, and a *recognition* passed between them, though of what, she felt unsure.

When the dance finally ended, Iona limped back to Fidelmus with the others, and took a long draught of her watered-down wine. Her old injury site ached dully, and her feet felt worse.

"I think it's time to call it a night. I must return to the priory for Evenchant, anyway," the prior said, rising to his feet.

"We ought to get going, too," Isobel agreed.

Bertrand attracted the seneschal's attention and asked for their carriages to be brought around to the keep entrance. The seneschal sent Lorcan to attend to it, and led them towards the duke's throne, where he had retired to sit during a lull in the dancing.

Surrounded by sycophants, Clovis waved his goblet at the group, who approached to pay their respects. "Leaving so soon? But the night is still young!"

"Sadly, I have a headache, and I believe the prior must get back for Evenchant," Isobel answered for them all.

"Madame Leon is correct. But thank you for your gracious hospitality," Fidelmus added and sketched the circle blessing on his forehead.

The duke wore a brooding expression, and his eyes flicked towards Iona. "It's been some time since I paid a visit to the priory. Perhaps you can return my hospitality soon."

Fidelmus tucked his hands into the sleeves of his habit and bowed. "It will be our pleasure to receive you."

Not mine! Iona thought as she backed away from the throne with the others, keeping her eyes down.

When they escaped into the portico area behind the open entrance doors, the Leon carriage waited at the bottom of the steps. Isobel clasped Iona's hands in farewell. "Perhaps you could accompany Robina when she delivers my latest order next week. We live in Tritaurium's merchant's quarter, the house near the fountain. We can talk at leisure then."

"Thank you. That would be lovely," Iona readily agreed, and waved goodbye to Bertrand and Alicia as they descended the steps.

As the carriage drew away to be replaced by the prior's, Iona remarked, "We must find a way into that tower and discover what Clovis is concealing as soon as possible. I don't want to be in his vicinity a moment longer than necessary. Oh, and if he visits the priory, I'll be busy washing my hair."

"*We*?" Shay said, eyebrow raised.

"Yes, *we*!"

Shay clamped his mouth shut as the Lady Madeleine suddenly appeared from the great hall, her tall, conical headdress almost scraping the archway's apex.

"I need a few words with the *Eterna*, if you don't mind?"

Shay and Fidelmus looked at Iona. "You two go ahead, I'll catch you up."

When the two men reached the stair bottom and entered the carriage, Madeleine came straight to the point. "What are your intentions?"

"Erm, I'm not sure what you mean."

"Don't play coy with me. You think you can use the mystique of your position to bedazzle the duke and supplant me in his affections? I know your type. You act the virtuous innocent to keep him keen until he'll offer you anything to make you succumb. So, I ask again, what are your intentions? Do you seek marriage or simply the wealth and power of a mistress? Something else?"

"Wow, you really are paranoid! Why would I want those things? I'm the *Living Aurigan*, *the Eternal Traveller*, sent here by the *Great Wheel*. In the fulness of time, I intend to return whence I came like the others before me."

"Goodwife Robina didn't. She resigned the position to stay here. How do I know you don't intend to do the same? A duke is a somewhat better catch than a beekeeper!"

At this point, Iona lost her temper. "For the last time, I have no interest in the duke and did nothing to encourage him. It's not my fault you can't keep him on his leash! Believe me, you'll do me a favour if you can bring him to heel!"

Two angry red spots appeared on Madeleine's cheeks, but before she could retort, Lorcan shot from a narrow service passageway and skidded to a halt. He smoothed his golden hair, flustered to be caught running. Madeleine ignored him and with an abrupt nod, muttered, "*Eterna*," and swept back into the great hall.

Iona turned to descend the steps, but Lorcan stayed her with a hand on her arm. "Where are Shay and the prior? Am I too late? Have they already left?"

"They're waiting for me in the carriage."

"I've tried to speak to Prior Fidelmus in private all evening and something's prevented me at every turn." Lorcan nervously glanced over his shoulder and suddenly thrust something into Iona's hands. "Give this to the prior. Don't let anyone see it!"

Iona gazed at the key she held in her hands, wound about with a strip of parchment fastened in place with cord. She remembered the last time someone had given her a key, and look where that had led…

Hearing footsteps in the passage, Lorcan whispered, "Quick, Quick! Hide it!"

Iona slipped the key down the bodice of her underdress, and when the seneschal emerged from the passage, said, "Alright Lorcan, I'll let Quintus know you asked after him. Goodnight, now!"

The seneschal bowed to her in a distracted manner, and said to Lorcan, "Did you tell the cellarer to replenish the mead, as I asked?"

Iona turned away and hobbled down the steps. Nothing in this world would make her wear these blasted poulaines again. The pain in her toes and heels made her gasp as Shay took her hand to pull her into the carriage. He shut the door, and as she collapsed onto the seat beside the prior, Shay banged on the roof to signal their readiness to depart.

"What did Lady Madeleine want with you?" the ranger enquired as the carriage lurched forward.

"Oh, nothing much. She warned me off encroaching on her territory." Iona gave a humourless laugh. "Ha! I wouldn't touch the lecherous scrote with a bargepole!"

"You certainly have a way with words," Fidelmus remarked, eyes bright with involuntary humour. "Was that Lorcan I glimpsed you speaking to in the portico?"

"Yep. I take it you planted him in the duke's service to spy for you? Risky business, that." Iona tsked.

Shay stiffened; his eyes wary. "What did he say to you?"

"It's more what he gave me," Iona replied and reached into the front of her dress. She fished out her prize and held it up. Shay reached for it, but Iona jerked it away. "I guess this might be *our* way into the Janus Spire?"

Shay held her gaze. "Alright, you're in. Now give me the key."

Iona handed it over and Shay unfastened the cord that bound the parchment. He unrolled it from the key's stock and squinted at the message in the meagre light. "It's a duplicate key for the tower's exterior door. We already know the guard positions, but from what I can decipher, Lorcan has provided us with the other information we asked for."

Fidelmus held out a hand and Shay surrendered the key and message. The prior tucked both into his belt pouch. "The hour grows late. We will meet in my office tomorrow – all three of us – to read the message and plan our next move."

Shay acquiesced reluctantly. Folding his hands, the prior leaned his head back against the headrest and shut his eyes.

"I didn't receive the impression that Lady Madeleine knows where I come from. She *might* just be a good dissembler, but if the duke knows, I would have thought she'd be in on it. What I *don't* understand is why no one asks me that question. *I* would, if I were them," Iona said.

The prior opened one eye. "The answer is defined as one of the sacred mysteries of our order, kept secret from the uninitiated and known only to those at the top of our hierarchy. Saint Aurigan decreed it so to protect the travellers. I believe he modelled it on the mystery religions and cults that existed within our two worlds in antiquity. He cited examples such as the cult of Isis, Mithraism, the early Christian church, and so on. No one would dream of prying into order secrets. Shay knows out of necessity. Saint Aurigan made provision in our charter for the initiation of essential outsiders into the 'mystery' where crucial to our cause." He closed his eye again and wiggled his shoulders against the backrest.

When they arrived back at the priory, Fidelmus retired to his office to prepare for Evenchant.

Feet protesting, Iona walked with Shay to their courtyard rooms. After they exited through the door of the main building into the quadrangle, Iona paused at the statue of Saint Aurigan, and leaning on the plinth, examined her feet under the light of the tall basket brazier that illuminated the saint at night. She rubbed a heel, and her hand came away sticky with blood. Shay took one look at it, and without warning, swept her into his arms. With her wrists around his neck, she inhaled the clean fragrance of his hair, wishing everyone here attended so closely to their personal hygiene. She debated whether to protest at his cavalier assumption of control, but didn't want to take the risk he would dump her back down onto her sore feet.

Shay shouldered open the tower gateway, and carried her to the well in the courtyard's centre, where another brazier balanced atop a pole. He settled her on the low wall that rimmed the well; her legs stretched out along it, and drew up a bucket of water. Sitting down beside Iona, Shay placed her feet in his lap, and with surprising gentleness, removed her shoes, revealing a bloody toe and two blood-soaked heels.

He dropped the poulaines onto the ground, muttering, "Absurd foolish things!"

"It wasn't *my* idea to wear them!"

"How did you dance for so long and not mention your pain?"

Iona shrugged. "Used to it. You've obviously never seen stilettoes." Though if truth be told, Iona couldn't remember the last time she and her friends had danced around their handbags; before the accident, anyway.

Shay selected a pan from the stack beside the well. He dipped it into the water bucket and placed it on the wall beside him. "You need to roll down your stockings."

Iona tensed for a moment, then reached under her dress to untie her garters. She rolled her stockings down to her ankles; absurdly glad she had shaved her legs. With gentle fingers, Shay unpeeled the stockings, stuck to her bloodied feet, and chucked them on top of the shoes. He withdrew a clean handkerchief from his belt pouch and dipping it into the water can, used it to bathe her feet.

"Oh, that tickles!" Iona giggled as a finger brushed the sole of her foot.

Shay glanced at her from beneath his lashes, and shook his head in a long-suffering manner. Iona leaned back on the heels of her hands, secretly enjoying his ministrations, a small smile hovering around her lips.

She wiped it from her face before Shay looked up. "That's the best I can do, for now. You'll need to send for Binny in the morning to bandage your feet."

Iona hoped Binny had re-invented plasters.

Shay dumped the poulaines and stockings in Iona's lap and stood. He bent down and easily scooped her into his arms to carry her the short distance to her room. Setting her down outside her door, he waited until she unlocked it before he bowed and turned towards his room.

"Thank you, Shay. Goodnight."

He paused and glanced at her over his shoulder. "Goodnight, Iona."

She felt pleased he hadn't called her '*Eterna*' – it was too impersonal.

Chapter 12

When Iona woke the next morning, she lay in bed and thought about Shay. She couldn't work him out; one minute abrasive and the next stiffly considerate. Had he tended to her feet out of duty? No matter the reason, he had, at last, consented to involve her in the plot he had cooked up with Fidelmus.

Binny arrived after breakfast, though Iona hadn't sent for her. "Shay sent Dara to fetch me. It gave Dara a good excuse to visit his new puppy without incurring Brother Ennis' wrath; as Shay well knew." Binny winked. "Anyway, sit on that chair and I'll take a look at your feet."

Iona obeyed, reassessing the ranger in light of this new demonstration of concern for her welfare and his small act of kindness towards the lowly acolyte. However, judging by their previous clashes, she knew her revised opinion might not last beyond their next encounter.

Binny heated water in a pot on Iona's small fire and set naturally antiseptic herbs and alum shavings to steep. Blisters had formed overnight on two toes, and the poulaines had rubbed both heels and another toe raw. After bathing Iona's feet, the former chemist applied poultices to the affected areas, held on with bandages.

"I need sandals. I doubt I'll be able to wear my boots without discomfort," Iona said.

Binny frowned in thought. "Hmm, perhaps I can alter those sheepskin bootees you wear as slippers. We can get you a new pair later, and I'm sure Alfred can make sandals if need be."

Iona told her where she had left the bootees. Binny fetched them, then removed a large pair of shears from her basket to cut out the heels and toes. Sliding them onto Iona's feet, she pulled the ankle drawstring tight, and Iona stood. "They feel okay, though I'm not sure how long the soles will last if I wear them outside."

"You won't need to wear them long; a couple of days at most. The poultices are pretty effective. It must have been agony walking back to your room after the banquet, though."

"Er, yes and no. Shay carried me most of the way."

"*Did* he now?" Binny drawled with a shrewd, narrow-eyed glance at Iona. "Eliza is dying to know all about the banquet. So am I, for that matter!"

Iona sat down again. "I don't know how I would have coped without Eliza's lessons! She'll be pleased to know I danced with the duke, though the pleasure was all his," Iona said with irony and regaled Binny with the duke's antics and Lady Madeleine's response.

"Bloody hell! You don't want to get mixed up in that ménage trois! I heard tell of a lady-in-waiting who'd grown a little too close to the duke. They found her at the bottom of the solar-turret stairs with a broken neck. Did she fall or was she pushed? I suspect Lady Madeleine knows..." Binny informed Iona in an ominous tone. "You had best steer well clear of the court!"

"I intend to, though Clovis threatened to pay a visit here... However, Shay has finally agreed to my inclusion in his scheme, and I can only hope I find a way home soon."

"Hmm, well, you can't bank on that," Binny cautioned and rose to her feet. "I'll take your banquet outfit home with me and give it a clean. How are you fixed for this afternoon?"

"I have a meeting with Fidelmus and Shay to discuss the plans for infiltrating the Janus Spire. Though I'm not sure what time. Oh, Isobel Leon has invited me to visit with you when you deliver her order next week."

Binny smiled. "Good. She must like you. The Leons are worth cultivating. They're good people with a great deal of influence. I'm hoping to strike a deal with Bertrand to distribute my wares once I'm in a position to manufacture on a larger scale. Well, good luck with your meeting. I expect I'll see you tomorrow."

Not long after Binny had left, Shay knocked on her door. Iona opened it to find him dressed in his usual leathers, his long hair plaited.

"Fidelmus is ready to speak to us now," the ranger informed. "Can you walk?"

"Just about! Why? Are you *offering* to carry me?" Iona joked since he hadn't *asked* her the last time, but winced at the unintended sarcasm in her tone.

"If that's what you need; though if you haven't healed when the time comes for action, I'm not sure how useful you'll be," he replied smoothly.

Iona scowled. "I'm fine!" She shut the door behind her and followed Shay across the courtyard, hobbling a little on her bandaged feet.

Despite his words, Shay matched his pace to hers, for which she felt thankful.

As Iona seated herself with relief before the prior's desk, she noted the key and parchment strip under his folded hands. Shay sat in the chair beside her's and waited for Fidelmus to speak first.

The prior smoothed out the curled parchment on the desktop and addressed Shay. "Before we discuss this, perhaps you should give Iona a summation of our game plan, thus far?"

Booted foot on one knee, Shay nodded but held his tongue as

someone knocked on the door. When Fidelmus bade the person to enter, Quintus slipped into the room.

"I'm sorry to interrupt, but this can't wait. The duke's major-domo is in my office. He delivered a gift for the *Eterna* and awaits her response." The guest master presented a carved wooden casket to Iona.

She curled her lip and drew back as though Quintus threatened her with a scorpion. "I want nothing from Clovis. Take it away."

"Ahem, there will be repercussions if you decline it. Take a look inside, at least," Fidelmus advised in a mild tone.

Iona glanced at the prior and, with great reluctance, took the casket from Quintus' hands. She set it on the desktop and opened the lid to reveal an extravagant gold and ruby necklace. *At least the jewels aren't black, blue and yellow...*

"There will be repercussions if I *don't* refuse it!" Iona slammed the lid shut and stubbornly folded her arms.

Quintus nodded thoughtfully. "Yes, *if,* as the duke intends, you accept it as a *personal* gift. However, if you welcome it as an offering to the *Living Aurigan*, it becomes a donation to the priory in exchange for the *Great Wheel's* benevolence."

Fidelmus nodded slowly. "Good thinking, Quintus. Such a compromise is better than outright rejection."

Shay snorted. "A man like Clovis will believe Iona is playing hard to get; it won't deter him."

"Perhaps, but what alternative do we have? We can't afford his enmity; especially now, and this will buy time." The prior reached for parchment and ink and pushed both across the desktop to Iona. He handed her a quill, saying, "Express how honoured you are that His Grace deems you worthy of such munificence. In the spirit of reciprocity, the *Living Aurigan* humbly accepts this donation in return for the chaplain's special intercessory meditations on behalf of our esteemed duke."

"Meditations? Not prayers?" Iona asked, head tilted in question.

"The *Great Wheel* is a symbol, not a god."

Iona nodded. She dipped the quill in the ink and held it poised above the parchment. "Repeat that, please. Not so fast this time."

Fidelmus dictated as she wrote and then sanded the completed message. He affixed a wax seal stamped with the priory's *Great Wheel* sigil and passed it to Quintus for delivery to the waiting major-domo.

Once the guest master departed, Iona shoved the offending casket across the desktop to Fidelmus, who placed it in a drawer. She turned to Shay and met his contemplative gaze. "You were saying?"

"I was *about* to confirm that our primary objective is access to the Janus Spire to determine what Clovis conceals. To gain entry, we must first reduce the number of elite men-at-arms who guard it."

"What do you mean by *reduce*? How?" Iona queried nervously.

"As Jake wrote, the off-duty tower guards congregate in the *Black Cockerel* tavern. The night before we make our move, an… *associate* will arrange a brawl of the type that should put the respite shift out of action before the guard changeover."

Iona noticed the prior's pursed lips. "I take it you do not approve?" she asked him.

Fidelmus sighed. "Shay assures me they will keep traumatic injuries to a minimum. However, since some participants will be kinsfolk of the kidnapped villagers, I fear this brawl will leave more than sprained wrists and sore heads."

"If they wish to discover the fate of their kin, they won't jeopardise our mission. However, anything can happen in the heat of the moment. That is a risk we must take." Shay shrugged. "The tower guards are not innocents. They're complicit in the sackings and kidnaps perpetrated by the duke's knights."

The prior nodded unhappily.

Shay continued, "With half the elite guards out of action and the rest on double-shift, Clovis perforce must pad out the ranks with regular guards, though he's unlikely to station the uninitiated *inside* the tower. This means we must take advantage of the situation on a day when his regulars are stretched too thin to bolster the depleted tower force. Therefore, the tavern brawl will occur the night before the castle fair."

"The fair where Binny will have a stall?" Iona enquired.

"Yes. Ducal guardsmen police the thrice-yearly fairs. Most activities will take place in the main courtyard before the keep. There'll be huge crowds, making it easier for us to blend in and avoid unwanted notice. Our 'friends' will create a minor diversion to draw the remaining tower guards away long enough for us to slip inside."

"I've so many questions that I don't know where to start," Iona said and, chin in hand, tried to arrange her thoughts. "By *us*, you mean you and me?"

Shay nodded. "The prior has convinced me I'll need you to interpret anything we might encounter from your world that I don't understand, otherwise I might miss its significance."

Iona glanced at Fidelmus, who heaved a huge sigh. "I'm not altogether happy about sending you with Shay, but your argument for inclusion swayed me. Quintus thinks the risk is too high, but the decision is yours."

"Who is this *associate* and the men he controls?"

Shay crossed his arms and shook his head. "I'm not sure it's wise to tell you."

Iona rolled her eyes. "Hm, let me guess. I assume it's a man. He's either a lord or baron with a grudge against the duke or a shady, underworld contact with criminal connections."

Shay looked at her askance, and Fidelmus gave a startled chuckle. "The *associate* is close to your second description, but how did you guess?"

"Since coming here, I feel like a character in a novel – that's a storybook, in case you don't know – mainly because dragons don't exist in my world, but *are* staples of fantasy literature. My guess is based on the character tropes in such books," Iona said with a wry smile. "I imagine his paid underlings will comprise most of the brawlers, but who leads the kinsfolk of the missing?"

Fidelmus and Shay exchanged a glance, and Iona persisted, "Come on; you either trust me fully or not at all. I'm part of this conspiracy now, and it's senseless, even dangerous, to send me on this mission with only half the information."

The prior steepled his fingers beneath his chin and studied her. "Alright. Quintus is the only other person who knows what I'm about to tell you, and the knowledge must stay in this room. You cannot even tell Binny, though she's aware we plan to gain admittance into the tower."

"I promise not to tell anyone," Iona replied.

"Their leader is Will Copeland, a blacksmith from Mallowbrook. His wife, Clare, is one of those kidnapped from the village during its sacking. She's the niece of Bertrand Leon, who, incidentally, will supply the materials to create the diversion."

Iona sucked in a breath. "Well, I wasn't expecting that! Hasn't Bertrand petitioned the duke for his niece's release?"

"Though Clovis won't admit it, Clare's capture was a mistake. He denies all knowledge of the sacking and claims the attackers masqueraded as his knights to implicate him. However, Will recognised their leader as Sir Norris, the duke's master-at-arms. Bertrand must tread carefully despite his status. Like most merchants, he's a self-made rich man without a title. If he persists, he could end up in the tower with his niece; presuming she's still alive," Fidelmus replied with a sad headshake.

He poured water from a jug into a beaker and offered some to the others. Shay declined, but Iona nodded. The prior filled another beaker and passed it to Iona, who took a sip before she asked, "How much does Bertrand know?"

"His concern is with the missing. He knows nothing about the *trisiks* operation."

"And the diversion you mentioned; what form will it take?"

"Black powder firecrackers imported from the East. They make loud bangs and whistles and emit coloured flashes, flames and smoke."

"Fireworks?" Iona frowned dubiously.

Fidelmus smiled. "Although virtually unknown in the West, colourful firecracker displays are a staple in the entertainments of the eastern potentates. The illuminated explosions will draw the tower guards forth, believing the spire is under attack. By the time they discover the eruptions are an 'impromptu' demonstration of a surprise gift for His Grace, you and Shay will have slipped unseen into the tower. That's the plan, anyway. The disruption may anger the duke, at first, but it won't last once he discovers he's the recipient of something no other Beretanian noble owns."

"Once inside the tower, how do we navigate it and then leave undetected?"

Fidelmus picked up Lorcan's message. "Hopefully, the answer is in here." The prior cleared his throat and read aloud,

'I've determined the top floor and dungeon within the Janus Spire are inaccessible behind sealed doors, so these are the areas of interest. I also discovered the guard presence inside the tower is negligible, although I don't know why. Instead, the elite men-at-arms concentrate in numbers outside to prevent incursion. Although there's a guardroom on the ground floor, it should be clear on Fair Day if all goes to plan – with the ranks decimated, the captain will require all available hands to man the perimeter. There's no cause to fear you may encounter recuperating brawlers, as the guardsmen's living quarters are in a separate, dormitory building. A door on the tower's second floor accesses the curtain wall battlements, where more guards patrol. However, this is your best means of egress since you can time your departure between patrol circuits.'

"It seems the answers we seek lie beyond the two locked doors Lorcan mentions, but how are we supposed to gain entry? We only have a key to the ground floor exterior entrance," Iona fretted.

"Don't worry about that. Leave it to me," Shay replied laconically.

Iona didn't bother asking how he would contrive access – his quiet confidence convinced her he had the means.

Three days later, Agnes delivered Jake's altered garments. The seamstress had performed an excellent job, and they fitted Iona to perfection. She decided to wear them on the *mission* since the impracticality of managing all those narrow tower stairs dressed in a kirtle filled her with dread. Alfred arrived with her new boots later that afternoon. Her feet had healed sufficiently for her to try them on, and she felt delighted with the fit.

The following day, she wore the boots beneath her kirtle for a couple of hours to wear them in, but her heels and toes still felt a little sore, and she changed back into the cutout bootees.

Iona had almost lost track of the days but refused to give in to the panic that often lay close to the surface. She dared not entertain the idea they barked up the wrong tree. The duke *must* be behind the *trisik* business – if not, they had no other leads. Thoughts of the dangerous task ahead filled Iona with nervous anticipation, but scriptorium sessions helped her relax for a short while. When she finally returned to her old life, Iona knew she would miss the camaraderie of the illuminators who had made her one of their own.

Although they each laboured on separate manuscripts, they all contributed to a group project (a history of Saint Aurigan's Priory) initiated by Brother Ambrose, working on it between their commissions. When the armarius had asked Iona to paint a full-page illumination for this manuscript, Iona had felt honoured and touched by his faith in her ability. She had worked over four sessions on her depiction of the illuminators at their tall desks, pleased with how she had captured the light that flooded the tower room. Iona added the finishing touches to the illumination that afternoon and presented it to Brother Ambrose.

He beamed with delight. "It's marvellous! I recognise every brother!" Ambrose chuckled. "And there's me, peering over the top of my eyeglasses!"

As the illuminators gathered around, laughing and exclaiming at their likenesses, Iona felt a warm glow.

Returning to her room, Iona felt restless. On a whim, she swapped the bootees for the notched ankle boots Alfred had made and went for a walk by the river.

Unlike Iona's troubled mind, the area along the shoreline felt so peaceful. She watched a skiff loaded with grain sacks head downriver from the mill beyond the farm to the priory brewery, west of the infirmary, and returned the boatman's wave. As Iona's thoughts turned to the morrow and her visit to the Leons, two honking geese skimmed low over the water and landed with a splash. She drifted closer to the covered bridge and spotted Quintus talking to a soberly clad man on horseback. Quintus bowed, and the man inclined his head and turned his horse onto the bridge.

Catching sight of Iona, the guest master grinned and fell into step beside her. "That was Baron DeVry, here to talk terms with the prior. His son, Cahir, will soon arrive to begin his apprenticeship in the library."

"Dara will be pleased!" Iona said.

Quintus gave a rueful smile. "Me too, if I'm honest. I could use his help. Where are you headed?"

"Nowhere in particular; just out for a stroll."

"Mind if I join you?" Quintus asked.

"Not at all; I'll be glad of the company," Iona replied and turned at the sound of hoofbeats. A mule headed for the bridge carrying Brother Vincent, who wore a leather satchel across his chest. The library monk nodded in greeting and his mule clopped onto the wooden span. "I wonder where he's off to," Iona said idly.

"The castle. He's helping the duke's chamberlain to assess and catalogue the contents of the family archives and library. Ennis spares him for an hour or two each week." Quintus noticed her narrow-eyed expression. "He doesn't know about the role Lorcan plays for us, and he'd make a poor spy! His task for the duke is genuine."

They continued past the bridge, and Quintus said with studied casualness, "You appeared deep in thought before I joined you. Were you, perhaps, reconsidering your part in Shay's reckless strategy?"

"No, of course not. It's something I *must* do to stand any chance of finding a way back home."

"Pity... I hoped you might change your mind. Only... I *fear* for you. Is it really *so* terrible here that you would risk your life to return?"

Iona stopped walking and turned to face the monk. "Quintus, that is not the point. It's *far* from terrible here at the *priory*, but this isn't my home! My family will be worried sick, and I have clients I can't afford to let down. I *miss* my work and... and... listening to the music I enjoy and..." Iona threw her hands up in frustration. "The friends I've made here *are* important to me, it's just..."

"I understand; truly," Quintus said, his green eyes filled with sympathy that warred with sorrow. "You should know there'll *always* be a home here for you if it doesn't work out."

Iona clasped his hand impulsively. "Thank you."

Quintus squeezed her hand and turned away to mask his emotion. "Oh look! Yellow Flag Iris! It's a stunning flower, don't you think?"

Iona glanced at the clump of showy blooms growing near the water margin and nodded in agreement. Quintus plucked several and presented them to her. "They'll brighten up your room. Anyway, I've matters to attend to, so I'll leave you to enjoy your walk."

Iona gazed at his departing back and wondered if he was responsible for the flowers she often found in her room after the cleaners had gone.

After breakfast the next morning, Iona coiled her plait around her head and placed a linen coif over her hair. The green kirtle had seemed more suitable than the blue for visiting the Leon's in Merchant's Square, and she accessorised it with the leaf-green, embroidered shawl, which she had not yet worn.

Iona picked up the 'Thank You' card (or parchment rather) she had created for Eliza in gratitude for the dancing lessons and made her way to the bridge, where she had arranged to meet Binny.

Her friend arrived promptly driving a small mule cart, with a beaming Eliza seated beside her. The little girl scrambled into the back so Iona could take her place, talking nineteen-to-the-dozen about how she had impressed Madame Barreau when she told the teacher she had taught the *Living Aurigan* the dances for the duke's banquet.

Binny rolled her eyes humorously and said, "Don't worry, we're dropping Miss Chatterbox off at the dame school."

Iona laughed. "She has a right to feel proud." She handed the 'card' to Eliza. "This is what we give to each other in my world to show our appreciation for a helping hand or kind act."

Eliza squealed with delight when she saw the illumination of a lady in Iona's banquet outfit, dancing with a gentleman, who uncannily resembled Shay, and the vignette of a curled-up Smudge beneath the 'thank you' dedication. "I'll treasure it forever!" she exclaimed, clasping it to her breast dramatically.

Iona and Binny shared a fond grin as the cart clattered onto the bridge.

When they neared the town, Iona remarked, "This is the first time I've been back to Tritaurium since the day Jake stole the trike. The visit to the duke's castle doesn't count. I hope the stench isn't as bad as I remember!"

"I think you'll find it is. It's okay in Merchant's Square, but we must go through some pretty whiffy streets to reach it. I'm working on a solution via Fidelmus, who has the ear of the town council. Tritaurium requires sewers and proper sanitation, with access to clean water for all. The burghers of Glassnesse in Zephyrinus have made great strides in cleaning up their city, but Duke Clovis doesn't care." Binny reached into a pocket and withdrew a small, round wooden box. She handed it to Iona. "Here, rub some of this beneath your nostrils. I made it from baking soda and essential oils. Unlike Neutrolene, it doesn't completely eliminate odours, but it's better than nothing."

Iona applied the clear paste contained within and passed it back to Binny. "What's Neutrolene?"

"It's the stuff used by morticians and forensic pathologists to neutralise the smell of decomposing bodies."

"Nice!" Iona replied with a grimace. However, she felt glad of Binny's product when the cart entered the narrow streets, rumbling over the filthy cobblestones.

Binny dropped Eliza off at Madame Barreau's dame school, located in a salubrious cul-de-sac behind Merchant's Square, and continued to the Leons house. Entering the paved plaza, they passed the marble fountain that Iona remembered from her journey on the trike. The imposing Leon residence with its barley twist chimneys and decorative plasterwork resembled something from *Hans Andersen*. Binny drove the cart beneath an archway into a private passageway at the house's side, emerging into a backyard lined with warehousing and stables. The yard bustled with activity as workers loaded crates and barrels onto two large wagons, whilst another strapped down luggage onto the roof of the family coach. Bertrand Leon and a tall man stood before a small outbuilding that might be an office. The merchant shook hands with the fellow, who Iona recognised as Aylard Quillen, the prior's lawyer. As Aylard passed them on his way from the yard, he doffed his hat, and Bertrand hastened forward to hand Iona and Binny down from the cart.

"We're in something of an upheaval preparing for our journey to Saint Lexis Priory in two days," Bertrand explained.

"Oh, the trade delegation to the dragons is now a reality?" Iona asked, intrigued.

Bertrand smiled with satisfaction. "Indeed! Prior Faolan of Saint Lexis replied to my sounding-out letter, confirming that the dragon council has agreed to hear me out. Isobel insists on being present. So, we are packing up the household and travelling to our residence in Glassnesse; it's closer to the dragon territories and Bel thinks we would all benefit from the sea air."

Binny manoeuvred the basket containing Isobel's order from the cart and said wryly, "And no doubt she'll be keen to investigate the Zephyrinus marriage market. I hear there's a dearth of suitable suitors for Alicia here in Kentauros."

"Yes, there's that too!" Bertrand chuckled. "My agent in Glassnesse informs me the *Appollonia* is due to dock any day; hopefully with your order from Truscaromia onboard. Aylard Quillen and Mr Payne, my foreman here, will handle business during my absence. They're aware of our future joint venture, so you can speak to them if the need arises before I return."

Bertrand instructed a stableboy to take care of the cart and escorted the two women into a parlour with linenfold-panelled walls hung with richly-coloured tapestries, where Isobel and Alicia waited. The busy merchant withdrew, leaving the ladies to their chatter.

"Sorry about the mess. We're all in a dither with the packing. Bertrand arranged this trip so last minute," Isobel apologised.

"Oh, don't mind us!" Binny replied, unloading her basket. "Everything you asked for is here, including the new face cosmetics. Just in time for all the parties Alicia will no doubt attend in Glassnesse!"

Alicia grinned. "I can't wait to leave this provincial backwater. The city by the sea is worldly and elegant, and when the tall ships dock, it's so much fun to hear the sailors' tall-tales and the reports from Papa's agents! I love watching them sail forth to exotic destinations and imagining all the adventures they might have." She clasped her hands in delight and then gave a small moue. "It's just a pity we're leaving on the same day as the castle fair. I was quite looking forward to that."

"I'm sure there'll be better and more exciting fairs in Glassnesse," Binny consoled, at which Alicia perked up.

A maid served small pastries with a delicious new tea from the East, and talk turned to the dragons.

"I've persuaded Papa that, as the heir to his trading company, I must attend the talks with the dragon representatives. If Papa manages to strike a deal, it will be the most important trade concession he's ever negotiated. Besides, unlike humans, dragons regard males and females as equal," Alicia informed with an edge of defiance, glancing sidelong at Isobel.

"You'll get no argument from me unless the middlemen at Saint Lexis have the final say in the delegation's composition. To the best of my knowledge, it's been years since anyone has dealt with them and we know little about what goes on there," Isobel cautioned.

"Have you ever met a dragon before?" Iona asked.

"Once, when I was a little girl. My father was an impoverished minor baronet, with a small estate adjacent to the territories, several miles west of Saint Lexis Priory. A low wall defines the border there, and one day, whilst playing catch with my cousin, we ventured too close to it and my ball sailed into the trees on the other side. I thought I had lost it forever, but a Venator youngling – one of the middling-sized dragons – appeared from the treeline and tossed it back to us. I had never seen a dragon up close before, though I often watched the Alphas' from afar when they performed their aerial dances at sunset," Isobel said with a nostalgic sigh. "Anyway, we played catch with the youngling, throwing the ball back and forth across the wall, until we heard Mama calling for us. Though I often returned to the spot before we moved to Glassnesse, I never saw the youngling again."

"What a lovely memory to have, though. Do you know if the Lacunae dragons' alleged ability to teleport is true?" Iona enquired.

"Teleport? I don't know that word," Isobel replied with a puzzled frown.

"Sorry, I forgot... erm, can they disappear into thin air and reappear wherever they choose?"

"Oh, I see. Yes, they can. At least, that's what my parents taught me, though it *does* seem improbable. Perhaps they're just very good at disguising themselves!"

When Iona and Binny finally prepared to leave, Isobel said, "I've just remembered to ask if Clovis has bothered you since the banquet?"

"Sort of, and I had words with Lady Madeleine after you left," Iona replied and quickly filled her in on the unpleasant exchange, and the duke's subsequent presentation of the necklace.

Isobel shook her head. "You might want to consider staying with the nuns at Glassnesse Abbey for a while. Clovis has no jurisdiction there. Duke Alvaro rules Zephyrinus. You could travel with us."

"Hopefully, my rejection of the duke's gift has cooled his ardour. Fidelmus has been good to me, so I'd like to stick it out. If things get ugly, I'll certainly take your advice! The prior will ensure I travel there safely. But thanks for your kind offer; there's no one I'd rather journey with," Iona stalled.

Isobel nodded. "Well, if you're sure, but please don't underestimate Lady Madeleine's influence…"

"I won't!"

Chapter 13

Late the next morning, Iona sat down at the knee-hole desk. Since the attempt at infiltrating the Janus Spire would occur on the morrow, she thought it advisable to write her deposition for the leather folder, just in case things went tits-up……

She had done no more than sharpen a quill when a knock sounded at her door. Iona's visitor was Shay, of whom she had seen little since their conversation with Fidelmus. No doubt he had kept busy in the interim, plotting with Will Copeland and his unnamed 'associate'.

Iona invited him in, and Shay said, "We've decided its best you're not seen arriving at the fair with me. Instead, you'll travel with Binny. You must stick with her until I signal it's time to make our move." He plonked a large canvas and leather backpack onto the table. "This is for you. We must prepare for any contingency. Pack what you'll need in the event we cannot immediately return to the priory after our mission."

"Cannot return? What do you mean?" Iona asked in trepidation, though she half-guessed.

"If all goes according to plan, we'll be in and out before anyone suspects. However, if we don't make a clean getaway, we cannot afford to draw pursuers to the priory, implicating Fidelmus. Even if we're recognised, the prior can claim he had no knowledge of our intentions. Clovis may not believe him, but he'll have no proof Fidelmus is lying."

Iona snorted and said facetiously, "Knowing the duke, he'll think we've eloped together, solving Lady Mad's imaginary problem. Where will we go if we can't return to the priory?"

"That will depend on what, if anything, we find in the tower. I don't plan on getting caught, but it makes sense to go prepared in case we must lie low for a while. If you've got cold feet, there's still time to withdraw, and I'll go in alone."

"Never! Not after the job I had of persuading you to include me!"

Shay shrugged. "Fine; if you're sure you can follow my orders?" When Iona gave a grudging nod, he continued, "We'll travel light. Don't pack anything impractical like the banquet gown. I'm sure your normal clothes will suffice for an elopement wedding," and with a sardonic twist of the mouth, he departed.

"Huh! Sarcastic much! Bighead!" Iona said to the empty room.

After completing her deposition, Iona organised the backpack. Since she would wear the black knee boots Alfred had made, she placed the notched ankle boots at the bottom and added the altered jerkin and one of the two shirts – she intended to don the other with the breeches on the morrow. Binny had given her a black skirt that, for ease of movement, could be hitched above one knee via a hook and eye, which Iona planned to layer over the breeches to avoid drawing the fairgoers' attention to her manly garb. After all, it wouldn't do to appear too conspicuous. Iona added underwear and a nightshift and, on impulse, removed her own clothes from their hidey-hole. She returned the hoodie to the secret compartment, but stuffed everything else into the backpack – she could wear them beneath other attire if comfort became a priority. Though she hoped her preparations would prove unnecessary, Iona knew she must be ready for any eventuality.

Iona next packed her sanitary items, thankful she had just finished her period, and stowed a selection of Binny's toiletries and medicines in a padded linen bag she discovered inside the backpack. Her hand paused over the pouch of contraceptive leaves, and though she didn't need them, Iona added the pouch to the bag without analysing her reasons. On a whim, she included the cosmetics – they didn't take up much space. Inserting the linen bag into the backpack, she slipped hairpins and ties into a side compartment, along with the pack of chewing gum from the hoodie pocket. She'd add her toothbrush, hairbrush, and comb in the morning.

Iona slept little, too keyed up to relax, and rose early – Binny must set up her stall before the fairgoers arrived.

Clad in the shirt and breeches, Iona reached for a leather belt once owned by Jake. Joss had shortened it for her, and she strung her belt pouch onto the supple leather before buckling it on. The black skirt fastened with ties, making it easy to whip off if it later became too cumbersome, but she left the hem down, for now.

After a hurried breakfast, she slotted the last items into the backpack and reached for the black cloak. From the doorway, Iona gazed back at the room, which she now realised felt like home, and wondered if she would ever see it again.

She found Quintus outside, bearing a water flask and a linen-wrapped package. "Morning Iona. I just came to give you these; food and water to take with you in case..." The guest master's implication seemed clear, but he amended, "Well, they'll be safer to consume than anything you'll find at the fair."

"Thanks, Quintus, I appreciate it," Iona said and stowed the items in her backpack. The guest master helped her hoist it onto her back, and she adjusted the shoulder straps.

"I'd walk with you, but I'm needed at the stables to greet Cahir, who's just arrived," Quintus explained, regret clear in his green eyes. "There's still time to pull out—"

"No, Quintus," Iona interrupted, shaking her head. She stepped closer to him, and laying a hand on his shoulder, kissed his cheek in farewell; she might never see him again.

Quintus embraced her, the backpack making it awkward, and one arm slid down to her waist. "Please be careful," he murmured in her ear, and Iona felt his heart racing in his chest. He stepped back, his cheeks flushed, and unable to meet Iona's eyes, he wished her luck and hastened towards the passageway down the side of the bathhouse.

Iona stared after him as a suspicion dawned.

Fidelmus waited for Iona in the vestibule behind the front door.

As she stepped towards him, he said, "You've just missed Shay. He reported the brawl casualties amongst the guards are enough to make a real difference to the numbers guarding the tower, as we had hoped." He sighed with mixed feelings and handed Iona a small pouch that clinked in her hand. "You'll need some money for the fair and... if you can't return to us straight away."

"I can't accept this! You've given me so much already," Iona protested.

Fidelmus drew his hands behind his back when she tried to return it. "You're one of us now. If it makes you feel better, consider it payment for your illuminated contribution to Brother Ambrose's project." He smiled. "Besides, the ruby necklace is worth far more than the pouch's contents!"

"Very well. Thank you, prior," Iona conceded, and tucked the purse into her belt pouch.

Fidelmus took her hands in his. "Good luck, my dear. I'll appeal to the *Great Wheel* to return you safely to us."

Iona squeezed his hands, acknowledging to herself how fond she had become of this kind man.

Brother Hildebrandt, who peered from the door hatch, informed them that Binny had arrived. With a final squeeze, she withdrew her hands from the prior's and, with a nod to Hildebrandt, slipped through the door to descend the steps to Binny's waiting cart, piled high with wares to sell.

As the cart pulled away down the path, Iona turned to wave at Fidelmus who stood on the porch.

Binny glanced at her passenger. "You almost resemble a female version of Shay in that outfit!"

"Yeah, I just need a sword and some leather pants. Oh, and a supercilious sneer to complete the transformation."

Binny shook her head. "You two! You're as bad as each other. Both pushing one another away to keep the obvious at bay. You won't be able to deny it forever!"

"What do you mean?"

"Now is not the time. You'll work it out eventually…" Binny changed the subject. "I'm glad I've got some help to set up the stall. Joss and Eliza won't be along until later."

"Will the duke be there?"

"He'll put in an appearance at some point, but it's doubtful he'll browse the stalls! Just keep your head down and your hood up until Shay fetches you. I hope you know what you're doing!"

"I know I have to do it," Iona replied, thinking of Quintus' reservations, which led to thoughts of his reaction to her departure. "What do you know about Quintus?"

"About as much as I know about any brother. Although, Joss believes he has a *past*… He must be what, thirty? Perhaps a bit younger, but he joined the order relatively late. Most monks start as acolytes. Why?"

Iona shrugged casually. "Oh, I just wondered. He's um… very personable, good-looking even. It just seems a waste, if you know what I mean."

Binny gave a cynical half-smile. "He wouldn't be the first man to run away from his old life."

As they joined the procession of carts and wagons toiling up the hill to the castle, Iona dismissed Quintus from her mind to concentrate on the task ahead.

When they passed through the open gates into the courtyard, an official directed them to Binny's designated stall. With Iona's assistance, it didn't take her long to set out her wares. Vendors had travelled from far and wide to tout their goods, and Iona observed everything from textiles, leathers and furs to spices, perfumes, wood carvings, exotic fruits, cheeses, wine, and caged songbirds. Other traders readied snack and refreshment booths, and workers erected a beer pavilion hung with pennants and banners over a plank serving bar.

A short, dapper man approached Binny, who introduced him to Iona, "This is Timmo, an experienced barker. He'll extoll my wares from the stall front, receiving ten percent of the profits from sales made to any customers he attracts." She handed him a parchment sheet, on which she had listed the properties and benefits of various products.

Timmo had fifteen minutes to memorise it before a bell sounded to announce the fair's opening, and patrons streamed into the castle grounds.

With no shortage of entertainments, something caught Iona's eye wherever she glanced. She spotted jugglers, fire-eaters, magicians, and a band of strolling players enacting a drama on a gaudily decorated stage. Beyond the beer tent, contestants vied for prizes at an Aunt Sally and other games, including apple-bobbing, wrestling, and tug-o-war. In a side courtyard, musicians performed for merrymakers who danced the *Carole*, a social circular dance livelier than the courtly prancing Iona had learned.

She kept her eyes peeled for Shay amidst the crowds and tumult, but as the fair grew busier, she couldn't just stand idle behind the stall with business so brisk. Iona understood why Binny had hired Timmo, who, despite having only a short time to gen up on the products, drove customers their way with a confident spiel that promised much – but nothing the merchandise couldn't deliver. He tempted with exclusivity, injected humour where appropriate, and flattered the susceptible amongst the mostly female clientele.

Iona replenished stock from the cart when it grew low, and even sold items when other customers engaged Binny's attention, until, at last, she spotted Shay. With his cloak hood concealing his black hair, Shay examined a shortsword at the cutler's stall opposite Binny's. Placing it back down, he casually turned and, hands at his belt, unobtrusively flicked all fingers to signal Iona must join him in ten minutes. He moved on to the next stall and appeared engrossed in the tooled leather sword belts and horse harnesses on display.

Bending to hook up her black skirt in readiness, Iona failed to clock the browser, who moved on from the neighbouring stand to Binny's. She reached beneath the stall for her backpack and rose to discover Lady Madeleine staring at her with imperious disdain.

"Well, if it's not the *Living Aurigan* playing at trader! Have the monks thrown you out as an imposter?" She gave a false, tinkling laugh and sipped at the mead goblet she held in one hand. A lady-in-waiting and man-at-arms by her elbow smiled dutifully at the joke.

"*We* at the priory are not too proud to help out our friends," Iona replied with a dignity that belied her veiled insult.

"Is that so?" Madeleine replied, her eyes flicking to Binny. Iona wondered if she felt threatened by her association with the former *Living Aurigan* who had not left – perhaps she thought the urge to stay might be catching.

Binny's customer moved off in a hurry, and Lady Madeleine picked up a pot of face cream. "Maybe she'd rather be friends with your beekeeper! Oh no, I forgot; the *Eterna* aims higher."

Binny's face tightened as the noblewoman blatantly slipped the face cream into her belt pouch without paying. However, she could do nothing. The guards wouldn't uphold any complaint against the duke's paramour and might arrest Binny for slander.

A group of excited children ran past, and as the lady-in-waiting moved to avoid them, she jogged Lady Madeleine's arm. Taking advantage, Madeleine exaggerated the nudge's force, slinging the goblet's contents at Iona, who stepped back a little too late. Though she managed to dodge a faceful of mead, it splashed her cloak, and the sickly-sweet aroma of fermented honey overpowered all the other stinks.

"Oh dear, how clumsy of me," Lady Madeleine simpered.

Iona bent her head to a mead-soaked patch and inhaled. "Don't worry. That's better than a pomander at disguising *nearby* nasty smells."

She gazed directly at Lady Madeleine, whose face darkened at the innuendo. Before she could retaliate, a loud bang followed by a whoosh made Madeleine jump. As a red flame flower blossomed in the sky with staccato popping noises, another bang prompted the man-at-arms to lay hands on his charge and hustle her away from the perceived danger.

Binny hastily helped Iona don her backpack, and swiftly kissing her friend's cheek, Iona pulled up her hood. She rounded the stall towards Shay, almost tripping over the mead goblet, which rolled underfoot. The ranger grabbed hold of Iona's elbow to guide her at a weaving jog between the stalls towards the north curtain wall. They moved against the tide of fairgoers running away from the coloured smoke and scintillating flame projectiles erupting at the wall's foot in a terrifying cacophony of whizzes, drawn-out squeals and sudden bangs.

Altering course on a northeastern tangent, they skidded around the keep's corner, almost barging into two tower guards who had hung back while their fellows investigated the threat. "Quick! Quick! They went that way!" Shay shouted with panic as he pointed to the south. "Don't let them get away!"

The guards, substitutes pulled from the common ranks, responded to his urgency and gave chase without question, afraid of negligence accusations if the unidentified 'them' escaped. As they disappeared around the corner, Shay almost dragged Iona to the unguarded Janus Spire, key at the ready. He swiftly scanned the vicinity before inserting it into the lock. The heavy door opened silently on oiled hinges, and Shay drew his sword before they entered within. No one appeared to challenge them, and silence reigned inside the thick walls as Shay re-locked the door.

Iona panted from exertion, but Shay gave her no time to recover. "We'll check the guardroom first," he murmured, and breathless, she could only nod.

They crept to the closed guardroom door, just feet away. Shay gently drew back the shutter on a peephole grille set into it at head height. Peering into the windowless room, lit by a wall torch, he stepped back and gestured for Iona to look. She stood on tip-toes and espied a lone guard, reclining in a chair with his back to them. With one arm strapped to his chest, and a bandaged leg propped on a stool, she assumed him a walking-wounded casualty of the bar brawl.

Shay silently bade her to stand back and checked the door was unlocked. Nodding to Iona, he sheathed his sword and withdrew a knife from his belt. With shocking suddenness, he burst into the room and reached the man in two long strides. One fist planted in the guardsman's hair; Shay held the knife to his throat with the other before the hapless man could do more than lower his leg from the stool.

Iona watched from the doorway as Shay demanded, "What lies hidden in the dungeon and on the top floor of this tower?"

"I d-don't know!"

Shay increased the blade's pressure on the man's neck. "Wrong answer."

"I h-honestly d-d-don't k-know! Only t-the duke, S-S-Sir Norris and Lord P-Peregrine are allowed b-b-behind t-the locked d-doors! Not even the c-c-castle m-marshal has p-permission!"

"How many key sets exist?"

"F... three."

Shay smiled grimly. "You sure there aren't four? An extra set for emergencies? That set hanging from your belt, for instance?"

The man nodded in defeat and instantly regretted it as the blade nicked his flesh, drawing a trickle of blood.

"Remove the keyring from your belt and drop it beside this chair," Shay commanded.

One-handed, the man did as the ranger bid, and Shay kicked the fallen keys towards Iona, who snatched them up.

"Your superiors trust you not to sneak a peek behind the doors?"

Speaking clearly now, as though resigned to his fate, the guard replied, "Yes. I have no desire to satisfy my curiosity after what happened to the last key guard who disobeyed. It's not worth the risk."

The guardroom contained several restraining devices, and Shay instructed Iona to fetch him a coil of rope. After binding the guardsman to his chair, he asked a final question. "What happens to the kidnapped villagers?"

The man shrugged. "Your guess is as good as mine. They're herded into the dungeon, but never come out again."

Shay stiffened at the man's uncaring attitude, and Iona detected anger in the set of his broad shoulders. He wordlessly gagged the guard and filched the wall torch, leaving him in darkness when they departed the room.

The ranger pointed to a recessed door opposite and murmured,

"That probably leads to the dungeon." A key on the guardsman's ring opened the locked door, and they descended the narrow, winding stairs beyond a landing.

Though Iona had felt shocked at first by Shay's method of questioning the guard, she recognised he had no choice. With the limited time available, it was the only way to gain the answers they needed and prevent the man from raising the alarm. As she followed Shay, his sword held at the ready, the pack on her back seemed to grow heavier. Round and round they trod until the ranger reached the end, halting before a set of double doors. He slotted the torch into a wall bracket and, sheathing his sword, waited for Iona to catch up. With two steps left to go, she overbalanced in her haste to gain the bottom and pitched forward. Shay caught her in his arms before she could face-plant in the floor, and Iona clung to him, her legs trembling with adrenaline.

His arms tightened around her reassuringly, but his words did more to dispel her fright. "You smell like a brewery. Lady Madeleine *really* doesn't like you."

Iona pulled away, indignant, and caught a hint of amusement in his *(annoyingly arresting)* dark eyes.

While she still sought a comeback, Shay turned to the tall, wide doors and selected a key from the ring. "Looks like this'll fit." Slotting it into the keyhole, he nodded and reached for his sword.

The doors swung open silently to reveal a silvery, brushed-steel wall stretched across the passage, inset with a handle-less door fitted so seamlessly, that it barely appeared distinguishable from the wall.

But it was the ATM-like wall recess beside the door that grabbed Iona's attention.

Chapter 14

Iona gazed at the glowing yellow monitor light on the touchscreen frame, her eyes roaming over the keypad and fingerprint scanner beneath, and the biometric, iris-scanning device above. "We're fucked."

Shay glanced from the interface to Iona, wariness replacing his initial shock, his stance alert. "You know what this is?"

Iona nodded. "This is technology from my world. There's no way we're entering through that door. It will only open for authorised persons who pass the eye and fingerprint recognition scans, making a full guard presence inside this tower unnecessary. Sorry, you probably didn't understand half of that."

"I understood enough. Jake explained some of the computer science of your world to me. But I thought it required power unavailable here?"

"Yes; electricity. Perhaps they have a generator or something; I don't know. At least this proves a connection with the *trisik* operation."

"I wonder if we could force the door or disable the... *machinery*."

Iona shook her head. "I wouldn't advise it. Destroying the circuits will likely jam the door and set off an alarm. Besides, I hazard this wall is bomb-proof. I doubt you could even dent it with an axe, and the noise will draw the attention of anyone on the other side."

Shay stood hands-on-hips; his head bowed in thought. He finally nodded. "Alright. Let's check the locked doors to the top floor."

"Okay, but I won't be surprised if we discover another wall like this behind them," Iona opined, and slipped off her backpack to rotate her aching shoulders. She untied the black skirt and bundled it into the pack – after her stumble, she had no wish to catch her heels on the trailing back hem with such a long climb ahead of her.

Shay closed and locked the heavy wooden doors that concealed the metal wall and adjusted the straps of his backpack. He helped Iona shoulder hers and said, "I need my hands free to fight, if necessary."

Iona guessed that was his way of saying he would carry her backpack if he could. "I know."

The ranger removed the torch from the bracket and, sword in one hand, torch in the other, he mounted the stairs with Iona at his heels.

Iona found balancing the backpack easier when climbing upwards, although it required less effort to walk downstairs. Even so, she felt glad of her trike sessions by the time they returned to the vestibule. They located the staircase to the upper floors in a deep archway and continued their ascent.

When they reached the first floor, Shay checked the rooms to ensure no guards lurked, but found them empty. He did likewise on the second floor with the same result and returned to the landing, where Iona waited by the small door that accessed the curtain wall walkway. "The fireworks have stopped. We'd better hurry before the guards return to the tower," she advised, turning from the narrow, lancet window beside the door.

Shay peered through the window at the two sentries patrolling the walkway, their attention fixed mainly on the knot of guards gathered around the spent firecrackers at the wall's foot. He turned towards the final stair flight, and they began the ascent, Iona's legs trembling with fatigue before the halfway point.

The ranger halted and suggested, "Why don't I sprint on ahead while you follow at your own pace? There are enough arrow slits this high up to light your way. If there's another metal wall behind the doors, I'll return immediately. It will save you from needlessly toiling all the way to the top. However, if I find a normal door, I'll wait for you to catch up."

"Okay, that makes sense," Iona agreed.

As Shay disappeared around the next bend, Iona struggled with her disappointment. The prospect of returning home had buoyed her up, but the metal wall had confounded her expectations and home seemed even farther away than before. Hands-on-knees, she rested for two minutes with her back to the wall before continuing.

Iona had not progressed far when she heard Shay's booted feet on the stairs. He appeared from the gloom, shaking his head. "It's the same. Another metal barrier with an identical contraption to open the door."

Though Iona had expected it, she still felt crestfallen and stood aside to allow Shay to take the lead back down the stairs. But he thrust the guttering torch into an empty wall bracket and took her arm to lend his support, sword still grasped in his other hand.

On reaching the second-floor landing, they scanned the walkway through the narrow window beside the exit, alarmed to discover a knot of men fighting at the stairhead leading down off the wall to the courtyard. A figure burst from the melee and ran towards the door. "It's Lorcan! What's he doing here?" Shay exclaimed.

Shay snatched up the keyring and found a key that fitted, unlocking the door just as Lorcan reached it. "Rawley has betrayed us! He delayed until the duke could catch you red-handed! We must leave now!" Lorcan gasped.

"Leave *how*?" Shay demanded over the clash of swords at the stairs.

Lorcan lifted off the rope coiled from shoulder to hip across his body. "Over the wall," he nodded towards the roadside cliff and gestured to the fighters. "Will Copeland and his men will hold the guards off as long as they can; 'twas him who warned me, but we've no time to lose!"

Shay nodded once and turned to lock the door behind them – it might slow down any pursuers who came at them through the tower.

As Shay tied the rope securely around the nearest merlon, Iona peered over the crenellated edge, horrified at the long drop to the bottom. If they didn't break their necks on the climb down, they must then traverse from the castle base to the hilltop brink; the distance short, but exposed. She could see the menhir at the roadside below the steep cliff they had to negotiate, almost directly beneath the tower.

"You can't be serious! There's no way I can do it!" She turned to Shay and her eyes widened. Behind him, she observed Will's men pushed back, two guards breaking through the cordon. "Sh–" she began, but the ranger had read the message in her expression and already spun towards the sprinting men, sword drawn. He moved to meet them, and blade flashing, despatched them with a ruthless efficiency that stunned Iona.

Shay swiftly wiped the sword on their clothing and sheathed it. He tugged on the rope, testing it, ignoring the groans of the downed guards. Turning to Iona, he gripped her shoulders. "I'll go first. You don't need to climb; Lorcan will lower you down to me. You've got no choice unless you want to take your chances with the duke. Do you trust me?"

Iona glanced at Will's men, who had rallied, and nodded uncertainly. Shay swivelled her around and stripped the backpack from her shoulders, handing it to Lorcan, who donned it instead. Without further ado, Shay flung the end of the rope from the battlements. Iona watched it slither down the external wall, coming to a halt about ten feet from the ground. That didn't deter Shay, who grasped the lifeline and lowered himself over the edge. Hand-over-hand, he shinned down the rope dangling between his knees, his feet 'walking' the castle's outer face. Iona watched, heart-in-mouth until a fresh uproar drew her attention.

A stream of pitchfork-wielding peasants, pursued by guards, burst from the tower at the walkway's other end. As the serfs ran roaring to join their comrades atop the stairs, Iona fleetingly wondered about the true extent of unrest within the duchy. Despite the din of full-scale battle, fear for Shay forced her eyes back to him. He neared the end of the rope, and letting go, he dropped to the ground with a graceful somersault, landing on his feet like a gymnast.

Lorcan immediately pulled up the rope and wound it loosely around the merlon, leaving enough free to fashion a loop with a slip-knot. "Step into this, please," he requested. Iona gazed at the flimsy-looking sling, her heart thundering in her chest. "It's perfectly safe. I'll use the merlon to belay your weight and gradually pay out the rope. You'll need to jump the last few

few feet, but Shay will catch you."

Against her better judgment, Iona stepped into the loop, and Lorcan showed her how to release the knot before he tightened the sling around her waist. "Hold on tightly with both hands at head level. It'll help reduce the deadweight if you 'walk' down the wall as Shay did."

"I'm not a fly," Iona muttered nervously, but hoisted herself onto the ramparts beside the merlon. "I feel sick."

"Don't look down," Lorcan advised as he removed a pair of gauntlets tucked behind his belt and slipped them on.

Iona hesitated, frozen to the spot, her legs turned to jelly. A sudden hammering on the locked tower door, followed by silence, spurred Lorcan to speak with urgent bluntness. "C'mon, move! They'll be back when they've found another key, and I can't climb down until you're safely at the bottom."

As Lorcan gripped the rope, ready to control its release, Iona knew she must literally take the plunge, or else she might become responsible for the young man's capture and possible execution. She straddled the rampart, her left leg hanging over the abyss, and crouching low, held onto the rope one-handed. Digging the fingers of her right hand into the mortar on the walkway side, she raised her right leg and, hugging the stones, shifted to face Lorcan as she lowered it over the rampart. Lorcan nodded and, gorge rising into her throat, Iona released her grip on the wall, grabbing the rope with both hands.

She dropped the length of her height, her stomach swooping, and came to a juddering halt, swinging a little before Lorcan lowered her farther in increments. Iona, stiff with fear, gazed up at him rather than look down and saw him mouth *feet*. She adjusted her position and raised her feet to 'walk' down the castle's façade.

Iona had five feet left to go before the rope reached its extent, when it gave a sudden jerk, dislodging her boots from the stones, the slip-knot catching on her belt buckle. As Lorcan fought to free the snag, Iona swung dizzily on the rope's end, sobbing in terror, eyes squeezed tightly shut. With another jerk, Lorcan released it from the obstruction and she dropped another three feet. Feeling a slackness around her waist, Iona glanced down and, to her horror, saw the slip-knot unravelling, pulled apart by the opposing pressures of her buckle and the force of her descent. She made a desperate, one-handed grab for the knot, her left hand, still on the rope, strained beyond endurance as the knot came loose.

With a piercing scream, she fell twelve feet into Shay's waiting arms. Though he staggered backwards, he didn't drop her. An image of the scaffolder who had fallen upon her from a great height flashed through her mind and, heart hammering, she buried her face in Shay's neck and tried to control her relieved sobs.

Shay gently set her down, and she turned in the circle of his arms to observe Lorcan, already gliding down the rope like a monkey, his technique different from Shay's. With the gauntlets to protect his hands and the rope coiled around one leg, he slid rapidly downwards, his agility and competence unexpected from a man in his job.

With Lorcan still twenty feet from the ground, a guard burst through the tower door, closely followed by the duke and another two guards armed with bows. As they gathered by the merlon, Shay dragged Iona towards a large bush flush against the castle wall, six feet from the dangling rope. They peeked from its shelter in time to see Clovis produce a large knife, which he used to saw at the tough lifeline. Aghast, Iona clutched Shay's arm, her eyes wide with alarm. However, her fear turned to incredulity as she watched Lorcan sway backwards and forwards, gathering momentum as he swung the rope in an increasing arc. The duke had paused to watch, and realising what the young man intended, renewed his efforts with the knife – too late. The rope swung towards the bush, and though it remained two feet short, Lorcan launched himself into a dive, landing atop the shrub and bouncing off unharmed.

Mouth agape, Iona stared at the seneschal's erstwhile assistant until Shay hauled her across the grass to the cliff edge. An arrow whizzed past her ear, concentrating her attention. Weaving as they ran to present less of a target, the trio reached the brink and slid down the slope on their asses, arrows flying harmlessly overhead. The incline levelled out, arresting their impetus, but the hill's brow would conceal them from the castle walls until they gained the gentler gradient near the road, by which time they should be out of arrow range.

Iona rolled onto her hands and knees and glanced fearfully upward.

"They'll not come at us from behind. Apart from a shallow maintenance culvert with a rusted grate at the wall's base, there's no access to the hilltop from this side of the castle," Shay reassured.

"Still, we've no time to dally. The duke will despatch a force down the castle road to hunt us down," Lorcan advised, running a hand through his tousled, golden hair. He bounded to his feet and scampered down the hillside, surefooted as a goat.

Iona stared after him with a perplexed frown as Shay helped her stand. "Lorcan is no soft court official. He's an ex-child acrobat who turned things on their head by running *away* from the circus. Fidelmus took him in, but he was never going to become a monk," the ranger explained with a half-smile. "Let's go. We need to keep moving."

Shoulders aching and legs trembling with exhaustion, Iona did her best to keep up. Her old injury had flared to life and she couldn't manage the steepest parts of the hill unless she hugged the ground on her hands and knees. "I need to rest for a while, Shay," she pleaded.

The ranger squatted and passed her his water canteen. "I'm sorry, but we don't have the luxury of time. We must reach Dumatha Village before Clovis catches up with us. I have a safe house there where we can rest up and plan our next move. Our best bet is to cross the border into Zephyrinus; perhaps lay up at the motherhouse for a while."

"Glassnesse Abbey?" Iona shook her head. "We can't, Shay." She fumbled in her pouch and withdrew the parchment scrap given to her by Sister Honoria. "I surmise the man who betrayed you is the *associate* responsible for starting the brawl. Lorcan called him Rawley?"

Shay gave a cautious nod, and Iona handed him the parchment. "Sister Honoria said if I ever wanted to transfer to the abbey, I must ask their agent in Tritaurium to arrange it. His name and address are on there."

The ranger unfolded the parchment and read aloud, "Garrett Rawley." His lips tightened. "It's the same man. It may mean nothing, but I don't understand why you couldn't just ask Fidelmus to organise it."

"Does Rawley know about me?"

"I shouldn't think so. I didn't tell him you were coming to the tower with me, and he may still not know if the duke didn't recognise you from such a distance..." Shay trailed off in thought. He gave back the parchment and abruptly stood. "We have to go. You've been very brave, but I must ask you to be brave a little longer."

Was that grudging respect? Iona thought as Shay lifted her onto her feet.

She almost made it to the hill's base, but Shay had to carry her the last few yards. "This is becoming a habit," he remarked sardonically as he set her down by the menhir, where Lorcan waited.

"Oh, I always get injured just so you can carry me," Iona replied airily and noticed Shay's mouth twitch.

"There's a wagon train heading our way," Lorcan warned.

They huddled behind the menhir, and as the leading vehicle drew nearer, they all recognised the Leon family coach transporting Isobel and Alicia with their maids. Bertrand rode beside it on horseback, and two covered wagons followed the coach.

Iona remembered the family had planned to set out on their trading mission today, and knew they travelled to Glassnesse. Shay stepped out from behind the menhir and she joined him with hesitance as Bertrand spurred his horse towards them.

"Quick! Quick! Into the wagons! The duke is not far behind us!" Bertrand ordered as he dismounted. He pushed Lorcan towards a servant who had jumped from the second wagon's front seat. "The box," he said succinctly to the man, who appeared to understand his master's command. The servant hustled Lorcan into the back of the rear wagon, and Bertrand ushered Iona and Shay into the other. With the aid of a manservant who rode within, he pushed several crates back from the wagon bed's centre, and lifted a section of the floor to reveal a rectangular, box-like cavity. "False floor," he explained.

Shay peered within, noting the tight space, and removed his backpack and cloak. Lorcan still had charge of Iona's pack, but she, too, slipped off her cloak, and the manservant stowed pack and cloaks amongst the gear in the wagon. Shay jumped into the cavity and lay down. Bertrand handed Iona in next, and she half lay atop the ranger, her back pressed against the box's side. As Bertrand and his man replaced the false floor section and crates, she noticed the airholes in the cavity's sides, which admitted pinpricks of light.

When the wagon lurched into motion, Iona sighed. "It looks like I'm going to Glassnesse, after all. Isobel will be pleased *if* we don't get the Leons into trouble for this."

"Bertrand knows what he's doing. He supplied the firecrackers, remember?"

"Does Rawley know?"

Iona felt Shay shake his head. "No. Will Copeland knows, but not Rawley."

"Who set off the fireworks?"

"Mr Payne, Bertrand's foreman, and another of his staff were supposed to perform the 'demonstration', and then present the duke with a crate of firecrackers as a surprise gift from Bertrand. Hopefully, Will warned them in time. With our mission uncovered, the duke is bound to suspect the display was a diversion. I reckon the plan changed. Bertrand didn't appear concerned for his own safety, only ours."

"What will happen to Will and his men?"

"They will attempt to fight their way free. I won't be surprised if they receive covert aid from a few fairgoers and stallholders……"

"I hope Binny is okay."

"She'll be fine. She knew what we planned, and if she was sensible, would have packed up and left as soon as the fighting started."

"I'm thirsty."

Shay passed Iona a hip-flask, and she took a mouthful. "That's not water!"

"It's peppermint cordial with a hint of parsley; a refreshing palate cleanser."

"Hmm, tastes like mouthwash to me," Iona grumbled, but took another generous swig and passed it back to Shay, who did the same.

"Shay?"

"Uh-huh?"

"My neck's getting stiff. Can I rest it on your shoulder?"

Iona saw the gleam of Shay's eyes in the dark as he shifted onto his side. He gently pressed her head into the hollow beneath his throat, and she automatically draped her arm around him. It felt good pressed up against him like this……

"Shay?"

"Yes?"

"Is that your sword digging into my—"

The wagon came to a sudden, jarring halt, and Shay pressed a finger to Iona's lips. Soon after, they heard footsteps and thuds above them, and Iona held her breath. It seemed to go on forever, although only ten minutes passed before the footsteps receded, the searchers evidently satisfied no fugitives hid within. Another ten minutes later, the wagon set off again, and Iona sighed in relief.

She wondered when Bertrand would deem it safe to release them from their hidey-hole, but found she didn't mind if he delayed a bit longer……

"Shay?"

"Yes, Iona?"

"About that sword—"

With a judder, the wagon bounced over a large rut and into a pothole, flinging Shay on top of Iona. Their mouths brushed in passing, sending a bolt of electricity through her; or so it felt. As though magnetically drawn together, their lips met again in a kiss so intense that heat flooded through Iona's core, stronger than anything she had ever experienced with anyone else. Her arms circled Shay's back, her fingers digging into his taut muscles as their tongues intertwined in unbridled passion. With his fingers laced in her hair, he stroked down the length of her body with his other hand, her back arching to meet him.

A thump from above recalled them to their senses, and Shay pulled back at the sound of more thuds and a scraping noise. "I'm sorry. I shouldn't have done that. It won't happen again," he apologised, his eyes heavy with desire and regret.

"Eh?" Iona replied, dizzy from lust, her brain clouded with confusion.

Light flooded the cavity as the manservant lifted the false floor section. "Master Leon says it's safe for you to come out, now."

Chapter 15

The manservant closed the trap but left the crates scattered around its periphery rather than moving them back on top. "Master Leon thinks it's wise for you to stay inside the wagon until we cross the border into Zephyrinus. We should reach it by nightfall. He doubts the duke's men will search our transports again, so it's just a precaution. I've left the box easy to access in a hurry, just in case. Master Leon will remain on alert outside and says he'll confer with you once we're over the border." The man drew Iona's attention to a barrel, and she noticed her backpack leant against it. "From Lorcan. He said you might need what's inside. He'll remain in the other cart, for now."

"Thank you," Iona replied, still reeling from her intimacy with Shay, and his subsequent remorse (*rejection of her?*)

The fellow departed to sit up front with the driver, and Iona lowered herself to a crate. She studied Shay, who sat on the floor with his back to a barrel, one leg drawn up, elbow resting on his bent knee, staring down at the wooden planks.

"Why are you sorry? I'm not, or at least I wasn't until… Is there someone else? Is that it?" Iona asked, trying, and failing, to keep her voice level.

Shay shook his head in denial. "Isn't it obvious?"

"Not to me, it isn't."

"Iona… we come from different worlds, and you intend to return to yours." Shay looked up at last, anguish warring with steely determination in his molten gaze. "I forgot myself in the heat of the moment, but I think we both know *that* kind of relationship between us could never be casual. I won't set myself up for heartache, or do that to you."

She knew he was right – had known it from the start – and cursed her fate. It seemed typical of her luck that she must journey to another reality before she found (*the one?*) Iona knew little about Shay, but it didn't matter; she could no longer deny what Binny had discerned. Yet, she *couldn't* stay here as her friend had done. Her family…

Iona nodded and bowed her head. After what they'd discovered today, the odds of her returning seemed longer, but Shay understood she wouldn't give up.

There *had* to be a way to make it work.

When they finally climbed from the wagon bed, sunset stained the sky.

The vehicles had turned off the road onto a flat patch of grassland before halting for the night. Bertrand stood talking to two armed men and turned as they approached with Lorcan. "These two gentlemen are Hugh and Gil, security from my Glassnesse office, whom I arranged to meet with here. We're just three miles over the Zephyrinus border, but they'll guard our small convoy overnight, and we'll continue to Glassnesse in the morning." The merchant regarded Shay and Lorcan from beneath beetled brows. "And now, we have much to discuss, not least the reason for the *Living Aurigan's* presence on your… *venture*."

Bertrand led them to a small, collapsible pavilion, beneath which Isobel and Alicia sat on folding stools. He dismissed their two maids to the campfire, where another servant prepared the evening meal.

Alicia eyed Iona's breeches with thinly veiled perplexity, and she could tell the young woman was beside herself with curiosity. Bertrand directed Iona to an empty campstool, and the three men seated themselves on barrels. She and Shay had already discussed how much to tell Bertrand about her role in the affair and agreed they must give him enough to explain the barrier that denied them access to the kidnapped villagers, assuming they still lived.

"Well, who's going to enlighten me about why Iona is here?" Bertrand began.

"Me. I will tell you as much as the order rules allow. As you know, the *Living Aurigan's* origin and purpose are part of the order's sacred mysteries and cannot be shared with the uninitiated," Iona replied.

Bertrand nodded. "Go on."

"You are aware the eternal travellers are… *called* here from… well, I'm forbidden from divulging that. Let's just say we come from an advanced civilisation whose science might seem like magic to outsiders. Anyway, an unknown person or persons have found the means to interfere with the… summoning process, and falsely *called* some of the former *eterna* incumbents here. Prior Fidelmus traced the source to the Janus Spire and believes there may be a connection with the kidnapped villagers. I volunteered to accompany Shay as a consultant since my knowledge might prove invaluable," Iona simplified.

"Hmm, it's beyond my comprehension but it sounds like a rum do… Did you find the missing? My niece?"

Shay shook his head. Bertrand closed his eyes in despair, and Isobel squeezed her husband's arm. "However, we confirmed the kidnapped citizens *are* incarcerated in the tower dungeons on arrival. Unfortunately, if still alive, they remain out of reach behind an impenetrable steel wall, its door controlled by unintelligible devices," Shay explained.

"The devices Shay refers to originate in the *Living Aurigan* realm, and before you ask, the wall is impervious to destruction by any means *here*. We discovered three people are… *keyed* to these devices and only they can pass through the door," Iona added.

"Poor cousin Clare! It seems wrong to continue about our own business whilst she remains trapped in the tower," Alicia decried.

"There's nothing you can do for her until we find a way to penetrate her prison," Iona said with gentle logic.

"Who are these three people who can access the dungeons?" Isobel asked.

"Clovis, as you would expect, plus Sir Norris and the duke's brother-in-law, Lord Randolph Peregrine," Shay answered. "I know not if Lady Madeleine is privy to their scheme."

Lorcan cleared his throat. "She may not necessarily be aware of what goes on. Despite how it seems, her husband is the *real* influence over the duke and spends far more time in the tower than Clovis. He, er, took a fancy to me, and I often acted as his runner or serving boy at court events. Such frequent proximity enabled me to observe his attitude toward his wife's er, *relations* with Clovis. Their distraction with each other allows him to pursue his own illicit liaisons, and whatever occupies him in the Janus Spire. He may seem like a grovelling sycophant, but the man is a snake whose attentions I'm relieved to have escaped. It was getting harder to fend him off... I'm not that way... not that I've anything against it... I'm just... not that way..." he stuttered with a glance at Alicia, who unaccountably blushed and lowered her head shyly.

"I must get a message to Fidelmus, letting him know we are safe," Shay said into the ensuing silence as everyone digested this new information.

"After the wagon search, I took the liberty of sending a runner from our party to inform him of the situation. If necessary, you can send Fidelmus a message from Glassnesse. I assume you will stay at the motherhouse with Iona?" Bertrand said.

Shay shook his head. "We can't take the risk."

After he explained why, Isobel exclaimed, "I hardly think the abbess would be involved in anything shady. Mother Wilfrida is a highly principled and devout woman. It's more probable that Sister Honoria acted on her own behalf, though for what purpose, I cannot imagine."

Shay sighed. "I tend to agree, but I'll not take Iona there until I've done a bit of snooping into Sister Honoria's background and recent activities."

"In that case, you can all stay with us until you're satisfied the abbey is a safe environment." Isobel offered.

Iona noticed Alicia's half-smile and the furtive glance she exchanged with Lorcan before they both quickly looked away, and smiled to herself.

As the servants approached with the evening meal, Shay asked

Bertrand, "I take it Payne got away safely?"

"Yes, he escaped with help from my nephew-in-law, Will, who warned him in time. Luckily, the guards seemed loath to approach until all the firecrackers Payne lit were spent, by which time he and his assistant had scarpered. I'm hopeful Will and his men won free. Payne said an uprising seemed to be underway when he himself fled."

After they had eaten, Iona bedded down in the now-curtained pavilion with Isobel, Alicia, and their two maids. With limited space in the wagons due to their cargo of supplies and trading goods, most of the men slept on the ground outside the pavilion.

"You will travel in the coach with us tomorrow. We can talk properly then," Isobel said, flicking her eyes meaningfully at the maids.

Iona surmised that meant the maids would travel on the coach's rear external seat to give them privacy. "I guess that will be more comfortable than the smuggler cavity in the wagon," she joked.

"Smuggler? I don't know what you mean, I'm sure," Isobel retorted.

"Oh, come on, Mama!" Alicia scoffed and turned to Iona on the neighbouring sleeping pallet. "It's the only way to avoid the duke's double taxes on certain foodstuffs that we distribute to the poor. We couldn't help nearly so much otherwise."

"I'm glad it has airholes, at any rate!"

"Oh, they're for chickens! Some serfs don't even have a fresh supply of eggs," Alicia explained.

"Well, I'm thankful someone cleaned out the chickenshit!"

The next morning, Iona used the latrine area a manservant had dug out behind a stand of bushes near a narrow creek that bounded the campsite. She considered it no worse than the facilities at a couple of music festivals she had attended.

After performing her ablutions in the swift-flowing creek, she returned to the pavilion and donned the tie-skirt with a clean shirt – the breeches were filthy after yesterday's escapade. She settled on the notched ankle boots – the black knee boots also required a good clean.

Though she had not expected to sleep with the Shay conundrum weighing on her mind, the previous day's exertions had worn her out so much that slumber had claimed her quickly. Now, she covertly watched him as they ate a hurried breakfast before continuing their journey. Iona could no longer lie to herself; Shay took her breath away. However, she *really* didn't need this added complication. The ranger seemed to sense her regard and glanced expressionlessly at Iona, but she detected the bleakness in his eyes. He, too, had stopped lying to himself......

Once aboard the coach, Alicia's high-spirited chatter masked Iona's silence as the convoy turned back onto the road. They had not travelled far when Alicia leaned forward in her seat and, eyes sparkling, said, "I've been dying to hear how you escaped from the tower!"

"It was pretty hair-raising," Iona replied and regaled them with the story.

"Who'd have thought that Lorcan could be so... heroic?" Alicia exclaimed. "I'm not surprised by Shay's derring-do, but... Lorcan!"

"Hmm, he sure impressed me! It appears he's a man of many talents. Quintus thought highly of his administrative and 'people' skills. They're why the duke recruited him from the priory," Iona gilded the lily. Though Lorcan came from humble beginnings, so had Alicia's father...

"Ah, Quintus..." Isobel murmured with a faraway expression.

Iona regarded the woman seated beside her. "What about Quintus?"

Isobel shook her head as though returning to the present. "A sad story. I once knew his family. Quintus is the youngest son of a baron. He fell madly in love with Iseult, a baronet's daughter, and she returned his feelings. However, their families had betrothed her in childhood to his eldest brother, the heir to the baronetcy. I'm not clear about whether they forced her to marry him, or if she did so voluntarily. But Quintus, just nineteen at the time, vowed never to wed another. He couldn't bear to remain in the same household with his new sister-in-law and ran away. I believe he joined a mercenary band before he ended up at Saint Aurigan's."

"But... he's the most cheerful monk in the priory!" Iona declared.

Isobel shrugged. "Who knows what goes on in people's heads? Still, it *was* a long time ago; ten years, I think. Time enough to get over his loss?"

"Oh, that's so sad!" Alicia interjected.

At first, Iona struggled to reconcile the urbane man she knew with the spurned suitor, but remembering their parting, she discovered it wasn't so difficult......

At midday, they stopped for lunch.

Before they returned to the coach, Iona and Isobel left Alicia chatting with Bertrand and Lorcan and took a short walk to stretch their legs.

"Tell me if I'm being too nosy, but what is going on with you and Shay? I've seen how you avoid each other and the way he looks at you," Isobel said bluntly.

Though tempted to change the subject, Iona decided she might profit from the older woman's advice. "We have... *feelings* for each other... *strong* feelings, but we can't afford to... to *indulge* them."

"Whyever not?"

"Well, I'm... unable to return home just now, but I fully intend to do so when... when the way becomes clear."

Isobel raised an eyebrow. "Ah! It was not just former *Eternas'* who heeded the false summons; you did too and find yourself trapped."

Iona nodded. She might have known she couldn't fool such an astute woman.

Isobel halted and turned to face Iona, who mirrored her. "Do you love Shay?"

"Yes, I think I do." As soon as she confessed it out loud, she knew it was true.

"And he feels the same way about you?"

"I believe so."

"Binny resigned the *Living Aurigan* position for love."

Iona shook her head to indicate that wasn't an option, but Isobel appeared undaunted. "Your situation isn't as impossible as you think. I gather you have loved ones back home, but if your return to them depends on overturning the machinations of the evil cabal behind the kidnaps, you may have to wait a long time. In the meanwhile, why deny yourselves to no good purpose? These things have a way of working themselves out. If the opportunity to return arises, perhaps Shay will go with you, or you may discover a way to travel back and forth – you are the *Eternal Traveller*, after all!"

"I suppose, tis better to have loved and lost than never loved at all," Iona quoted Tennyson and added, "Though Quintus might dispute that."

"Quintus had little control over his own destiny, but it doesn't have to be the same in your case. Neither of you can know what you *really* want or are prepared to sacrifice when the time comes unless you allow the relationship to develop. You don't want to live the rest of your life regretting what might have been. Besides, let's face it, you may be stuck here forever, so what's the point of repudiating a chance at *some* happiness for a reality that may never happen?"

"I dare not think like that! There must be another way to penetrate those metal walls; I just have to find it. Still, you've given me much to mull over," Iona conceded and glanced back up the road at Shay, remounting Bertrand's spare horse. "Looks like they're preparing to move out. We'd better get back, but thanks, Isobel."

Back in the coach, Alicia fanned herself with a ledger-like book. The day had grown hot, and Iona scented the difference in the air as the highway turned northeast and she caught her first glimpse of the sea. As the road curved to parallel the coast, a refreshing zephyr wafted through the open windows.

Iona inhaled the salty tang and gazed at the foam-tipped waves glittering in the sunshine.

Still pondering ways and means to access the areas behind the tower's metal walls, she glanced at the book in Alicia's lap. "What's that you're reading?"

"This? Oh, it's just Papa's notes, and information from various sources about dragonkind; customs, etiquette and so forth. I must swot up on it before the trade meeting," Alicia informed, and noting Iona's curious interest, passed her the ledger.

Iona flipped through the well-thumbed pages, pausing at a height comparison sketch of two Lacunae posed beside a human figure. The dragon marked 'male' appeared equivalent in size to a Shetland Pony, whereas the smaller female roughly equated to a Great Dane. She read three, mostly speculative paragraphs about the Lacunae ability to transition instantly from one place to another, regardless of barriers. Iona wondered if they could carry passengers during the transfer, and a mad idea took root.

It smacks of desperation, and Shay will think I'm crazy but– "What is it?" Alicia enquired, noting Iona's distracted expression.

"Oh, nothing," Iona replied with a smile and handed back the book.

Chapter 16

When Glassnesse appeared on the horizon, Iona leaned from the coach window for a better view.

It bore little comparison to Tritaurium or any of the small settlements they had passed through. The city, built on a terraced hill that swept down to a horseshoe bay, gleamed white in the late afternoon sun. Iona gazed awestruck at the Romanesque buildings and wondered if they might be a survivor or late-flowering of an earlier architectural style. Seagulls swooped over the masts of tall ships moored alongside fishing vessels in the harbour and drifted on thermals above a promontory on the bay's northern side. An imposing gothic edifice stood upon this headland, contrasting starkly with the city's classical lines, and Iona guessed it must be the abbey.

A floodplain stretched beyond the ness, and Iona glimpsed an aqueduct behind the city-hill's shoulder.

Entering the city from the south, the little convoy wound its way up the main thoroughfare, which circled the hill. The terracing ensured the avenue remained level, though it rose on a gentle gradient when it switch-backed up to the next tier. Shops, houses and public buildings lined the central road, with stairways connecting the levels, plus side streets and alleys branching off at intervals. The coach wheels occasionally passed between stone slabs, spaced to allow vehicular passage. These slabs, of equal height to the raised pavements, acted as stepping stones, allowing pedestrians to cross the road without getting their feet wet or dirty. Though less mucky than Tritaurium, the city suffered from an inadequate sewerage network, but as Binny had mentioned, the duke's engineers made steady progress in its modernisation.

Most citizens wore the same fashions as prevailed in Kentauros, but Iona observed a wider variety of dress; from a woman in billowing, ankle-cuff trousers and a multi-hued shawl to a brown-skinned man in a striped robe and turban, a sheathed scimitar belted over his waist sash. This evidence of a more cosmopolitan culture seemed consistent with Glassnesse's position as a port city, and Iona hoped it meant she could wear her breeches without raising eyebrows.

Two tiers up, the vehicles crossed a forum-like square with a central, white basalt fountain, and took a shortcut up a stone ramp to avoid circling the city again. The buildings became grander the further they climbed, milky limestone and marble replacing the white stucco of the lower levels. Iona gazed up at Duke Alvaro's palace, crowning the hill's apex, shading her eyes against the dazzle of sunlight on snowy marble.

"I don't get this place. Why's it so different from everywhere else I've seen?" she queried.

"This is the former capital of the Truscaromian invaders who once ruled much of Beretania before the fall of their empire. Duke Alvaro is a descendent of the last governor, and his noble forbears always took pains to maintain the city; even during the dark age that followed the Truscaromian withdrawal," Isobel explained as the coach halted before a pair of tall gates that faced the harbour.

The passengers alighted from the coach and wagons, the vehicles pulling into a side yard beyond the gates where the teamsters would offload the luggage and supplies before driving the wagons with their remaining cargo down to the Leons dockside warehouse.

A groom took Shay's horse and Isobel led her three guests through the gates to a walled yard, an archway at one side providing internal access to the side yard and stable area.

"Welcome to Villa Leon," Isobel said.

Iona followed her hostess up a path lined with flowering shrubs to a two-storey dwelling. Alicia explained the layout as they entered the vestibule, "That doorway on the right leads to the kitchen and servants' quarters, and the stairs to the upstairs rooms are through the doorway at left."

From the vestibule, they proceeded to a mosaic-floored atrium surrounded by rooms, with an impluvium in the floor's centre – a small, rectangular, stone-lined pool for collecting rainwater through a shuttered roof opening. Skylights in the ceiling shed light on the walls, painted with colourful frescos of ancient Truscaromian life. A door in the rear wall led to a peristyle courtyard planted with trees and box hedges, a hexagonal pond at the centre where fish darted between the waving fronds of water plants. Marble benches and elegant statuary bordered the peristyle – a continuous porch formed by a row of columns surrounding the courtyard's perimeter, behind which Iona spotted more doors, storage rooms, perhaps.

"Wow, this is beautiful!" Iona exclaimed in delight, feeling they ought to don togas to complete the picture.

"Yes, isn't it!" Alicia agreed and grabbed Iona's hand, pulling her back into the atrium and through a doorway. "Isn't this grand?" she beamed.

Iona could only nod as she gazed around the room in which they stood. A sunken bath dominated the space, with a stone dolphin at one end, a pipe protruding from its open mouth, presumably to convey water. The blue-painted walls frescoed with sporting merpeople competed for charm with the mosaic design of dolphins and fish covering the floor.

"The aqueduct brings fresh water into the city for baths, fountains and drinking water. This villa even has an underfloor heating system called a hypocaust to heat the rooms in winter, and also our piped bathwater," Alicia informed proudly.

"How does that work?"

"It's a system of hollow chambers between the floor and the ground, heated by gases from a furnace below. We could learn a lot from the ancient Truscaromians if most of our nobility weren't so averse to bathing and afraid of anything new! Though it isn't *really* new, of course. Many of the Truscaromian practises fell into disuse during the Dark Age. Come on! I must show you the latrines!"

Iona shook her head and gave an ironic half-smile. "I can't wait!"

Alicia dragged her into the next room, where Iona surveyed a row of four marble boxes, a keyhole shape cut into the top centre-edge.

"Apparently, the ancient Truscaromians enjoyed a chat while they... *did their business*," Alicia said with a delicate shudder. "Papa plans to partition them, though. He only bought this property a year ago and there's still work to be done. However, Binny will be pleased to learn they empty into a cesspit connected to a sewer. Talking of ancient Truscaromian inventions, it was *my* idea to add a little crushed eggshell or seashell to her new toothpaste as a mild abrasive. That's what they did! They had famously white teeth, you know! Did she give you some?"

Iona laughed. "I can see Binny has made a convert out of you! Yes, she gave some to me and Shay before we left." Iona eyed the latrines. "Well, they're certainly an improvement on the garderobe, but that marble looks awfully chilly!"

"It is, rather. Papa plans to get varnished wooden seats fitted."

Isobel appeared in the doorway. "What on earth are you two doing in here? Are you planning to revive the old Truscaromian tradition of conversation on the *necessary*? Come, Iona; I'll show you to your room."

When Iona woke the next morning, she stretched luxuriously in the surprisingly soft bed and peered at her surroundings.

The green walls, frescoed like all the villa's rooms, bore botanical studies with nymphs and fauns peeking from the foliage. Filmy drapes covered the half-glazed door onto the balcony that surrounded the villa's upper storey on three sides. *If I have to remain stuck in this primitive reality, this is the place to be*, she decided, although part of her missed the priory and her friends there.

She discovered warm water in an ewer that a servant must have left while she slept, and washed in a marble basin, clad in her nightshift. After her bath the night before, a maid had taken away Iona's clothes for washing, leaving only her leggings and Jake's altered jerkin, plus some clean underwear. *I hope the leggings and jerkin don't earn me too many hard stares*, she fretted.

A knock sounded at the door, and Iona called, "Come in!"

Isobel entered the room, a lavender kirtle and white linen chemise draped over her arms. "I thought this might fit you. I commissioned it on my last visit to Glassnesse, but it's a little too large for me and requires alterations."

Iona hoped it would; Isobel and her daughter shared the same slight build. She accepted the kirtle and held it against her. She thought it might fit if she laced it loosely. "Thanks, Isobel. I really appreciate all you have done for me."

"Oh, nonsense! *Thank you* for the risk you took seeking the missing. Though Bertrand puts on a brave front, he's very concerned about his niece's fate."

"I'm sorry we didn't find them, but I've thought of a way we might penetrate the tower barriers. It may not be viable, and I must discuss it with Shay first."

"Shay has already left for the abbey to discover all he can about Sister Honoria. Come join us for breakfast when you're dressed."

Isobel departed, and Iona found, to her relief, that the kirtle fitted. It came with a matching belt onto which she strung her pouch before fastening it on.

As Iona slipped on the notched ankle boots, she reflected that her old life had come to resemble a dream. This thought alarmed her and renewed her determination to find a way back before she lost herself entirely.

On her way out, she passed a maid who had arrived to collect her chamber pot. The woman informed her that the family breakfasted in the small Triclinium, the informal dining room off the atrium.

When Iona arrived at the same time as Alicia, Isobel glanced up from her bowl with a smile. "Oh, good, the kirtle fits! The colour suits you."

"Thanks, Isobel!"

"Where's Papa?" Alicia queried.

"His lookouts sighted *The Appollonia* off the coast and he's left for the docks."

"Oh, he could have told me! I wanted to be there when it puts in to harbour!" Alicia pouted with vexation.

"I expect he thought you would be occupied with our guests," Isobel replied.

"Is *The Appollonia* Merchant Leon's trading vessel?" Lorcan enquired.

Isobel nodded. "One of them; we have two."

"I would be happy to escort Alicia to the docks. Perhaps Iona might like to come, too?"

Iona guessed he needed her to act as a chaperone. Isobel might not assent otherwise. "It would be good to see something of the city," she agreed.

"Oh, please Mama! Say yes!" Alicia pleaded.

"I'm not sure it's safe to visit the docks unaccompanied by your papa," Isobel stalled, and then sighed. "Bertrand has taken the small cart, so I suppose you can use the coach, but take Hugh with you and go straight to our warehouse."

Alicia beamed. "Oh, everyone at the docks knows me, but we will, I promise! Thank you, Mama!"

"I won't let anything befall Alicia; or Iona, of course," Lorcan reassured Isobel.

Breakfast consumed, Hugh, one-half of the Leons Glassnesse security team, brought the coach around to the front gates, and Alicia hopped aboard with her two guests.

The streets, busier at this time of day, teemed with people going about their business, and they progressed slower than they had on arrival. Alicia fidgeted with impatience as they crossed the forum, their way impeded by street hawkers selling their wares from handcarts or colourful blankets laid on the ground.

When they finally arrived at harbour level, the coach had first to negotiate the wholesalers' yard, crammed with stalls selling imported fruit and vegetables, before cutting through the fish market to reach the waterfront. They had cleared the yard when Hugh yanked on the horse's reins and brought the coach to an abrupt, juddering halt. Yells and curses from up ahead drew the passengers' attention, and they leaned out the windows to ascertain why their vehicle had stopped.

The drivers of two wagons in front of the coach had dismounted, gesticulating at a third whose cart had overturned ahead of them, the victim of a broken wheel axle. Plump canvas sacks thrown from the cart lay where they had fallen. A handful had split, littering the ground with iron nails, rivets and roves. Another wagon had pulled up behind the coach, and it seemed obvious to Iona they were stuck until the unlucky carter retrieved his sharp, scattered cargo, and hauliers had removed the broken vehicle blocking their passage.

"I'll miss the docking at this rate!" Alicia fretted, her fingers tapping on the window frame in frustration. She reached a sudden decision, and opening the door, said, "It'll be quicker to walk," and jumped out.

Lorcan frowned with concern but followed suit. "I'm not sure this is wise. I promised your Mama I'd look after you."

"Oh, we haven't far to go. *The Apollonia's* mooring berth is near the warehouse," Alicia said dismissively and held out her hand to Iona. "Are you coming?"

Iona didn't fancy remaining cooped up in the coach by herself and allowed Alicia to assist her down.

Hugh was not happy. "Your parents will have my guts for garters if I let you wander off! Please, get back in the coach."

"Oh, don't be an old silly! We'll be fine! Lorcan is with us."

Hugh couldn't abandon the coach and horses, and although he grumbled, Iona suspected he might have objected more strenuously if not for Lorcan's presence. She gave him a sympathetic smile and hurried after the others who had slipped behind the fishmongers' stalls to avoid the obstruction.

As they emerged from the market, Iona wrinkled her nose at the combined aroma of decaying fish, seaweed, brine and tarred logs underlain with the stink of rotting garbage. Boatyards, and workshops housing sail, net and rope manufactories lined the waterfront, with a warren of alleys behind containing chandleries, taverns, and sailors' dosshouses. A few small boats tied to pilings dotted the waterline, but the deeper anchorage lay northwards near the warehouse district to which they headed.

The harbour bustled with activity. They zig-zagged between a motley crew of newly disembarked sailors' intent on reaching the nearest tavern, and a stevedore team rolling barrels into an alley too narrow for their cart to enter. Iona stared at the tangle of masts and rigging in the near distance, and part of her understood why the sight made Alicia's heart stir.

"I can see *The Appollonia*!" Alicia pointed. "Look, there! It's tacking around the headland!"

Iona gazed out to sea at the ship that hopefully carried Binny's botanical specimens, when three ragged, barefoot children barrelled into them, one snatching at Alicia's belt pouch. She stared down at the cut strings, but Lorcan had already given chase, and everyone in the vicinity had stopped what they were doing to watch.

Alicia moved forward for a better view, and Iona felt herself grabbed from the rear, a hand covering her mouth before she could scream. She struggled ineffectually as the assailant yanked her backwards behind a teetering stack of crab pots and held a knife to her ribs.

Another unseen person forced a musty sack over her head, and a female voice said, "Come quietly, and you won't suffer harm. Do you understand?"

The knife dug harder into her ribs. Iona nodded and allowed them to tie her hands behind her back. They pushed her down into what she assumed was a handcart or barrow and covered her over with sacking.

As the cart moved out, Iona fought to sit up, but a hand pushed her back down. "Last warning. I won't hesitate to stick you unless you cooperate," the woman spoke again. She left her hand atop Iona's shoulder as she walked beside the barrow, and Iona surmised the man (?) hauled it.

Iona's stomach clenched in fear. She didn't *think* they had targeted her randomly. The woman's voice seemed familiar, but she just couldn't place it. The cutpurse incident smacked of a setup; a diversion to lure Lorcan away. They should have listened to Hugh and remained in the coach.

The sound of the wheels switched from a low-level rumble to an uneven chunter, indicating a change of ground surface, and through a slight gap between the sacking and the hood covering her eyes, Iona sensed a darkening of the light. Had they entered one of those narrow, grimy alleys? The barrow halted, and Iona strained her ears. She heard the metallic scrape of a bolt drawn back and the squeak of rusty hinges as a door opened. Hands pulled her upright and dragged her forward, her shoulder brushing a doorframe. A door slammed behind her and the smothering hood was suddenly removed. She gasped for air and wished she hadn't as the stale reek of damp rot, boiled cabbage, and human filth assailed her nostrils. A stocky man, his muscles turning to fat, stood before her, but of the woman, there was no sign. Leaving her hands tied, he forced her up a flight of cramped wooden stairs enclosed between clammy walls, his knife pressed against her spine. Flecks of daylight pierced chinks in the wattle-and-daub partition to her right, barely sufficient to light their way. The man opened a door at the stairhead and pushed her into a dingy room, only slightly less dark than the staircase.

"Who are you? What do you want from me?" Iona demanded.

However, the man said nothing. He used his knife to cut the rope binding her hands and shoving her onto her knees, quickly backed from the room, locking the door behind him.

Iona scrambled to her feet, and though her wrists felt numb, she banged on the door. "Let me out! You can't do this!"

Realising the futility of her protests, she listened to the footsteps receding down the stairs and the bang of the street door closing. She turned around, back against the door, and surveyed her prison. A pallet with a moth-eaten blanket lay on a plank floor littered with rat droppings. The only light came from a smoky tallow candle on a rickety table; necessary, since a barred wooden shutter covered the single window.

Iona crossed to the window, opposite the door, passing a stained wooden bucket she guessed served as a toilet. To her surprise, the bar unlatched easily, but the shutter wouldn't open. Holding her kirtle above the filthy floor, Iona fetched the candle, and via its meagre illumination, saw someone had nailed the shutter closed. With no hope of attracting the attention of passersby, Iona swallowed back a sob and returned the candle to the table. She needed to sit down and think but eyed the (probably vermin-infested) pallet with distaste. Her eyes scoured the room's gloomy corners, and she spotted a three-legged stool with two unlit candles lying on top. Moving it near the light source, she placed the spares on the table and sat.

Her chances of rescue seemed slim. No one knew where her captors had taken her. Who were they, anyway? She concentrated on her memory of the woman's voice, but her brain, fogged with fear, couldn't conjure up where she had heard it before. Her mouth felt dry, and remembering the chewing gum in her pouch, she cracked open the packet and popped a piece between her lips.

Iona held her head in her hands and stifled her useless tears. What would Shay do when he learned she had vanished? What *could* he do? No one had witnessed her kidnapping. She was on her own. Though she suspected this was just a holding room, Iona had no way of knowing how long her captors intended to keep her here. Raising her head, she noticed the light had dimmed as the smoke from the cheap tallow candle intensified. It required trimming, but she had nothing to trim it with.

Her eyes snagged on an infinitesimal pencil of light coming through the shutter's centre that she hadn't noticed before. Iona rose and lit one of the spare candles from the sputtering flame. She extinguished the old candle and replaced it with the new one. Tarnished metal candlestick in hand, she crossed to the window and held it close to the tiny hole in the shutter, centred in a wood-knot. The area around the knot appeared rotten; no surprise in such damp surroundings. Iona pressed her fingers to the wood and felt a sponginess. Could she knock a hole in the shutter? She glanced around the sparsely furnished hovel, her eyes alighting on the stool.

Placing the candle on the table, Iona picked up the stool. She twisted it in her hands, experimenting with her grip, and returned to the window. Hands wrapped around the seat edge; she rammed the legs into the shutter's weak patch. Again and again, she bashed the wood, until one of the stool's legs snapped in half. Though splinters poked from the shutter's surface, it continued to hold firm. She whacked it twice more, and another leg fell off, though it remained intact. Iona scooped the leg from the floor and used it like a hammer. More splinters flew from the rotted section, but a crack zig-zagged up the stool leg. She needed something harder and more obdurate. The candlestick! However, Iona required the candlelight to see by, and couldn't extinguish it anyway without the means to relight it. Perhaps she could make a tallow pool on the table to hold it upright? No, she wasn't sure if that worked with tallow as it did with wax and she couldn't risk setting the table on fire. And then the solution came to her. She removed the chewing gum from her mouth and stuck it on the tabletop. Iona pressed the candle into the gum until she felt satisfied it had adhered.

She hefted the candlestick, testing its weight on her palm, then took an almighty swing at the shutter. Though her arm tired, Iona continued until, with a rending smash, the candlestick passed through the wood. She yanked it out, long splinters coming away from the gap's edges. Another two swings later, and the hole had widened. Iona used the candlestick's pointed end to prise away loosened wood and put her face to the aperture, unsurprised to find the window unglazed. In the poorer areas of this world, shutters alone often covered casements, though hides, cloth or oiled parchment sometimes replaced window glass.

Iona gazed down on a street not much wider than an alley. Her prison faced a closed apothecary's shop, its shutters down, and to her left, she could just make out a tavern sign gently swaying on its pole. The room with its enclosed staircase appeared tacked onto the tavern's side. She couldn't see much to her right as the adjoining building's eaves blocked her view.

Two men staggered out of the tavern singing a sea shanty, arms draped around one another's shoulders.

Iona cupped her hands around her mouth and hollered, "Help! Help me!"

However, they remained oblivious, their song drowning out her cries. She emitted a piercing scream of frustration, and at last, they looked up. Unfortunately, the drunkards couldn't seem to pinpoint the shriek's source, though Iona waved her hand through the hole. Her captors could return anytime, and it would take too long to widen the gap while she waited for someone less inebriated to pass. Picking up half of the broken stool leg, she dropped it from the hole, only narrowly missing one man, but it got their attention.

Iona shouted, "Please, help me! I've been kidnapped! Please alert Merchant Bertrand Leon at his warehouse!"

One man scratched his head and squinted up at the face that peered through the gap. "K-Kidnapped, you s-s-ay?"

The other man swayed, but more lucid than his friend, added, "Will Leon reward us?"

"Yes! Yes! Please hurry!"

"How do I know you're not lying?"

Iona resisted the urge to scream again and fumbled in her belt pouch for the money Prior Fidelmus had given her. "Here's a silver each for your trouble." She threw two coins out of the hole and watched the men scramble to retrieve them. "They're additional to your reward. The first man to reach Merchant Leon will also receive this bonus." Iona thrust her hand through the hole, and a stray beam of sunlight glinted off the gold coin pinched between her thumb and forefinger.

The two sots exchanged a glance and broke into a lurching run, the less intoxicated man elbowing his 'friend' aside as he overtook him. The shoved man spun in a half-circle but managed to stay upright and stumble on.

When the sound of their cursing faded away to her right, Iona assessed the distance to the street below and shook her head – even if she could enlarge the hole enough to fit through, the drop might kill her. However, it seemed foolish to rely on the two drunks, and Iona continued to bash the shutter. Her chance of attracting attention would be higher if she could at least stick her head through the gap. Anxiety knotted her stomach each time she checked the empty street below. A barefoot child ran past before Iona could call out to him, and she gave up her weakening efforts when the wood surrounding the rotted area proved too resistant. Iona wondered at the dearth of pedestrians, but the apothecary's shop remained shut, and the buildings to each side of it appeared derelict. Iona's discouragement grew when another man exited the tavern but hurried away to its left without passing beneath her window.

She estimated twenty minutes had passed when she spotted the stocky man who had incarcerated her wheeling his barrow into the passage between the enclosed staircase and the building to its right, accompanied by a cloaked figure whom she guessed must be his female accomplice. *Damn! Any rescue party, if it's coming, will be too late!* Thankfully, the pair didn't glance up and spot the hole in the shutter. As they disappeared from view, Iona knew she only had minutes before they exited the passage into the alley at the staircase's foot and reached the room. Iona took one last, desperate peek through the hole, and positioned herself behind the door with the battered and bent candlestick raised above her head in a two-handed grip.

Her arms ached, and she wondered why her captors took so long. They should have arrived by now. When Iona finally heard footsteps on the stairs, she adjusted her stance. Standing spread-footed, she listened as someone inserted a key into the hovel's door lock.

When Shay burst into the room, Iona just managed to pull her swing with the candlestick.

Chapter 17

Shay whirled, sword in hand, and the candlestick thudded to the floor as Iona released her grip.

"You took your time," she quipped with a tremor in her voice.

The ranger sheathed his weapon and pulled Iona unresisting into his arms. He buried his face in her hair as she clung to him tightly, forgetting for that moment the impossibility of their love.

Shay gently cupped Iona's jaw in his hand and gazed into her eyes. "Did they hurt you?"

She shook her head. "Apart from manhandling me like a sack of potatoes, no. But can we leave this stinking hellhole now?"

The ranger nodded and stepped to the table, where he wrenched the candle from the chewing gum with a grimace. "Urgh, what's this stuff?"

"I'll explain later. Can we go?"

With the candle to light their way down the murky stairway, Shay took the lead and guided Iona around the prone figure of her kidnapper, who lay dead at the bottom.

As they exited through the door, Lorcan approached at a jog, shaking his head. "I lost her. She had a horse on standby two alleys over."

"Lost who?" Iona asked.

"Sister Honoria," Shay growled in vexation.

"Of course! *That's* who it was! I *knew* I'd heard the woman's voice before! But why?"

"Let's get you to Bertrand's warehouse first, and then I'll tell you what I discovered," Shay suggested.

The Appollonia rested at anchor when Iona arrived at the warehouse with Shay and Lorcan.

Bertrand waited in the internal office with Hugh and a contrite Alicia, who had received a rare scolding from her father. The ragged cutpurse sat on a stool under Hugh's watchful eye – it appeared Lorcan had managed to catch *him*, at least.

Alicia leaped to her feet when she sighted Iona, guilt warring with relief on her face. "Are you alright? I'm so sorry! I shouldn't have disobeyed Mama's instructions. You're not hurt, are you?"

"No, I'm fine. I could murder a drink, though."

"Murder?"

"Never mind; it's just a colloquialism from my world. A way of saying I'm thirsty."

Shay handed Iona his hip flask, and she eyed it with suspicion. "This isn't more of that so-called *refreshing* cordial, is it?"

"No," he replied, his eyes glinting with amusement.

Iona took a swallow and gave a spluttering cough. "Brandy? Well, it's an improvement on the other stuff, anyway." She necked another swig and, wiping her mouth on the back of her hand, passed the flask back to Shay.

"Come, sit down," Bertrand urged, pushing a chair towards her.

Gil, the other half of Bertrand's security team, appeared in the doorway, the two men Iona had bribed at his back. "These two reprobates say the lady promised them a reward for alerting you to her situation."

"Not forgetting the bonus owed to whoever arrived here first. That would be me," the previously drunker man of the two added.

"You?" Iona said in surprise, noting his friend's scowl. Their race appeared to have sobered them up. No doubt they would soon remedy that with the reward money.

"Yep. I hitched a cart ride."

She glanced at Bertrand, who nodded in confirmation. Extracting the promised gold coin from her pouch, she extended it to the winner, but the merchant raised his hand.

"Put that away. The onus is on me after… *our* failure to protect you," Bertrand insisted, his eyes flicking towards Alicia, who blushed. He dipped into his pouch and slapped a gold coin into the man's outstretched hand. Turning back to Iona, he asked, "How much did you pledge?"

"I didn't specify an amount, though I gave them a silver each in good faith."

Bertrand's lips thinned as he again reached into his pouch to withdraw two silvers. When he faced the two men, Iona realised he felt annoyance with them, not her. "Thank you for raising the alarm. However, it grieves me to reward men who demanded payment before helping a lady in distress. Your reward would have been greater if you had come to her aid out of the goodness of your hearts. Here's another silver apiece; count yourselves lucky I'm giving you anything at all."

The pair shuffled their feet in discomfort, and tugging their forelocks, backed from the room with downcast eyes.

The merchant regarded Alicia. "Well, daughter. I believe you owe recompense?"

Alicia plucked two silvers from her restored belt pouch and pressed them into Iona's hand.

"There's really no need. I could have stayed in the coach. It was my decision to leave with you," Iona protested as she tried to give them back.

Alicia shook her head. "Papa is right. I should have looked after you better. You came with me because I assured you there was no danger."

"You weren't to know a *nun* would attempt to kidnap me!" Iona said, but accepted the coins to ease Alicia's distress at her refusal.

Gil returned after seeing the two men out, and pointing to the urchin, asked Bertrand, "What do you want me to do with him?"

"Find him a job in the warehouse for now to keep him out of trouble. I'd like you and Hugh to take responsibility for his training. He appears to have skills that require re-directing."

The boy slipped from his stool and bowed. "Thank you, guvnor! I would'na dunnit only they made me; honest!"

As Gil ushered the child from the room, Iona raised a quizzical eyebrow.

"Honoria's henchman threatened harm to the boy's little sister if he didn't comply with their scheme," Bertrand enlightened.

Iona curled her lip in contempt and said, "I don't understand what Honoria wants with me. What did you discover, Shay?"

"I don't know, either. Sister Honoria upped and left the abbey four days ago. She's the missionary type who regularly travels the realm, but in this case, she didn't seek Mother Wilfrida's permission and she cleared out her cell. My contact suggested I ask around the docks. Her informant recently sighted a woman of Honoria's description twice in the Black Barnacle Tavern, dressed like a civilian. That's the tavern with the annexe where she imprisoned you. I had just dropped into the warehouse for Bertrand's advice on who I should talk to when Alicia and Lorcan reported you missing."

"So, my kidnap may not be why she left the abbey. If she's been hanging around the docks, she may have heard the *Living Aurigan* arrived with the Leons or even spotted me in the coach when we arrived," Iona speculated.

"It may well have been an opportunistic kidnap. Even though the identity of the Leons guest isn't common knowledge, she could have discovered it easily enough from the household servants, perhaps at the market or baths. My instinct tells me she's left the city now. The Rawley connection suggests she may head for Tritaurium, but why is anyone's guess." Shay shrugged.

"I'll ask Bengo, my overseer, to question his contacts in the dockside community after he's despatched a couple of riders on fast horses to attempt an interception of Honoria along the highroad. However, chances are, she has taken to the lanes, in which case, we've lost her," Bertrand advised. He stood and through the open door, beckoned to Bengo across the warehouse floor and issued instructions.

As Bengo hurried away, Bertrand said, "Hugh, please drive the ladies back to the villa. Perhaps Shay should ride in escort. Lorcan, I'd like you to remain here, if you please. With my overseer otherwise engaged, I'll need a man of letters and numbers to assist with the docking formalities and *The Appollonia's* manifest and bills of lading."

Iona observed Alicia appeared torn between jealousy and gladness that her father had assigned Lorcan duties she enjoyed helping with. Yet, now Lorcan had left the duke's employ, he required a temporary position, at least, until he found another role befitting his skills.

Bertrand sighed at his daughter's downcast expression and alleviated her punishment. "Alicia, you can attend the meeting on the morrow with our newly returned agents and *The Appollonia's* captain."

Hugh left to ready the coach, and leaving Lorcan and a mollified Alicia talking to Bertrand, Iona followed Shay as he went to fetch his horse.

"Do you think Honoria is part of the *Trisiks* conspiracy?"

Shay nodded. "There's a strong possibility. Before I left the abbey, I spoke to Mother Wilfrida in my capacity as Prior Fidelmus' envoy. It appears Honoria turned up out of the blue twenty years ago, which coincides with the start of the *Trisik*s operation as near as we can tell. The abbess asked very few questions, which isn't unusual. Many women with a 'difficult' past join the order and face no pressure to tell their story until they are ready. Mother Wilfrida advises you to maintain a low profile, for now, until she has conferred with Prior Fidelmus."

"Okay, but we need to speak later. I've had an idea for gaining admittance into the sealed-off tower areas," Iona confided.

On the trip back to the villa, Iona questioned Alicia, "When do you all leave for Saint Lexis Priory?"

"In five days. We have a dinner engagement this evening, and tomorrow, we're attending a ball at the ducal palace. I told Mama it shouldn't be hard to acquire an invitation for the *Living Aurigan*, but she thinks you and Shay should keep out of the public eye, for now. Anyway, we'll spend the following three days preparing for our trip. Papa has arranged for us to travel north on a coastal barque since it'll shorten the journey. We'll transfer to wagons when we disembark at Bywhitt near the border. I wish you could come with us, but at least you'll have somewhere to live until we return."

"It's very kind of your parents to allow us to stay at the villa in your absence; though I hope Mother Wilfrida doesn't insist we move into the abbey now she knows we're in Glassnesse."

"I know you miss Binny and Fidelmus, but it's too risky to return to the priory. With Shay and Lorcan wanted men in Tritaurium, the abbey will provide sanctuary if Clovis pursues a vendetta. In fact, Mama and Papa have discussed moving to Glassnesse permanently. I'm all for it, as you can imagine." Alicia grimaced in self-reproach. "Speaking of Lorcan, he's mortified that he fell for the diversion that enabled your kidnap, but the fault is entirely mine."

"There's no point dwelling on it; what's done is done, and all things considered, I escaped lightly."

"Hm, I wonder if Honoria intended to haul you back to Tritaurium?"

"Maybe." Iona shrugged and changed the subject. "So, who are you dining with this evening?"

"Oh, a minor lord and his family. He has a son of marriageable age..." Alicia stared gloomily from the window and fell silent.

As Isobel and Alicia dressed for dinner, Bertrand and Lorcan returned from the docks. The merchant had information for Iona and Shay. "Bengo discovered Honoria and her accomplice lodged at the Black Barnacle under the names Madam Apsion and Brigges, her manservant. They stabled a wagon and horses at a livery owned by the proprietor, who identified the dead kidnapper as Brigges. One horse is missing." Bertrand glanced at the water clock. "We can discuss it tomorrow. I must get changed now, otherwise we'll be late for our dinner engagement."

Bertrand hurried away, followed by Lorcan, who carried a sheaf of documents Bertrand had instructed him to deposit on his desk in the Tablinum, Bertrand's home office.

"This news makes Alicia's theory sound plausible," Iona said.

Shay nodded. "They may have been waiting for nightfall before they moved you. It would be too conspicuous to bundle you into a wagon in a busy livery yard during the day."

"But why? Honoria seemed so keen for me to relocate to Glassnesse Abbey."

"A ruse? Perhaps she hoped her note might sow suspicion of Fidelmus in your mind, encouraging you to leave the safety of the priory and contact Rawley as she instructed. What easier way to deliver you into his hands? Yet I doubt she had any real expectation you would bite, though she may have thought it worth a gamble."

"I still don't understand *why*, though."

"Until we discover what's behind those walls, trying to guess *why* is pointless. Though we've no *real* evidence Honoria is involved with the *trisiks* scheme, my hunch tells me she is. Even so, she may be working to her own agenda. There's been nothing in Clovis' behaviour towards you that indicates he's a party to your attempted kidnap."

A maid summoned them to dinner before Iona could share her thoughts on broaching the walls, and she had no wish to discuss it in front of Lorcan, who sat down to eat with them in the Triclinium.

Alicia popped her head around the door to bid farewell to the three guests and departed in a haze of perfume.

"Alicia looks lovely tonight," Iona remarked.

Lorcan stabbed at his meat as though killing it again. "I don't know why she's gone to so much trouble for a foppish lordling."

"How do you know he's foppish?" Iona asked, hiding a smile.

"Aren't they all?" Lorcan replied scornfully and rose from his seat. "Please excuse me. I think I'll accept Gil's offer to show me the liveliest taverns."

As he stalked from the room, Shay also rose. "You'll have to excuse me, too. There's someone I must speak to. Hugh has set a night watch, so you'll be safe here in the villa."

"But… but aren't you worried about Lorcan?" Iona queried.

Shay shook his head. "No. Gil will look after him."

When Shay departed, Iona threw her napkin on the table in frustration.

After his display of emotion when he'd rescued her, Shay's demeanour towards her had reverted to semi-formality. However, she had believed he would only sustain it in public. Now, she didn't feel so sure. His departure had thwarted her plan to confide her idea for their next course of action, compounding her exasperation.

Iona drifted to the family room and picked up a book Alicia had loaned her. However, after she'd read the same sentence half a dozen times, she gave up and asked a maid to prepare her a bath – the woman would feel insulted if Iona did it herself.

As she relaxed in the hot water and gazed unseeing at the mermaids and mermen painted on the walls, her thoughts strayed to her family, whom she rarely allowed herself to dwell on for fear that sorrow would incapacitate her. She must remain proactive to find a way back to them, but despite what had happened today, she no longer knew if she missed her old life as much as she had thought. Yes, she longed to see Skye and her dad, but she felt less detached from life than she had back home.

When Iona dried herself on the linen sheet provided, she pined for the fluffy towels of her modern world and shook her head at her contrariness. Dressed in her nightshift, she brushed out her plait, leaving her long hair to tumble around her shoulders, and draped herself in the soft wrap Isobel had loaned her.

She stepped from the bathroom into a shaft of orange light, reflected from the coloured glass oil lanterns a servant had lit against the night in the peristyle courtyard. Through the open doors, she discerned a figure sitting upon an outsize throw cushion, one of several scattered around the fishpond, his back against a marble bench. Iona's pulse quickened as she recognised Shay, returned from his mysterious errand.

Her steps carried her into the courtyard, seemingly of their own volition. As Iona hesitated beside Shay, she saw his fingers worried at something in his hand. He glanced up at her, his sultry brown eyes honeyed by the lamplight, and he nodded at a cushion beside him. She dragged it into a position facing him and sat down.

Shay spoke first. "Last night, after you'd gone to bed, Isobel found me out here and she said some things about, er... us."

Iona remembered the advice Isobel had given on the road to Glassnesse, and replied, "Probably the same things she said to me."

"She spoke with wisdom, but..." Shay gazed up at the stars, and then back down at the item in his hand. "I have something to show you. It belonged to my late mother."

He passed Iona the object, a bracelet constructed from multi-coloured, braided cords, strung with charms and beads. It reminded her of a cheap bracelet she had purchased at a music festival, and Iona gasped when she spotted an enamelled CND symbol and a plastic daisy amongst the charms. "This comes from my world!"

"I guessed as much. My mother wears it in my earliest memories. I must have been six when she put it away."

"Who is your father?"

"I don't know, but I was seven or eight when she married Charol, a Zingari sword dancer, who treated me like his own son." Noting Iona's puzzled expression, Shay explained, "The Zingari are nomads who live and travel in elaborately painted wagons. Yet, I have a faint recall of *other* house wagons, unadorned and horseless, *before* we lived with the Zingari, though mother always said I dreamed them. My earliest *clear* memory is of the menhir stone outside Tritaurium, but it's overlain in my mind with another location. I see it in *two* different places. The horseless wagons seem to pre-date that; *if* they're true memories."

Iona took a deep breath and tried to order her thoughts. "You were six when your mother stopped wearing the bracelet? How can you be so sure?"

"Because that's how old I was when we joined the Zingari, and she never wore it again after that."

"How old are you now, Shay?"

"Twenty-six."

"So, twenty years ago, something changed for you and your mother, and Honoria appeared at the abbey twenty years ago when the *trisiks* operation started. I can't believe it's all a coincidence."

"I don't remember any trikes, as you call them, only the menhir stone."

"Hm, according to the Saint Aurigan biography, *he* first appeared in this world close to the menhir stone, which just happens to be located below the Janus Spire."

Shay scrubbed a hand over his face. "So, the horseless wagons? Do they exist in your world?"

Iona nodded. "They sound like caravans. If your mother was a gypsy or traveller, she would have adapted well to the Zingari lifestyle. Is your stepfather still alive?"

"No. Charol died when I was twenty-two, a couple of years after my mother, and gave me the bracelet on his deathbed. I tried to question him, but he rambled unintelligibly in fever dreams. The only clear words he spoke made little sense; *'You must never go back! It will kill you! If you return, you'll die!'*."

"Why didn't you tell me this before?"

"I had no reason to until..." Shay held Iona's gaze, and she understood. Assuming his mother *had* crossed from Iona's reality, had Charol tried to warn his stepson that danger awaited him there? Unless they discovered the nature of this peril, it might scupper any hope Iona nurtured of Shay returning with her, as Isobel had suggested.

"Don't you want to know the truth?" Iona asked.

"*This* is my world... the truth; well, it didn't matter until... us."

Iona suddenly had enough of skirting around their feelings and, inching closer to Shay, laid her hand atop his. "There's too much we don't know to say with any certainty there's no future for us. I may never find a way home, or Charol's warning might just have been part of his fever dream, with no real substance behind it. But if it wasn't, we'll cross that bridge when we come to it, and damn well find a way to stay together!"

Shay smiled and cupped Iona's face with his free hand. He drew her into his side, where she nestled in his arms.

"Charol's Zingari clan is temporarily encamped on the plains north of the city. They performed their traditional dances in the forum tonight. That's where I went after dinner, hoping to arrange an audience with the Madjia, the clan's mystic, and oldest living member. I thought she might remember something... or know the meaning of Charol's last words to me. I didn't expect her to be at the performance, but the Madjia confided she saw me in a vision and knew she must attend."

"What did she say?"

"Something strange... the Madjia claimed the answers I seek lie with the dragons, and I must beg an audience with Hyraxus, the Keeper of Mysteries, a dragon of the Alpha species."

"Really? How peculiar... Still, that fits rather well with the idea I have for penetrating the tower's barriers. All the sources agree that the Lacunae species can instantaneously transpose from one place to another regardless of obstacles. I know it sounds nuts, but I thought…" Iona shrugged.

Shay raised an eyebrow. "You thought we could ask one to have a quick look-see or convey us behind the walls – if that's even possible – or… what exactly?"

"I haven't hammered out the specifics, but I thought we could petition for an audience to ask if there's any way a Lacunae might help. Desperate times call for desperate measures," Iona replied, though even she thought her idea sounded daft.

"Even if a Lacunae *could* help, why would they?"

"I don't know, but if your request to see Hyraxus is granted, we must travel to Saint Lexis Priory to speak with him, and there's no harm in asking for Lacunae assistance while we're there. They can only say no."

Shay gave a sudden grin. "Fair enough, since I don't have a better idea. We can't just turn up at the priory uninvited though, so I'll write an audience request letter to Prior Faolan on the morrow."

"Won't that take ages to arrive and then another age before we receive his reply? I sort of hoped we could travel with the Leons…"

"Not necessarily. We'll visit Mother Wilfrida tomorrow morning. I'm sure she'll allow us to use a messenger bird."

"Messenger bird?"

"Yes, the abbess of Glassnesse and the prior of Saint Lexis communicate via a carrier pigeon system. Since you're the *Living Aurigan*, you're entitled to use it."

"Great! Well, now that's settled…" Iona caressed Shay's chest and raised her face to his. Eyes gleaming in the lamplight, he lowered his mouth to hers, the touch of his lips sending a thrill from her toes to her hair roots. Their kiss deepened, and Shay pulled Iona onto his lap, her legs straddling his hips. Iona moaned as he stroked a hand down the length of her spine, and she twined her hands in his hair.

Voices penetrated her awareness, and drawing back, Iona reached for the wrap that had slipped from her shoulders. She shared a rueful smile with Shay as she slid from his lap. When Isobel walked through the open doors from the atrium, the pair sat demurely side-by-side, but Isobel's arch smile told Iona they hadn't fooled her, and she looked pleased they had taken her advice.

"Did you have a good evening?" Iona asked politely.

"Yes, we did, thanks. Griffin, Lord Tyrwhitt's son, is a most charming fellow."

Alicia appeared then, and asked in an indifferent tone that didn't kid Iona, "Where's Lorcan?"

Drunken singing reached them from the front door, and Iona

replied, "I think that's him, now."

Alicia scowled as Lorcan staggered into the atrium, supported by a shame-faced Gil who explained, "It's my fault. I didn't know he hadn't drunk Zingari firewater before."

As Iona and Shay joined the others in the atrium, Alicia begged Gil, "Get him up to his room before Papa sees him. He's just conferring with the night watch and will be back at any moment."

Shay briefly rested his hand on Iona's back before he went to help Gil with Lorcan.

"Well, I'm for bed," Isobel said, to nods of agreement from Alicia and Iona.

Soon after Iona retired to her room, the bedchamber maid popped her head around the door to ask if she needed anything.

"If it's not too much trouble, I'd like a beaker of hot water and a stirrer, please."

When the beaker arrived, Iona dug out the bag of ground contraceptive leaves Binny had given her, and stirred the required measure into the hot water, grateful for her friend's foresight……

Chapter 18

Iona and Shay informed the Leons of their new plan over breakfast the next morning.

"If you receive a favourable reply from Prior Faolan before we depart for Saint Lexis, you can, of course, journey there with us. My fears for my niece, Clare, grow with every passing day. I very much hope the dragon council will allow a Lacunae to lend assistance, though I must admit, I'm struggling to see why they might get involved. Still, it's certainly worth a shot," Bertrand said.

"Thank you, sir. We'll leave for the abbey shortly. The sooner we get a bird to Faolan, the sooner he'll reply," Shay responded.

Bertrand nodded and stood. "My agents will arrive soon with their report. If you still wish to attend the meeting, Alicia, please join me in the Tablinum office in ten minutes."

"I wouldn't miss it for the world," Alicia replied with a bright smile.

Bertrand turned to depart but paused. "Oh, by the way, my men found no sign of Honoria along the highway. I expect she's well on her way to Tritaurium now via the back roads."

"Thanks for trying anyway, Bertrand," Iona acknowledged.

As Bertrand crossed the atrium to his office, Iona noticed Alicia cast another covert glance at Lorcan, as she had throughout the meal. Apart from a paler than usual complexion, he appeared none the worse for his over-indulgence the night before.

"So, do you have your outfit planned for the ball tonight?" Iona asked Alicia.

"I'm thinking the yellow satin," Alicia replied, swirling her uneaten porridge with her spork.

"The rose damask suits you better. You must look your best tonight. Don't forget, Lord Tyrwhitt and his family will attend, and you've promised Griffin the first dance," Isobel reminded as she rose from the table and, nodding to her guests, departed for her own small office.

Alicia dropped her spork into the bowl with a clatter, and refusing to meet Lorcan's eyes, hurried through the open door and across the atrium to join her papa.

Lorcan gazed after her with a pained expression and opined in a bitter tone, "Lord Twit is only interested in her inheritance, and Twit Junior could never understand her as I do. He seeks only to make an advantageous marriage. Alicia will be nothing but an ornamental broodmare to the likes of him. He'll crush her adventurous spirit and disallow her from taking any part in the business when she inherits."

"They've only met once! She's not engaged to him yet! If you feel that strongly about her, you mustn't give up without a fight. I hear you performed your new duties admirably yesterday. Make yourself indispensable to the Leons and show them you'll be a better partner for her *and* the business! But no more drunken escapades! Perhaps you ought to solicit for a place amongst their crew on the journey to Saint Lexis," Iona advised.

Lorcan nodded slowly. "Yes, you're right. I'm working with Bengo today. We're meeting potential buyers. Perhaps I can work my vaunted people skills and experience of dealing with difficult nobles to our advantage."

Iona heard the irony in his voice and patted his hand. "Well, that's your chance to prove what you're made of! Let Alicia enjoy her ball guilt-free. She's had little fun these past few months confined to Tritaurium. Believe me, it's *you* she wants. Don't make things difficult for her, and she'll love you more!"

Shay stood and said, "Iona, we'd better get going. I'll just go and check the cart's harnessed and ready."

Iona gave Lorcan a smile of encouragement and hastened to her room to slip a starched coif over her hair, coiled neatly atop her head. She hated the thing, but it seemed appropriate for visiting an abbess. She smoothed down the skirt of the lavender kirtle worn over a clean chemise and decided she looked presentable enough.

Though Shay preferred travelling on horseback, on first hearing of their plans, Isobel had suggested they take the cart in deference to Iona, who had not ridden a horse since her teens.

When the Leon villa disappeared from view, Iona inched closer to Shay on the driver's perch. Not taking his eyes off the bend ahead, he smiled and eased the horse around the turn.

The improved sewers, in combination with the light sea breeze, meant Glassnesse smelled less rank than Tritaurium, and Iona discovered she enjoyed the ride in the open air. The cart offered a better view than the enclosed coach, and Iona gazed at the colourful street scenes they passed.

"Shay, you never told me why you left the Zingari."

"You didn't ask. I got the impression you'd had enough of talking and would rather engage in another activity instead, so I obliged."

Iona felt her cheeks grow warm. She had found it hard to stop thinking about their interrupted intimacy and didn't need any reminders. "Well, *you* didn't require much persuasion."

Shay took his eyes off the road long enough to give her a slow, sultry smile. "I look forward to continuing where we left off." He faced forward again and added, "I left because it felt like the right thing to do. I have an older stepbrother, Dareesh, Charol's son, by his first wife, who died in childbed. My stepfather was the Barozi, the clan leader, and by tradition, any sons over the age of twenty-one must challenge each other for the title on the Barozi's death. This ensures the strongest and most skilful brother becomes the new clan leader. The challenge is called *The Inferno* and is the most difficult and demanding of the Zingari sword dances, often resulting in death. I knew I would beat Dareesh, and so did everyone else. However, challenging my stepbrother felt wrong. Dareesh was Charol's son and Zingari by blood. Besides, he'd always looked out for me, and I didn't want to maim or kill him. So, rather than challenge him, I left. If I'd stayed, it would have undermined his leadership since an element in the clan believed the title was mine for the taking."

What a barbaric custom! Iona mused. Zingari sword dancing sounded nothing like the dances performed by Morris Men or kilted highlanders in her world. "Did Charol challenge a brother for the title?"

"No. His older brother, Shanahan, automatically inherited the Barozi title on their father's death since Charol was only seventeen, and therefore too young to challenge him. However, just twelve years later, the clan travelled along the dragon borderlands when a thick fog descended. After it cleared several hours later, they discovered they had accidentally strayed a long distance over the border. With their bearings lost, they halted the wagons, and the four best trackers, including Shanahan, set off in different directions to scout out the quickest way back to human lands. All the trackers returned except Shanahan. Since it's forbidden to enter the dragon realm uninvited, the clan departed via the route one tracker had located, leaving two men behind to wait for Shanahan, their return path mapped out on parchment. They hid in the vicinity for two days before giving up. However, the clan remained near the border for a month before moving on. With Shanahan still missing one year later, the clan declared Charol the Barozi by default, as his brother had no living sons to inherit the title."

"Wow, that's quite a story! I wonder if Hyraxus knows what happened to him," Iona speculated.

"You don't think it's a coincidence that Shanahan vanished in the dragon lands and the Madjia has urged me to ask Hyraxus the meaning of Charol's last words?"

"Maybe, maybe not." Iona shrugged.

Shay fell silent as he pondered the possibility. "Well, we won't know until we get there," he said, at last.

When Shay finally directed the cart onto the road connecting with the headland, Iona gazed down at the waves rolling onto a narrow strand below the promontory's northern side. A multitude of jewel-like pebbles littered the rocky beach, a rainbow of colours sparkling in the sunlight.

"Oh, that's pretty!" Iona exclaimed, half-standing in the cart for a better view.

"Ah, yes. That's the famous glass beach for which the city and abbey are named. The pebbles form from glass and ceramic trash; old bottles, jars, and broken vessels, thrown into the sea by shore-dwellers or from boats. They become smoothed over time by the tumbling action of salt water, waves, and sand, losing all their sharp edges until the corners become smooth. The frosted appearance is due to sand etching the surface. It's thought the tidal currents around the ness deposit them here, although superstitious sailors call them 'mermaids' tears'," Shay explained.

"How wonderful that the ocean recycles human rubbish into something so beautiful!" Iona remarked, sitting back down as the road curved towards the headland's centre, cutting off the view.

The track merged into an avenue lined with trees, bent and twisted by the prevailing wind off the ness. Iona stared ahead at the grey stone abbey, the Lancet style of its gothic architecture more austere in appearance than Saint Aurigan's Priory, yet softened by the sprawl of buildings that surrounded it.

"How much does Mother Wilfrida know about recent events?" Iona queried.

"I had to tell her everything. She is, after all, the head of the order, sworn to protect the *eternal travellers* and guard the *ways* between worlds, as Saint Aurigan mandated. However, like Prior Fidelmus, she knows nothing about the *ways* and agreed we must wrest control of the *trisiks* operation that appears connected to them. You can speak freely in front of her."

Shay drove into a stable yard and, dismounting, threw a copper to a groom, who took charge of the cart. Swinging Iona down, Shay led her past a glaziers' workshop, from which a woman emerged bearing a tray of colourful glass fragments. She wore a leather apron over a knee-length maroon tunic paired with matching breeches, a simple linen coif concealing her hair beneath a leather skullcap.

Iona tried not to stare, but once out of earshot, Shay answered her unspoken question. "That's Sister Gerda, chief glassmaker and manager of the abbey's stained-glass manufactory. It's equivalent to the priory's illuminated manuscript business and earns the abbey a tidy sum."

"She wore breeches…"

"The abbess allows the female glassmakers, even the nuns, dress concessions for practical purposes."

Iona smiled in approval and wondered how many of the beach's glass pebbles were by-products of the workshop.

On reaching the abbey's main entrance, Iona gazed up at the stained-glass rose window dominating the wall above it, observing the central pane depicted the faceless Saint Aurigan. The doorkeeper greeted Shay by name and admitted them instantly, murmuring to a grey-robed acolyte, who hurried away. They waited in the vestibule until a maroon-habited nun glided down a corridor towards them. Iona gazed at the face beneath the oversized starched wimple, recognising Sister Bedelia, the young nun who had accompanied Honoria to Saint Aurigan's Priory.

The sister beamed and said to Shay, "I hear you followed up on my information."

"Does nothing escape you?" he replied with a wry smile. "If you know that, then you'll know what happened."

"Naturally," Sister Bedelia said and glanced at Iona. "I'm glad the *Living Aurigan* survived unharmed. Mother Wilfrida will no doubt wish to hear the details. Sister Honoria's treatment of our saint's living representative is a serious offence against the order. Come, the abbess' visitor is just leaving."

Iona frowned at Shay in puzzlement as the young nun set off at a brisk pace. They soon arrived at a solid oak door, and telling them to wait, Sister Bedelia knocked and entered within.

"*She's* the contact you mentioned? But she looks so young!" Iona whispered.

"Don't let that fool you. Her father runs a network of informants from *The Tipsy Tuna*, his dockside tavern."

They fell silent as the door opened, and Sister Bedelia emerged. "The Mother's visitor is still here, but she'll see you now." She showed them into a wood-panelled office, and sketching the circle symbol on her forehead, hastened away.

Mother Wilfrida, a woman in late middle age, sat behind an oak desk. Iona wondered how she could hold her head up beneath her wimple, which towered to twice the height of those worn by the other nuns. Her saucer-sized *Great Wheel* amulet reinforced the wimple's message of its wearer's importance. Despite this, the abbess' office was simply furnished and neat as a pin in contrast to Fidelmus' cluttered sanctuary, where scrolls, books, and curiosities littered every surface.

However, Iona only had eyes for the abbess' visitor, who rose from his chair with a grin. She remembered her manners enough to perform a curtsey to their host before she burst out, "Brother Quintus! What are you doing here? Is everyone alright at the priory?"

They took a step towards each other but stopped, as though resisting the urge to embrace in front of the abbess.

"They're all fine! We had some trouble from Duke Clovis, but the prior denied all knowledge of Shay's... *escapade*, and though it's doubtful the duke believed him, he has no proof that Shay didn't act behind Fidelmus' back. He knows about Lorcan, of course, but hasn't connected you with the hooded woman seen fleeing with them. Clovis demanded to see you, but the prior pleaded indisposition on your behalf. However, I'm not sure how long he can maintain the charade before the duke becomes suspicious. He sent me here to get an update on your situation and discover if you wish to return with me."

The abbess pursed her lips at this last remark. "That would be most unwise. Even if the duke does not suspect her involvement, there's no guarantee you can protect *The Living Aurigan* from his lecherous advances. The safest explanation Fidelmus can supply is the *Eterna* has moved on to the motherhouse."

Quintus glanced at Iona, who nodded. "He may not suspect me now, but he soon might if Honoria is part of the conspiracy and tells him I arrived in Glassnesse with Shay and Lorcan."

The monk hid his disappointment. "Yes, that's true. Mother Wilfrida told me about the attempted kidnap."

"Won't you all be seated, please? I'd like to hear about the unpleasant incident directly from the victim," the abbess said.

When her visitors had taken chairs before her desk, Mother Wilfrida addressed Iona. "So, we meet at last. The motherhouse will welcome you with open arms if you wish to remain here."

"Thank you. I'm most grateful and will keep that in mind for the future. However, I must soon travel onward in search of a way to penetrate the Janus Spire's mysteries. Shay and I have another plan, but first, I'll tell you what happened with Honoria," Iona answered diplomatically, careful not to antagonise the woman whose carrier pigeons she needed.

After she'd recounted her experience with the rogue nun, the abbess stood and moved to peer sightlessly from the window, tucking her hands into the voluminous sleeves of her habit. "What is Honoria up to?" she muttered in a vexed tone before turning back to her chair. "Sister Bedelia informed me that Honoria displayed some odd behaviour on their visit to Saint Aurigan's Priory, twice rising in the night when she thought Bedelia slept. Both times Bedelia followed her to the library, which is locked at night. However, someone within admitted her, locking the door behind them, though Bedelia only saw a cloaked figure in the shadows. I would have dismissed it as insomnia and the need for a book to help her sleep, except for Bedelia's insistence that Honoria did not need to knock for admittance since her visitee appeared to expect her. Still, even if she pre-arranged the assignations, I believed there might be a perfectly reasonable explanation."

"Perhaps she's having an affair with Brother Ennis," Iona said facetiously, and could have bitten her tongue. "Sorry, I don't think he likes me."

However, Mother Wilfrida snorted. "The librarian doesn't like anyone! Brother Quintus, tell Prior Fidelmus to put a discreet watch on Brother Ennis. Now, Iona, what's this plan you've cooked up with Shay?"

When Iona had explained why they needed to send a messenger pigeon to Saint Lexis Priory, the abbess stared thoughtfully at Shay, her hazel eyes boring into his. "I didn't know your mother came from the *Living Aurigan's* world."

"Neither did I. Well, I suspected, but I didn't really know until last night."

Mother Wilfrida nodded, redirecting her gaze to Iona. "Begging a Lacunae to help bypass the tower barriers seems a desperate measure, but Saint Aurigan charged the order to guard the *ways*, and so far, we've failed through ignorance. If there's any chance the answer lies within the tower, then we must do all we can to remedy our lack of knowledge." She opened a desk drawer, and removing a long parchment strip, reached for a quill. "I'll write the message to Prior Faolan using the shorthand code only he and I share. That way, he'll realise its importance and will press the dragon council to approve your joint request. I'll emphasise the need for haste due to your travel arrangements with the Leons."

With the message written and sanded, the abbess rolled the parchment tightly and pushed it into a tiny metal tube, which she also extracted from the drawer. She stood and commanded, "Shay, walk with me to the pigeon loft. I expect Iona wishes to speak to Brother Quintus before he departs."

Quintus stood and exchanged circle signs with the abbess who admonished him to take care on his journey before she swept from the office, Shay trailing in her wake.

"When did you arrive?" Iona asked the monk as he sat down beside her.

"Yesterday afternoon. I overnighted in the abbey guest wing, though I felt a little disappointed to discover you weren't staying here as I expected."

"It's good to see you, Quintus. I'm so glad to hear no one at the priory suffered as a result of the failed mission. Do you know if Will Copeland and his men escaped?"

"Will and most of his men fought their way free with the help of a disgruntled populace. Although the duke eventually quelled the uprising, unrest simmers beneath the surface, just waiting for a spark to reignite it."

"I can't wait to tell Bertrand his nephew-in-law evaded capture.

He'll be so relieved."

Quintus leaned forward and clasped Iona's hands. "I'm worried about you. This scheme with the dragons… you could be pushing your luck."

"I might be, but we've had this argument before, Quintus. I haven't changed my mind. I *need* to do this, and the abbess agrees."

He sighed and nodded, squeezing her hands before he released them. "Fidelmus will agree, too."

"If the dragons' assent, we'll return to the priory in secret, and make our move from there. Tell Fidelmus to watch out for us."

"I will… Iona, I know it's none of my business, but can I ask you something personal?"

"Go ahead, Quintus, ask away."

"Are you and Shay… are you a couple now?"

"Yes, I think we are. I'm sorry." Iona didn't know what she apologised for.

Quintus held up a hand. "No, that's good if it means he'll take extra care of you."

"He'd do that anyway, Quintus."

A knock at the door heralded the appearance of Sister Bedelia, who addressed Quintus, "The guest mistress asked me to escort you to your horse whenever you're ready. She's already loaded your pack and some food supplies for the journey. I'll wait outside the door." The nun tactfully withdrew to give them privacy to say their goodbyes.

Iona and Quintus stood.

"I'm sorry we didn't have more time to talk," Iona said, thinking of the story Isobel had told her about his lost love, Iseult.

"Me, too. Please take care, whatever happens next."

"I'll try. If all goes well, I'll see you back at the priory." Iona rested her hand on Quintus' shoulder and kissed him on the cheek.

Quintus embraced her and stepped back, his cheeks dimpling in one of his infectious grins, though it didn't quite reach his eyes. "I'll look forward to it. Good luck!" he said in a cheerful tone, assumed for Iona's benefit.

When Quintus departed with Bedelia, Iona sat back down, hopeful he would soon accept it might be time to relinquish the monastic life that had once been a refuge, but now held him back; acknowledging his readiness to love again. He had so much more to offer and deserved to be happy.

She didn't have long to wait before Mother Wilfrida breezed back into the office with Shay in tow. "The message is sent. Now, are you sure you don't want to stay here until we receive a reply?"

"Since we'll travel with the Leons, it makes sense to continue boarding with them and help with the journey preparations. Plus, we'll have a few of our own to make. But thanks for the offer," Iona replied.

"Alright. I'll send a messenger to the Leon residence as soon as I receive word from Prior Faolan. Of course, I can't guarantee he'll answer before the Leons depart. In that case, we'll need to make alternative arrangements."

Iona nodded. "I understand. Thank you for all your help."

The abbess blessed Iona and Shay before she instructed an acolyte to escort them to the vestibule.

As they walked back to the stables, Iona said, "I forgot to ask how long it will take the pigeon to wing its way to Saint Lexis Priory."

"Oh, no time at all! Homing pigeons can fly seven hundred miles in one day! If we're lucky, it will arrive there early this evening," Shay reassured.

"Wow!" Iona exclaimed and added in afterthought, "Mother Wilfrida isn't nearly as scary as the monks at *our* priory made out."

"Perhaps, but woe betide anyone who gets on her wrong side. She asked me a lot of questions about my mother and wanted to know if I remembered anything about the *Living Aurigan's* world. I think she felt disappointed that I recall next to nothing. I guess it's natural she's curious about her saint's realm, but etiquette and custom prevent her from questioning the *Living Aurigan*."

"I've told Fidelmus a fair amount about my world, but then, he didn't ask outright. He either hinted at his questions, or I volunteered the information. I imagine the previous *Living Aurigans* also told him stuff. I suppose he has the advantage over the abbess in that regard."

"Indeed. Anyway, I'll drop you back at the villa, and then I need to pay my respects to Dareesh at the encampment. The clan will soon travel on."

When the Leons departed for the ball an hour before sunset, Iona, already bathed and changed for bed, watched the progress of all the coaches and carriages that climbed the hill to the ducal palace on the summit. She had a good view from the balcony that circled the villa's upper floor on three sides, easily accessed from her bedroom.

The palace already blazed with lights, and part of her felt regretful she couldn't attend. However, the other part didn't envy Isobel and Alicia in their uncomfortable poulaines. When the last carriage disappeared into the palace grounds, Iona moved to the balcony's south side, facing the sea. She gazed down at the city, where lights twinkled against the coming darkness. Lorcan dined tonight with Bengo and his family, and she could just make out the overseer's small villa one level below the Leon residence.

Iona surveyed the sweeping panorama of city, ness, and sea before returning to the balcony's eastern side, the location of the guest rooms. As she turned the corner, Shay's balcony door opened, two rooms down from hers. She hadn't known he had arrived back from the Zingari encampment, and as he stepped through the door, Iona saw he, too, had changed. Barefoot, he wore low-slung, black cotton trousers, his chest bared beneath an unlaced white shirt worn loose. His black hair, unbound from its customary plait, fell in soft waves around his shoulders.

Iona tore her eyes away from Shay's tanned, hard-muscled torso, her stomach somersaulting at his slow, seductive smile. He reached Iona in three strides and crushed her against him, his mouth seeking hers. Heat flooded through her as she returned his kiss with equal ardour. Grabbing one of the hands exploring her body, Iona pulled Shay into her room, nudging the door closed with her foot without breaking their kiss......

Later, naked bodies entangled, black hair mingling on the pillow, they lay spent after discovering each other with slow, sensuous pleasure following the wild abandonment of their initial coupling.

Nothing in Iona's previous experience came close to how Shay made her feel. She couldn't conceive of parting from him, and it seemed more urgent than ever to find a solution to their predicament. Iona knew Shay felt it too. He had understood, long before she did, that acting on their need would seal the bond neither had sought – or had they? In the corner of her mind that still half-believed this world a fever dream, Iona wondered if they had conjured up one another from their deepest longings.

Euphoric in the afterglow, they clung together with no need for words, their mutual avowals already made. But at last, Iona reminded, "The Leons will be back soon."

"I'll stay until then. By the way, we've received an invitation from my step-brother to visit the Zingari encampment tomorrow evening," Shay said, his hand warm on her hip.

"We?"

"Well, Dareesh asked why I'd left the priory, so I told him I still worked for Fidelmus, who sent me on a quest with the *Living Aurigan*. The Madjia listened in and insisted he also invite you. I remember how you complained about the 'boring' court dances you had to learn, and I think you'll find Zingari dancing more to your taste." Noticing Iona's expression in the lamplight, Shay appended, "Don't worry, the dancing is strictly for entertainment!"

Intrigued, Iona assented to accompanying him. She felt inquisitive about the people and lifestyle of his formative years, and with *The Inferno* off the cards, curious to see Zingari dancing.

The noise of the Leons return filtered up the staircase. With a rueful smile, Shay kissed Iona tenderly and gathered up his clothes, slipping out the door and along the balcony to his own room.

Feeling like a naughty teenager, Iona extinguished the lamps so no light showed beneath the door to reveal her wakefulness, and drifted off to sleep reliving her steamy session with Shay.

Chapter 19

The next day, Isobel and Alicia took Iona shopping.

Operating on the assumption she would gain an audience with the dragon council, they insisted she required a suitable outfit for the meeting.

Iona felt as though they prepared her for a job interview, but since she had not spent a single coin of the money Fidelmus had given her, she might as well purchase new clothes. "I could do with another kirtle, even if the council declines my petition."

"Oh, they're bound to approve it since Mother Wilfrida wrote the message herself!" Alicia assured optimistically.

Isobel nodded. "It improves the odds, but with so little time left before we sail, you can't afford to wait until the abbess receives a reply."

Though 'off the peg' fashion barely existed in Beretania, they took Iona to an exclusive dress shop on the street level above their villa, where pre-made gowns and kirtles hung ready for adjustment and embellishment to the customers' size and taste.

"These look expensive," Iona whispered to Alicia as she flicked through a rack of sumptuous gowns, stopping at an emerald-green silk kirtle, simpler than the rest.

"They are, but don't worry about that! Papa supplies fabrics and trims to this establishment, and I negotiated a deal with the proprietor last year. Mama and I receive a healthy discount whenever we shop here!"

"*You* negotiated the deal?"

Alicia nodded and smiled with pride and satisfaction. She was her father's daughter, and Iona thought how tragic it would be if a future husband barred her from involvement in the business.

The shop owner, Madame Clemence, disappeared into a fitting room with Isobel, who had chosen a kirtle for the Leons own audience with the dragon council. Iona took the opportunity to ask Alicia, "How was the ball last night? You didn't say much at breakfast."

"I had a marvellous time, but er, didn't want to upset Lorcan by banging on about it at breakfast. Griffin Tyrwhitt is handsome and an elegant dancer, but he made no effort to woo me and acted like we were already engaged. I expect he thinks a merchant's daughter will fall over herself to marry a lord's son with no effort on his part! Still, I didn't let him spoil my enjoyment and danced with others, though he tried to monopolise me."

"Damn cheek!" Iona said indignantly.

"You *do* have a way with 'naughty' words!" Alicia giggled.

An assistant glided up to ask if they required help, and Alicia pointed to a bronze satin kirtle. "I'll try that one." Her selection made, Alicia took her turn in the fitting room with Madame Clemence, while Iona sat on a high-backed settle with Isobel.

"Judging by your attentiveness to each other at breakfast, I assume you have reached an… understanding with Shay," Isobel said delicately.

"Is it that obvious?" Iona smiled wryly.

Isobel returned the smile. "Only to the observant. I'm glad for you."

"We are visiting his family at the Zingari encampment later."

"It must be serious then!" Isobel quipped and then sighed. "Alicia hasn't taken to Lord Tyrwhitt's son as much as I hoped. She'll become an old maid at this rate! Still, she met other eligible bachelors at the ball. There must be one amongst them whom she'll look upon with favour!"

"I don't think Alicia *wants* to become an old maid, but perhaps she feels that's better than marriage to a man who won't value her acumen and skills as Bertrand values yours."

"I can't say I blame her. She likens it to a transaction – her future wealth in exchange for a title. However, an influential husband could be of great benefit to the commercial enterprise she'll one day inherit – if he doesn't run it into the ground through lack of judgment. A title is worth nothing without money, as I should know." Isobel sighed again, and Iona remembered her former status as a penniless baronet's daughter.

"Alicia greatly admires her Papa's enterprising spirit and models herself on him rather than me. He's worked hard to get where he is, and the last thing either of us wants is a son-in-law who'll fritter away all we've built. Sadly, this world is not yet ready to accept a woman at the business helm," Isobel continued.

"Hm, it seems to me that a man sharing Alicia's love of commerce, whom Bertrand can mould, might be worth more weight in gold than an 'influential' lord who may not prove as susceptible to training and instruction."

"I gather you've noticed Alicia's interest in Lorcan! Bertrand thinks he has great potential and we're aware of how swiftly he rose to a place at court. As Bertie reminded me, I'm hardly a shining example since *I* married 'beneath' *my* station. However, Alicia barely knows the lad! Still, Bertrand will include Lorcan in our Saint Lexis Priory retinue to judge how well he conducts himself. *I'm* hoping Alicia might give Griffin another chance when we return. Unlike most of his peers, he's a sensible young man who recognises his inexperience, and seems willing to take advice."

Iona smiled crookedly. "That's *something* in his favour at least, though I don't think Alicia appreciated the way he took their union for granted. As for Lorcan, who can fathom the laws of attraction? Sometimes you just *know* when you meet the right person and length of acquaintance seems immaterial."

"Is that how it was with you and Shay?" Isobel smiled.

"Yes, though I didn't admit it to myself for a long time."

After Iona chose the emerald-green silk and took her turn in the fitting room, the three women returned to the coach. Madame Clemence had promised to deliver the kirtles on the morrow after her dressmakers had reworked them and hid her disappointment when Iona declined a pair of matching poulaines.

Isobel directed the driver to convey them to the main forum three levels below, so they could browse the market-day stalls.

As they strolled past a florist's stand, Iona inhaled the scent of late-summer blooms, which cloaked the less appealing smell of the public convenience opposite. A red and blue striped awning attached to the side of a fortune-teller's booth caught her eye, and wandering nearer, Iona noticed a young Zingari woman had set up stall beneath. Iona smiled with delight at the selection of white cotton, ribbon-tie blouses adorned with colourful embroidery, that reminded her of her favourite boho, 'gypsy' top. The young woman, sensing she had an eager customer, quickly found a blouse she judged would fit the woman with long black hair like hers, though her punter's pale skin and blue eyes hinted at Goidelic heritage.

Iona also chose a dark-green fringed shawl, beautifully embroidered, and, pointing at a pair of leather shoes with criss-crossing leg ribbons similar to ballet slippers, asked if they came in other colours.

While the stallholder rootled through a crate, Alicia whispered, "Are you sure about this? I admit the garments are pretty, but they're barbarian fashions, albeit the blouses are expensive cotton."

Iona grinned. "Yes! Pretty, *almost* practical, and best of all, those shoes look miles more comfortable than the horrible poulaines you're so fond of!"

"Fair enough!" Alicia held up her hands.

The young woman turned back to her customer, holding several pairs of shoes. Though Iona had petite feet by the standards of her world, most women here took an even smaller shoe size, but she found a black pair that fit. After the stallholder demonstrated how she could alter the shoes' appearance by changing the ribbon laces, Iona chose three lace sets in green, black, and gold.

When Iona had paid for her purchases, she asked the young woman, "Are you with the Zingari encamped west of the city?"

"Yes?" the woman replied with a questioning lilt.

"I might see you this evening in that case. I'm visiting the encampment with Shay Hawksmoor."

"*You're* the *Living Aurigan*, Shay's ves'tacha?"

"Vest... what?"

"Ves'tacha. His beloved."

Iona dared not look at Alicia. "Erm, yes. What's your name?"

"I'm Rena, the Madjia's granddaughter. My mother is the fortune-teller," the stallholder nodded towards the booth behind her.

"Well, it's lovely to meet you, Rena. Until later, then?"

Rena nodded and smiled; her dark eyes alight with curiosity.

As the three women walked back to the coach, a bug-eyed Alicia exclaimed, "Did I hear right? You're Shay's *beloved*?"

Isobel rolled her eyes. "*Do* keep up, dear! Of course she is!"

"Erm, I didn't mean to imply *he's* a barbarian. I only meant the clothes are... peasant dress... no, that's wrong... er, foreign? Different?" Alicia tried to extricate herself.

Iona laughed. "Don't worry! Shay will likely regard the term as a compliment!"

After an early dinner, Iona retired to her room to dress.

She paired the pretty blouse with the black skirt Binny had given her, hitching it above one knee via the hook and eye fastening to show off the green ribbon-lacing of her new shoes. After fastening Jake's black leather belt at her waist, Iona adjusted the blouse's elbow-length puffy sleeves and off-the-shoulder neckline. She then applied a little of Binnie's make-up and perfume and brushed out her plait, so her hair lay loose down her back. The green shawl completed her outfit, and after slipping everything she might need into her belt pouch, Iona descended the stairs to the vestibule, feeling comfortable in a skirt for the first time since her entrapment in this reality.

As she entered the atrium, Shay appeared in the family room doorway and walked towards her, his eyes aglow with appreciation, a sensual smile playing around his lips. Iona ignored the sudden heat that coursed through her and exchanged farewells with the Leons through the Triclinium's open door.

Shay boosted Iona onto the cart seat, his hand lingering on her waist, and jumping aboard, steered the horse from the stable yard to head west around the city to the road stretching across the grasslands beyond.

With the floodplain on their right, Shay kept the horse at a steady trot and, glancing at Iona, said, "You look beautiful. The blouse suits you."

"Thanks. This attire feels more like my normal clothes." She fingered a sleeve and added, "The fabric is lovely, but Binny told me cotton is really expensive here, so although this top wasn't cheap, it didn't cost as much as I expected."

"Ah, the Zingari are traders in addition to entertainers; mainly horses and dogs, but also leather, metalwork, and firewater. The clan no doubt bartered the cotton from the Sirengi, the Zingari's distant cousins, at one of the big trade meets."

"The Sirengi?"

"Yes, half spend their lives at sea, and the other half roam the inland waterways on houseboats, trading the seafarers' merchandise."

Though Iona looked forward to visiting the encampment, she felt nervous and fidgeted with her shawl.

Shay slowed the carthorse to a walk and, holding the reins one-handed, put his arm around her. "There's no need for anxiety. The Zingari hold Saint Aurigan in high esteem. As wanderers themselves, they feel an affinity with the *Eternal Traveller* and his living representative."

"And they see no problem with our relationship? They don't think it wrong that your Ves'tacha is the *Living Aurigan*?"

Shay appeared momentarily startled. "Where did you hear that word?"

"Rena, the Zingari girl who sold me these clothes."

"I see. Well, I didn't shout it from the treetops, but Dareesh and the Madjia know we're a couple, and since Rena is her granddaughter..." Shay shrugged. "No, they approve. Their people will deem it singularly fitting that even an adopted Zingari like me should become the *Living Aurigan's* consort. Even if they didn't, it doesn't matter what they think; you *are* my Ves'tacha." Shay gently squeezed Iona's waist, and, taking the reins in both hands, sped up towards a track on their left, which meandered into a stand of trees.

The encampment occupied a large clearing in the wood's centre, the brightly painted wagons grouped around a central firepit. Halting on the periphery, Shay leaped from the cart and swung Iona down as two grinning lads hastened towards them. Leaving the boys to take charge of the equipage, Shay led Iona between two wagons into the firelight, where many eyes stared at her with open but friendly curiosity.

A man strode up and clasped arms with Shay, turning to regard Iona. "Dareesh, this is Iona, the *Living Aurigan*. Iona, my step-brother, Clan Leader Dareesh," Shay introduced.

Tall like Shay, but leaner of build, Dareesh wore his hair in a long plait, as did most men in the encampment, though some sported a top-knot, or 'man-bun' in the jargon of Iona's world. He bowed to her with aplomb and said, "Welcome, *Eterna*. I'm glad you could grace us with your presence tonight since we move on tomorrow."

"Thank you for inviting me; I feel honoured to meet Shay's kin.

Where do you journey next, if I may ask?"

"Prior to recent, er, events, Duke Clovis invited us to perform for his court in Tritaurium. The engagement is in eight days', but we'll travel there by a circuitous route, stopping to trade with the Sirengi at the confluence of the Taurion and Rinusi rivers, on the Northern border of Kentauros and Zephyrinus. Oh, and pick up my wife, who's half Sirengi. She's visiting with her relatives," Dareesh explained and led them to a wagon magnificently decorated with a forested landscape on one side, and two hawks soaring over moorland on the other. Two trees, one painted on each side of the door, twined their branches above it, and another hawk perched amongst the foliage. Iona wondered at the symbolism, connecting it with Shay's family name, *Hawksmoor*.

Dareesh directed them to seats arranged before the wagon's fold-down doorsteps, offering Iona his own carved and painted, high-backed chair. "I hope you'll enjoy tonight's performance in your honour," the clan leader said, and called for wine.

Iona gazed with interest at the gathered Zingari, noting Shay didn't appear out of place amongst them. If she didn't know better, she might have thought Dareesh and Shay were blood brothers since they shared the same high cheekbones and dark eyes, although the ranger had a squarer jaw. However, though Shay looked Zingari, he had crossed to this reality at age six, which meant that, like his mother, his father must also be native to Iona's world.

"Does Duke Clovis know about your connection to Shay?" Iona asked the clan leader.

"Not as far as I know, but Shay warned me to be on my guard inside the castle." Dareesh snorted. "I'm not afraid of Clovis. My sword-dancers are more than a match for his knights if trouble should arise. However, I'm not expecting any, and the duke's paying us too well to consider backing out for no reason."

Dareesh's confidence, reflected in his relaxed body language, reassured Iona. Yet, despite their camaraderie, she felt a smidgeon of restraint between the step-brothers and wondered if Shay's refusal to challenge for the leadership had left something unresolved. However, two small children pelted towards them, accompanied by a barking lurcher, dispelling any lingering tension as they flung themselves upon Shay, who grinned with pleasure to see them.

"My children, Fernamo and Villette, or Letty as we call her," Dareesh introduced with an indulgent smile.

Iona laughed at the enthusiasm with which the youngsters greeted their Uncle Shay, and when they turned big, shy eyes upon her, she asked questions about their dog to put them at ease.

"Off with you, now. Go and sit quietly with the other children until after the performance," Dareesh directed as a fiddler began to play a plaintive air.

Women dressed in flounced skirts with sash belts in primary colours streamed from between the wagons to dance languidly around the banked, central fire. Their balletic footwork mirrored the graceful undulations of their arms and hands as they swayed and stepped in synchrony. A zither-like fretboard instrument joined the fiddle, plus two guitars and a flute, and the dancers trod faster as the cadence increased. Rena suddenly emerged from a wagon painted all over with dragons large and small and pirouetted down the steps. She circled the dancers, who broke away one by one to follow her to a clear space before the clan leader's wagon, none of them missing a step. This seemed the signal for another tempo increase, and the women leaped and spun like dervishes, maintaining their elegant posture lines. The music came to an abrupt halt, the women holding their poses with one leg thrust forward, until a lone drum began to beat, to which they rotated their hips in time whilst remaining rooted to the spot. The beat intensified as two more drums pitched in, and bare-chested men flowed in two columns from behind the fire, colourful sashes tied beneath their sword belts. They twirled towards the women, and matching with their partners, picked them up from the rear in a spinning, cross-body manoeuvre as the two guitars, the fiddle, and then a trumpet and shawm accompanied the drums in an urgent, driving rhythm that propelled the dancers onward.

Iona watched in wide-eyed amazement as, hand in hand, the partners danced a series of fast, side-rocking steps, and weaving their legs together, gyrated their hips and shoulders as they swayed back and forth. The coordinated dance steps and full-body movements appeared to her eyes like a cross between the *Flamenco* and the *Salsa*, totally unexpected in this reality, especially after the stiff court dances she had witnessed. Iona's foot tapped in time to the urgent beat, and she hardly noticed when Dareesh came to Shay's side and spoke into his ear.

Shay frowned and shook his head, but Dareesh spoke some more and, at last, Shay nodded and rose to follow his step-brother, raising his hand in a stay gesture to Iona. She gave him a thumbs-up and transferred her gaze back to the lively group dance. The tempo gradually decreased, and the partners slid together, rotating slowly as the music quietened, until only the fiddle remained to play a melancholy air. As the women broke off and melted away, the men faced forward and, standing spread-legged, drew their swords and raised them two-handed above their heads.

A solitary drum beat a foreboding rhythm, the men stamping in time, and then Shay and Dareesh appeared from the shadows as the other drums joined in. Shirtless like his fellow dancers, Shay wore an emerald green sash beneath his sword belt. As the guitars struck up a counter-rhythm, the step-brothers whirled, their swords whipping from their scabbards. The dance that followed took Iona's breath away, and she barely registered Rena, who ghosted up to sit beside her. She witnessed a mock group swordfight, choreographed to full musical accompaniment; balletic, athletic, acrobatic, terrifying and exhilarating, the dancers leaping and swirling, swords flashing a hairsbreadth from each other. Eyes riveted on Shay as he rapidly switched his weapon from hand to hand in a series of lightning-fast wrist movements whilst executing a hands-free somersault, Iona sat mesmerised.

With a final skirl of melody, all but the drums ceased, and spinning on the spot, blades held overhead, the dancers glided together back-to-back in a circle, and sheathed their swords on the last drumbeat.

Clapping her hands vigorously, along with the other spectators, Iona took a generous draught from her winecup and turned to Rena. "Wow! That was... wow!"

"Fear and desire," Rena summarised, her eyes crinkling with amusement.

"Yes! I think I salivated at one point, but that was bloody dangerous!" Iona responded with a mock shiver. Yet, if *that* was a 'mere' exhibition dance, she dreaded to imagine what *The Inferno* entailed. She glanced towards Shay and Dareesh, slapping each other on the back, and as Shay shook the other dancer's hands, he caught Iona's eye, winking in a most un-Shay-like manner when he read her expression.

Before long, the musicians began a new tune, similar in cadence to the mixed couples dance, and most of the women returned to the floor, freestyling with their partners. Shay stepped towards Iona and held out his hand. She didn't require any persuasion, and slipping off her shawl, joined him with alacrity.

Her knowledge of salsa helped immensely, and they adapted to one another's style with ease, melding together in near-seamless syncopation. She had loved to dance before her accident, but never had a partner as proficient as Shay, and with regular applications of Binny's salve, her leg no longer troubled her. When Iona dared a grinding hip movement, Shay's eyebrows shot up, and he reciprocated with a wolfish grin. As the tune transitioned into a slower tempo, Shay guided her in a dance that resembled a rumba, his eyes smouldering with contained fire. Losing her inhibitions like everyone else, she gave herself up to it with joyous abandon, weaving around Shay with one hand trailing over his bare torso.

When the music finally wound down, the couples dispersed. "It's time we left," Shay murmured into Iona's ear.

With the children long since abed, and their farewells made to the dancers and musicians, they retrieved Shay's shirt and Iona's shawl. Spotting Dareesh exit the dragon-painted house wagon, they approached to say their goodbyes.

"I hope the dancing met your expectations?" the clan leader asked Iona, a twinkle in his eye.

"More than! I had a truly wonderful evening!" she replied.

Dareesh beamed, and jerking his thumb at the dragon-decorated wagon, said, "The Madjia would like to see you before you leave," and bowed low over Iona's hand. "Good luck with your quest. Fare thee well until we meet again."

"You, too. Thanks for your hospitality," Iona responded and watched as the step-siblings embraced in a quick man-hug.

Still high on adrenaline, Iona followed Shay up the wagon steps, where he knocked on the door. A reedy voice bid them to enter, and they crossed the threshold into the dim-lit interior. A single lamp burned low atop a painted cupboard, providing just enough illumination for Iona to discern the elderly woman with long white hair propped up in a narrow bed, covered with a tapestry counterpane. Her milky eyes signalled blindness, and Iona realised the lamp shone for her visitors' benefit.

Shay knelt beside the bed and took the Madjia's hands in his. "Iona is here with me. You wished to speak to us?"

"Ah, I thought I recognised your step, Shay! You always did move with feline grace." The Madjia slipped one hand from Shay's and beckoned to Iona, somehow aware she stood beside the painted cupboard. "Come closer, my dear. With your permission, I'd like to 'read' your face."

Iona knelt beside Shay and took the Madjia's free hand in hers, placing it on her cheek. The old woman ran her fingers lightly over Iona's visage and smiled, her resemblance to her granddaughter, Rena, suddenly evident.

"Pretty indeed! However, you are not of this world, so your thread is missing from the tapestry that connects me to all the souls woven into its fabric. I cannot prophesy your future, but I sense you'll have a choice to make that will have far-reaching consequences unless you reconcile your heart with your conscience."

"Far-reaching for whom?" Iona asked, goosebumps prickling down her spine.

"For you, certainly, but also perhaps for many others; this world, even." The Madjia then addressed Shay, "Despite your otherworld heritage, your connection to this one is stronger, though imperfect, like a loose thread. Your fate is also hidden from me, but I scry a quandary ahead, unrelated to the *Living Aurigan's*, and you, too, must make a decision based on your conscience. Though some might say it's my job to speak cryptically,

I assure you it's unintentional; I simply cannot interpret the pattern. However, I believe Hyraxus will make things clearer to you."

"Why? Did you see that in a vision?" Shay probed.

"Goodness, no! Your mother, Audrey, entrusted me with the task of referring you to Hyraxus if a time ever came when you needed to learn about her past. She called it her failsafe in case she wasn't around to tell you herself."

His face and body immobile, Shay appeared stunned, having taken it for granted the mystic had acquired her knowledge via her usual methods.

"Don't concern yourself with it now; there's time enough for that tomorrow." The Madjia's sightless eyes glanced from Shay to Iona. "I *saw* your bliss together this evening, and the night is not yet over. My daughter and Rena have prepared *Aurigan's Grotto* for you. I suggest you take full advantage." The Madjia smiled impishly. "Go now, I must sleep."

Shay rose to his feet and kissed the Madjia's temple. Iona also stood, deciding she didn't wish to know *how* the old woman had *seen*.

When they emerged from the wagon, Iona asked, "What is *Aurigan's Grotto*?"

"You'll see!" Shay replied with a smile that suggested he had taken the Madjia's advice and would worry about her revelation another time.

As they crossed the clearing, a man threw a log onto the fire, sending a shower of sparks high into the night sky, the motes glittering like golden stars.

Shay drove the cart southward along a low riverbank on the wood's western boundary until he sighted a packed-earth incline down which he guided the horse. They continued southward on the river's foreshore of sandy soil, the bank rising higher on their left.

"Do you miss the Zingari life, Shay?" Iona ventured.

He shrugged. "Sometimes, but it's not always like tonight. It's often a hard life, especially in the winter. Though serfs or freemen beholden to a lord lack the Zingaris' independence, the clans are bound by their own traditions, and freedom is relative. When I left, I could have joined another clan with ties to mine, but I wanted to become my own person and find my own way, and in the process, discover if I'm truly Zingari by inclination, and not just adoption."

"And did you?"

Shay gave a wry smile. "Put it like this – I don't miss the clan enough to return, though there are times, like tonight, when I'm reminded of the lifestyle's best parts. Still, I have liberty working for Fidelmus from whom I've learned a great deal. He values my input, and the job allows me to keep my skills honed and my blade sharp. I've found my niche, though that's not to say I won't move on if it feels right."

Iona smiled inwardly at that admission and hoped it meant what she wanted it to mean.

The bank now towered above them, and Shay halted the wagon before a verdant rockface. Jumping down, he unharnessed the horse and left it on a long tether near the water's edge. Iona stood beside the cart, gazing around uncertainly. Taking her by the hand, Shay led her around a buttress of rock, and she discerned a muted yellow glow beneath a mass of trailing vegetation in the corner where the outcrop extended from the bank.

"The Zingari have used that site in the woods for two centuries. Its proximity to a water source makes it ideal. What I'm about to show you has long been associated with Saint Aurigan in their legends," Shay explained, and lifting the curtain of ivy and creepers, revealed the entrance to a small cave. He gestured for Iona to precede him, and entering, she gasped with wonder.

A low, natural rock ledge surrounded the semi-circular perimeter, upon which a multitude of wax candles shed golden light upon the walls above, decorated with shells in intricate, unmistakeably Zingari patterns. Here and there, the artists had incorporated the pearly, nacre interiors of abalone and molluscs into the design, their highly polished surfaces glinting pink, blue, and green in the candlelight. Rena, or her mother, had swept the sandy floor clean, arranging a nest of new-looking blankets in its centre. A large rock, carved into a seat and draped with a soft rug, stood behind the blankets, a bowl of water, linen cloths, and a wine carafe with two goblets on the ground beside it. With the creepers concealing the entrance, and the river's soothing burble the only sound, the cave had a cosy, intimate ambience in the warm night.

"According to clan folklore, Aurigan rested here on his journeys, though Fidelmus found no mention of it in the archives. The Zingari made it their own and maintain it whenever they pass through Glassnesse. Those who follow the way of the *Great Wheel* use it for meditation, though it also has other purposes…" Shay said softly.

Iona turned to gaze at him, his beautiful dark eyes liquid in the candle-glow, and standing on tip-toe, she twined her arms around his neck. "It's perfect. Goodness knows when we'll next get an opportunity to be alone together."

"Indeed," he murmured, nuzzling her ear, pressing her tight against him. They kissed with pent-up passion, and Iona's legs felt watery when Shay finally drew back. He led her to the rock seat, and lowering her onto it, removed his sword belt and boots. Kneeling before Iona, Shay lifted her left foot onto his knee, and untying her leg ribbons, slowly unwound them to remove her shoe, stroking her leg from thigh to ankle. When he moved on to her right foot, Iona's core burned with anticipation. The shoe discarded, Shay unbuckled her belt and brushed his mouth over hers, teasing, until with hungry demand she caught his lips with hers. Breathing fast, they at last drew apart, and Shay reached for the front ties of her blouse……

Afterwards, nestled in the blankets, they remained until the candles grew dim, and the first light of dawn blushed the sky with rose.

Chapter 20

A message arrived from Mother Wilfrida at sunset the following evening, confirming the dragon council had granted Iona and Shay an audience. They had felt tense and anxious all day, worried they wouldn't receive a response before the Leons sailed for Bywhitt on the next morning's tide.

Iona hastily packed all her belongings in the small trunk borrowed from Isobel, placing the rucksack at the bottom in case she needed it later. She opted to travel in comfort and laid out her leggings and soft, notched ankle boots, ready for the morrow. Though the weather held fair, it might be colder at sea, so she added Jake's altered jerkin to her selection, dismissing the notion she'd resemble an extra from *Robin Hood*.

The Leons were now accustomed to Iona's 'eccentric' clothing choices and hardly batted an eyelid when they all assembled in the Triclinium the next morning, although Alicia studied the leggings' fabric with interest.

As the sky lightened, Iona entered the coach with Alicia, Isobel and their lady's maid for the ride to the docks.

Alicia could hardly contain her excitement at the prospect of her first sea-going trade mission, even though it only entailed a journey along the coast and not a voyage to foreign climes. She constantly peered through the window to check their progress, drummed her fingers on her knee, rifled through her dragon portfolio, and asked rhetorical questions, most beginning, "I wonder if…" or "Do you think…" until Isobel reprimanded, "Enough, Alicia. It's too early in the morning for this assault on our senses."

Iona sympathised with Isobel, but at least Alicia's chatter kept her thoughts at bay. The immediacy of her situation warred with the unreal, storybook nature of her plight. Now that she actually journeyed to a meeting with creatures considered mythical in her world, the small part of her still resisting belief in this reality wondered when she would wake up. What would her sister, Skye, say if Iona ever got the chance to tell her about this bizarre adventure? But she couldn't think like that. She must stay in control and not waver in her determination to see this through to the end. At least she had Shay… could she simply concede defeat and settle here with him? No. Though it might seem the easy thing to do, she could only make that decision by *choice*, and not because she had no other option. She must fight to the bitter end to regain mastery of her own destiny.

Forcing herself to abandon these fruitless musings, Iona asked Isobel, "How long will it take to reach Bywhitt?"

"If the winds favour us, it should take approximately twenty hours. Bertrand estimates we'll arrive at around three in the morning. We'll lay up in the *Golden Gannet* inn until midday tomorrow, before continuing our journey to the priory via wagon."

"Did Bertrand decide which trade goods to offer the dragons?" Iona asked.

"We're hoping they'll tell us what they want, although we're bringing a selection of merchandise Bertrand believes might interest them—"

"Toothpaste!" Alicia interrupted Isobel.

"Sorry?" a puzzled Iona questioned.

"Binny's toothpaste. It was Lorcan's idea. He borrowed my dragon manual to seek inspiration and read an old report by Friar Botolph who studied them before the Arcem Treaty which established the current borders. According to the friar, the Alphas spend hours cleaning their teeth. Due to their peculiar internal combustion physiology, which enables them to spew fire, a sooty cinder residue gradually coats their teeth, which, if allowed to build up and harden, interferes with their ability to chew and eat."

"Hm, I see... and will you also provide them with giant toothbrushes?" Iona asked sceptically.

"We'll cross that bridge *if* we come to it," Alicia declared in an airy tone. "*My* idea was books. Dragons adore stories, apparently. Perhaps we could even commission new stories especially geared to their tastes and invest in one of the new printing presses! I think we should do that anyway, and make affordable books available to everyone; well, to those who can read."

Isobel rolled her eyes. "Our sample wares also include more practical items, such as liniments for wing membranes; horse harnesses specially sized and adapted for dragons to carry things in flight; forged metal claw guards; and for the luxury market, golden vessels and decorative claw guards embedded with gems unavailable in the dragon lands. It's well known that dragons love gold and jewels."

"Mama *also* had a whimsical idea, though she hasn't mentioned it!" Alicia smirked.

"Ah, yes. I've never forgotten how much the Venator youngling enjoyed playing with my ball all those years ago. We've packed a crate of various-sized balls as a gift for the dragon council's offspring. Mayhap it will help oil the wheels of commerce."

Iona grinned, and let herself become infected by Alicia's excitement; it seemed preferable to stewing in her doubts and fears.

The coastal barque *Calpurnia* lacked the sleek lines of the Leons ocean-going vessels, but the single-master appeared sturdy and well-maintained. Its owner, Gideon Marchmont, a haulage operator who plied the eastern coast, had also arranged their wagon transportation onward from Bywhitt.

With the luggage, supplies, and trade goods already stowed aboard an hour before dawn, Bertrand, Shay and Lorcan escorted the women over the gangplank to join Gil and four other employees chosen to act in a dual capacity as guards and wranglers. Gideon himself captained the barque on this trip, and as he took the helm, the sailors cast off.

Iona stood at the rail with Shay, staring back at Glassnesse, and wondered if her circumstances might have changed when she next beheld it – *if* she ever saw it again. Sensing her mood, Shay placed a hand over hers where it rested atop the taffrail, and she reversed her palm to lace her fingers through his.

As the *Calpurnia* tacked around the headland, Iona transferred her gaze upward to the abbey and fancied that Mother Wilfrida watched their departure from her study window. When she sighted the glass beach glittering in the sun on the ness' northern side, her spirits lifted. It's accidental creation by humans and the sea made its beauty seem even more wondrous. Despite her situation, she felt a sense of privilege that she journeyed to visit creatures that most fantasy literature aficionados would give their eye-teeth to encounter. Past caring what anyone thought, Iona withdrew her hand from Shay's and slipped her arms around his waist.

Shay didn't seem to mind this open display of affection and wrapped his arms around her. His eyes gleamed softly in the water-reflected sunlight as he smiled down at her, tendrils of hair escaping his loose plait in the gentle breeze.

When they had sailed past the river estuary and Glassnesse disappeared into the distance behind, Isobel, Bertrand, and the captain retired to the window-surrounded great cabin, which spanned the upper stern's width, leaving the bosun to take the helm. Shay excused himself to speak to Gil about the security arrangements for the wagon train, and Alicia took his place beside Iona at the rail.

They watched the coast slide past in silence, but Alicia could never stay quiet for long. "So, you and Shay… will you follow Binny's example?"

"You mean get married and settle down here? We haven't planned that far ahead. At the moment, we're just taking things as they come until we find a solution to the Janus Spire problem," Iona temporised, not wishing to discuss such a sore point. Much to her relief, Lorcan provided a welcome distraction.

She nudged Alicia's arm, and her friend turned to see what Iona stared at. Agile as a monkey, Lorcan climbed up the mast ratline and crawled out onto the top yardarm, seemingly unfazed by the barque's rolling pitch. Iona observed money exchange hands between a sailor and a

Leon wrangler, and she guessed Lorcan had performed the stunt for a bet. Ignorant of Lorcan's former child acrobat career, the sailor must have accepted the landlubbers' wager with smug confidence.

Lorcan spotted Alicia's admiring gaze and swung from the yardarm one-handed.

"It looks like your father's new apprentice is trying to impress you," Iona said with a wry smile.

"Consider me suitably impressed," Alicia replied, and smiled coyly, peeking at Lorcan from beneath lowered lashes before she turned away with fake disinterest.

However, the bosun, responsible for passenger safety, didn't share Alicia's admiration and angrily shouted at Lorcan to come down.

Alicia couldn't resist turning around to watch Lorcan's flamboyant descent, although a worried frown creased her brows. "I hope my parents didn't see that through the great cabin windows; they're likely to view it as irresponsible showing off."

At midday, the passengers partook of lunch in the great cabin, although Iona, Shay, and Alicia returned to the deck afterwards. Lorcan made to follow them, but to Alicia's dismay, Bertrand requested a word with him first – it appeared the merchant had either witnessed or heard about Lorcan's antics.

Iona had experienced no seasickness, though a wrangler and Sybile, Isobel's maid, looked decidedly green. She enjoyed observing the verdant coastal scenery and the sparkle of sunlight on water, and found the snap of billowing sails oddly soothing.

However, towards mid-afternoon, the sea suddenly became dead calm. The captain ran a hand over his tanned, bald pate as he studied the storm-glass with a perplexed expression. "The wind hasn't dropped enough to account for this. I wonder... the sandbar blocking the river Colfair where it enters the sea a little farther up-coast has threatened to collapse these past three seasons. If it finally succumbed, the release of all the pent-up silt and water, and its dispersal into the ocean, might cause a localised dead calm. If that's the case, it shouldn't last long."

While Bertrand and Isobel conferred with Captain Marchmont by the helm, Iona wandered to the starboard rail, squinting at the empty horizon, and thought she detected wave movement farther out. Her vision suddenly snagged on a long, V-shaped wake cutting through the glassy surface towards them. "Look at this!" she yelled to no one in particular.

Shay and Lorcan stood nearest and rushed to the side with a deckhand. Iona felt convinced the unknown creature would collide with the barque, but it veered away at the last minute. As it curled back on itself, she glimpsed a scaly, sinuous coil beneath the still water.

"Sea serpent!" the deckhand hollered.

The captain hastened to the rail in time to witness the wake heading away before it abruptly disappeared. "The wyrm has dived. Keep your eyes peeled; it might resurface." He addressed the deckhand, "Are you sure you saw a sea serpent? They're deep-sea creatures. I've never heard of one coming this close to land!"

"I'm sure, alright! I served on the *Calliope*..."

This appeared to be the only explanation the captain required, and he turned to the bosun. "Get everything tied down—"

However, he got no further when Lorcan pointed and shouted, "I can see it!"

A serpentine coil arched above the water, close to the waves farther out, its scales glinting dully in the sun, and plunged back beneath the sea. As the wake again moved towards them, Iona clutched Shay's arm. "Sea serpents are mythical..."

"Like dragons, you mean?" he replied with a sardonic smile. "Actually, scholars believe sea serpents are distantly related to dragons, although they lack sentience and speech."

The wake drew closer, curving around to the bow, and the captain urged everyone back towards the stern cabin.

"Why doesn't he order us below?" Iona asked Shay as they moved backwards, keeping their eyes on the wake.

"It's safer up top. If the wyrm holes the vessel below the waterline, it'll flood quickly."

However, Shay's calm exterior didn't deceive Iona. Though he held onto her with one hand, the other gripped his unsheathed sword.

The wake vanished, and Iona stifled a scream when a huge, wedge-shaped head atop a barnacle-encrusted columnar body rose above the bowsprit, water cascading down its greenish sides. A sail-like fin fluttered behind each yellow, saucer-sized eye. Two fleshy horns surmounted its skull, their bulbous tips reminiscent of lollipops, though one appeared blackened and oozed ichor. More barnacles rimed the wyrm's long snout, and with disinterest in the humans, it rubbed them on the spar that extended forward from the prow.

"Do... do sea serpents eat people?" Iona queried tremulously.

"Occasionally; if they're starving. Their favoured prey is other marine species, especially giant squid and small cetaceans," the deckhand replied, his gaze never leaving the intruder.

Iona feared for the bowsprit's integrity as the serpent increased its efforts to dislodge the snout barnacles. It scraped with vigour, and the barque rocked back and forth, causing unsecured equipment to slide about the deck. Everyone grabbed onto whatever fixed feature came to hand to avoid the same fate. Lorcan and the deckhand seized hold of the starboard rail. Shay, forced to sheathe his sword, gripped the mast one-handed, holding Iona tight against him with the other. She peeked from the shelter of his arm and saw Isobel and Bertrand in the knot of people clinging to the port taffrail. Others had retreated to the great cabin, and she spotted the top of Alicia's head above the rear hatch, where she lay on the slanting ladder-like stairs that accessed the hold, arms and legs hooked through the treads.

The serpent looped a flipper-like appendage over the prow for greater leverage, and the bow dipped. Iona's feet scrabbled for purchase, and Shay wedged her between the mast and his body, gripping it with both hands as she wrapped her arms around his waist.

However, Alicia wasn't so lucky. She had crawled from her vulnerable position to drag herself towards the great cabin when the barque's abrupt downward pitch rolled her over, and screaming in fear, she slid rapidly towards the bow before anyone could grab her. The bowsprit finally gave way under the pressure, and snapping upwards from its mount, flew over the prow to land beside the forward hatch, just missing Alicia as she hurtled past.

The serpent tracked its trajectory, and spotting Alicia, used the dinghy-sized appendage to scoop her from the deck, the barque bobbing back up as the pressure upon it decreased. Bertrand roared in anguish and Isobel wailed as the wyrm drew Alicia close to one yellow eye. It studied her briefly before dipping its head over the bows in search of more appetising prey. Having once raided a whaler and attacked a deep-sea fishing vessel, it knew these floating islands sometimes contained freshly dead marine life, conveniently there for the taking. Cradling Alicia in its flipper-like swimming paddle, it held her in reserve high above the prow, its snout questing inches above the deck.

Alicia's piercing screams changed to heartrending cries of "Papa!" before they abruptly ceased, as though she thought better of drawing the beast's attention. In tears, Iona didn't know what she feared the most. Though the serpent might lose interest and dash Alicia to the deck, or even retreat with her beneath the waves where she'd quickly drown; on balance, both seemed preferable to being eaten alive.

With the vessel now on an even keel, Lorcan's gaze switched from frantic to calculating, and he darted to the cleat that attached the topmast stay to the deck. Unfastening it, he glanced from Shay to the captain and raised his voice so all could hear. "I'll retrieve her, or die trying. Keep it distracted, but don't harm it yet lest she's put at risk! You'll need a net to catch her in when I'm done." He pointed to a spot on the deck and added,

"Hold it ready there."

Although Shay didn't know Lorcan's plan, he had a fair idea and trusted in his capabilities. "I'd advise you to do what he says and do it quickly. It may be Alicia's only chance," he spoke forcefully to the captain as Lorcan moved to the mast, the stay looped around his chest, the other end still attached to the mast top.

As the sea serpent sniffed at the forward hatch, Captain Marchmont grunted, "Bertrand?" The merchant nodded once, giving his permission, his devastated gaze never leaving his daughter, a blanched-faced Isobel clinging to his arm.

Lorcan wasted no time and scurried up the main shroud ratline. Estimating height and distance, he wound the excess rope around the top yardarm's centre and securely tied the end of the remaining long length around his right ankle. Swinging out onto the arm, he dangled from it in a two-handed grip and swayed back and forth like a trapeze artiste.

In the meantime, the deckhand fetched a cargo net, and heart-in-mouth, Iona watched Shay and Gil approach the sea serpent. The beast withdrew its head from the hatch, scenting nothing of interest within, and transferred its baleful glare to the two men. Gil circled to the left, and Shay to the right, where he drew his sword and *danced*. He leaped and spun, drawing the wyrm's attention, avoiding its snapping serrated teeth, sometimes by inches. Gil snatched up the broken bowsprit, using it like a spear, making quick jabs to irritate it without causing injury.

With the serpent's concentration engaged elsewhere, and the safety net in position, held fast by Bertrand, Captain Marchmont, the bosun, and three sailors, Iona crossed to Isobel, and they clung together.

When Lorcan's oscillation gained maximum height and speed, he released his hold on the yardarm, and twisting midair, made a lunging dive towards Alicia, swinging like a pendulum from the rope attached to his ankle. Flying over her, he made to grab Alicia on the backswing, but the sea serpent's paddle-flipper dipped as its head thrust towards Gil, and Lorcan missed. Contorting in flight, he seized the yardarm as he swung back and readied himself for another attempt.

The serpent's maw clamped around the bowsprit wielded by Gil, lifting him from his feet. With a crunch of its powerful jaws, the spar broke, dumping Gil onto the deck. Shay darted in with his sword, stabbing at the beast's snout, and backed off with alacrity when Gil rolled clear. The security chief snatched up a boathook, its pike-like staff shorter than the bowsprit, and both men again circled the beast's head.

With the serpent's swimming paddle two feet lower, Iona could see it might be a stretch for Lorcan to reach Alicia in her crouched position, but with no time to make adjustments, he swung out again. As he passed overhead, Alicia rose to stand shakily on the flexible appendage and raised her arms to their fullest extent on his backswing. This time, he caught her hands in a firm grip, and she bent her knees to clear the cupped paddle, the additional weight on the rope slowing its momentum, making it easier for Lorcan to target the net with accuracy. As he released her hands, Alicia inhaled a scream and the net bearers shuffled forward, making a small compensation to catch her in its centre. As they gently lowered her to the deck, Lorcan almost missed the yardarm, his hands slipping on the spar, strained muscles screaming. He inched to the ratline, and untying the rope from his ankle, hugged the mast wearily, his chest heaving. Descending slowly, he gained the deck, and Alicia almost bowled him off his feet as she flung herself upon him, tears leaking from her eyes. Bertrand hustled them both to the great cabin, a relieved and grateful Isobel hurrying to join them.

Iona knew Lorcan had won over Alicia's parents the moment he rescued their daughter from a horrific death, perhaps even before that when he declared he'd die trying. With Alicia safe, the wranglers and crew made a concerted effort to repel the sea serpent, who didn't even appear to notice the absence of his backup meal. Using all manner of weapons and tools, they danced in and out of its ambit, stabbing and slashing. Iona retreated to the wheel, where the knowledgeable deckhand had taken the helm to steady the vessel, which now rose higher in the water as the waves gradually picked up.

"I don't understand why the beast is so slow. Last year, one decimated an entire crew armed with harpoons. It must already have been in a weakened state before it attacked," the deckhand confided.

As though to contradict his words, the serpent pounced on a sailor who hadn't retreated fast enough, crunching his leg between its jaws. Iona uttered a small scream as Shay nipped in, jabbing at the beast's sensitive nostrils, forcing it to release the sailor whose shipmates hauled him back, his leg a mangled wreck. Shay only avoided the same fate by somersaulting onto the serpent's snout, hacking at the fleshy 'lollipop' protuberances on its head, before sliding down its neck to the deck behind it.

"What are those antenna-like things on its head? One of them looked damaged when the sea serpent first appeared," Iona enquired.

"The learned Friar Botolph who studied dragons, penned a treatise on sea serpents, and mentioned the dragons referred to the 'things' as *navigation horns*."

"Echolocation! *That* explains why a deep-sea creature ventured so close to shore! The damage to the 'horn' must have mucked up its sonar!"

"Echo what?" The deckhand asked, but they both forgot the question when the serpent lowered its now-empty paddle to sweep a handful of men off their feet. As they tumbled away, Gil darted in with his boathook and made a lucky strike at the beast's right eye. As the head reared back, taking the boathook with it, the other paddle-flipper rose briefly from the water, and Iona noticed its ragged appearance before it resubmerged. It seemed the deckhand had made a correct assessment of the wyrm's health.

The beast's head lowered again to the deck, and Gil jumped up to push the boathook further into its eye. It exhaled a stinking breath that Iona smelled from her position at the stern, and withdrew towards the bow, taking a section of fore-rail with it as it slid back into the waves. The serpent headed out to sea on a tangent but sunk out of sight just yards from the barque. If not for Alicia, Iona might have felt sorry for it.

She stumbled across the deck to Shay, legs trembling in aftershock. He hurried to meet her, and she threw herself into his arms, relieved he had escaped the encounter unscathed.

The barque limped away from the battle site, and passing the collapsed sandbar, the captain weighed anchor so the crew could make temporary repairs at sea, including jerry-rigging a bowsprit and attaching new stays to the mast, which had taken on a lean after Lorcan's heroics.

As the wranglers helped to straighten out the tumbled mess of equipment above and belowdecks, Iona sat in the great cabin with Alicia and Isobel.

Alicia assured her she felt fine apart from sore shoulders, and Iona joked, "I hope the experience hasn't dampened your adventurous spirit!"

"It will be a fine tale to tell our grandchildren," Alicia replied with a watery smile. "And now you've explained *why* you think it was a freak occurrence, I won't let it deter me from sailing the coast again. Although I hope Papa doesn't confine me to home after this."

"*Our* grandchildren?" Iona said with a twinkle in her eye, making Alicia blush.

Bertrand joined them after inspecting the cargo hold and reported, "The trade goods and supplies all appear undamaged, although the crate containing Isobel's gift for the younglings burst, and balls were rolling underfoot all over the hold! I think we've managed to round the lot up now!"

By the time the barque set sail again, they had eaten the evening meal.

Isobel retired with her maid, Sybile, to one of the two small belowdecks cabins set aside for the women, each with a latrine stool that emptied into the sea; primitive, but a vast improvement on the 'head' the sailors used. Bertrand would bunk down with Shay, Gil and Lorcan in the great cabin, the wranglers sharing the crew's quarters.

Iona stood beside Shay at the starboard rail, watching the sun cast a fiery track across the sea as it descended to the horizon.

Snuggled into his side, she leaned her head on Shay's chest and listened to his heartbeat. He had become her touchstone with reality, and she found the sound reassuring after the risks he'd taken that day, and the fantastical nature of the sea serpent encounter, which had played out like a movie scene. Though Iona felt happy to share a cabin with Alicia, she wished she could spend the night in Shay's life-affirming embrace.

Shay pointed towards the northeast, and Iona's eyes widened to behold two distant draconian shapes performing an aerial dance, limned by the sunset.

Chapter 21

The barque ghosted into Bywhitt at five in the morning, two hours later than planned. The wagons stood on standby, ready to receive the cargo from the vessel's hold, after which Gideon Marchmont's dockers would drive them to his secure warehouse where they'd remain until the Leons departure for Saint Lexis Priory.

With the local barber-surgeon rousted from his bed to attend to the sailor maimed by the sea serpent, passenger carts conveyed the Leon party to the *Golden Gannet*, the best hostelry in the port town. Having slept for some hours onboard the *Calpurnia*, they intended to stick to schedule and lay up at the inn only until midday.

Iona huddled beneath her cape on the cart seat beside Shay, shivering a little in the misty pre-dawn. Raising his cloak, Shay drew her into his side and wrapped it around them both. The charcoal-grey gloom made it difficult to discern much of the town, but in the light cast by the carter's lantern, Iona observed it bore a closer resemblance to Tritaurium than Glassnesse, with half-timbered buildings and narrow, cobbled streets. The briny tang that travelled on the fresh breeze off the sea partially disguised the usual, less wholesome smells Iona associated with this world's human settlements.

Accustomed to the vagaries of current and weather, the innkeeper seemed unfazed by the party's late arrival, and with the night porter's assistance, showed them to their ready-prepared rooms.

Iona shared a chamber with Alicia and Sybile, where they could doze for a while before breakfast and freshen up later for the next phase of the journey. She inspected the canopied double-bed for bugs and declaring it vermin-free, she and Alicia sank into it, the maid taking the truckle-bed at its foot.

Almost two hours later, Iona heard Bertrand and Isobel stirring in the next-door room, and shaking Alicia awake, they prepared to descend to the large, private parlour where the innkeeper's wife served the Leon company with a hearty breakfast of sausages, bacon, eggs, crusty bread, kippers, and porridge. Though Iona eyed the sausages with dubiousness, Isobel assured her they contained quality meat and were safe to eat. Iona washed the food down with tea from the Leons personal store, not fancying the ale or cloudy apple cordial that arrived with the food. What she would give for a glass of orange juice!

Meal consumed; Bertrand took Lorcan with him when he left for Marchmont's warehouse with the wranglers. Iona noticed the young man's grimace as he rolled his shoulders with discomfort and nudged Alicia. "I think Lorcan's suffering from even worse muscle strain than you! Perhaps you should pass on the pot of Binny's muscle rub I gave you. He might need help to apply it, though," she said with a wink.

Alicia blushed, but staring after Lorcan with a gleam in her eye, said, "But don't you need it back?"

"It worked such wonders on my leg that I no longer use it."

Iona admired Alicia's fortitude after her terrifying ordeal and hoped she wouldn't experience a delayed reaction and suffer from nightmares. Hopefully, her budding romance with Lorcan would take her mind off it.

Isobel rose from the adjoining table. "I don't know about you two, but I could do with a walk after that gargantuan breakfast. Perhaps we might take a stroll down to the jetty at the end of the street? It'll take too long to walk to the main docks."

Iona and Alicia agreed. With Shay and Gil in escort, the women ambled from the inn. The early mist had dispersed, and the sun shone from a near-cloudless sky. Though Bywhitt's position made it an important transit point to the Dragon lands, the fishing industry employed a majority of townsfolk, and several boats bobbed at the jetty, with others presumably still out fishing.

Close to the waterfront, Iona observed women surrounded by fish drying on racks, gutting and salting herring at trestle tables, the cobbles beneath slimy with fish guts. The work looked hard and grim, but despite their red-raw, chapped hands, the women sang in harmony to keep up their spirits, their sense of community evident. Even the gulls that hovered above seemed part of their system, politely waiting for the workers to finish, so they could help themselves to the discarded innards.

Walking back between tar-coated net sheds, Iona gazed up the street to the inn, admiring the top floor's golden-brown timbers against mellow-ochre plasterwork, the contrast more subtle than the black and white facades of Tritaurium's projecting upper storeys. The two wooden tubs of steaming hot water awaiting her and Alicia in their room, each surrounded by a tapestry screen, impressed her even more.

After her bath, Iona dressed in Jake's breeches and white shirt and gathered her belongings. A porter took care of their luggage, and she descended to the parlour with Alicia. They found Isobel peering from the window, observing the arrival of the three covered wagons that would transport them onward.

Gideon Marchmont had supplied a driver named Roscoe, who knew the route, to take charge of the leading wagon, which contained the trade goods.

With Bertrand on the seat beside the driver, and a wrangler/guard riding inside with the merchandise, the wagon set out towards the northwest, followed by the wagon bearing Isobel, Alicia, Sybile, and another guard named Bilston; driven by Shay, with Iona perched beside him. The luggage and supplies occupied the rear wagon with the other two wrangler guards, Lorcan seated beside Gil, who drove it.

"Roscoe said it will take seven hours to reach the priory! Won't that be a strain for the horses?" Iona asked Shay.

"Yes, which is why we'll change horses at Winternola, a small town halfway along the route. It's all arranged," he replied.

As the coast fell away behind them, they turned due north onto a packed-earth road between fields of near-ripened wheat and barley, purple-green mountains hazy in the distance.

"You drive this wagon with great confidence, Shay."

"I should do after the years I spent travelling in Zingari house wagons!" He smiled wryly. "Tell me about the *carz* of your world."

"Cars," Iona corrected, and attempted to explain the internal combustion engine and the vehicles it propelled.

"I think I have a vague memory of my mother's wagon, or caravan, as you called it, attached to such a conveyance when we lived in your world. What are movies?"

"Movies?"

"You compared our tussle with the sea serpent to a movie."

"Ah, yes. That's because things like that only happen in books or movies in my world. You seem very interested in it all of a sudden?"

"It always seemed such an abstract, like the God-worshippers' vision of heaven and hell, until I came to Saint Aurigan's priory and met the trikers. Jake told me about computers, but even then, it all felt a bit fantastical; not dissimilar, I suppose, to how you view dragons and sea serpents. But when *you* happened along... and when I knew for sure my mother came from your world, it started to become real. I think perhaps I need to learn more about it before our interview with Hyraxus. So, what are movies?"

The miles flew past as Iona answered Shay's questions the best she could, describing all the 'wonders' of her modern world until, three hours later, they turned west onto a road paved with irregular stone slabs.

"We've passed into the duchy of Hymborum, ruled by Duke Theobald. Winternola is just six miles down this road," Shay explained in a distracted tone, still musing on all he had learned.

"So, what are your thoughts about *my* reality? Do you... do you think you could live there? It's where you were born, after all," Iona asked nervously, biting her lip.

Shay hesitated before he answered, "I don't know. You seem to have a lot of labour-saving devices and things I can see no real use for except to while away time. Have people forgotten how to do things for themselves?"

"I don't *think* so. It's just they don't *need* to. Those women salting fish at Bywhitt? Well, in my world, they'd be working in a factory, wearing protective gloves provided by their employer. Machines would help with the salting process. They'd work reasonable hours for a wage agreed by their union, take regular breaks, and have health and safety rules to protect them. Surely that's an improvement on the conditions those Bywhitt workers must put up with?"

"Yes, I can *see* that, but still... what would *I* do there? What use is a sword dancer in a world like yours?"

"I can think of one," Iona replied, remembering the display by the Chinese Jian Wu sword dance company she had watched on YouTube. Shay's phenomenal skills would break the internet... "But you're so much more than 'just' a sword dancer turned ranger. It would be a different life, but you'd have so many options open to you, all unavailable here."

"Well, there's no point discussing those options until we know if I *can* return. Don't forget Charol's warning, and *that's* assuming we can find a way to go back."

"I haven't forgotten. Let's hope Hyraxus can shed light on Charol's words. But you'll think about it?"

"Iona, I'll do whatever it takes to ensure we stay together; you know that. I *love* you." Hands still on the reins, Shay leaned down and kissed her.

Winternola, a town of circular, wattle-and-daub dwellings with thatched roofs, huddled against a hillside, the main road paralleling a stream below a steep bank. A half-dozen rectangular, brick-built buildings stood on the outskirts, and it was to these they headed, passing a demolished roundhouse and another new-style building under construction.

They only stayed long enough to change horses at the *Four Arrows* hostelry, since the *Golden Gannet's* proprietors had provided them with a huge picnic of pasties, pies, bread, cheeses and cold meats to sustain them on the journey.

Iona estimated the time at around five when they left the town behind and again headed north. An hour later, the mountains loomed closer as they drew nigh to the border with the dragon lands. The road turned west between green moorland hills, and gradually narrowed as they closed in around it, giving the impression they travelled along a ravine.

The wagon ahead rolled to a stop, and Bertrand jumped down, walking back to confer with Shay, who halted their vehicle. "Roscoe says this stretch of road was rife with robber bandits until Duke Theobald's knights flushed out their lairs. Nevertheless, he recommends we stay alert. It might be advisable for Iona to swap places with Bilston."

Shay nodded, and Bertrand strode to the rear wagon to convey the information to Gil and Lorcan. Iona and Bilston exchanged places, the guard's sword unsheathed and held ready for trouble.

Iona settled herself in the wagon beside Alicia, who sat near the rear, where she'd unlaced the back opening of the canvas hood that enclosed the interior, partially drawing back the flaps to ventilate the inside and allow light to enter. It meant she could observe the passing scenery, although Iona noted it also gave Alicia a good view of the rear wagon, or rather, Lorcan, perched on the driver's board beside Gil.

The wagons lurched into motion, and Iona gazed up at the rugged green hills that might conceal any number of watchers. When a drizzly mist descended, she felt glad to be under cover of the oiled canvas. The mist soon thickened into a grey fog, and all three wagon drivers lit lanterns to ensure they didn't stray from the road, reminding Iona of Shay's tale of the Zingari who did just that, losing themselves in the forbidden dragon lands.

Iona heard a muffled *thunk*, and a break in the fog revealed an arrow stuck in the canvas just inches from Gil's head. He reined in the horses and hunkered on the footboard, pulling Lorcan down beside him. Iona bellowed, "Shay, we're under attack!" at the same time as Alicia yelled, "Stop!"

As another arrow thudded into the canvas side of the leading transport, Shay pulled on the reins and shouted through the front flaps, "Lie down and keep low!" causing the women to flatten themselves against the wagon bed.

With the three wagons halted in the road, the men all leapt to the ground. Noting the unknown archers had fired from the northern hills, they crouched beside the nearside wagon wheels that faced south, weapons drawn, knowing the swirling fog made them difficult targets.

As they peered around their makeshift barriers, straining their eyes for movement in the gloom, another arrow clattered into the road, just missing the rear wagon's offside horse.

Iona stayed down but risked a peek over the backboard in time to witness a huge jet of orange flame that lit up a wide swathe of hillside and road. Something tumbled down the hill to join the arrow, and to Iona's horror, she realised it was a man, blackened to a crisp. Another jet flamed, followed by a rending scream, and as the light died, leaving an after-image on her retinas, she heard the flap of sail-like wings fading away to the north before silence descended.

When no more arrows materialised, Roscoe rose from his crouch and sprinted to the dead man who lay in the road. Gazing down at the husk, he remarked, "It appears someone, or rather, some *dragon*, took steps to ensure you reach your destination. Your mission must be important."

Iona wondered *which* mission – the Leons, or her and Shay's.

"Official permission to cross the border works both ways. Luckily, our rescuer didn't need to; it's just over this hill," Roscoe continued.

Taking up lanterns, Bilston and three other guards scoured the hillside, discovering another two barbecued victims, and six feet from them, a half-cooked man, one shoulder and arm unburnt, his bow still clutched in his hand. Reporting back to Bertrand, they surmised he had run faster than his fellow casualties, but not fast enough.

Leaving the dead attackers where they lay, the party regrouped and proceeded onward in a pensive mood. The road climbed on a gentle gradient, widening as the fog lifted and the hills gave way to misty fells. Half an hour later, it traversed high moorland, wending northward towards two foothills and the shallow valley between that straddled the border. Saint Lexis Priory, a glorious structure of flying buttresses and gothic arches, occupied the valley's centre. The widely spaced, carved-stone buildings that surrounded it extended to the foot of both hills, upon which structures chiselled out on two levels appeared grown from the cliffs themselves. Both hills supported an arched bridge on their topmost levels, terminating in wide twin balconies beneath the roof of the priory's eastern and western facades, picturesque against the valley's mountainous backdrop.

Isobel drew back the canvas front flaps so the women could peer out, craning to see over Shay and Bilston's shoulders, the leading wagon partially obscuring their view. The road, level with the valley, passed beneath an arch higher than the retaining wall, merging with a forecourt beyond the open gates. A green-habited monk waited to greet them, perhaps warned about their approach by the Venator dragon that lifted from the eastern hill's summit and flapped away to the north, its copper scales glinting in the mist-filtered light of the descending sun. Iona gazed after it, her eyes alight with wonder, and fancied the Venator flew to inform the dragon council of their petitioners' safe arrival.

Bertrand dismounted from the lead wagon, and the monk sketched the wheel symbol on his brow before addressing him. "Welcome to Saint Lexis Priory. I'm Brother Devine, the guest master. If you could please be so good as to show me your credentials, I can then escort you to Prior Faolan."

The merchant withdrew a small parchment scroll from the leather satchel he wore slung across his chest and handed it to the monk. "I'm Bertrand Leon. Here's my permit signed by the prior on behalf of the Dragon Council."

Brother Devine scanned it briefly for form's sake and passed it back. "Excellent! I believe you have petitioners in your party who are here on a separate matter?"

Shay had already alighted from the second wagon and, signalling for Iona to join him, approached the monk, proffering Prior Faolan's reply to Mother Wilfrida's message, which her courier had delivered to the Leon residence. "I'm Shay Hawksmoor and this is Iona Abernathy, the *Living Aurigan*. Here is our authorisation for an audience with Hyraxus, Keeper of the Mysteries."

"Very good. That all seems to be in order," the brother replied as he returned the parchment strip. Turning back to Bertrand, he gestured towards a tall, long-faced monk who hurried down a side path towards them. "Brother Edric, our quartermaster, will show your employees where to secure the wagons and merchandise, and where to convey your personal luggage if the delegates would like to follow me?"

Iona hoped the wranglers would take good care of the valiant horses who had pulled the wagons such a long distance and not startled at dragon fire.

Brother Edric climbed onto the driving board beside Roscoe on the lead wagon. With Sybile accompanying Gil and the wranglers to supervise the luggage's disposition, the quartermaster directed Roscoe to drive down the side path, the other wagons following behind, Bilston at the reins of the second vehicle.

Shay, Iona, and Lorcan tailed Brother Devine down the main path with the Leon family, passing a huge monument dedicated to Saint Lexis. According to the inscription, which they paused to read, the dragon saint's adherents had buried his heart beneath it. The rectangular granite plinth, carved on each side with the *Great Wheel* ouroboros symbol, supported a colossal marble sculpture of Saint Lexis, with Jaellin, the order's founder, standing beneath the shelter of one outspread wing.

Iona remembered her surprise to discover the existence of a dragon saint after an illuminator had shown her his depiction of the pair, Jaellin wearing a vivid green robe. She had come a long way since then... *how little anything surprises me now*.

However, when they walked through the priory's vast halls, she discovered this world *could* still challenge her preconceptions. Although the Saint Aurigan and Saint Lexis orders practised the *Great Wheel* creed, the maroon-habited monks and nuns of Saint Aurigan served in separate communities. Yet, Iona spotted several women clad in the green robes of the Saint Lexis order, wearing simple white coifs beneath their cowled habit hoods, instead of the oversized wimples sported by the Saint Aurigan nuns. But this mixing of the sexes wasn't the real jaw-dropper; that honour went to Iona's observation that dragons also appeared to serve the priory.

After a Venator and then two pewter-hued Lacunae passed them in a wide cloister, all wearing green fabric bibs with the *Great Wheel* symbol embroidered in gold thread, Alicia questioned Brother Devine. "How come I've never heard of dragon monks or nuns before?"

"We are isolated here and receive few visitors. It's a tradition for young Venator and Lacunae to serve here as acolytes for a time, although only a handful stay on to take their vows. My assistant, Sister Myriax, whom you shall shortly meet, is one such."

Not wishing to appear rude, Iona had tried not to stare at the fabled creatures, containing her avid interest in the Lacunae, the species she hoped could help her and Shay gain access to the sealed-off areas within the Janus Spire.

Brother Devine ushered the visitors into an audience chamber, although the splendid wooden throne carved with dragons on the backrest and arms stood empty on its dais. A slightly built man of indeterminate age rose from behind a desk scattered with scrolls and parchments, whom the monk introduced as Prior Faolan.

However, Iona's gaze had immediately fastened on the bronze-scaled Venator who sat on her haunches behind a large lectern, wings folded neatly along her spine. Her front limbs, shorter than her back legs, ended in flexible, claw-tipped 'hands' that busily sorted through a pile of lists and charts. She appeared smaller than the average Venator, and Iona surmised her stunted growth might be a contributing factor in her decision to remain with the order, for she guessed her identity right away.

"And this here is Sister Myriax, who will show you to your quarters after we've taken care of the formalities," Brother Devine continued, confirming Iona's supposition.

The dragon-nun inclined her head, using a claw to sketch the circle symbol on her scaly forehead between two short, spiralled horns.

Prior Faolan gestured to the six chairs arranged before his desk, and with the guests comfortably seated, Sister Myriax edged from behind her lectern. Walking on her hind legs like a miniature T-Rex, she crossed to a table laden with bottles and goblets. "You must be thirsty after your journey. We have a selection of cordials, if anyone wishes to partake?"

Though not expecting such a melodious voice to issue from Myriax's fanged jaws, Iona only felt mild surprise; it seemed she had become inured to the strangeness of this world.

Once the guests had chosen their cordials, Brother Devine did the honours since Sister Myriax's clawed hands made pouring drinks a delicate operation.

Prior Faolan remarked, "I *do* hope your journey wasn't too arduous?"

"It was an adventure, to put it mildly! But apart from attacks by highway robbers and a sea serpent, it was not unpleasant," Bertrand replied with irony.

"A sea serpent attacked you?" Sister Myriax interjected; her glowing amber eyes fastened on the merchant. "I would be most interested to hear the story later, if you have no objection?"

"My esteemed assistant has made quite a study of the dragons' distant cousins," Brother Devine explained.

The dragon-nun folded her hands together. "Recent reports of sea serpent beachings prompted my research, and I discovered no one has studied them since Friar Botolph one hundred years ago. I *do* hope the encounter has not disposed you unfavourably towards draconian-kind?"

"What? No, of course not. In fact, who knows what might have happened if an Alpha hadn't intervened to halt the robbers in their tracks?" Bertrand replied.

Prior Faolan exchanged a glance with Sister Myriax and turned to Bertrand. "Intervened, you say?"

Bertrand described the incident, and the Prior studied his hands. "Most unusually, the dragon council ordered their sentries to patrol that stretch of road after authorising the *Living Aurigan's* and Mister Hawksmoor's interview with Hyraxus. That's all I know. Their meeting with the Keeper of the Mysteries is scheduled for tomorrow afternoon, and depending on the outcome, they may face the dragon council afterwards. Your trade delegation will appear before the council the day after tomorrow. However, I see you have four delegates in this party. I'm afraid the permit only covers three, although the council *may* allow an additional representative after the initial talks."

"Alicia will be the third delegate. I'm just along for the ride," Lorcan said.

"And thank goodness you were!" Isobel exclaimed.

Prior Faolan nodded, making a note on a form. "Very well. The council will gather in the Aerie of the Sun, reachable via the eastern bridge. Brother Devine will escort you to the balcony that accesses the span, and Venator acolytes will convey examples of your trade goods across." He turned then to Shay and Iona. "You must go to Hyraxus in the Archives of Infinitude. They are located in a cave system to the northwest, accessible from the western hill via a tunnel. Now, I'm sure you must all be tired and hungry after your journey. If you follow Brother Devine and Sister Myriax, they will show you to your quarters."

Chapter 22

They emerged through a back door onto a paved garden walk at the end of which Brother Devine turned to the Leons. He pointed to a slate-roofed building with dragons carved around the lintels. "I have placed a suite in our guesthouse at your disposal. You will find your luggage in your rooms. However, since the *Living Aurigan* and Mister Hawksmoor have an early start in the morning to reach the archives, I thought it expedient to allocate them a suite on the west hill from whence they must journey. If they could be so kind as to follow Sister Myriax?"

After so long in the Leons company, separation from them felt strange. Iona had no time for more than a hurried farewell before Brother Devine swept the family away with Lorcan. She and Shay followed the dragon-nun to a waiting pony trap driven by a fresh-faced young monk, and found their luggage in the back.

With Sister Myriax flying ahead at a leisurely pace, the trap wended westward through the village-sized settlement that surrounded the priory. Iona gazed with fascination at the myriad of fine, dressed-stone buildings with scalloped roof tiles that resembled fish scales.

"The dragon council appears to have had a vested interest in our safe arrival. I wonder why?" Shay mused.

"The brigands? Yes, it does seem that way. I'm not sure whether to feel heartened or worried. I expect we'll discover the reason tomorrow."

When they arrived at the western hill, the trap halted before a wide, pillared doorway carved into its northwestern face at ground level. Iona stared up at the structures on the first and second levels, accessed by a series of stone staircases. Their columned facades appeared almost temple-like, perhaps influenced by the ancient Truscaromian architecture of Glassnesse's public buildings, and she wondered if they pre-dated the priory.

The young monk hoisted Iona's trunk onto his shoulder, leaving Shay to manage his backpack. Trailing Sister Myriax through the door, they passed down a hallway lit by torches in iron wall brackets, the dragon-nun's clawed feet clicking on the flagstones. She led them right at a short corridor, then left into a passage lined with pilasters, stopping halfway down at a recessed double door topped with an architrave.

"Here is your suite. I hope you will find it comfortable," the sister said as she opened the door and gestured for them to enter.

Iona beheld a sitting room furnished with two upholstered wooden couches and a table bearing covered food bowls, with carafes of wine and water. A lidded earthenware pot that emitted a delightful aroma hung from a hook over a small, niched fireplace, keeping warm over a bed of partially banked coals. She peeked through a door on the left-hand wall to discover a compact bedroom, fitted out with a half-tester bed. Shay opened another door in the north wall, and his intake of breath brought Iona to his side. They surveyed a huge space with a low, round, almost nest-like bed in one corner, piled with cushions. On the left, three open arches divided the room along its length, through which they saw a gently steaming pool in the rock floor, its water cascading over one lip into a slightly lower pool. A series of half-glass, sliding doors lined the back wall of both sections, beyond which they observed a narrow, roofed gallery extending the room's width, supported by ivy-festooned columns on the outer side. Iona gazed out at the stunning view of forested mountains in the gathering dusk, grateful for the abundance of lamps that lit the otherwise windowless rooms beneath the hill.

"These pools look natural," Shay remarked, peering up at a near-hidden ceiling vent above them.

"Yes, the upper pool is a thermal spring, although the smaller pool is cooler and has undergone alterations to catch the overflow as part of our sewage works. The spring is perfectly safe to bathe in if you so wish. This whole area is dotted with springs and underground streams, which we have taken advantage of for separating fresh water from waste," Sister Myriax explained.

"Sewage works? That seems quite advanced compared to other places I've visited in Beretania. Er, does that mean there's a garderobe here somewhere that's connected to the system?" Iona voiced the thought that always surfaced first when she recced new accommodations in this world. It had become a near-obsession that she couldn't quite overcome.

"Yes, indeed. It is located in an alcove on the far left of the gallery." Sister Myriax gestured towards the sliding doors, and Shay hid a grin. Iona's fixation on 'proper' toilet facilities amused him.

"I will leave you to eat your dinner now, but will return after breakfast tomorrow morning to escort you to Hyraxus. In the meantime, if you require anything, ring the bell in the sitting room to summon assistance. The bell pull is connected to another in a service area." The dragon-nun bowed and departed, chivvying the young monk from the living room, where he had deposited Iona's trunk.

Iona and Shay looked at each other, both thinking the same thing. Although the guest master had provided two bedrooms, as only proper, they doubted Sister Myriax would condemn them for impropriety if they shared a bed – dragons didn't understand the moralistic gatekeeping over the natural sexual impulse practised by most human societies.

"Well, this is a stroke of luck!" Iona grinned saucily.

Shay glanced through the open bedroom door at their dinner warming on the hearth, and then over his shoulder at the enticing pool. He turned back to Iona wearing a matching grin. "I'm sure whatever's in that pot will keep a bit longer."

As he unbuckled his sword belt and kicked off his boots, Iona slipped through the door and retrieved her toiletry pouch from the trunk. Returning to the bedroom, she found Shay already in the pool, his clothes in a heap on the floor. He sat on a submerged, natural rock ledge, arms stretched to each side along the pool's rim, the water level with his sternum. He gave Iona a lazy, seductive smile. "Come on, jump in. The water is *just* the right temperature."

At the sight of Shay's tanned, muscled chest and biceps, Iona dropped the pouch and quickly stripped off. She dipped her toe in the water to test Shay's claim and sat down on the edge. Shay glided towards her and, catching her around the waist, pulled her against his chest and into the water, their lips locking together.

Iona, her back spooned against Shay's chest, opened her eyes to the dim, early morning light, filtered through the foliage that draped the columns beyond the sliding doors. She smiled in remembrance of the night before. Despite their apprehension over the audience with Hyraxus, they had left their cares behind to fully embrace the unexpected opportunity.

Careful not to wake Shay, Iona shifted around to face him in the strange, oversized round bed. Its dimensions had led them to suspect its creator had originally designed it for a Venator. Iona raised herself onto an elbow and stared down at Shay's sleeping face. A stray lock of his unbound hair had fallen over one eye, and she gently brushed it back. When he smiled and flipped her onto her back, she knew he'd been awake all along……

Rising at last, Iona bathed and then stood indecisively before the green gown, hanging from a wall hook. Though she had purchased it for her interview with the Dragon Council, she wouldn't meet them today, if at all. The gown seemed impractical for a journey underground to the Archives of Infinitude, so Iona donned the breeches with a fresh shirt instead.

A knock at the outer door heralded breakfast, served by a green-habited nun and a Lacunae. Though she longed to question the small dragon about its abilities, she didn't wish to give offence, so refrained. She would hopefully learn soon enough from Hyraxus.

However, Shay didn't seem to share her compunction. The Lacunae held out a tray, onto which the nun stacked their dinner dishes from the previous night. "Please excuse my curiosity, but will you *displace* yourself straight to the kitchens with that lot to save you the walk? Or the flight, perhaps?" Shay asked the hound-sized dragon.

"Oh no! That would be impolite to my mentor, whom I must shadow at all times during my training period. I'm not yet old enough to transpose Sister Clothilde with me," the little dragon piped in fluting tones, glancing towards the nun, uncertainty clouding his innocent eyes when she frowned, as though he'd said something wrong.

Sister Clothilde motioned the Lacunae towards the door. "Sister Myriax will arrive in half an hour," she informed Iona and Shay, and inclining her head in farewell, left with the little dragon.

Iona raised her eyebrows at Shay, who shrugged. "I guess admitting the truth about Lacunae abilities is against order policy. While the rumours remain hearsay, or just a tale to scare naughty children, they'll not become a subject of *interest* to a superstitious populace, or the unscrupulous who might think to use them despite the Arcem Treaty. Since you're the *Living Aurigan*, perhaps the acolyte didn't class you as a *complete* outsider and thought it permissible to answer my question. But we now have confirmation that the Lacunae can transport others with them when they… teleport? I think that's the word you used?"

"Yes, that's right. Or at least the adults can if I understood the acolyte correctly. It's useful to know that before we meet with Hyraxus……"

When Sister Myriax arrived, she led them farther along the pilastered corridor to another set of double doors near the end, which opened on a wide staircase leading down.

On descending to the bottom, they found themselves in a vaulted basement, and the dragon-nun ushered them into a tunnel in the north wall, large enough for a Venator to fly along. Though torches lined the walls at long intervals, dimness prevailed between each sconce, lit only by a faint phosphorescence.

However, they hadn't gone far when another Venator appeared from the gloom, and Sister Myriax gestured towards a strange, two-seater contraption that resembled a wooden settee positioned between two overlarge wheels. "It is three miles to our destination, and not an easy route for humans in the poor light. However, if you would seat yourselves in the chaise, Tunnel Porter Abraxius will tow you there," she explained.

Only then did Iona notice the strap arrangement attached to the high seatback. She shared a dubious glance with Shay, and they gingerly seated themselves on the low chaise, which faced the way they had come, with the wheels beyond each armrest higher than their heads. They rested their feet on a footboard, and Abraxius, larger than Sister Myriax, gathered the straps in his claws, and flew at a steady pace down the tunnel, keeping low to the ground.

Iona clutched Shay's hand. Although they moved backwards, the jaunt reminded her of the Funfair ghost train, which, when children, had scared her and Skye silly. Sister Myriax's eyes, gleaming in the semi-darkness as she followed behind, merely strengthened this impression. However, with Shay's arm around her shoulder, Iona soon relaxed and even enjoyed their passage along the smoothed-rock floor.

When at last the light grew brighter, Abraxius slowed down, and descending to the ground, grasped the chaise to halt its now reduced momentum. Iona and Shay stepped from the conveyance, thanking their haulier before they followed Sister Myriax through an archway and up a ramp onto a wide landing. She led them next up a flight of stairs and they entered a vast cave via a door at the top. Another ramp circled its perimeter, winding in a spiral around the walls, ascending almost to the ceiling. Iona spotted other cave mouths off landings at different ramp levels and craned her head back to stare at them in wonder.

"Some of the caves housing our libraries are natural, but most are dragon-hewn. The ramp is mainly for the benefit of our human allies, who do not have wings like us," Sister Myriax informed. However, she bypassed the ramp's foot, leading them onward through the central cave, which, unlike the tunnel, was brightly lit, augmented with shafts of light that pierced through vents in the high ceiling.

They traversed the levelled floor to a pillared archway in the back wall, wide enough to admit an Alpha, passing two Venator archivists sorting scrolls on a stone table, and a Lacunae librarian balancing a pile of books in his arm-like forelegs. With a little jump, the librarian suddenly vanished before their eyes. Iona and Shay shared a meaningful look but forbore to comment.

The archway led to another cave system, this one all on ground level, the central passageway of boulevard-width. Iona peered into the cave mouths they passed but saw nothing except soft lights shining through the curtained-off entrances. The passage terminated at another cave, before which Sister Myriax halted. "This is the domain of Hyraxus, Keeper of the Mysteries. Please wait here while I announce your presence."

The dragon-nun slipped behind the curtain and returned shortly to say, "Hyraxus will receive you alone. Please go through; I will wait for you out here."

A gigantic, semi-circular stone desk dominated the area beyond the curtain, littered with parchments and writing slates, a tray of inks and outsize writing implements resting on one end, and a dragon-sized lectern on the other. Scroll racks covered the right wall, and folding doors, man-made in appearance, closed off another cave mouth on the left. A tall pilastered archway beyond the desk led to a cave room crammed with bookcases and racks, from which a huge Alpha dragon emerged, bearing something between his front claws.

The enormous creature, his green scales darkened with age, stooped to peer at them from slightly rheumy green eyes. "Ah, my two supplicants. I am Hyraxus and am very pleased to meet you both. Please help yourself to drinks from the yonder table and take a seat."

Shay poured water into beakers, and handing one to Iona, perched beside her on a human-sized wooden bench before the desk.

As Hyraxus placed the objects he held onto the work surface, Iona noticed his shortened claws. Perhaps he cut them to make handling delicate parchments easier. However, she found the objects of more immediate interest; two hot-pink box files, obviously manufactured in *her* reality. "How did those files get here? They're not of this world!"

"Audrey Hawksmoor lodged them with me. They contain her family documents, which go back as far as her ancestor, Aurigan Aurelius, otherwise known as Saint Aurigan."

Shay almost spilt his water. "What?!"

"It is true. The saint is your ancestor, and tasked his descendants to guard the portals between worlds and keep their secrets."

"I know nothing about portals or secrets, but... those boxes tug at my memory... their colour... I had forgotten them, but I now recall my mother poring over their contents. I think they stood on a shelf in our caravan before we crossed to this reality."

"Why did Shay's mother give them to you?" Iona asked Hyraxus.

The Alpha sighed, a wisp of dark grey smoke coiling from one nostril. "The story is long and complicated, but I knew this day would come and practiced my words. I will assume you know little and start at the beginning. There are two portals between the Primary and Secondary worlds; one within a cave in the dragon-lands, and the other is the menhir stone in Kentauros–"

"But *I* didn't come here through a *portal*!" Iona interrupted.

"Yes, I know about the *trisiks*, but that is another story. Let us deal with this one first," Hyraxus said sternly.

"Sorry!"

The dragon nodded and settled more comfortably on his haunches. "The cave portal is only active for a day every one-hundred-years and debouches into a hidden cavern in the Scottish Grampians, located in the Primary world. The menhir stone works differently, and is active at a variable rate, as recorded by each descendent of Aurigan chosen to become the Watcher. Their charts are in here." He tapped the topmost box. "We are uncertain if the menhir has a twin in the Primary world, or if it exists in *both* worlds at the same time. A node between them, if you like. Whichever the case, the connecting menhir in the Primary world is situated in England, on private land in Wiltshire. When Aurigan first encountered it as a boy, his uncle owned the land on which the menhir stood, hidden in a tree thicket. He recorded that he first visited the Secondary world at seventeen years of age and stayed for two days. After that, he had to wait twenty-one years before the way 'opened' again. This time, he intended to stay for good. His wife had died, and he suffered disappointments in his career. Blaming himself for his failures, he sought redemption in a world that would benefit from his knowledge. He entrusted the secret to his eighteen-year-old son, who shouldered the task of recording the menhir's activity, noting that the *way* remained open for three months after his father passed through. He eventually inherited the land from his childless great-uncle, but by the time your mother, Audrey, inherited the mantle of Watcher, the family had fallen into penury, and bailiffs had seized the estate."

"Did they know about the other portal in the Grampians?" Iona asked.

Hyraxus nodded. "Aurigan learned of it from my predecessor, who had similar concerns about protecting the portals from those who might seek to misuse them. Fifty years after Aurigan crossed to this reality, the menhir *way* opened again. Time runs at the same rate in both worlds and, despite his advanced age, he passed through to see his son for a final time. He gave him rough coordinates for the Grampians cave portal, as supplied by the incumbent Keeper of the Mysteries. Aurigan's grandson eventually found it during *his* term as Watcher, and henceforth, all the Watchers after him, whose tenure coincided with its 'opening', journeyed there to remain on guard until it closed again. As it happens, Audrey's watch concurred with its brief centenary activation. With the menhir land and attached house the subject of a legal dispute, she had taken to the traveller way of life, intending to return when her calculations, based on the charts compiled by her precursors, indicated the menhir *way* would reopen. At the time she left for the Grampians, this would not occur for another eight years."

Hyraxus lowered his head and contemplated the two humans through partially slitted eyelids. He eased down onto the floor, coiling his tail under his forelimbs like a cat, and absently ruffled his wings while he chose his next words with care.

Though Iona felt thankful she didn't have to crane her head as high to study the dragon's face, she found herself gripping Shay's hand in unease, intuiting that Hyraxus was about to tell them something distressing.

In a seeming change of subject, Hyraxus continued, "Shanahan Hawksmoor, Zingari leader of your stepfather's clan," he waved a claw at Shay, "had become lost in the dragon lands after the clan's wagon train accidentally crossed the border in thick fog. Leaving the halted wagons, he searched for the quickest way out, but spotting two Alphas flying overhead, he hid in a cave because the treaty forbids humans from entering the dragon lands uninvited. However, the cave he chose is the portal site through to the cavern in the Grampians, and by a strange twist of fate, the portal happened to be active. When he stepped through to the cavern, he did not know he stood in another reality – one cave is much like another. However, when he judged it safe to return the way he came, hoping the Alphas had gone, he found the way blocked – the portal had closed and would not reopen in his lifetime. Audrey observed him emerge onto the hillside, his torch almost spent, and realised he came from the Secondary world. She had no choice except to succour him until his only way back, the menhir portal, would open eight years in the future. Shanahan joined Audrey on her travels, and they fell in love. Their child, Shay, was born two years later."

Hyraxus paused to give them time to digest the implications. Shay's hand tightened on Iona's. "Shanahan, my stepfather's brother, is my father? But that's..."

"Didn't your stepfather, Charol, become the Barozi by default after Shanahan disappeared? Doesn't that make *you* the hereditary clan leader?" Iona asked.

Shay nodded numbly. "As Shanahan's only son, with no brothers to challenge for the leadership, the title is mine by right. That must be what the Madjia meant when she foresaw that I would have to make a decision based on my conscience."

"As a child of both worlds, it may also explain why the Madjia likened your connection to this reality as a loose thread on the tapestry, whilst my thread is missing entirely," Iona mused and then had a sudden thought. "Hyraxus, why did Charol warn Shay he must never return to his mother's world?"

"Ah, here is where we come to the difficult bit. Are you ready for me to resume the story?"

Iona and Shay nodded, though trepidation made Iona's stomach roil.

"Alright. Those who cross from the Primary world endure in the Secondary without any ill effects, or no more than they might naturally succumb to in their own reality. However, the reverse is not true. Although Audrey had documentary evidence of this from previous Watchers, she could only hope that Shanahan would survive long enough to return through the menhir portal. However, it was not to be. Though Shanahan lasted longer than most, within three years he began to *fade*. He grew thin and insubstantial until his substance disintegrated and his essence floated away."

"What? How…" Iona said fearfully, her stomach clenching.

"Dragonkind philosophers posit that the Secondary reality formed from the dreams of those who inhabit the Primary world." Hyraxus' wings rose and fell in a non-committal shrug.

"But Shay…"

"Audrey believed Shay's half-Primary heritage would protect him, and indeed, he showed no signs of his father's malaise until he turned six. When the first symptoms appeared, Audrey knew her son had little time, and thanked the fates for the menhir portal's imminent opening. She sold the Aurelius family jewellery and plate to invest in precious gems that she could barter for Beretanian currency. However, with the legal dispute now resolved, a company named Borderland Incorporated had purchased the manor house and attached land. Audrey stationed her caravan on common land adjacent to the lea where the menhir stood, and when the *way* became active, broke into the now fenced and guarded grounds. With Shay in his pushchair, and the box files in her backpack with the gems, she could not move fast enough to avoid detection, her unauthorised entry having set off an alarm. However, she knew the land better than her pursuers and reached the menhir *just* ahead of them. Snatching the half-conscious Shay from his pushchair, and heedless of the witnesses, she pressed her body against the stone, and immediately found herself on the other side. No one followed her through. Shay revived almost at once, and Audrey knew she had done the right thing, even though her crossing had broken the Watcher chain – for she could never return."

Iona glanced at a tight-jawed Shay, who sat stiffly erect, his hands clenching and unclenching. "Are you saying I'm not…*real*? That none of us are except Iona and Binny?"

"Binny?" Hyraxus waved his own question away with a flick of a claw. "No, that is not what I am saying. All Secondary worlders are real – so long as we remain here."

Iona felt sick. Shay would die if he returned with her. She imagined his atoms dispersing one by one, blowing away like bubbles on a breeze. "When is the menhir portal due to open next?"

Hyraxus sighed, another smoke spiral curling from a nostril. "Let me see, according to Audrey's records, fifty years after the last time, minus twenty years since then, so that makes it thirty years hence – if nothing interferes with the cycle. Perhaps you can return the way you came, but I wouldn't bet on it unless you discover *how*."

"Interferes with? What do you mean?"

"I was getting to that bit. Shall I continue?"

Iona nodded.

"Audrey's charts told her the portal would remain open for five months, and she felt duty-bound to stay nearby and check on it daily until it closed. She rented a room in Kentauros, but to her shock, the *way* deactivated after three months. Not long after that, the first of the *trisiks* arrived. With Shanahan's stories of his Zingari life still vivid in her mind, she knew where she could find his clan at that time of year, and journeyed to their summer encampment outside Glassnesse. Audrey spoke a phrase to Charol that Shanahan had taught her, a private password between brothers, and the rest of her story, you know. I'm not sure how much she told Charol, but enough that he knew the danger to his nephew should he return to the place where his father had died. I believe the Madjia divined Shay's identity – Audrey told me he bears a strong resemblance to Shanahan. After her marriage to Charol, the clan again travelled the border of the dragon lands. With no Watcher on the portals' Primary side, and unable to bequeath the role to Shay, Audrey knew she must turn her files over to someone with knowledge of the portals' existence. Remembering Aurigan's record of his consultations on the subject with the Keeper of Mysteries, she detoured to Saint Lexis Priory and begged an audience with me."

"What did she know about the trikes, or the *trisiks*, as you call them?" Iona asked.

"Nothing, though she suspected they originated with Borderland. The Company's head honcho, as she termed him, trained as a Quantum Physicist, although he had business interests in a number of scientific fields."

"I didn't understand a word of that last sentence," Shay confessed.

"I barely comprehend it either, but it's all in the files. Your mother added her own reports and explained some things to me. I'm merely repeating what is in here." Hyraxus tapped the boxes again.

"The trikes *do* originate with Borderland; it was them who provided me with mine. What do *you* know about them?" Iona asked Hyraxus.

"I only know what Mother Wilfrida confided to Prior Faolan. As a fellow *Great Wheel* practitioner, he feels duty-bound to keep abreast of the Saint Aurigan order's *eterna* incarnations. Unfortunately, the Secondary worlders cannot *see* the *trisiks* whilst they travel through this reality. I do not know why. Nevertheless, they appear to emit a powerful repelling force which makes other road users avoid the invisible machines, taking pains to swerve from their path."

"Yes, that was my experience," Iona confirmed.

"The menhir projects a similar force when it is active. *My* view is the *trisiks* appear to be some kind of mobile portal, although I did not tell Prior Faolan that. As Keeper of the Mysteries, I head a select coterie of philosophers and councillors in the dragon hierarchy that shields the dangerous knowledge of the portals' existence from the human and dragon masses. In fact, some of us speculate that the Lacunae ability to *transpose* has a certain affinity with the portals, though on a different scale."

"The Lacunae... that's why *I'm* here," Iona said.

"Tell me first what *you* have learned about the *trisiks*."

Iona swallowed most of her water, and setting the beaker on the bench beside her, folded her hands in her lap to hide their tremble. She summarised her own story and those of the previous trikers who had left their depositions in the folder she had discovered under the mattress at Saint Aurigan's priory. Moving on to Prior Fidelmus' and Shay's suspicions about Duke Clovis, the man responsible for the villager kidnappings, Iona described her and Shay's doomed attempt to penetrate the Janus Spire's sealed-off areas. She concluded with Honoria's failed attempt to kidnap her. Iona felt strangely detached from her tale; the wind taken out of her sails by the knowledge that Shay couldn't return home with her, and more sceptical about her chances of returning – or at least not for another thirty years – than she had been before.

"Let me guess, you believe a Lacunae or two can *displace* you behind the impassable walls?"

"That's what we hoped; yes."

Hyraxus looked away, tapping the box files in thought. Turning back to his supplicants, he remarked, "I doubt the duke is *behind* the operation, exactly, but it seems highly probable he *hosts* it. The menhir portal is directly below the Janus Spire. No, the instigators are from *your* world; they must be. The truth is, we have been most concerned about the *trisiks* business and its possible interference with the menhir portal. What do the perpetrators wish to achieve? Will this constant... *blending* of our worlds via the *trisiks* threaten the Secondary world's stability? We have known for some time that we need to intervene, but unfortunately, we could not do so without an invitation, otherwise it would break the Arcem Treaty. When we received your application for an audience, we hoped it might be the opportunity we sought, and took steps to ensure your safe arrival."

"The robber bandits?" Shay queried.

"Yes. We knew a band had survived Duke Theobald's purge." Hyraxus rose onto his haunches. "We will require a formal invitation to aid you in this endeavour. Though it would normally come from the Duchy concerned, in this case, we can hardly expect Duke Clovis to issue one to us! However, by edict, the *Great Wheel* orders are semi-autonomous, and it is within the treaty terms to accept an appeal for help from them. Although Prior Fidelmus heads the chapter at Tritaurium, it will be quicker to go through Mother Wilfrida, who is the supreme leader of Saint Aurigan's order. Prior Faolan can get a bird to her before the day is out. If you agree to this, I will confer with the Dragon Council about the best way to proceed."

Iona and Shay had not expected Hyraxus to grant them help so easily, if at all, and shared a quick look of surprise. Iona nodded, and Shay said, "We agree."

Hyraxus lifted the box files from his desk and handed them to Shay. "These are yours. I have copies of everything they contain. Return to your quarters, and I will send you a message after I have spoken to the Council. Oh, by the way, alone in the Saint Lexis order, the scholarly Sister Myriax knows the secret of the portals. You can trust her."

Chapter 23

The lunch hour had come and gone when Iona and Shay arrived back at their suite. A cold repast awaited them in the sitting room, which they ate in a state of stunned bewilderment. Although they had achieved their goal, Hyraxus' revelations overwhelmed their victory.

Iona settled on what seemed the safest topic to discuss. "Will you claim the clan leadership?"

"No. I never wanted it. *That* hasn't changed *just* because I'm the rightful heir. Dareesh has led them well since Charol's death; it would be wrong to snatch the Barozi title from someone who *does* want to lead."

"You told me that, as the stronger sword dancer, you didn't want to challenge Dareesh for the title and risk killing him in the *Inferno*. Now, you could take the leadership without bloodshed. You're Shanahan's true heir, with no brothers to contest your claim."

Iona glimpsed the hurt in Shay's eyes when he gazed into hers. "That may have been the main reason then, but I've since discovered my path and know the Zingari life is not for me. Do you *want* me to claim the title? Will it be a sop to your conscience if you find a way to return home, leaving me behind?"

"How can you say that? I only tried to gauge your feelings now you know who you are." Tears trickled down Iona's cheeks. "I can't bear the thought of you flying apart as though you never existed! I love you and the idea of us parting kills me!"

Huge sobs racked Iona, and Shay suddenly knelt by her side. He pulled her from the dining chair into his arms and stroked her back. "I'm sorry, I'm sorry," he murmured into her hair.

When Iona's tears quietened, Shay raised her from the floor and settled her into his lap on the couch. He cupped her chin and gently turned her face to his. "I won't stand in your way if there's a chance for you to return home. It will shatter me to lose you, but you're here by default because you've no other choice. I'd rather you *chose* to stay, with no regrets, if given the opportunity to leave."

Iona opened her mouth to protest, but Shay laid a finger on her lips. "It may never happen, so let's not muddy the waters. Despite everything, I'm still committed to discovering what happened to the villagers and the other trikers. And if Hyraxus believes the trike operation's continuance will endanger *this* world's integrity, then I have a duty to stop it; I owe it to my mother, who gave up so much for me."

Nestled in his arms, Iona asked, "Will you tell Dareesh what you learned?"

"I may have to. He's in Tritaurium now, and we might need his sword dancers to aid us in the conflict with the duke."

"Even if we must destroy the trikes," Iona gulped, "At least it will prevent Borderland from tricking more suckers, like me."

"Let's not get ahead of ourselves—"

A knock at the door interrupted Shay, who lifted Iona from his lap to answer it. Sister Clothilde stood without and handed Shay a message. "From the Leon party," she explained. "I will wait here for your reply."

Shay thanked her and closed the door. He unfolded the message and scanned it. "It's an invitation to dine with them this evening. Their audience with the Council is tomorrow, and I expect they're curious about our interview with Hyraxus. What will we tell them?"

"Everything. I think we owe it to them," Iona replied.

Shay nodded. "Alright, so be it. Depending on how quickly things move for us, it may be our last chance to speak to them before we leave. Prior Faolan implied their negotiations with the Council might go on for days. I'll tell Sister Clothilde we accept."

After Shay had spoken to the nun, he returned to the couch. "We shouldn't mention the dragon philosophers' theory to our friends; it's not a good feeling to hear you might just be a figment of a collective imagination."

"Oh Shay, I don't believe that! Your mother carried you in her womb for nine months in the Primary world, and you survived there for six years. Don't tell me that's not real!"

Shay shook his head. "I don't know… *Evaporating* to nothing is hardly a normal way to die…"

Iona wrapped her arms around him. "You feel real enough to me." Straddling his lap, she kissed him with passion. His response made her smile with pleasure. "*More* than real……"

As they relaxed in the pool an hour later, Shay remarked, "Mother Wilfrida and Prior Fidelmus know the trikers come from *somewhere*. As devotees of Saint Aurigan, they have a *right* to know about the portals since they're the reason Aurigan *founded* the order."

"Yes, to safeguard the *ways*, as Fidelmus said. Besides, we can hardly form a cohesive plot against Duke Clovis without telling them everything that's at stake," Iona agreed. "If we *do* discover a way to cross back, we must also warn Binny. She's happy here, but if she decides Eliza might be better off in the modern world…"

Bertrand and Isobel also knew the *Eterna's* came from *somewhere*, but had never questioned this 'sacred mystery' of Saint Aurigan's order. However, they had already learned enough from Iona to accept the truth with less shock than they might have done when Iona and Shay enlightened them over pre-dinner drinks.

Iona couldn't help feeling a little relieved at Alicia and Lorcan's absence. They had gone to watch a candlelit procession of Saint Lexis' effigy, with Sybile, Gil, and the wranglers. She felt more comfortable letting Alicia's parents decide whether to share the knowledge with their daughter and her beau.

With Alicia and Lorcan's return, they all sat down to dinner, Alicia enthusing over the picturesque cortege. "The acolytes carried streamers of red and yellow silk 'flames' atop wooden poles, and incense smoke escaped through the painted-wood effigy's nostrils. Musicians flanked the column and— Oh! Lorcan, tell them about the dragon choir!"

Iona listened with half an ear; glad she had not put a dampener on Alicia's high spirits with depressing talk of an alternate reality that annihilated its twin's people.

Alicia at last asked Iona and Shay, "How did you fare with Hyraxus?"

"He agreed to my request for assistance to penetrate the Janus Spire's impassable barriers," Iona replied with a bright smile and, as planned with Bertrand and Isobel, resolved to stick with this aspect of the Hyraxus interview.

"That's wonderful! It gives me more hope we may finally discover what happened to Cousin Clare," Alicia said.

"I wish I could be there when the time comes… perhaps when this mission is over…" Bertrand fretted.

"I don't know, Bertrand. I've got a feeling the dragons will move fast," Shay cautioned.

With dinner consumed, they retired to the sitting room of the six-room suite. While the others discussed how Saint Aurigan's priory might host the Lacunae, assuming Hyraxus concurred with Iona's plan and didn't have another in mind, Isobel and Iona talked quietly in a corner.

"I'm so sorry for you and Shay. You must both feel devastated," Isobel sympathised.

"We do; our choices are so limited. But it may not matter if there's no way back. We'll just have to cross that bridge if we come to it."

Isobel nodded and patted Iona's hand. "From a personal point of view, I won't be sorry if you must stay, but I can imagine how keen your loss will feel either way. Duke Clovis and this Borderland group have a lot to answer for."

"Yes, but I could never regret meeting Shay; he's the missing part of me. And I feel lucky to have discovered true friends here; you, Binny, and many others whom I'd never have met otherwise. If this is the last time that I see you until… well, I'm not sure… please know how much I appreciate everything you've done for me."

A knock at the door signalled the pony trap had arrived to return Iona and Shay to their rooms. Iona and Isobel stood and embraced with tears in their eyes. Iona hugged the others, wishing them good luck in their trade mission.

"The best of luck to you and Shay, too, my dear; the very best of luck," Bertrand responded, and cleared his throat.

Back in their rooms, Shay unlaced Iona's emerald-green gown. She had worn it to dinner, having bought it specially for this trip.

"You looked beautiful tonight," he said as the kirtle slipped to the floor.

Iona reached up to remove the ebony hair stick that held Shay's hair in a knot atop his head, his locks cascading down in a fragrant waterfall. "Hm, you've been using Binny's shampoo."

He gave a crooked grin. "I know how sensitive you are to bad smells."

"They aren't nearly so bad here at Saint Lexis. Or maybe I'm just getting used to them."

"Never! Shall I help you out of that corselette?" Shay said huskily, running his fingers down Iona's bare arms, leaving a trail of goosebumps.

"There are times when I miss the humble zip, but this is not one of them," she replied, raising her arm so he could reach the side laces……

Iona leaned on the gallery's stone balustrade, gazing out at the mountains in the early morning mist.

The sliding door opened, and a bare-chested Shay emerged, his hair loose around his shoulders. He embraced Iona from behind, and she curved her body into his. "It's beautiful here," she murmured as an Alpha winged across her field of vision, disappearing behind a forested peak.

"I think you've fallen in love with this place."

Iona nodded. "It's… special." She sighed. "I wonder how long before we hear from Hyraxus?"

"Not long, I should think. Hopefully, he'll receive the invitation from Mother Wilfrida later today."

"Perhaps we ought to look through those box files while we wait."

After breakfast, they took a box each. Iona's was so crammed with documents that the spring mechanism had broken, and someone had wound twine around the box to keep its contents intact.

Half an hour later, Iona broke the silence. "Listen to this. In 1896 –

that's around one-hundred-and-twenty-seven-years ago in the Primary world – a woman named Adeline Davis, nee Aurelius, held the Watcher title. She had one grown-up son, Arthur Davis. When her husband died, she married a man named Jeremiah Gordon. Arthur describes him here as a rogue and a bounder, who conned his mother into believing he loved her, but he only loved her money. Adeline stupidly confided the secret of the portals to Jeremiah, and although he didn't believe her, it gave him the ammunition he needed to have her committed to a lunatic asylum. He gave its director copies of her portal activity charts as proof of her mad delusions. Jeremiah had already tricked Adeline into signing over the estate to him, bypassing her son. Though Arthur contested the new ownership, his mother's committal put him in an awkward position. Though he knew the truth of her claims, Arthur couldn't prove them, since the menhir wouldn't become active for another twenty years. He didn't admit he shared her beliefs, knowing Jeremiah would also accuse *him* of insanity, declaring him unfit to manage the estate. However, in a change of fortune, the asylum director supported Arthur, declaring Adeline mentally incompetent to dispose of the estate in a rational manner. As a result, the court case went in Arthur's favour, and he regained his inheritance, becoming the new Watcher. The asylum director returned the menhir chart copies to Arthur on request, but Arthur suspected he'd made copies of the copies for his case notes. Jeremiah turned up dead a year later, shot through the head by a person unknown. Wow! You sure have a colourful family background, Shay!"

"A lunatic asylum? Is that like a madhouse?" Shay asked.

"Yes, although by 1896, I believe doctors referred to the inmates as patients and made *some* attempts to treat them."

"A sad tale. I suspect Arthur served the scoundrel his just desserts. Presumably, not with an arrow."

"No, a gun, like those I described to you."

They spent most of the day poring over the documents, fascinated by the menhir charts, which each Watcher updated until, over a centuries-long span, an activation pattern emerged.

Early that evening, Sister Myriax arrived with news.

"The dragon council has received a formal request for assistance from Abbess Wilfrida. She invites their emissaries to present themselves at Glassnesse Abbey, where they will proceed to Saint Aurigan's Priory. You will both be included in this party. The dragon council deliberates on a plan with Hyraxus tonight and will discuss this with you tomorrow morning in the Aerie of the Sun. You must come prepared to leave for Glassnesse immediately afterwards."

Iona and Shay exchanged a surprised glance at the speed of events.

"Get some rest. I'll come for you in the morning," Sister Myriax advised.

As she turned to leave, Iona asked, "Do you know how the Leons fared with their trade proposals?"

"Yes. The first phase of the negotiations proceeded most satisfactorily. The council seems particularly enamoured of the toothpaste, and the proposition to supply books to dragonkind. They will meet again tomorrow afternoon for the second phase."

"I'm glad to hear that," Iona said.

When the dragon-nun departed, Iona remarked, "We'd better get packing. The box files should fit in my trunk."

Shay nodded. "It won't take long. Let's make the most of our last night here." He gazed at the pool through the open bedroom door, regret clouding his eyes.

Though Iona shared the feeling, with the dragons' help, her limbo state might soon end, and the question of whether she could return home resolved once and for all. Skye and their father must have given her up for dead by now, and the thought of their grief hurt. However, no matter what happened, she would never forget this interlude with Shay in these rooms. He had mixed feelings, like her. Though eager to stop Duke Clovis and Borderland in their tracks and rescue the kidnapped villagers, Iona knew he dreaded the answer to *that* question, despite his brave words yesterday.

That night, they made love with frantic urgency, clinging together afterwards as though they would never let go……

Sister Myriax arrived after breakfast, and Shay shouldered his backpack before he picked up Iona's trunk.

A pony trap waited outside the hill entrance, driven by the same fresh-faced monk who had dropped them at the door three nights ago. Alighting from it at the priory, they trailed Sister Myriax through the west door and along a cloister that ran the building's width. A door at the eastern end accessed an abutment containing stairs that spiralled up to a great height. The dragon-nun took Iona's trunk from Shay and glided up the steps as they followed behind. By the time they had climbed halfway, Iona felt nostalgic for the lifts and escalators of her world.

The stairs terminated in a wood-panelled room with half-glass double doors on the outer wall, through which Sister Myriax led them onto a wide balcony and the bridge to the Aerie of the Sun on the eastern hilltop. Iona stared in wonder at the stunning view as they crossed the span, forgetting her aching legs.

Entering the council chamber via another balcony, Iona surmised the Alphas must access it through the huge, semi-circular arch cut into the left wall, beyond which she noticed a cluster of Lacunae reclining on a flat plateau or dragon landing area. However, Iona only observed this incidentally, her attention focused on the four Alphas' flanking Hyraxus. They reposed sphinx-like on shallow stone platforms, shafts of sunlight from the open archway striking glints off their lustrous green scales. Awestruck, and a little intimidated, Iona inched closer to Shay, who squeezed her waist reassuringly.

"The council bids you welcome. However, we will try to keep this consultation brief," Hyraxus said. "Imbolyx, our chief tactician, has questions for you." He nodded to the dragon on his left, whose ridged horns swept back and up to an impressive length.

Iona had a feeling the Leon trade delegation had not dealt with *these* particular councillors.

"We have settled on sending four experienced Lacunae to lend assistance. What other support can you rely on? Do you have fighters, for instance?" Imbolyx asked, moving his head sideways to peer at them from a lambent, green eye.

"William Copeland, Bertrand Leon's nephew-in-law, and leader of the Kentauros villagers' resistance, will place his fighters at our disposal. Their friends and relatives number among the kidnapped, so they have a high stake in this operation's success. I also dare to believe Dareesh Hawksmoor's Zingari sword dancers will join us in a coordinated assault on the Janus Spire," Shay replied confidently, shoulders back and his head held high.

"Zingari sword dancers, eh? Against trained knights and men-at-arms? No contest!" The councillor on Hyraxus' right exclaimed and showed his fangs in a dragonish grin. Iona noted he could do with some of Binny's toothpaste. As if to emphasise her thought, he suddenly belched a cloud of black smoke, and thumping his chest, said, "Pardon me."

Imbolyx made a noise much like a tut and turned back to the two humans. "Very good – if you can persuade the Zingari to take part. Sister Myriax will accompany you in a double role. The abbess' invitation, penned on a messenger bird strip, is only semi-official in the eyes of your lawmakers. As the ambassador from one *Great Wheel* order to another, Sister Myriax will accept a properly stamped and sealed version from Mother Wilfrida's hands, and act as strategy adviser and liaison between your mission leaders and the Lacunae. Do you have any questions?"

Iona held up her hand. "Yes. How will Shay and I travel to Glassnesse?"

Gesturing towards the open arch and the basking Lacunae, Hyraxus answered, "By *transposition*."

He nodded at Sister Myriax, who instructed, "Come, it is time to leave."

Iona took her lead from Shay, who bowed to the council, and with a 'Good luck' from Imbolyx, they followed the dragon-nun through the arch and out onto the plateau. The four Lacunae stood and moved towards a tall, wickerwork receptacle resembling a hot-air balloon basket. Iona looked at Sister Myriax with uncertainty, noting the long drop to the valley floor.

"There is no cause for concern," the nun reassured as two of the Shetland pony-sized dragons, larger than Sister Clothilde's young assistant, stepped forward to take their luggage. They deposited it in the basket, and one returned to stand beside Sister Myriax.

"How do they know where to go? Is the transfer instantaneous? How will it feel?" Iona asked in a nervous scattershot.

The Lacunae beside the nun answered for her in warbling tones, "I am Calixo. At the point of transition, we will arrive at our destination between one breath and the next; too quickly for you to feel anything. You may experience vertigo and see spots in your peripheral vision for a minute afterwards, but nothing more serious. The Lacunae are born with an intimate connection to this world. Just as you *know* every part of your body and use your limbs without thought, the world is our greater 'body'."

"So, when you transfer to any part of this world, you are 'using' that part without conscious thought?" Iona asked, frowning in her attempt to understand.

"More or less; it is the closest analogy I can think of."

Iona wondered if it might be more akin to human dreams, where the subconscious could instantly take the dreamer anywhere.

Sister Myriax gestured to the three Lacunae by the basket. "Karnax, Flix, and Belonyx are ready for you. Calixo will *transpose* me."

The three dragons held straps in their front claws, the other ends attached to the basket at different points. Shay ushered Iona towards it, and boosting her over its lip, jumped in beside her. Hyraxus emerged from the council chamber to see them off, and although not a member of the order, he traced the *Great Wheel* symbol on his forehead.

Calixo and Sister Myriax joined hands. They leaped from the plateau together and vanished.

"Close your eyes," Karnax instructed, and obeying, Iona gasped and gripped Shay's bicep as the Lacunae trio launched into the sky.

Chapter 24

Iona opened her eyes to find the basket had already touched down. The imposing gothic buildings that surrounded them swayed dizzily, and dots like TV static flickered in the corners of her vision. She guessed if she had not closed her eyes during the abrupt change of scenery, the effects might have been worse. Iona shut her lids for a minute, and when she opened them again, the architecture had stopped moving.

They occupied the centre of a courtyard, and as Shay helped her to stand, Iona saw Sister Bedelia slip through a door. Perhaps she had watched for their arrival and gone to fetch the abbess. Shay vaulted from the basket and lifted Iona out. They joined Sister Myriax who stood nearby.

Before long, Mother Wilfrida emerged with Sister Bedelia, who gazed wide-eyed at the Venator in the green bib worn by all dragon members of the Saint Lexis order. Sister Myriax and the abbess both inclined their heads to each other and traced the *Great Wheel* symbol over their hearts.

Mother Wilfrida handed the dragon-nun a rolled scroll, the official invitation that Imbolyx had mentioned. "Welcome to Glassnesse Abbey. It does my heart good to see a *Great Wheel* representative of dragonkind here, at last."

"I am honoured, and grateful for the opportunity to meet the head of another order that shares our creed," Sister Myriax replied, and ceremoniously unrolled the scroll to read the invitation, complete with its formal stamps and seals.

"This courtyard is the oldest part of the abbey, but the order outgrew the rooms abutting it years ago. They are now disused, and no one ever comes here. Due to the nature of your mission, I thought it wise to keep your visit low-profile. I've learned my lesson after Sister Honoria's betrayal. You've heard about that?"

"Yes, Hyraxus briefed me. Perhaps when all this is over, we can plan an open celebration of our solidarity."

"It would be my pleasure!" The abbess gestured at a building on the courtyard's eastern side. "We have prepared accommodation for you and the Lacunae in the old chapter hall over there. I hope it meets with your approval. Feel free to use yonder spring for drinking water." She pointed to a weathered stone basin with an ornamental fountain in its centre by the north wall.

"So, we'll be here for some time, then?" Shay queried.

"Four, maybe five days at most," Mother Wilfrida replied. She waved towards the courtyard's colonnaded western side. "Shall we adjourn to the former refectory? I thought we could use it as our meeting room."

Everyone followed the abbess into the cloister, fronting a long room with double-leaf doors, the entrance wide enough to admit a Venator.

Stepping within, Iona noticed scrape marks on the swept floorboards and guessed them the ghostly imprint of the form benches that once surrounded the long-gone refectory table. "I wonder if Saint Aurigan ate here?" she whispered to Shay. "It feels weird to think of you as his descendent. And they call *me* the *Living Aurigan*!"

"I'm having trouble getting my head around that, myself," he murmured.

A sizeable stone hearth dominated the north wall, with two high-backed, pew-like settles arrayed before it. Unlit candles in metal holders and an earthenware water jug with beakers stood on a table pushed against the western wall, a tub of apples for the omnivorous Lacunae on the floor beside it.

Mother Wilfrida and Sister Bedelia shared one settle, and Iona and Shay the other. Sister Myriax and Calixo settled onto their haunches beside them, with the other three Lacunae disporting themselves beyond.

"I despatched a messenger to Prior Fidelmus immediately after I sent the bird to Saint Lexis Priory. Since Hyraxus implied in his message that you would return swiftly after the receipt of my invitation, I warned Fidelmus to expect your arrival before the week is out. By the time we reach the priory, he will have prepared quarters for the Lacunae in a discreet location," the abbess informed.

"We? Are you coming with us?" Shay asked without surprise.

"Of course. Sister Bedelia and I will both make the journey. It's incumbent upon me as head of the order to be present at an event that might deepen our understanding of Saint Aurigan's founding directives."

"What we have to tell you will do that," Iona remarked.

The abbess shifted on the wooden settle, and folding her hands in her lap, said, "Let's begin with that, shall we?"

Iona straightened the maroon counterpane covering the bed in the room Sister Bedelia had assigned her in the guest wing. The gold-embroidered *Great Wheel* on the coverlet's centre gleamed in the early-morning sunlight refracted through the stained-glass window.

Though fit for a queen, much less the *Living Aurigan*, the chamber felt empty without Shay, who occupied a room down the corridor. Iona had spent the lonely hours' last night tossing and turning, half-hoping he'd risk discovery and sneak into her room. However, he esteemed Mother Wilfrida too much to disrespect her hospitality.

Buckling on her belt, Iona wondered how soon a return message would arrive from Prior Fidelmus. They couldn't *transpose* to the priory until they knew where they must *appear,* besides which, the prior might have news they must heed before they blundered in unprepared.

She couldn't wait to see Binny, Eliza, Fidelmus, and all her other friends, surprised at how much she had missed them. Thinking of Binny reminded her she ran low on the contraceptive powders; perhaps it was just as well she and Shay must sleep apart, for now. Besides, her period had started... at least she carried a good supply of Binny's pads.

Iona pulled on her boots, musing on Mother Wilfrida's reaction to the account of their discoveries. She had thanked them for their honesty and said she now had an enhanced understanding of Saint Aurigan's mandate for the order. However, she remained uncertain if the portal secret had become lost or deliberately hidden by one of her predecessors to better protect the knowledge. Iona smiled at the memory of the abbess' face when she learned of Shay's relation to her saint. She had never seen Mother Wilfrida flustered before, torn between genuflecting to him or allowing her good sense to prevail – thankfully, she had chosen the latter – much to Shay's relief.

As Iona stepped from the room, she saw Shay sauntering down the corridor towards her and waited for him.

Pulling her against him, Shay murmured, "I missed you so much last night. It took all my willpower to not come to you."

"Me too. I guess our stay at Saint Lexis Priory spoiled us. Perhaps we can take a little stroll to a secluded spot later for a cuddle," Iona suggested coquettishly, peering at him beneath her lashes.

Shay sighed with regret and shook his head. "Though the abbess hasn't forbidden us from wandering around, I think she'd prefer it if we kept a low profile. Apart from a handful of dockers, few know we left for the dragon lands with the Leons, but our sudden appearance here might raise a few eyebrows, especially since we have no mounts in the stables."

"Although no one saw us arrive, maybe they'll assume someone dropped us off, or we came here on foot," Iona conjectured and, hearing a door open down the corridor, pulled away from Shay.

They breakfasted alone in the abbess' private dining room, a chamber she used rarely, preferring to take her meals in the refectory with the other nuns. Sister Bedelia waylaid them as they left and asked them to come with her to the abbess' office.

Taking the proffered chairs before her desk, Iona and Shay waited for her to speak.

"After your revelations yesterday, I feel an urgency to set out for Saint Aurigan's Priory today and confer with Prior Fidelmus before your arrival. It will take me a day and a half to journey there, and I'd rather not arrive too long after you, which will be the case if I wait for Fidelmus' message. On receipt of that communication, you can follow with Sister Myriax and the Lacunae. It's a shame the situation prevents me from openly presenting the sister to the brotherhood with all the pomp and circumstance her advent demands." Mother Wilfrida sighed.

"If you wait for the messenger, perhaps the Lacunae could *transpose* you and Sister Bedelia there first, then come back for us? You might still get there quicker than you will if you leave today via the road," Iona proposed.

The abbess suppressed a shudder at the thought, and Sister Bedelia interjected, "Sadly, that won't work. The Mother Superior travels everywhere in her official coach. Too many questions will be asked if she simply disappears, with the conveyance still inside the coach house. It is much better for our purposes if she is witnessed leaving on a formal inspection of the priory under her auspices. They are due a visit, anyway."

"It's all in hand. Mayhap I'll pass the messenger on the road. Sister Bedelia will remain here to companion Sister Myriax and will follow on later. I must go and pay my respects to her now before I leave. Incidentally, due to the dangers of falling masonry, I have decreed the old courtyard and adjacent structures out of bounds until remedial work is carried out," the abbess informed as she stood to leave.

"They looked in pretty good nick to me!" Iona smiled wryly. "I guess the *Great Wheel* teachings permit a little white lie in the cause of the greater good."

Mother Wilfrida regarded Iona serenely. "Well, they *could* do with a revamp. Let Sister Bedelia know if you wish to call on the dragons; I'm sure they'd appreciate it."

At mid-morning two days later, Iona and Shay chatted with the Lacunae in the courtyard. Less intimidating than the Alphas, and not just because of their smaller size, Iona found the Lacunae friendly and curious, their fearless and laidback attitude perhaps not surprising considering they could disappear at will. She thought their trilling, bird-like voices beyond cute, but kept it to herself.

Calixo appeared to be their leader and had just told them Belonyx and Flix (the lone female) were siblings from the same clutch when Sister Bedelia burst through the door in the southern building, formerly a workroom.

She waved a sheet of parchment and cried, "Prior Fidelmus' message, at last!"

Iona and Shay crowded around her as Sister Myriax emerged from the old chapter house.

"It says here they've made provision for their *guests* in the old tithe barn at the edge of the priory farm. An enclosed yard fronts it, plenty big enough for the dragons to set down in," Shay said.

Fidelmus had provided a rough sketch of its location in relation to the priory, which Sister Bedelia handed to Calixo.

The Lacunae closed his eyes. "Yes, I can see it," he advised enigmatically and opened his lids, handing the sketch to Karnax, who did the same before passing it on to the others.

"Fidelmus says your Zingari clan is encamped beside the path that leads down to the covered bridge over the river," Iona noted, reading over the nun's shoulder.

"Good; that's close to the priory," Shay replied. "He also writes that Duke Clovis hasn't bothered the monks since he told him you preferred to live with the sisterhood at Glassnesse Abbey and won't be returning. I wonder though... did Honoria tell him about your real situation? Assuming she's part of the conspiracy..." Shay mused.

"The prior concludes by saying he has sent an alert to Will Copeland, whom the duke has declared an outlaw. He believes he'll have no difficulty smuggling him into the priory for meetings. Meanwhile, Fidelmus has two monks taking it in turns to watch for your arrival at the tithe barn," Sister Bedelia informed Sister Myriax as she folded the message. "I'll make preparations to depart for the priory as soon as you all leave."

"Why not come with us? There is room in the basket for one more, and someone as slender as you cannot weigh much," Sister Myriax invited.

Sister Bedelia glanced at Iona and Shay, who nodded in agreement. She gave a sudden grin. "Alright! We'd better get our things then, and leave straight after. As Mother Wilfrida's spymistress, the nuns are used to my sudden disappearances!"

As Shay helped her and Sister Bedelia from the basket, Iona saw a familiar figure approach.

"Quintus!" she exclaimed, forgetting to address him by his 'brother' appellation.

Shay stood back stiffly as they embraced, and Iona recalled the tension that had existed between the two men over the dangerous nature of the Janus Spire mission Shay had allowed her to take part in – despite Quintus' fears for her safety.

Pulling away, Quintus bowed to Sister Myriax, unfazed by her presence. "The abbess arrived last eve. She and the prior have decided to make your visit here known to all in the priory, although the Lacunae must stay hidden, for now," he said with an apologetic glance at the smaller dragons.

"We understand," Calixo replied, and signalling to the other Lacunae, they unloaded the luggage and carried the basket into the tithe barn, where they remained out of sight.

Sister Myriax nodded. "That makes sense. As the representative of an order affiliated with yours, and invited here by the abbess to renew and celebrate our ties, any comings and goings from my quarters," she gestured at the tithe barn, "will arouse no suspicion."

Brother Quintus smiled at the dragon-nun and turned to Shay. "Your position here is compromised since Duke Clovis declared you an outlaw along with Will Copeland. The prior offers you two choices. The tithe barn will become the site of our confidential meetings, and you can either remain hidden here with the Lacunae or apply for Sanctuary. If you choose the latter, you will have the freedom of the abbey, but cannot leave its grounds until we make our move."

Iona detected no malice in Quintus' tone, but was that a flash of satisfaction in his green eyes?

Shay stood with his shoulders back, thumbs hooked into his sword belt. He stared expressionlessly at the monk, but a muscle jumped in his jaw. "As the ranger here, I'm aware the abbey limits extend to the end of the footpath beyond the bridge, where the path meets the main road. That is sufficient for my purposes, therefore I'll accept Sanctuary."

Iona remembered the Zingari had encamped beside that footpath, hidden from the road behind the hill.

"How will the prior explain our sudden arrival, unnoticed by anyone?" Shay asked.

Quintus pointed to the stables abutting the enclosure's south wall. "Four saddled horses await within. One is mine, and the other three are for you, Iona, and Sister Bedelia. The Abbess has already proclaimed Sister Myriax's imminent arrival. The story is, Sister Bedelia and the *Living Aurigan* are Sister Myriax's assigned assistants. *You* still work for the order, but are now based in Glassnesse Abbey. You escorted Iona and Sister Bedelia from Zephyrinus, travelling here on horseback. However, because of your 'wanted' status in Kentauros, the three of you crossed the river at Dumatha to approach this location via the northeastern back roads, thus avoiding the highway. On arrival, you waited here for Sister Myriax to fly in from Glassnesse during the night, reducing the chance of any uninformed citizens spotting her." Quintus reached into his belt pouch to withdraw a small scroll. Handing it to Shay, he explained, "Prior Fidelmus anticipated you would choose Sanctuary. This is your copy of his *Sanctuary Grant Declaration*."

"I detect Mother Wilfrida's devious mind behind *that* story!" Iona said wryly.

"She and the prior cooked it up between them. Fidelmus is no slouch at concocting a fiendish plot, when necessary! I'll ride ahead to inform them of your arrival. Give me half an hour before you depart, so they can arrange a suitable reception committee," Quintus advised.

"Who else knows the real reason we are here?" Shay asked.

"The three senior scriptorium monks – Brother Ambrose, Brother Oisin, and Brother Anselm. Plus, Brother Florian, the infirmary head. Binny and her husband, Joss, also know."

"Not the head librarian, Brother Ennis?"

Quintus shook his head. "Not at this time. The others have known since the abbess warned Fidelmus of your impending return. However, although he trusts Ennis, others don't, including me. On my return from visiting Glassnesse Abbey, I related the tale Mother Wilfrida told us about Honoria's midnight visits to the library, witnessed by Sister Bedelia when both nuns stayed here. The prior put a discreet watch on Ennis as the abbess instructed, but he's done nothing untoward. Still, that proves nothing. Fidelmus is exercising caution by keeping Ennis in the dark, for now."

"Good. One more question before you go. Where do our mounts come from?" Shay jerked his head towards the stables.

"Mine belongs to the priory. Don't worry, no one will recognise the others; we hired them from a livery yard."

After Quintus rode out, Shay turned to Sister Myriax. "I doubt these horses are accustomed to dragons, unlike those that pulled the wagons to Saint Lexis. It might be best if you stay downwind when we travel to the priory."

Sister Myriax sniffed the air. "I'll fly behind you, so they can't see me."

The dragon-nun removed herself behind the barn when the time came to depart. Shay strapped Iona's trunk onto a docile-looking mare and led her from the stables. He held the reins while Iona rubbed her nose. "It's been a long time since I rode a horse. I'm glad I'm wearing breeches at any rate."

"You've no cause to feel nervous. I'll take the lead, and Bedelia the rear. We haven't far to ride, less than two miles, and your mare will follow her stablemate with little direction from you."

Sister Bedelia already sat confidently astride her horse, her habit tucked around her legs, holding the reins of Shay's mount in one hand. Shay boosted Iona into the saddle and passed her the reins before he leaped onto his horse.

As they set off, Iona's reflexes took over, ingrained through her teenage riding lessons. She surmised that, like riding a bike, one never forgot the technique once learned. Sister Myriax flew at a safe distance behind them, gliding rather than flapping to create less air disturbance.

They rode down the narrow farm lanes towards the river path without seeing a soul, and drawing level with the covered bridge, turned up the track connecting it with the priory. As they neared the long infirmary building that paralleled the track, jutting from the priory façade at a right angle, Iona observed the two columns of people flanking the path to each side of the entrance steps. Mother Wilfrida and Prior Fidelmus stood foremost amongst the group that awaited them in the entryway, the double doors behind them flung wide open.

Shay raised his hand in the halt signal, and Iona tugged on her reins. He vaulted from his mount and caught Iona as she slid awkwardly from the saddle before turning to help Sister Bedelia dismount. Three stableboys came running to lead the horses away, and Sister Myriax closed the distance between them, settling on the ground between Iona and Bedelia as they had arranged.

With Shay in the lead acting as herald, and the others walking three abreast behind him, they processed down the path to the steps. Unsure where to look, Iona kept her eyes fixed on Fidelmus who, catching her gaze, smiled at her like a proud father.

As Shay made the formal introductions, Iona spotted Binny and Joss near the head of the column on her right, an awestruck Eliza peeking wide-eyed at the dragon from the shelter of her father's arm.

With the formalities complete, Sister Myriax turned to the crowd and, sketching the *Great Wheel* symbol over her heart, bowed to each column as the musician monks led by Brother Riordan struck up a joyful tune.

Iona's glance fell on a cluster of acolytes, amongst whom she clocked Dara and Tynan, the talented boy training to become an illuminator. Tynan gave her one of his irrepressible grins, and she knew that, like her, he recalled the day she had gifted him with the dragon illumination she had painted in Brother Oisin's masterclass. Her subject choice now seemed prophetic.

Brother Quintus raised a golden sceptre mounted with the *Great Wheel* Ouroboros symbol, and the group in the entryway parted as Sister Myriax climbed the steps and followed him through the doorway, trailed by Sister Bedelia. Before Iona could do likewise, she heard a high-pitched voice cry, "Iona! Iona!" and she turned to see Eliza break away from Joss. Eliza flung herself into Iona's arms, and as Iona hugged the little girl, Binny hurried over to retrieve her, glancing up at the abbess, whose frown at the impropriety suddenly changed to a smile.

Iona included Binny in the hug. "I have so much to tell you!"

"You still have your old room. I'll come and see you this evening."

Chapter 25

Iona stood outside the door of the *Living Aurigan's* room and turned to survey the deserted square in the pre-sunset light.

Unlike the God-worshippers, *Great Wheel* adherents didn't pray, but they meditated and performed chants and rituals similar to some religions in Iona's world. After hosting Sister Myriax in the chapter house, Mother Wilfrida and Prior Fidelmus led the gathered monks to the chapel for celebratory rites in honour of Saint Lexis, the patron saint of Sister Myriax's order. At this point, Iona had slipped away, eager to freshen up before Binny arrived. Shay had disappeared to the Zingari encampment an hour earlier; he had a lot to discuss with Dareesh, the step-brother who was also his cousin. She doubted she would see him until the morning.

Iona glanced towards the bench outside his room at the cloister's end. The first time she had set eyes on him, he had sat there oiling his sword. Lifting her gaze to the library, Iona observed Thomasine, the cat, sitting on a windowsill, peering at her from behind the glass. Brother Ennis, currently attending the rites in the chapel, had avoided her in the chapter house during the reception. However, the other monks' response to her return had warmed her, Iona's friends from the scriptorium hoping she had come back to stay. A moist-eyed Prior Fidelmus had embraced her, and resting her head on his shoulder, Iona had blinked tears from her eyes as he patted her back.

Clutching the room key Fidelmus had returned to her, Iona regarded the square a final time, struck by the impossible feeling she had come home.

Iona found the door unlocked, and the heady scent of roses, underscored by beeswax and lemon, tickled her nostrils as she entered the room. Iona wondered if Quintus had left the blooms arranged in a vase on the table, but the spotless surfaces must be Binny's work. She slipped behind the screen and saw someone had deposited her trunk beside the freshly made bed. A cauldron of water kept warm over the small, part-banked fire, enough for a stand-up wash. Clean towels and underwear lay on the bed, and Binny had replenished her toilette supplies.

Iona opened the armoire doors and fingered the red and gold banquet gown that hung there with her spring-green and blue kirtles. It almost felt like she had never been away. She removed the maroon robe and laid it on the bed before pouring warm water into the basin for her ablutions.

Washed, and dressed in the robe, she lifted her Zingari outfit, Jake's jerkin, and the lavender and emerald-green kirtles from the trunk, marvelling at the number of clothes she had accumulated in her short time here. *Hmm, it's been a month, at least, since my entrapment. My awareness is now so heightened, and the experiences I've had so intense, that it feels much longer*, Iona mused as she shoved her washing into a laundry sack.

Though dinnertime had passed, Iona felt no hunger, having eaten at the reception, the food miraculously provided by the priory cooks at short notice. A knock at the door heralded Binny, who arrived with a wine carafe and two goblets.

They sat at the table and, as Binny poured the wine, she asked, "How are you, Iona?"

"I'm fine, physically. Mentally? I don't know…"

"Quintus told me you and Shay… I wasn't surprised; I knew how you felt about each other."

"Do you believe in fate?"

Binny sipped her wine and stared at Iona over the goblet rim. "My old, research chemist self would have said no. But now…" she shrugged, "I feel Joss and I were meant to be together."

"I feel the same about Shay, but it's more than that. I wonder if there's such a thing as fated friends. It's just… I've only known the people I care about here a short time, but it seems like I've known you all for ages. Why do I feel like I belong here, yet my mind rebels against the very idea?"

"Only you can answer that. Fidelmus told me a little of your adventures, but I'd like to hear the full story from you."

When Iona had told her everything, Binny leaned across the table to grip Iona's hand. "I'm sorry for you and Shay, but do you really believe there's a chance of returning home?"

"I don't know, and I'm no longer sure what I'll do if presented with it."

"I *have* theorised what *I* might do if you found a way for us to return, and though I've no desire to go back, part of me felt it would be selfish to deny Eliza the opportunities unavailable to women here. But now I know the consequences of taking Eliza and Joss to our world…"

"I don't think you need to worry about Eliza's future. If Bertrand pulls off this trade deal with the dragons, in which your toothpaste and wing liniments play a large part, he'll help you scale up production. You'll become a very rich woman in a position to give Eliza a life independent of the social norms here. I can even see her and Alicia doing future business together!" Iona chuckled. "Changing the subject, will you be at the meeting in the tithe barn tomorrow afternoon?"

"Yes. Fidelmus said I have a right to be involved in this, considering my origin. Joss wants to come too, but someone needs to stay at home to mind Eliza. I'd normally leave her with Fidelmus or Brother Ambrose, but they'll also be at the meeting."

Iona nodded. "Good, I'm glad you're coming. So, do you have any news or gossip for me?"

"Nothing exciting… Oh, I forgot, Dara has asked if he can apprentice to Joss and learn beekeeping and chandlery. He's doing well and is much happier under Brother Quintus, but he wants a family life. A monk's existence is not for him. However, his parents apprenticed him to the priory, as they couldn't afford to feed and clothe him."

"So, there's no hope for him?"

"There's always hope." Binny gave a determined smile. "Since Joss is the priory beekeeper and candlemaker, it could be argued that Dara will still work for the order, just in a different role. If my product lines take off as I expect, we'll need the apprentice Fidelmus promised me. Quintus told him he's happy to allow Dara to split his time between him and Joss until the boy is older. Although, I've a feeling Quintus won't stay with us much longer…"

"Me too," Iona replied.

Binny polished off the wine in her goblet. "I'd better be off. I promised Quintus I'd help out with Mother Wilfrida. She and Sister Bedelia are staying in the rooms on each side of yours. I'll see you at the meeting tomorrow."

Shay knocked on Iona's door after breakfast the next morning.

They sought privacy in the garden behind their cloister rooms and perched on the bench where they'd sat together once before. Their closeness now couldn't be farther than their animosity then.

"What will happen when the duke learns you've returned to the priory?" Iona asked with a touch of anxiety.

Shay shrugged. "There isn't anything he *can* do. He can't touch me while I'm protected by Sanctuary law. Not unless I leave the priory environs. However, I expect *that* won't prevent him from trying. Hopefully, we'll have made our move before he discovers I'm here."

"Did you tell Dareesh everything?"

"Yes. I spoke to him and the Madjia together."

"Will he help us?"

Shay nodded. "I believe he feels he owes it to me for not contesting his leadership of the clan, despite my prior claim. Besides, the Zingari honour Saint Aurigan…"

"And the clan who aids his descendent will earn honour in return?"

"Something like that, but more importantly, the Madjia told Dareesh, in no uncertain terms, that he *must* help. As you know, the clan is camped near the footpath that runs along the hill's flank down to the bridge. The menhir stone is just a few yards along the main road from the hill face, beneath the castle hill on the other side. From the moment they settled so close to the menhir, the Madjia had trouble accessing the *tapestry*, and disturbing visions have assailed her. She refuses to share them, but prophesied harmful consequences for this world's people if the 'interference' is allowed to continue."

Iona shivered and blocked the image of her friends dispersing particle by particle.

"To be honest, I think Dareesh welcomes the opportunity to test his sword dancers in a real fight – it's been a long time... He'll come to the meeting this afternoon," Shay confirmed.

The garden gate opened, and Sister Bedelia appeared at the entrance. "We're leaving now, Iona," she called out.

Iona and Shay stood, and the sister politely averted her eyes when they embraced. As one of Sister Myriax's appointed 'handmaidens', Iona must leave early for the tithe barn, travelling with Mother Wilfrida and Bedelia in the abbess' official coach.

Benches ringed a cleared space in the barn's centre, with the Lacunae sleeping stalls beyond.

Mother Wilfrida stood flanked by Sister Myriax and Calixo near the back of this circle, while Sister Bedelia and Iona waited together by the door. Iona nervously smoothed down a fold of her blue kirtle. She could hardly believe her nebulous idea involving the Lacunae had led to this.

Binny arrived first with Brother Quintus, quickly followed by Prior Fidelmus, Brother Ambrose, and Brother Florian, the infirmarian. Shay turned up next, accompanied by Dareesh, and their similarity struck Iona anew, only this time she knew why Shay resembled the Zingari.

Everyone took a bench while they awaited the arrival of Will Copeland and his second in command, a man named Royston Hamm, a former miller turned outlaw.

Dareesh gazed at the dragons in fascination. Myriax and Calixo sat on their haunches at each side of the bench occupied by the abbess and Sister Bedelia, the other three Lacunae lounging beside the carrier basket at the barn's rear. Iona had grown used to them, but Dareesh's wonderment recalled her own.

They didn't have long to wait before Brother Kian, the mute bathhouse supervisor, ushered two men through the door. Though Iona had not known about the large monk's involvement in their conspiracy, she felt no surprise. Tynan had confided to her that the man who led the village raiding parties, Sir Norris, the duke's master-at-arms, was responsible for the loss of Brother Kian's tongue. The mute monk slipped back out the door, presumably to remain on guard outside.

Bertrand's nephew-in-law, Will Copeland, warily surveyed the gathered conspirators, but seeing no one whom he didn't expect to be there, he visibly relaxed. Bowing to the abbess, he stared with open curiosity at the dragons as he took a bench near the door, Royston Hamm joining him.

Will, a former blacksmith, had shaggy blonde hair and brawny arms corded with muscle. He nodded to Shay and Iona, who wouldn't have escaped from the Janus Spire without the aid of his resistance fighters, and turned to Fidelmus. "You stated in your message that the dragon council has sent us help to storm the Spire. I'd like to know why they're involving themselves in human affairs."

Sister Myriax stepped forward. "I will answer that, if I may?"

Prior Fidelmus nodded his assent, and with help from Iona and Shay, the dragon-nun explained to him and Royston what everyone else at the meeting already knew, and why the trike operation posed a threat to all citizens of the Secondary world.

"Do you think the villains are using my Clare and the other kidnapped villagers for some nefarious purpose?" Will asked, a hand tight-fisted on his knee.

Sister Myriax resumed her former position as Fidelmus answered. "We don't know for sure, but that's the implication."

Will glanced at Royston, who nodded. "You can count on us and our fighters. I heard the duke doubled the tower guard after Shay's incursion, but our ranks have swelled since then. However, the castle's main gates are now manned, and locked to those who can't produce a pass."

Dareesh spoke up. "I've been thinking about that. Duke Clovis has asked us to dance for his court again tomorrow evening. I have a pass for my troupe that includes a permit to park our wagons in the side court. The set begins, as usual, with a performance by the female dancers, before the men join in. Whilst the women entertain the duke, the sword dancers will gather in the foyer behind the main doors, ready to make our dramatic entrance into the grand hall to partner with the women. It should be easy enough for half to slip out the door and overwhelm the gate guards, leaving the other half to deal with any resistance in the hall. We'll open the gates to your men and join you in subduing the tower guards. Our women are more than capable of keeping watch over the assembly tied-up in the hall."

Will smiled in a predatory manner. "Now, *that* sounds like a plan!"

"Can your people be ready at such short notice?" Shay asked him.

"Oh, yes! We started preparing as soon as I received the Prior's first message."

"What about the Lacunae?" Iona queried.

Shay leaned forward, elbows on knees. Iona noticed he held his mother's festival bracelet between his hands. "The Lacunae must stay hidden until we've flushed the guards from the tower. More guards might lurk behind the metal walls we need to penetrate, but we'll deal with that as it comes. Perhaps we can send a signal when it's time for the Lacunae to join us. They could wait concealed on the covered bridge; there won't be any traffic on it at that time of day. If Quintus watches for the signal from the path head near the road, he can return to the bridge to inform the Lacunae. We'll have to decide on a signal, though."

"Oh, that's easy! I have some of Uncle Bertrand's firecrackers. I could ignite one of those shooting star illuminations from the curtain wall abutting the Janus Spire. Quintus won't have a problem seeing *that* from his position!" Will said with a grin.

"I can fight too!" Quintus protested, and Iona recalled Isobel telling her that Quintus had enlisted with a mercenary band before he joined the order.

Fidelmus stared at him askance, but Quintus held his gaze. "I *want* to do this. It's time I stopped hiding here."

The prior sighed and nodded. Iona sensed he had known this day would come.

"I'll do it!" Binny piped up. When everyone turned to stare at her, she shrugged. "*I'll* watch for the signal. I'm not letting Iona have all the fun!" She winked at her friend.

Iona chuckled. "Where will I be positioned? And Shay?"

"I'll join Will's people for the initial assault. Quintus, too, if he insists on fighting," Shay replied.

Quintus gave a curt nod.

"Iona can travel with me, and stay hidden in my wagon until Will sends up the signal," Dareesh suggested and smiled at Iona. "We'll disguise you as a dancer, just in case the gate guards check inside. You'll pass muster with that black hair if no one looks too closely."

"She'll be safer on the bridge with the Lacunae. They can *transpose* her to us when the time comes to access the areas behind the metal walls," Shay countered.

Calixo stood. "Karnax and I transposed to the hillside above the menhir late last night when humans lay sleeping. We wanted to assess the Janus Spire with our own eyes. The closer we drew to the tower, the more we sensed a strange eroding of our abilities. It did not prevent us from transposing back here, but it left us unnaturally weak in a way we have never felt before. We feel fine now. However, transposing with a passenger near to the interference field will deplete our energies – energies we must preserve to carry you through the barriers close to the source of the abnormality."

Shay's brow furrowed with concern. "Can you still do it?"

"Yes. If we fly to the tower instead of transposing, we should have energy enough to each transpose a person behind the metal walls and bring them back, if necessary. Though closer to the interference, the transposition distance is negligible – a journey from one side of a wall to the other. However, we are uncertain if we can make that journey twice. This is something totally out of our experience. We must physically carry you, since we cannot use the basket in such close confines. Though we always *see* our target, making the transition inside an unfamiliar building might pose a problem as the structure will overlay our *earth sight*. It would help us all if we knew *where* to materialise behind the walls."

"If I'm not mistaken, we hold architectural floor plans of the castle in our library. They're bound to include the Janus Spire's layout. Assuming the villains haven't altered it too much, the plans might prove useful," Brother Ambrose suggested to nods from Shay and Calixo.

"It appears Hyraxus' concerns are well-founded. This 'interference' to Lacunae abilities is without precedent," Sister Myriax remarked sombrely.

Iona twisted her fingers together in anxiety. "What the hell are they *doing* in that tower?" She glanced at Dareesh. "It looks like I'll be travelling with you, after all."

Chapter 26

Leaving Shay and Quintus to discuss strategy with Dareesh, Will, and Royston, Iona returned to the priory with the others.

Mother Wilfrida had arranged an after-dinner internal synod in the chapter house to discuss the comparative similarities and differences between the Saint Aurigan and Saint Lexis *Great Wheel* teachings and practises. She and Sister Myriax would both preside, and expected all the monks to attend. Despite the Janus Spire mission's unexpectedly near imminence, she could hardly cancel the synod without raising suspicions.

With Shay and Quintus planning to depart that evening for the villagers' resistance hideout, Iona had volunteered to locate the castle plans in the library.

Binny rode back in the abbess' coach, and they dropped her off at her riverside home.

When the coach pulled up before the priory doors, Iona went straight to the square that housed both the library and her cloister room.

She glanced towards Brother Vincent's desk as she entered the library foyer, hoping he might still be around in case she required help to find the plans. However, his chair stood empty, though Thomasine, the cat, sat on the desk, washing her face with great concentration.

Iona wended her way through the stacks, making for the section that contained the maps on the assumption it seemed the likeliest place to find other large charts and drawings. She had a rough idea of where to go, having visited the map area once before. Though she took a couple of wrong turns in the labyrinth of shelving, she found it at last.

Iona riffled through the charts that hung suspended from rows of hinged rods, but discovered nothing except maps, some detailed, others large in scale. She turned to the tall plan chests arrayed against the wall behind and opened drawers at random. Silence reigned heavily in the building, and she guessed the librarians, including Cahir, Dara's replacement, whom she'd yet to meet, dined in the refectory before attending the synod.

She flicked through a stack of navigation charts and tide tables before closing the drawer and moving on to the next. Iona searched methodically until she found what she sought in the third cabinet. Beneath a pile of ancient schematics for the priory, the parchment brown with age, lay five vellum sheets covered with drawings of the castle at different elevations, the Janus Spire on a separate sheet. Not wishing to orphan it from the others, Iona pulled out all five sheets and, placing them atop the plan chest, rolled them up together for easy transportation.

A sudden footfall behind her sounded loud in the oppressive silence, but before she had time to turn around, a hand clamped over her mouth, a maroon habit sleeve draping over her chest. Another arm snaked around her waist, pinning her arm to her side, and the plans fell to the floor. *"Ennis!"* Iona thought as she beat futilely at his arms with her free hand. She struggled to break loose as he dragged her backwards until, releasing his hold on her midriff, he pressed a dagger against her lower spine.

He hauled her unresisting through the stacks, her back against his chest. Emerging into the clear space near the loans desk, he retreated towards the foyer when the office door behind the desk opened. In sudden confusion, Iona observed Brother Ennis stride forth, carrying a heavy tome. He stopped in his tracks and, outraged, demanded, "What is the meaning of this? Release the *Eterna* at once!"

Caught in the act, Iona's assailant moved his hand from her mouth to her neck. "He's got a knife!" she croaked.

Ennis took two steps forward, and her captor stepped back, dragging her with him. "Come any nearer, and I'll stick it in her!"

The nasal voice sounded familiar, but too stressed to place it, Iona concentrated on drawing breath because the man had shifted his grip on her neck into a chokehold. He continued to back towards the door, and she stared at Ennis with desperate eyes.

"Brother Vincent, this is madness! I order you to let her go!" Ennis commanded.

"Go to hell!" Vincent retorted.

Brother Vincent?! But... but he's a cat lover! Iona thought absurdly, as if that precluded him from villainy. And then a fleeting remembrance chased it – *On the other hand, Hitler liked dogs*.

As though Iona's incongruous musing had conjured her, she suddenly felt Thomasine's tail flick her leg as she wound around her to rub against the back of Vincent's calves. The monk, still inching back, tripped over the cat, who yowled indignantly and streaked away into the stacks.

Vincent tumbled backwards, pulling Iona with him, instinctively thrusting his knife hand behind him to break his fall. Iona landed half on top of him, and Ennis was suddenly there. Lifting his heavy tome, he brought it down on Vincent's head. The grip on Iona's neck loosened, and she rolled away as the head librarian gave her attacker another whack. Iona struggled to her feet as Ennis stooped to bash Vincent again. However, the half-stunned monk raised his knife and thrust it into the head librarian's shoulder.

Ennis staggered back, dropping the book, the dagger embedded almost to the hilt beneath his collarbone. Vincent turned over onto his hands and knees, but before he could rise, Iona drew her foot back and booted him in the backside. He face-planted onto the floor and, snatching up the fallen book, Iona finished what Ennis had started. When Vincent lay still, she let fall the tome and knelt before the head librarian, who had sunk to his knees.

Blood leaked around the blade, but Iona envisioned a torrent gushing from the wound if she pulled it out. Feeling helpless, she bit her lip. "I'm afraid to remove the knife in case it's pierced an artery or something."

A grey-faced Ennis nodded, but before he could reply, they heard running footsteps, and Cahir appeared from the foyer, calling out to the librarians, "The prior says you must hurry; the synod is about to start and…" the acolyte skidded to a halt, registering the tableaux with an expression of open-mouthed horror.

"Brother Vincent attacked us. You must fetch Brother Florian, but do it discreetly. Make sure he has his medical kit," Iona instructed with a calmness she didn't feel. Glancing at Vincent, she appended, "We'll need two litters with bearers, and a strong arm to restrain Vincent in case he comes around. Go now! Hurry!"

Cahir took to his heels, and as the sound of his footsteps faded, Ennis whispered, "That volume… is the only copy of…" he swallowed, "Brullio's *'Gamino Rexus'* in… existence."

Iona glanced at the battered tome; its spine broken. "I'm sorry. Is it very important?"

"Some th-think so. It's pr-pr-pretentious tr-tripe, if you ask me."

"Well, at least it proved good for something. The quill is mightier than the sword," Iona paraphrased Bulwer-Lytton inanely, believing it best to keep Ennis talking.

Brother Ennis gave a rictus grin; the first time Iona had ever seen him smile. "M-must w-write that d-down." His eyes rolled back in his head and he toppled forward.

Iona caught him around the biceps and, trying not to jog the knife, manoeuvred Ennis onto his back with great difficulty. *Don't die on me,* she thought, sorry for her former suspicions. She glanced at Vincent, still out cold, knowing *he* must be the person Honoria had secretly met in the library.

As she wiped her blood-smeared hands on her handkerchief, Iona heard the patter of running feet. She sighed with relief when Brother Florian hurried towards them, followed by four infirmary assistants bearing two litters. Iona backed away to give Florian room as he knelt to examine Ennis.

"The knife doesn't appear to have pierced anything vital, but the wound is deep. I must treat him here in situ to prevent further injury," Florian declared and sent a litter bearer to fetch hot water and clean cloths. As one of those trained by former triker, Doctor Dennis Cleary, he knew the importance of hygiene in treating wounds.

With the knife removed, Brother Ennis swam in and out of consciousness as Brother Florian stitched him up and bound his shoulder. The infirmarian only turned to scrutinise Brother Vincent once the assistants transferred Ennis to a litter. "This one has a concussion and must join Brother Ennis in the infirmary. At least we don't need to tie him to the litter to stop him from escaping."

The assistants rolled Vincent onto the other litter, and taking up their burdens, carried the two librarians to the door just as Shay and Quintus burst through with Cahir, sent by Fidelmus to fetch them. However, they'd already started back for the priory to collect their gear, leaving Will and Royston in the tithe barn to await their return. Cahir, riding fast, had met them near the bridge.

Shay jogged to Iona and hugged her tight. "Are you alright? Vincent didn't hurt you?" he asked anxiously, noticing the bloodstains on her kirtle bodice.

"I'm fine! None of this blood is mine. It's all from Brother Ennis. We were wrong about him, Shay. He saved me! Him and Thomasine."

Ennis stirred on the litter, his eyes fluttering open, and he beckoned weakly to Cahir, who rushed to his side. "Thomasine... make sure..." he gasped, unable to finish.

Iona stepped to his side. "I'll look for her now and check she's unharmed."

The head librarian nodded and closed his eyes.

With the synod in session, and Fidelmus unable to leave without causing a stir, Quintus took charge and sent Brother Kian to the infirmary to stand guard over Vincent.

"Did you find the castle plans?" Shay asked Iona.

"Yes, but I dropped them in the struggle with Vincent. I'll go fetch them."

Shay followed Iona into the stacks, both keeping an eye out for the cat.

"I thought Ennis didn't like Thomasine! Perhaps he doesn't want the bother of interviewing a new mouser!" Iona joked.

"He has a responsibility towards *all* members of his team." Shay shrugged. "With everyone at the synod, Vincent probably couldn't believe his luck when he found you here alone. If Ennis hadn't been running late, this second attempt to kidnap you might have succeeded."

Iona heaved a huge sigh. "First Honoria, now Vincent..."

Coming to the map section, Iona retrieved the plans and handed them to Shay.

"I'll go over these with Calixo before leaving with Will."

They resumed the hunt for Thomasine, finally locating her perched atop a scroll rack. Shay lifted her down and passed her to Iona, who buried her face in the cat's fur, kissing the top of her head. Thomasine appeared unhurt and welcomed the attention, allowing Iona to carry her back to the loans desk. Since the acolytes had no obligation to attend the synod, Quintus had left Cahir in charge of the library. Iona placed Thomasine in his arms and followed Shay out the door.

It took Iona a moment to recognise Quintus, who appeared from the quadrangle archway. He had replaced his habit with clothing not dissimilar to Shay's, a sword strapped at his waist. She tried not to stare; he looked so different, so… himself? Iona couldn't think of a more accurate word.

While Shay fetched his gear, Iona stood with Quintus. "So, you are really going to do this," it wasn't a question. "Are you sure you're doing the right thing?"

Quintus' cheeks dimpled in the smile she loved. "Yes, *you've* made me sure."

"Me?" Iona cocked her head, but then realised she didn't need to ask what he meant. She suddenly knew his feelings for her had made him grasp he was over and done with Iseult and the events of his past. Iona returned his smile; he'd make the right woman very happy.

Shay returned quickly with his weapons; the castle plans thrust through the straps of his backpack. Quintus moved discreetly away to give them privacy. Taking both of Iona's hands in his, Shay said, "I trust Dareesh to keep you safe, but don't take any risks, Iona." Moving a hand to the back of his waistband, he produced a sheathed knife and held it out to her, hilt first. "Take this."

Iona hesitated, but thinking of how Vincent had threatened her, took the knife from Shay's hand. "I'll look in at the infirmary on my way to the Zingari encampment tomorrow. I've got a lot of questions to ask Vincent if he's recovered from his stupor by then."

"I doubt he'll answer them, but there's no harm in asking," Shay opined and drew her into his embrace.

They clung tightly together, and Iona murmured, "I know you're a superior swordsman and all that, but please, please take care."

"You don't need to worry about me. I'll see you tomorrow," he replied and kissed her goodbye.

Late the next day, dressed in her Zingari clothes, the knife sheath strung onto her belt by its loops, Iona entered the long, low infirmary building, a place she'd never visited before.

The monks had taken Doctor Cleary's teachings to heart, and the recovery room appeared clean and well-ventilated, the astringent odour of herbs permeating the air. Brother Florian looked up from a patient, a young lad with bandages covering both arms, and moved to greet Iona where she stood hesitating in the doorway.

"If you've come to question Brother Vincent, we've put him in a separate room with Brother Kian on guard. However, although he's regained consciousness, he's still very woozy, and not yet capable of responding to an interrogation."

"Hmm, I'm not so sure. *Brother* Vincent thoroughly deceived everyone and must be one hell of an actor to have kept up the charade for so long. How is Brother Ennis?"

Brother Florian smiled. "He's doing well and will make a full recovery if no infection sets in." He gestured to a bed at the room's end. "He's sleeping now, as you can see, but I could pass on a message when he awakes."

Iona considered. "Do you have parchment and quill?"

Brother Florian nodded and led her to his office, where she penned a short note – *Dear Brother Ennis,*

Thomasine is in good health, and Cahir told me she caught two mice today.

Thank you for coming to my assistance; I won't forget it.

I hope your recovery is swift.

The quill is mightier than the sword – Iona, the Living Aurigan.

Folding the parchment, she handed it to Brother Florian. "Give this to Brother Ennis, please."

He accepted the note and sighed. "I fear I will have many customers after the action this evening. Still, it can't be helped. Good luck in your endeavour." Brother Florian sketched *the Great Wheel* symbol over his heart.

Iona returned it and departed for the Zingari encampment.

She crossed the covered bridge where the Lacunae would hide later, and making her way along the path, sighted the brightly coloured Zingari wagons in the near distance.

A figure ran across the grass towards her, and Iona recognised Rena, the Madjia's granddaughter. "I've been keeping an eye out for you," Rena explained when Iona left the path to meet her. "Come; Linessa, Dareesh's wife, is dying to meet the woman who finally conquered Shay! She thought it would never happen!"

Iona remembered Dareesh's wife had been away visiting relatives when Shay had taken her to meet his clan near Glassnesse. She blushed a little at Rena's words and hoped Linessa wouldn't find her a disappointment.

Much to Iona's surprise, she spotted Sister Myriax when they entered the wagon circle. The dragon-nun lounged in the grass beside the Madjia, who, ensconced in a comfy chair outside her dragon-painted wagon, appeared engrossed in their conversation. They remained an oasis of calm amidst the bustle of preparations for the coming conflict, and the toing-and-froing as the non-combatants moved from the wagons selected to transport the troupe into those that would remain behind.

Dareesh's two children, Fernamo and Letty, played with their friends near the Madjia, unperturbed by the dragon's presence. Iona waved to Sister Myriax as Rena escorted her to the Barozi's wagon, the nun bowing her head in acknowledgment.

A smiling woman stood at the open door. She beckoned to Iona, who climbed the steps, turning to thank Rena before she disappeared into the tumult.

"I'm Linessa, Dareesh's wife, and you must be Iona, the *Eterna*?"

"Yes. I'm pleased to meet you, Linessa. Thanks for allowing me to travel with you. Just direct me to a quiet corner, and I'll stay there out of your way," Iona replied to Shay's sister-in-law-by-adoption, a tall, striking woman with lovely, amber-flecked brown eyes.

"Oh, nonsense! There's no need to hide away just yet! Please, come in and we'll sort out your clothes."

Iona followed Linessa into the wagon, impressed with its orderly interior, the furniture fitted to make maximum use of the small living space.

"Dareesh is just attending to last-minute details but will return when it's time to hitch up and be on our way. Right, let's see. You already have the correct blouse, shoes, and shawl, but we'll need to change that skirt, and re-plait your hair the Zingari way." Linessa rummaged in a closet and, removing a red, flounced skirt, examined it with a critical eye. "This one should fit you." She glanced at Iona's green leg ribbons and selected a green waist sash to match.

Relieved her period had ended, she allowed Linessa to help her dress. Once suitably attired, Iona sat on a stool whilst Linessa re-braided her hair, weaving a strand of iridescent, pearl-like beads through the plait styled to hang over one shoulder.

"There! Apart from those blue eyes, you look like a Zingari now!"

"Thanks, Linessa. I'm very grateful to your clan for the risk you're taking on Shay's behalf."

"Not *just* for Shay, if our Madjia is right about the danger to us all, and she's never wrong." Linessa placed her comb on a table and turned to face Iona. "But Shay is taking this risk for *you*. Oh, he wants to save the villagers and our world, but he's mainly doing this for his *Ves'tacha*, the person he thought didn't exist. He'll be destroyed if…"

Iona held Linessa's gaze. "Shay is my soulmate, and his destruction will also be mine. But I can't make promises I may have no control over."

Linessa studied Iona's face and finally nodded. "I believe you."

Iona felt she'd passed a test, but her shoulders slumped with relief when Linessa looked away, saying, "I need to say goodbye to my children. They'll stay with the Madjia and her daughter, Rena's mother. I won't be long."

When Linessa left, Iona stood in the doorway, watching the men hitching horses to the wagons that would convey the troupe to the castle, an atmosphere of excitement palpable in the air as the sword dancers and female performers hurried to take their places in the transports.

Chapter 27

As the convoy wound its way up the castle hill, Iona peered from a side window in the wagon's wooden walls, moving to the back when it approached the castle gates.

Two other performers travelled with Dareesh and Linessa in the leading wagon, the full complement of twenty-four dancers and seven musicians distributed amongst six wagons in total. The twelve sword dancers carried two blades each, and the twelve strong, female group bore ornate, curved daggers – and knew how to use them.

Four pikemen stood before the closed gates, and sentries manned the walls above, with most concentrated around the Janus Spire.

Dareesh leaned down from the wagon seat to show the guard captain his pass. Expecting the Zingaris' arrival for their second performance, the captain and his pikemen made only a cursory inspection of the wagon interiors, not clocking they contained an extra performer.

The gates opened with a ponderous rumble, and the wagons passed through to the side courtyard allocated for their use. Its location at the castle's southeastern side meant Iona wouldn't witness the fighting, since the central keep stood between the courtyard and the Janus Spire.

With practised ease, the drivers lined up the wagons, three to each side of the courtyard's northern and southern perimeters. They outfitted the horses with nosebags, and blinkers to keep them calm, before threading their reins through metal rings in the walls.

As the performers poured down the wagon steps and executed a series of stretching exercises, Dareesh popped his head through the door of his wagon and instructed Iona, "Stay here until the fighting is over. Don't leave until someone comes to get you."

Iona agreed, and Dareesh shut the door behind him, plunging the interior into gloom, though twilight had not yet surrendered to full dark. She couldn't risk lighting a lamp; its radiance spilling through the two small, gauze-curtained windows might betray her presence.

Iona nervously paced up and down the confined space. She estimated twenty-five minutes had passed, and the women must be well into their dance routine by now. It wouldn't be long until the sword dancers, gathered behind the castle's main doors, opened the gates to Will's fighters.

Anxiety clenched her stomach, and she peered from the back window, which faced the well-lit courtyard. Iona craned her head towards the arched entrance, straining her ears for any sound of fighting. Although Dareesh's wagon stood farthest from the entrance, close to a low doorway near the eastern wall, she could still discern the archway's outline in the light from the basket braziers that stood on tall poles to each side.

Two men clad in chainmail suddenly emerged through the opening, and Iona shrunk back from the window. However, fearful curiosity drew her back and, to her dismay, she saw them split up to examine the wagons parked on each side of the archway. They thrust lanterns beneath to study the undercarriage, and then the man on her side of the row disappeared from view as he moved to the wagon front, which faced the wall. However, Iona could still see the guard opposite when he copied his colleague. Though he appeared a mere shadow on the wagon steps, she saw the unlocked door fly open, and the shadow enter within.

When both men moved on to the next wagon in their respective rows, Iona knew they would search inside every single one. It seemed the laxity of the gate guards had lulled Dareesh into a false sense of security. She gazed at her dim surroundings, looking for somewhere to hide, but couldn't see anywhere the guards wouldn't search. Iona gripped the hilt of her sheathed knife in a sweaty palm and stared at the door. Although she could bolt it from the inside, that would be a dead giveaway that someone hid within. Fleeing seemed her only choice, but she didn't have much time. She inched the door open, and peeking out, saw the open entry of the wagon beside hers. She had to move before the guard emerged, but where could she go? Remembering the postern in the wall just yards away, she slipped out and scurried down the steps. Iona sprinted to the low door, glancing over her shoulder as she grabbed its iron handle, praying it wasn't locked. Though the ring latch turned easily, she had to wrench the warped wood open, the hinges squealing loudly. Alarmed that she had given herself away, Iona pelted through the entrance and found herself in an alley that ran behind the castle.

The sound of fighting suddenly drifted clearly on the night air, and Iona stumbled to a halt. Surely, the two guards would abandon their search to investigate? Perhaps she should return to the wagon and wait it out as planned. However, a figure appeared in the doorway, chainmail glinting in the light from his lantern. Iona took to her heels and ran. The cobblestones felt hard on the thin soles of her Zingari shoes, and a swift peek over her shoulder confirmed the man was gaining on her. Dispensing with caution, she put on a desperate burst of speed, but couldn't sustain it when a painful stitch pierced her side. The alley appeared to run the castle's length, and she knew the guard would catch her before she made it to the end.

Iona snatched her blade from its belt sheath, and staggering to a halt, turned side-on, her knife hand facing away from the guard and concealed in her skirts. She raised her other hand to signal her surrender, and then cradled her side-stitch, panting loudly as she leaned over, head hanging. As the man drew near, hand outstretched to grab her, Iona's eyes, level with his knees, flicked sideways. His chainmail shirt reached only to mid-thigh, leaving his legs unprotected. She lashed out with her blade, slicing it across the back of his knee. Bellowing in surprised pain, the guard's leg gave way, but he controlled his fall by shifting his weight to the other leg, dropping his pierced-metal lantern to put out a steadying hand. Rising from the cobbles, the man reached for his shortsword, but Iona had already sprinted away. When he tried to follow, blood pumping from the knife wound, he fell to the other knee, and risking a glance back, Iona guiltily wondered if she'd slashed an artery.

She slowed to a jog, unable to keep up the pace, the sound of clashing swords louder as she approached the alley's end. With her back to the wall, Iona inched her head sideways to peer from the alley mouth and observed it terminated in an open courtyard, the Janus Spire on the opposite side. The tower guards had rushed forward to repel the attack, leaving just three men at the door. Iona glanced up at the curtain wall, thick with archers, pikemen and sword fighters in frenzied combat.

Withdrawing her head, she stood irresolute. Should she risk returning down the alley to the wagons in the hope her pursuer had crawled away, his medical needs taking precedence? Iona avoided the idea she had killed him; he'd know how to make a tourniquet… It might be advisable to remain here, watching the tower until the battle was decided. Agitated by her unforeseen situation, Iona clenched her braid, the knife held out defensively in her other hand.

She had just worked up the courage to take another peek around the corner when a shadow fell over her as a figure blocked the entrance. Taken unawares, she gasped when a hand chopped down on her wrist, and the knife clattered to the cobbles. Something hard pressed into her side, and a voice drawled, "Well, *this* is serendipitous! You won't escape this time!"

Iona looked up at the smirking face of a breeches-clad Honoria, and down at the small, pearl-handled pistol pressed against her ribs. Her mind wandered, as it often did when stressed, to the side issues. *How did the woman get hold of a gun in a world where the trebuchet catapult is the highest form of weapons technology?*

Honoria seized Iona's shoulder and, thrusting her ahead through the alley mouth, planted the pistol in her spine. "You're coming with me to the Spire. Don't do anything stupid unless you want a bullet in the back!"

With Honoria pushing her onward, Iona moved towards the tower on unsteady legs. She thought of the fallen knife with regret. Though useless against a gun, Shay had given it to her… She gripped her plait in distress, the beads hard beneath her palm, glancing fearfully at the knot of fighters drawing closer on her left. The guardsmen appeared outnumbered; the ground littered with bodies clad in the surcoats of the duke's elite, the white fabric stark against the torchlit paving. Iona felt something give under her hand and distantly registered she had broken the pearl strand threaded through her braid.

When they reached the tower door, Honoria lifted her hand from Iona's shoulder to fish in her pocket. Holding her gun hidden from view behind Iona's back, she passed a key to the remaining door guard, the others having joined the melee. He unlocked the door without question and handed back the key. Shoving Iona through, Honoria slammed the door shut. She re-locked it one-handed, keeping the pistol trained on Iona, and gestured with the weapon towards the stairs that led upward.

A bead from Iona's plait dropped to the floor, unseen by Honoria, giving Iona an idea born of desperation. No one would know where she'd gone when they discovered her missing, but perhaps she could leave a trail for Shay to follow. As Honoria forced her ahead up the winding stairs, Iona worked on her braid, unthreading the pearls from the broken string and dropping them, one by one, on the steps. Though Honoria didn't notice the tiny beads fall, Iona hoped their pearlescent sheen would attract the eye of anyone who actively hunted for clues. Though the thick tower walls muted the noise of battle, the beads fell soundlessly, too small to make an impact.

Although Iona tried to space the pearls sparingly, by the time they reached the landing before the final stair flight, she had run out. Honoria stopped to take a breather, and pushing Iona against the locked door to the curtain wall, pressed the gun muzzle between her shoulder blades. She peered out the narrow window beside the door to gauge how the battle progressed, and muttered, "Damn!" A telling indication it went badly for the defenders. With Honoria's attention elsewhere, Iona pulled on the now-empty string to release it from the braid and bunched it in her fist. When they started up the last flight, she dropped it on the second step.

On reaching the top landing, Honoria produced another key and ordered Iona to unlock the wide wooden doors that concealed the metal wall. With the pistol aimed at her back, Iona had little choice and, hands shaking in fear and anticipation, almost jammed the lock. Honoria's angry cursing did little to help her nerves, but the door opened at last. The erstwhile nun shoved Iona through the gap and, following behind, commanded her to relock it. Iona turned to obey in the narrow space, placing the key on Honoria's outstretched hand when she'd done. Gun targeted on Iona's chest, Honoria backed to the ATM-like niche in the wall and depressed a switch that emitted a buzz like a doorbell. She spoke into a microphone beside the monitor screen, "I'm back, and I've got a little present for you, Sir."

A camera near the ceiling swivelled, and a near-invisible door in the metal wall slid open. Honoria hustled Iona through, and the door swished shut behind them.

Iona gazed around the tower-top chamber in stunned astonishment. Lights pulsed from huge steel cabinets arrayed against the walls. A long console board with a slanted top stood beneath the shuttered windows, more lights blinking above switches, dials, and gauges. The room's centre contained a massive curved desk that held a bank of computers, their monitor screens displaying fluctuating graphs, scrolling readouts, and esoteric equations. Two men sat at the desk, their backs to the door. The technician hunched over his keyboard farthest from Iona didn't look up from his work, but the other man turned to face her, and she identified Lord Randolph Peregrine, the duke's brother-in-law, his mediaeval tunic and hose incongruous in such a setting.

He lounged with casual ease on the modern swivel chair, one hand resting on a strange executive toy, a centaur with wheels instead of legs. Iona recognised the Borderland Incorporated logo familiar from her trike monitor screen. He gently pushed it back and forth on the desktop as he regarded his prize. "Ah, our elusive *Eterna*. It was most inconsiderate of you to befoul our schedule with your refusal to vanquish the next traveller we entice. We can hardly have two *Living Aurigans!* If you had *even* declared your intention to retire gracefully, like Mistress Robina... But, oh no! You must interfere with our itinerary by declining to, er, 'move on' at the appropriate juncture. Still, you're here now. No doubt dear Clovis will be pleased to see you, though I hear he's a bit tied up at the moment." Randolph chuckled at his own joke. "It's even more fortuitous that dear Honoria has finally apprehended you," he gave Iona's captor a withering look, "since we require answers to some rather pressing questions."

Refusal to vanquish? Does he mean my reluctance to steal the trike from the next victim, as the others did before me? Iona wondered.

"I presume *you* were the woman who broached this tower with the prior's pet sword dancer? You must have seen our internal barricades and known you could not pass them. Therefore, what do you hope to achieve with this pointless exercise?"

I mustn't say anything about the Lacunae! Think! What do I tell him?
Honoria brandished her pistol and barked, "Answer!"
"The villagers wish to reclaim their people," Iona replied lamely.
Randolph tutted and shook his head. "That does not answer my question. Do not try my patience. The truth, if you please."

Despite his urbane exterior, Randolph's eyes glittered menacingly, and Iona decided she'd much rather face Duke Clovis, giant codpiece notwithstanding. In sudden inspiration, she falsely confessed, "We planned to capture the duke and force him to reveal the door codes at sword point, so we could access this room and the dungeons."

"Good luck with that! I changed the codes and disabled Clovis' fingerprint and iris recognition. Only me and Mrs Kuiper know the new code." Randolph stood. "The peasants can fling themselves uselessly at the spire to their hearts' content; we are safe behind our impregnable barriers. Still, I ought to make tracks to the dungeons now before they invade the tower. I need to recalibrate the collider arrangement."

"What about the duke… and your wife?" Honoria asked.

"Hmm, he must take his chances. As for Madeleine, I do not think they will harm her. I hope not, anyway! I will require her help with the regency, if it comes to that. Perhaps it is time to secure my nephews. A job for you, methinks. I doubt you will find any Zingari lurking in the nursery, but take Blaine as backup. You know where to secrete them."

Honoria nodded, but hesitated. "Vincent didn't warn us. He must have known *something* was up! He'd have informed us of the *Eterna's* return if nothing else. I'm worried about him."

"I am sure your husband is fine, and if he is not, there is nothing we can do for him right now." Randolph pointed to Iona. "Tie her up and get going." With that, he swept from the room.

Vincent is her husband? Iona couldn't believe her ears. *Who are these people?*

Honoria opened a drawer and produced a pair of modern handcuffs. She pushed Iona onto a chair and cuffed her to a desk leg, its footplate screwed to the floor.

When Honoria had gone, leaving her alone with the silent technician, Iona tested the cuffs, knowing it was pointless, but relieved the chain length allowed her to sit upright. If only she could open a window shutter to watch for the firecracker signal, she'd know when Will called the Lacunae. At least Honoria had left, taking the gun with her – the woman seemed the type to shoot unexpected threats on sight, and a dragon appearing from nowhere would certainly be a surprise. Iona glanced at the technician, hoping he was unarmed. Now she saw him in profile, he looked familiar. As though he felt her regard, the man turned towards her……

Chapter 28

Jake Halstead! The man who stole my trike! "You! You're one of them!" Iona accused.

"Not by choice." Jake shook his head in denial. "The trike didn't return to your place as I expected, but brought me to a room in the dungeons here."

"What about the others? Gavin Whyte, Bethany, the doctor, and the people before them?"

Jake looked down. "Dead; except for Doctor Cleary, who Peterson found a use for… like me."

"Who is Peterson?" Iona frowned in confusion.

"Randy Peterson, chairman owner of Borderland Incorporated, aka Lord Randolph Peregrine."

"What? So, he's from our world? Why is he doing this? The trikes… how? How does he even power all this?" Iona waved her shackled hands at the computers.

"Generators in the dungeons, along with a lot of other stuff," Jake replied in a dark tone. "It's all connected with that megalith stone by the roadside, where we… met up."

"Where you stole my trike, you mean."

Jake had the grace to look abashed. "Fat lot of good that did me."

"Has Peterson found a way to subvert the menhir portal's power for his own ends?"

"You know about the portal?" Jake wore a startled expression.

Iona nodded. "Well?"

"Perhaps you should tell me everything you've learned, so I know how much I need to explain to you."

"OK, but can you open a window shutter first?"

"Why? Peterson won't like it." Jake gestured at the electric ceiling lights.

"He won't know. He's in the dungeons, isn't he? Look, can you leave this room?"

"I don't have the admin rights to override the door code. I'm just as trapped as you."

"I can get you out of here, and free of this tower, at least. I won't tell you how just yet, but I must watch out for a signal; a firework. So, can you please open the northwestern shutter as I don't have X-ray vision?"

"You don't trust me enough to tell me how you'll get us out," Jake stated flatly.

"Nope. Would you in my position? You've already proven your

untrustworthiness once. How do I know you haven't thrown in your lot with these people? They might have left you here to extract information from me under false pretences."

Jake shook his head vehemently. "No, you're wrong! I *have* to get out of here! They *killed* the others! Only my programming skills and physics knowledge saved me. They could change their minds any time!" He stood and opened the shutter, turning off the overhead lights.

The glow from the monitors and steel cabinets bathed his face in an eldritch luminosity as he sat down closer to Iona. "Tell me what you know about the portal."

Iona complied, leaving out her information source from whom they'd obtained the box files.

"How do you know all this? Who gave you the files?" Jake asked when she'd finished.

"Let's just say we received help from an unexpected ally – for now. Right; it's your turn. How did Peterson discover the portal, and what's his game with the trikes?"

Jake fiddled with a pen as he ordered his thoughts. "I'll start at the beginning. Randy Peterson is an astrophysicist specialising in quantum theory, a brilliant maverick, but highly regarded in his field. He's also rich; a combination of family money and licensed inventions. He established his own company twenty-five years ago and was an early innovator in the AI market, although he merely considers it an additional revenue stream to fund his quantum research. He met Vincent Kuiper through Honoria, Vincent's wife, an employee in his company. The Kuipers were amateur astronomers with an interest in pseudo sciences; you know, ley lines, crop circles, and the like. Vincent had recently inherited a nineteenth-century property from an aunt. He discovered two crates full of old patient records in the attic, stored there by an ancestor, the director of a Victorian lunatic asylum. Vincent suspected they might be clandestine copies of the case notes that most interested his forbear, amongst which he found the records of a woman who claimed her family were the historical guardians of a portal to another world."

"Adeline Gordon! Saint Aurigan's descendent!" Iona exclaimed.

"You know the story? Then you might also know the asylum director had made copies of the menhir portal activity charts. For a man of Vincent's leanings, this was an exciting discovery, and when he showed it to Honoria, she knew it would interest her boss, who currently studied black holes and event horizons. To cut a long story short, it did. He believed the portal, if it existed, could be a mini black hole, one that cyclically opened and closed, something he had posited might exist, but never found evidence to prove."

"I don't understand. Aren't black holes a feature of Outer Space?"

"Space is all around us. Put simply, when matter falls into a black hole, it becomes isolated from space-time. Theorists have speculated that curved space within a black hole could open the doorway into another world, or its gravitational waves might spin human consciousness, at least, into another place. They speak of matter as a series of waves on a quantum scale, which can form a link between consciousness and quantum entanglement."

"Sorry; you've lost me."

"Quantum entanglement is a phenomenon that occurs when two particles are generated, interact, or share spatial proximity in such a way that the quantum state of each particle cannot be described independently of the other, including when the particles are separated by a huge distance."

"Er, so each half of the duet can exist in two different places, but are essentially the same particle?"

"Not quite, but near enough for our purposes. Anyway, with the black hole localised so accessibly, Peterson had the mad idea he could harness its power via a restructured particle accelerator of his own design. By diverting the portal's energy into a storage system that *recycled* it infinitely, the menhir *way* would close prematurely and permanently. However, the mini black hole, now re-sited in the contained space, could be accessed at will by siphoning off the stored energy into moveable portals connected to Peterson's system via quantum entanglement; portals which could travel between the two realities from programmed starting points."

"The trikes!" Iona exclaimed in sudden comprehension.

Jake nodded. "With the menhir portal charts to guide them, Peterson and the Kuipers knew they only had four years to build and test his visionary collider arrangement before the portal became active. They had no proof the menhir stone was anything other than an ancient monument, but if it *did* turn out to be what they hoped, they'd only have five months to work in before the portal closed again, not to re-open for another fifty years. Peterson, wealthy and crazy enough to take a gamble, purchased the old Aurelius property which, fortunately for him, had come onto the market when the family's fortunes declined. He turned the manor house into his new project's centre of operations, installing the Kuipers and a highly secret workforce, paid well for their silence. He fenced off the land where the menhir stood and set to work, building the accelerator and trikes. However, his calculations confirmed he must site the system in the Secondary reality for optimum efficiency, so he designed everything to come apart easily for reassembly in situ."

"Audrey stated in her testimony that the menhir portal closed two months early after she passed through, and we know the first trike took to the road shortly afterwards. How did Peterson manage to install himself in the duke's graces in a mere three months, let alone establish the operation so quickly?" Iona asked.

Jake gave a grim, tight-lipped smile. "Money; Peterson had plenty and Clovis… he wasn't poor, but he had less wealth than many of the merchant class here. Adeline's case notes prepared Peterson for what lay beyond the portal, but when he sent the Kuipers through to reconnoitre, he must have rubbed his hands in glee when they reported the culture had barely advanced in the three hundred years or so since Saint Aurigan's time."

Iona scowled. "Yes, I'm sure he figured how easily he could manipulate such primitives."

Jake nodded and continued, "The Kuipers immediately observed that the tower above the menhir stone that exists in both worlds, would make an ideal site for their great experiment. They discovered its owner, Duke Clovis, searched for a rich wife, and this is where Peterson's sister, Collette, enters the story. Ten years younger than him, Peterson virtually brought her up when their parents died in a car crash just after he turned twenty-two. She still lived with her brother, and he'd made her a director of Borderland, responsible for managing the Aurelius site. He posed as Lord Randolph Peregrine from Gallegia, a land to Beretania's south, who'd travelled north with his sister, Collette, in search of a husband with a title great enough to tempt her. Lavish gifts and the promise of a huge dowry soon had Clovis eating out of their hands, and the wedding took place two months later. Peterson asked for nothing more than exclusive use of the Janus Spire as his bride price."

"But how did they move the generator and all the machinery into it without attracting attention?"

"Easier than you might think! With just a hillside between the menhir and the tower, they didn't need to convey everything through the town or castle. At that time, a door in the Janus Spire's north side opened directly onto the plateau above the hillside, although Peterson had it blocked up afterwards for security reasons. His Aurelius site workers moved all the equipment through the portal, and up the hillside to the tower over the space of three nights, with sentries on duty to 'deal with' any citizens abroad in the vicinity so late. They had the whole rig assembled and running within ten days, and the duke, occupied with his new bride, remained oblivious. I won't confuse you with the mechanics of how Peterson programmed the collider to mimic the mini black hole's nuclear signature and relocated the portal's energy, via quantum entanglement, to his atomic storage silo. Suffice to say, the menhir portal closed, and Peterson now controlled the way between worlds."

"Hmm, I still don't get the business with the trikes. Oh, I know they're a means to travel between the Primary and Secondary worlds, but I don't understand why Peterson uses them to lure people like me and you into this reality."

"It's all part of his research into the link between consciousness and quantum entanglement. At a more prosaic level, the trikes are siphons. With the black hole 'contained', its electrons cannot escape as they would in free space, a process that shrinks the hole over aeons. No one has ever recorded or studied this type of black hole, which opens and closes cyclically. As a consequence of the recycling process, which artificially keeps it permanently open, it grows a little bigger with each revolution. To maintain it at a stable and manageable level, some of its energy is diverted to the trikes at structured intervals via the same process of quantum entanglement. Although programmed to remain static in the Primary world, once they're switched on, they enter the Secondary world and can move on a pre-determined track from any of the coordinates uploaded into the onboard computer, returning to the spot they 'travelled' from in the Primary world when switched off. Vice versa, of course, if they start out from this world. Peterson can manually recall them to the mother source via the computer network, as happened to me when I attempted to return to our world on your trike. He uses one himself to travel back home whenever he likes, and his workers employ trikes with trailers attached to transport supplies, and fuel for the generators from the Aurelius site directly into the tower dungeons. Whenever the silo requires siphoning, portal electrons are freed from the trikes to allow their reuse."

"Why can't the Secondary worlders see them, though?"

"Peterson fitted them with an advanced form of the cloaking technology used in military aviation, which is activated when the trike is switched on. They also feature a powerful repellent force that ensures other road travellers avoid them. However, the consciousness of all who use the trikes becomes linked to them on a quantum level, and they remain able to see the trikes even when the cloaking device is triggered."

"But why us? Why choose us?"

"Peterson's core workforce for this operation is necessarily small to maintain secrecy. He cannot afford to expend their time on running the trikes when he requires them for other tasks. Therefore, he uses free labour; people who unknowingly help him by participating in his post-injury fitness scheme. Peterson chooses them with care. Most who take part are already vulnerable and not much missed by others, even Gavin Whyte, the footballer, who retired from the public eye after his career-ending injury. They also act as Peterson's cross-section of test subjects whom he can monitor via the onboard sensors to gauge their mental and physical reactions to this alternative reality, a critical part of any scientific process that involves the effects of environmental change on humans."

Am I not missed? No, I can't believe that! Skye and Dad must be frantic with worry, Zara and my other friends, too… Iona fretted.

"Therefore, Peterson felt delighted when the Saint Aurigan's order adopted the stray trikers, ejected from the trikes by their predecessors, who invariably ejected their successors in their turn. It allowed him to monitor them in 'real-life' situations, contrasting with his test subjects who merely passed through what they believed to be a virtual-reality scenario. To this end, he planted Vincent in the priory, who could also alert him if any trikers decided to leave. The *Living Aurigan* tradition covered up Peterson's activities, and when the time came for a new incumbent, this system made it easier for him to place the new *Eterna* in the old one's path, returning the trike thief to the dungeon for disposal. Those who made it as far as Glassnesse, the limit of his operation, met with a fatal accident in the form of Honoria, planted in Glassnesse Abbey, the Saint Aurigan's motherhouse. As an 'outreach' nun, Honoria had more freedom to travel than Vincent, who lacked her stomach for 'protecting' their interests."

"My refusal to play the game must have infuriated Peterson…"

"It certainly messed up his system, and Honoria's failed attempt to lure you from the protection of the priory to Glassnesse, compounded by her thwarted kidnap attempt had him tearing his hair out!"

"So, this business has been going on for, what, twenty years or so? What is their long-term plan?"

"The experiment had several aims to begin with. Peterson speculated on the possibility of artificially replicating the mini black hole and creating other portals elsewhere. But first, he had to record any consequences of keeping the contained portal open beyond its natural cycle. How *real* is this world in relation to the Primary reality? Would overlap occur, and the two worlds bleed together at the edges? Would it affect the Secondary world's stability and its people's integrity? He sent the odd vagrant or hobo from this world through to the Primary as guinea pigs and imprisoned them in the Aurelius manor house. When he realised people from this world couldn't survive in ours, he became worried. His sister, who had died in childbirth, had given Duke Clovis two sons. Peterson never intended them to remain in this backward reality and now knew they'd die if they returned to their mother's world. Despite his megalomania, Peterson loved his sister, and treasures his nephews, aged five and seven. That was when the wholesale kidnaps began, with villagers tied to trikes and sent into captivity in the manor house. A dodgy doctor in his employ performs tests on those who last the longest in an attempt to discover why. Other villagers are sent back before they expire to see how long they take to recover.

Peterson has sent one group back and forth several times to determine if it's possible to build up immunity. Doctor Cleary tends to those recovering in the dungeons, and though a mild-mannered man, I believe he'd kill Peterson if he could."

Iona clamped her manacled hands over her mouth. "Oh, my God! Clare! Do you know if Bertrand Leon's niece, Clare Copeland, is still alive?"

Jake shook his head. "I've no idea; sorry."

Iona wondered if 'leakage' from her world had caused the weakening of the Lacunae transposition ability, an impossible skill where she came from. She shivered at the implications, but kept her thoughts to herself. What if Peterson watched and listened to their conversation from the dungeons? Iona glanced up, trying to spot any hidden cameras, but saw nothing obvious. However, that proved nothing, and she couldn't risk unintentionally warning Peterson about the Lacunae. *I hope Shay makes the transposition to this room first, so I can alert him to the dangers lurking in the dungeons. I bet Peterson and his lackeys are armed with guns, like Honoria.*

"I know you've been incarcerated here for over a month, but how do you know so many *details* about the operation?" Iona asked.

Jake sighed and leaned back in his chair. "Peterson is proud of his achievements, understandably so, in some ways, and takes great delight in telling me all about them when I'm forced to work alongside him. I think he's taken a… *liking* to me."

"Ah, I see. Do you have someone to miss you back home?"

Jake shrugged. "Only my mum and my boyfriend, Daniel, but I'm not so sure about him."

Although it seemed longer, Iona estimated they had only conversed for thirty minutes, but hoped the signal would ignite soon. Fear for Shay gnawed at her insides, warring with the knowledge that a way back home likely sat stationary in the dungeons……

The central monitor before which Peterson had sat emitted a beep, and Jake turned to look at it. "It looks like there's a new taker for the post-injury exercise program. Now he has you in his clutches, Peterson will be pleased your successor is lined up, ready and waiting." He shook his head in disgust.

"I named my trike Troy because the wheeled centaur logo reminded me of the Trojan Horse. The name was more appropriate than I ever imagined," Iona supplied.

"I called mine Chiron, after the centaur in Greek mythology. Peterson is a man of many aliases… I guess it was he we communicated with via the onboard computer."

"What's the deal with Lady Madeleine?" Iona changed the subject, the extent of Peterson's trickery too anger-inducing to contemplate now.

"She's a Secondary worlder and knows nothing about any of this. A man in Lord Randolph Peregrine's position is expected to take a wife, and she became a convenient screen to hide behind."

"And a diverting distraction for Clovis," Iona added. "What does the duke *think* his brother-in-law is up to in the tower? Does *he* know?"

Jake rolled his eyes. "He thinks Lord Peregrine is a magician, who can transmute base metal into gold. So long as Peterson keeps the gold coming, he doesn't interfere too much. Peterson has an agent in Glassnesse who buys ingots and gold artifacts for him in bulk off the merchant ships. As you can imagine, the 'exchange rate' between this world and ours is very favourable, so it's cheap at the price. He doles it out in stages, pretending it's a product of his alchemy lab on the top floor of the dungeons, the only area behind the metal wall he's allowed the duke to see."

"Peterson has an alchemy lab?"

"It's a stage set only to fool the duke, who believes the high-tech access system is magic. Though Peterson 'trusts' him with the door codes to keep him mollified, Clovis is too scared to use them unaccompanied by his brother-in-law, who knows how to tame the 'demon' inside the monitor screen. He's never been beyond the wall shielding *this* room, as he believes it harbours Lord Peregrine's 'familiar'. Peterson plays a dangerous game. 'Witchcraft and wizardry' are punishable by death in the law's eyes, but Clovis' greed protects him."

"And Sir Norris, the man behind the villager kidnappings?"

Jake scowled. "Sir Norris is a brute with no conscience. He and his blackguards receive handsome recompense for every village sacking. Peterson admits them behind the dungeon wall to deliver the 'sacrifices', but only to a holding room; they see nothing else. As a mark of his 'favoured status', Peterson gave Norris a golden key to the wooden doors that front the metal wall, but not the access codes. A symbolic gesture signifying an unspoken promise, false of course, to initiate Norris into the secrets of the internal sanctuary for his continued 'services'."

"So, the duke and Sir Norris believe Lord Peregrine sacrifices the villagers to… what? A demon?"

"Yes; to grant him more power. He saves the best gold plate and cut diamonds to present to Clovis to demonstrate the sacrifices work."

"No doubt Clovis commissioned a diamond-encrusted codpiece to display them to their 'best' advantage," Iona quipped sarcastically.

Jake guffawed in a release of tension, then jumped at a loud bang.

Chapter 29

The window lit up as the firecracker exploded, sending a bouquet of white sparks into the heavens.

"The signal at last!" Iona exclaimed and rattled her chains in frustration. "I need to get out of these manacles, and I doubt our rescuers will have a convenient hacksaw. Are you any good at picking locks?"

"I can't say I've ever picked a lock, but I know where Honoria keeps the spare key," Jake replied.

Iona glowered at him indignantly. "You know where the key is, yet you've left me chained to the desk all this time?"

"I couldn't be sure Peterson wouldn't come back." He raised his hands in surrender when Iona continued to glare daggers at him. "OK, but you'd better be right about these rescuers." Jake stood, and rounding the desk, pulled a box file from the shelf below the control board. He lifted out a bundle of papers, beneath which a tin box lay hidden.

"She doesn't know I know where she stashes the spares," Jake explained as he returned to his seat with the tin, which contained several keys, all unmarked.

He tried several before finding one that fitted. Iona sighed with relief when Jake removed the manacles, and she rubbed her wrists where the restraints had chaffed. "Is there anything to drink in here? I'm dying of thirst."

Jake crossed to where he'd originally sat and, switching on a desk lamp, reached beneath the worktop. Light bathed his legs as he opened a door and removed a can from a mini fridge. "Will Coke, do you?"

"You've got *Coke*?" Iona held out a hand, and Jake passed her the can, beaded with moisture. After so long without sugary drinks, it tasted like nectar.

She wondered if anyone had discovered her disappearance yet, and how long she must wait before they searched the spire. The Lacunae would fly into the castle grounds and glide up the tower stairway to preserve their teleportation strength. If only she knew what was happening outside of her prison. Iona suddenly remembered the camera positioned near the ceiling between the metal wall and the outer wooden doors. Honoria had communicated with Peterson via an intercom...

"Jake, we must watch the outer doors. Which of these monitors is linked to the intercom and external camera?"

"That one," Jake replied, pointing to a laptop beside the central desk monitor. With a few taps on the keyboard, he brought up a live image of the narrow space and gestured to a headset hooked over the screen. "

"Use that to speak to your friends."

As they sat side-by-side before the laptop, Iona had a sudden idea. "Are there any other hidden cameras positioned in this tower? What about the dungeons?"

"Let's see if I can find out," Jake replied, reducing the image size and moving it to the top corner.

It took him less than a minute to discover a feed that looked down into the tower vestibule, facing the front door, which rattled on its hinges under the pressure of an external force.

"They're breaking the door down!" Iona declared unnecessarily.

"It looks like Peterson installed *this* camera after you broke into the tower with Shay," Jake informed and shrunk the image, moving it to the other top corner.

Unexpectedly, the next camera feed gave a window into the castle's great hall. "This one's different; I guess because the hall is so large." Jake pointed to a virtual toggle onscreen. "I can pan the camera remotely." Despite a thirty-second time lag after each command, he swept the hall along its length, and they peered at the guests, tied up under the watchful eyes of the Zingari women. Clovis sat bound to his ducal throne, hands fisted on the armrests below his wrist shackles. Lady Madeleine occupied a chair beside him on the low dais, an expression of stunned disbelief on her face.

"I don't see Sir Norris," Iona said.

"I believe Peterson sent him on an *errand*. I doubt he'll return before daybreak."

"Okay, never mind them. We need to know what Peterson is up to; assuming he's not so complacent about waiting it out as he appeared."

"Give me a minute," Jake said, clearing the scene in the great hall from the screen. He tapped some more and muttered, "Yes!"

A huge metal silo covered in blinking lights filled the screen, and as Jake panned out, Iona observed it occupied the centre of a cement floor, a Faraday cage surrounding it. A tube-shaped machine bracketed it horizontally on two sides, and pointing it out, Jake explained, "That's the collider arrangement."

Two trikes resting on stands near a generator caught Iona's attention, but Jake panned upwards, and she observed a narrow metal gantry with a staircase leading down to the floor. A half-glassed wall at the gantry's rear reflected the lights from the room beyond, and Iona spotted Peterson through the window, manipulating unseen controls.

"He's still here, then," she remarked.

"Of course. He can trike out anytime he likes, but why should he?"

Why indeed? Iona thought as Jake dismissed the view.

"It looks like there are camera feeds for the dungeon's upper floors, too," Jake said, but before he could open them, they observed the tower door fly off its hinges. Jake hastily enlarged the window onto the vestibule, and Iona's heart leapt when she saw Shay outlined in the doorway. He stood spread-legged, sword thrust before him, his jaw clenched in grim determination. Shay entered within, followed by Calixo, Dareesh, and Will, Quintus bringing up the rear with the other three Lacunae.

Jake stared in pop-eyed astonishment. "Do my eyes deceive me? Dragons?"

"Yep, dragons. Lacunae, to be exact."

"Lacunae? Aren't they the type that can teleport? According to rumour, anyway."

"It's no rumour," Iona replied, a little smug.

Jake opened his mouth to ask why Shay had brought Lacunae, when understanding dawned. "They can teleport us out of here?" Jake queried instead.

"Oh, yes! Although this close to the corrupted portal, they must conserve their energies as it's interfering with their abilities." Iona's eyes hadn't left the screen, and she watched Shay move towards the guardroom, presumably to check for occupants. He reappeared from within, shaking his head at the others, and they spoke together. Iona wished she had audio to hear their conversation and tapped her fingers on the desk. "Come on, come on, choose up, not down!" she pleaded.

"Is that Quintus?" Jake asked, squinting at the screen, and then answered his own question, "It is! Why is he dressed like that?"

"He's no longer a monk," Iona said and merely responded with "Later," to his questioning look.

The men and dragons split into three groups, with Dareesh, Quintus, and Calixo taking the stairs upward, while Shay, Will, and Karnax disappeared through the recessed door that led to the dungeon stairway, leaving Flix and Belonyx in the vestibule.

"Looks like they're reconnoitring," Jake opined.

Less than a minute later, Calixo returned to the lobby area and glided through the open door to the dungeon stairway. Iona wondered if Dareesh had spotted the beads she had dropped, glinting in the light from his torch, and recognised they came from the braid decoration his wife had loaned her.

Calixo soon reappeared, followed by Shay, Will, and Karnax. Will remained in the vestibule with Flix and Belonyx, but the others shadowed Calixo up the stairs to the tower top.

"Yess!" Iona hissed in relief.

Jake banished the vestibule feed and enlarged the door area image.

He handed Iona the headset. "You'd better get ready to speak. Erm... you and Shay... is it serious?"

Iona knew why he asked, and she looked back at the screen, even though there was nothing to see yet. "Yes, it's... yes."

Jake looked at her with pity. "I don't blame you; he's gorgeous. Still, falling for him wasn't a wise move."

"You don't need to tell *me* that. By the time we discovered what would happen if he returned home with me, it was already too late. Shay knows something of our world, but I don't know how I'm going to explain all this to him, let alone the others." Iona donned the headset, and Jake flicked the switch above the earpiece to the 'on' position.

Through the intercom, Iona faintly heard a key turn in the lock of the outer wooden doors and remembered Shay still had the key bunch he'd stolen from the guard when they last entered the tower. It appeared Peterson had only changed the front door lock since their incursion.

As soon as Shay flung wide the doors, Iona near-shouted into the mouthpiece. "Shay, it's me, Iona! I'm in the room behind the metal wall. Jake Halstead's with me, but no one else. We're fine, but we're trapped here."

Shay and the others glanced around warily, searching for the source of the disembodied voice.

"It's really me, Shay! I'm speaking to you via an intercom. It's a simple form of the telephones I told you about." Though it wasn't, really, Iona went with what he knew rather than wasting time with long explanations. "You can talk back to me. Go to the monitor screen, and speak into the mesh panel above the red button." At least he knew about computers.

Shay still looked cautious, but complied. "How did you know I was outside?"

"We can see you. Look up to your right. That's a camera; I told you about those, too." Iona saw his upward glance and continued, "Honoria captured me and brought me here, but it's worked in our interests as I've discovered everything we need to know. Can our Lacunae friends get us out?"

Iona saw Shay briefly close his eyes and exhale in relief at the knowledge they really *had* found her. "One can get *you* out. We can't waste our resources on the man who stole your trike. Don't forget, the unusual conditions mean each Lacunae can only do this once. Getting three people into the dungeons instead of two will increase the odds in our favour."

"We *need* Jake, Shay," Iona protested, remembering his disgust with the trikers who had tried to save themselves at the expense of others. "You'll understand why when I tell you what I've learned from him."

Karnax stepped forward. "I can transpose them both together. Carrying two passengers out, instead of one passenger in *and* out, as originally planned, equates to the same thing in terms of the transposition strength required."

Calixo waggled a claw. "Not quite. You must still transpose yourself beyond the wall. Although it takes next to no power without a passenger, that won't be the case this close to the interference."

"I can do it. There's no great distance involved. I must only journey beyond this wall," Karnax insisted.

Iona strained to hear Quintus, farther from the intercom, as he sought reassurance that it wouldn't put her at risk. However, Karnax's confidence won the day, and Shay spoke into the mesh panel. "Get ready; Karnax is coming through now."

"There's a clear space where he can land before the sliding door," Iona replied.

Although Jake had only heard Iona's side of the conversation, she knew he had inferred enough to know he must justify his rescue. She threw down the headset and stood as Karnax popped into existence two feet above the floor near the door. As he settled onto his haunches, Jake removed the headset jack and unplugged the fully charged laptop from the mains.

Karnax, the largest of the four Lacunae, regarded them both. "You," he pointed at Jake, "Climb onto my back but be careful of my wings." The Lacunae lowered himself to the floor, and Jake passed Iona the laptop linked to the cameras. She didn't need to ask him why they must take it. When Jake gingerly settled himself full-length against Karnax's spine, his head between the dragon's shoulder blades, the Lacunae rose to his feet, Jake clinging to his neck. Karnax beckoned to Iona. "Stand before me, facing forward."

Iona obeyed; the laptop clutched against her chest. Jake gripped on with his knees as the dragon reared onto his back legs and, lifting Iona to his breastbone, *jumped*. They materialised beyond the wooden doors, Jake sliding two feet to the floor, before Karnax touched down, settling Iona onto her feet. She staggered forward a couple of paces as Shay rushed to her side. He gathered her into his arms, and she breathed in the scent and feel of *home*.

Karnax sat slumped, his head hanging. "That's me done for today. If that... *thing* can't be stopped and spreads its malignancy farther, the Lacunae are in trouble."

"You must return to the tithe barn, and recover your earth sense away from its pernicious influence," Calixo advised.

Quintus helped a winded Jake to his feet, and the former triker turned to Karnax as the dragon moved to depart. "Thank you for not leaving me behind."

"If you wish to thank me, help these people stop this. Those... *machines* in that room I plucked you from feel... *wrong*."

Jake nodded and stepped aside to let Karnax pass.

"You found my bead trail, then?" Iona asked Dareesh.

"Calixo did; his eyes are sharper than mine." The Zingari leader smiled wryly.

"I feared the worst when we found you gone from the wagon," Shay said, hugging Iona close, the laptop pressing into his stomach.

"Two guards began searching the wagons, and I had to make a run for it."

"Yes, we guessed that when we saw the open gate and tracked your passage through the alley. The blood smears going both ways had us worried, and then we found your dropped knife," Dareesh informed.

Iona described her encounters with the guard and Honoria, whose whereabouts she didn't know, and then asked how the fighters fared.

"We hold the castle, but unfortunately, although the Zingari sustained no casualties, Will lost half a dozen men," Dareesh supplied.

"Oh, no... that's... oh, no. Perhaps we should return to Will in the vestibule. I've news of the kidnapped villagers for him, and much to tell you all before we descend to the dungeons."

"How do you know Will is in the vestibule?" Quintus asked.

Iona held up the laptop. "Through this."

With everyone gathered in the lobby area, Iona passed the laptop to Jake, so he could monitor Peterson while she explained the situation as best she could. She described how Peterson had infiltrated the duke's court in the guise of Lord Randolph Peregrine, and the truth of Vincent and Honoria's identity.

"Peterson is a scientist who studies energy, force, space and time, and all that derives from these. The world of the *Living Aurigan*, on the other side of the menhir portal, is much more advanced than this one, and scientists like Peterson developed devices to examine these natural powers. Peterson built a machine that he used to steal the portal's energy, and trapped it in another machine in the dungeons. You might think it is magic, but it's just an elaborate tool. He borrows the portal's power to send the trikes back and forth between our two worlds. I believe his interference with the portal's natural cycle will soon affect *this* world's reality if it hasn't already exerted its influence. For example, the Lacunae's transposition difficulties."

"Can it be reversed? Is it possible to release the portal's energy from the machine and return it to the menhir?" Shay asked.

Iona looked at Jake, who placed the laptop on a stone bench built into the wall. "Yes, the process can be reversed. What's more, a dozen different computational algorithms all agree that the portal will automatically return to the menhir site if released from its prison, or if the silo is destroyed. Peterson made me run them as part of a risk assessment."

"So, we *can* stop this?" Shay persisted, some of Jake's words mere gobbledegook.

Jake shrugged. "Only if we wrest control from Peterson." He pointed at the laptop's video feed. "Six workers have arrived in the portal room from the manor house, three armed with guns. Your swords will be useless against automatic weapons."

"We'll see about that," Dareesh said darkly, forgetting the Lacunae could only transpose three people behind the metal wall.

"How is Peregrine using our kidnapped people in this devilish scheme?" Will asked.

Iona had dreaded this part. "As you know, people from this world cannot survive for long in the other. Peterson is on a mission to discover why, and if there's anything to be done about it. He uses the captured villagers as test subjects, sending them to his property on the other side via the trikes, where some are held prisoner until they die, whilst others are sent back here to recover their health before he returns them to my world."

"And Clare, my wife? Is she dead?" an ashen-faced Will asked.

"We don't know, but if she's alive, she might be one of those Doctor Cleary is forced to care for in the dungeons," Jake answered.

Will nodded. "Then I must be in the party that enters within."

Jake turned back to the laptop. "There's a camera feed on the floor where the villagers are held. You might see her if she's there."

As Jake diminished the portal room view, he clicked on the great hall feed by mistake. "Uh oh; we may have a problem. Clovis is gone from his throne."

The others crowded around him, and Jake paused the live feed to rewind back through the automatic recording, stopping at the point where the change occurred just ten minutes before. They observed a curtain behind the ducal throne flap as a door behind it opened. Sir Norris burst through with two knights, who quickly released the duke whilst the blackguard fended off the Zingari women with his broadsword. The men hustled Clovis through the door, Sir Norris making broad sweeps of his sword to keep the women at bay, before he, too, backed from the great hall, slamming the door behind him. Dareesh's wife, Linessa, attempted to open the door, but it wouldn't budge.

"Sir Norris obviously locked it. Jake, return to the live feed and pan the camera. We need to see the whole picture," Iona instructed.

Jake complied, and they observed Rena trying to pick the door lock, while other Zingari women worked on the locks of two other doors, including one in the minstrels' gallery. Six women wielded a bench as a battering ram against the main door into the great hall.

"Sir Norris and his men must have sealed all the other doors before they rescued Clovis. The women are trapped with the guests... Oh, shit!" Iona cursed.

She heard someone tsk loudly behind them and whirled to see Duke Clovis and Sir Norris standing in the wrecked doorway, with the two knights in the video.

Chapter 30

"Such unseemly language from our *Living Aurigan*. It appears I should have listened to Madeleine when she warned me you are a duplicitous whore," Duke Clovis drawled and pierced Iona with a hard stare. "So, my rubies weren't enough for you. *You're* the woman who broke into my tower with her outlaw lover to steal my gold."

Shay stepped forward, sword in hand, ready to cleave Clovis in two for insulting Iona, but she placed a hand on his arm. "Don't Shay, he's not worth it. The man's an ass if he can't see how Peregrine tricked him."

Clovis' eyes bulged in outrage, and he took two steps forward, his own sword rising. Something glinted at his crotch as he moved into the light, and Iona almost did a double-take – he really *had* used the diamonds to decorate his codpiece. She exchanged a glance with Jake, who stood on her other side, and despite his fear, his mouth twitched at the absurdity.

The duke frowned and appeared to notice Jake for the first time. "Two *Living Aurigan's*? How... what is this? Have you returned for my gold, too?"

"There *is* no gold. Well, none that your brother-in-law created by alchemy. He's not who you think he is! Randolph Peregrine isn't even his real name, *and* he's no lord! Just a trickster who used you for his own ends. He lurks safely behind his metal wall and has denied you access beyond it. If you don't believe me, try keying your door code. He's changed it and abandoned you to your fate. Come on, wise up! Your dear brother-in-law plots to rule as regent in your stead! He's already despatched Honoria to steal away your children!" Iona declared, her eyes darting around the vestibule. *Where had the Lacunae gone?*

Clovis hesitated as doubt shadowed his eyes, but Sir Norris moved to join him, unblocking Iona's view of the open door to the dungeon staircase, behind which she descried the glint of a scaly hide. *Good, the Lacunae must have hidden before the intruders spotted them*.

"Don't listen to the witch! By planting seeds of mistrust, she seeks to gull you and save the lives of her lover and his thieving cohorts! She's a deceitful bitch, like all women!" Sir Norris urged.

Shay stiffened beside Iona, and she gripped his arm in restraint. The duke frowned. Despite his own insults prompted by her rejection of him, respect for the *Living Aurigan* had become ingrained in Beretanian culture over the years. Still, two *Living Aurigan's* stood before him... that couldn't be right...

Clovis raised his sword higher, and suddenly caught sight of Quintus, whom he hadn't immediately recognised in his unaccustomed garb.

"Q-Quintus? Cousin? Why are you with these people? Does the woman speak true, after all, or has she beguiled you, too?"

Cousin? Iona knew Quintus came from a privileged background, his father a baron, but Clovis' cousin?

"*Third* cousin," Quintus said stiffly, distancing himself from the duke. "The *Living Aurigan* does not lie. My brothers-in-arms stand here as loyal patriots, ready to defend the duchy from those who would harm it, and the false Lord Peregrine is one such."

Although unwilling to believe his cash cow had forsaken him, perhaps the duke construed Quintus' words to mean they would defend *him*, the rightful ruler, against a usurper. Maybe his own suppressed misgivings had risen to the surface – though he'd condoned the kidnappings, he didn't share Sir Norris' sadistic glee at the villagers' fate. Only sheer avariciousness had enabled him to shrug off the disturbing knowledge that his dead wife's brother consorted with demons. For whatever reason, Clovis lowered his sword.

Iona's instincts had marked Sir Norris as the more dangerous of the two, knowing as he did that Clovis' capitulation would spell the end for him and his blackguards. Therefore, she felt no surprise when, observing how Quintus' words had swayed the duke, Sir Norris signalled to his men.

The two knights came to the fore, and Norris pushed Clovis behind him. "Never fear, Sire. We will protect you from the wiles of those who speak with the tongues of serpents."

Confident in his prowess with the broadsword, and not having witnessed the near-preternatural skill of Zingari sword dancers, he launched himself at Shay as his underlings went for Dareesh and Will.

The contest was short.

Dareesh laid out his opponent without breaking a sweat. Shay hamstrung Norris and almost casually near-decapitated Will's would-be adversary on the backswing. He stood aside to let Will finish off Sir Norris, the man who had led the sacking of his village and carried off his wife and neighbours.

A stupefied Clovis stared at Quintus, who sheathed the sword he had not needed to employ. "Norris was Peregrine's man, not yours," Quintus said with a shrug.

Shocked by the sudden violence, Iona averted her eyes as Shay and Dareesh wiped their swords on the fallen knights' surcoats. The moon had risen, rendering the courtyard outside the empty doorframe almost as bright as day. Her eye snagged on a maroon-clad figure who crossed the flagstones towards them, head bowed beneath her wimple, crossed hands buried in her trailing habit sleeves. For a confused moment, Iona figured it must be Bedelia who so openly approached the tower – their victorious fighters wouldn't contest a nun from the order that supported them. However, Bedelia lacked this woman's height. As the nun entered the vestibule, Iona realised her identity even before she raised her head.

Honoria, now sans-breeches, assessed the dead bodies in a single glance and, withdrawing one hand from her habit sleeve, raised her gun and shot Clovis in the head. He collapsed to the floor in a spray of blood and brains, stunning the men who had never seen a gun before, let alone witnessed a weapon with such lethal capabilities, requiring only minimal skill to wield.

"Why?" Iona gasped in shock.

"I hazard you told him too much. He's no longer useful. A regency will be much more convenient for our purposes," Honoria replied dispassionately and targeted Shay with her pistol. "Tell them to put up their weapons, or your dashing hero is next." Honoria side-eyed Iona. "Oh, don't worry, I won't shoot them if they behave. Their... *vitality* will make them better test subjects than those pathetic villagers."

"Do as she says'," Iona pleaded, terrified the madwoman would kill Shay on the spot.

Iona could hardly believe her eyes when a Lacunae suddenly popped into existence, head downward above Honoria. Iona recognised Flix, the lone female, who fell upon the unsuspecting nun, both taloned hands pushing her gun arm down while raking Honoria with her hind claws. A bullet discharged harmlessly into the floor and, engulfed by the Lacunae's wings, Honoria collapsed beneath Flix's weight, the gun spinning from her hand.

Iona darted forward and swept up the pistol, pointing it at Honoria as Flix climbed off her back. She had no experience of guns, having only seen them used on TV, so she'd just have to wing it.

The false nun pressed a hand to her claw-lacerated side and stared venomously at Flix. As the other two dragons emerged from hiding, she muttered to herself, "So, *that's* how they escaped from the control room!"

Honoria rose to her knees, and Iona levelled the gun at her head. "You will key in the code, and scan your iris and fingerprint to unlock the door to the dungeon levels."

"Or else? You'll shoot me? Don't make empty threats you don't have the guts to carry out," Honoria scoffed, and laughed derisively.

"You think? I battered your husband half to death with a library book," Iona replied with a nonchalant shrug.

Honoria's hands curled into claws and a snarl twisted her lips, but her eyes betrayed a new uncertainty. "What did you do to my Vincent?!"

"He's recovering in the infirmary. Come on, we haven't got all night! Get to your feet and do as I ask, otherwise *you'll* no longer be useful to *us*,"

Iona responded harshly, putting all her hatred of this woman into her tone.

Yet Honoria still hesitated, confounded by their reversal of position. Shay sauntered over and, one hand on a relaxed hip, casually rested his sword tip on her shoulder. "Do as she asks', or I'll sever your head from your scrawny neck."

Honoria took one look into his cold eyes and pushed herself off the floor.

"Before we proceed, I must send a party to release the Zingari women trapped in the great hall, and ascertain how Clovis and his knights slipped past the sentries," Dareesh said.

As he turned towards the outer doorway, a breathless messenger appeared in the opening. Dareesh moved to intercept him, and after a brief exchange, the Zingari leader issued instructions and returned to the vestibule. He shook his head. "As far as I can tell, they came via the alley behind the castle that connects to the tower forecourt. The body of a dead sentry attests to that. I'm sorry, Will; he was one of yours."

A thin-lipped Will nodded. "Let's end this now. My people have suffered enough."

Calixo took the lead, and Iona prodded Honoria behind him through the doorway to the dungeon stairs, and down the first flight to the wooden doors before the metal wall. Shay used his stolen key to unlock them, and with everyone gathered before the barrier, Iona pointed to the camera near the ceiling. "Jake, I assume Peterson can access the camera feeds from his lair?"

"Of course, but I'm the only one watching them just now. I'll know if someone else logs onto the system. Let's hope Peterson is too complacent to bother," Jake replied.

Iona nodded. "I'd suggest we take out that camera, except its viewpoint might come in handy later. Shouldn't we find something to keep the door open, so we can get the villagers out quickly?"

"The entrance is designed to jam in the shut position if the control panel is disabled with the door closed. Perhaps if we smash the controls while it's open, it will prevent it from closing?" Jake speculated.

Will unhooked a club from his belt. "Let's find out, shall we?"

Iona jabbed Honoria's spine with the gun muzzle. "Go on, do your stuff. Any tricks will earn you what you deserve."

Honoria eyed her darkly, but keyed in the code. A red light above the sliding door turned yellow, and her index finger hesitated over the recognition pad.

"Do it, or I'll cut off your finger and do it for you," Shay threatened.

The fake nun pressed the pad and put her eye to the scanner. The light flashed green and the door slid open. Dareesh stood in the gap to prevent it from closing again and nodded to Will, who raised his cudgel two-handed and smashed it down on the controls. He kept bashing until the light above the door winked out, the door remaining wedged in its wall groove.

Will backed away, his shoulders slumped, and then straightened, raising his eyes to Jake's. "Show me the room where these devils hold the village folk."

Jake balanced the laptop on the pulverised control board and brought up the feed that monitored the dungeon's second level. The fixed camera looked down upon an aisle, a row of cot beds on each side occupied by people who either lay or sat upon them. A man stood before a door at the far end, his hand resting on a gun butt protruding from a hip holster.

Will groaned in anguish. "I can't see Clare. It's harder to make out those farthest away, but I don't think she's amongst them."

Shay placed a sympathetic hand on Will's shoulder, when a man and woman, their backs to the camera, came into shot from the bottom of the screen.

"That's Doctor Dennis Cleary and the woman Peterson spared to act as a nurse. The camera is above the entrance to an outer room outfitted as a lab, where Dennis also bunks. We can access his room via another door on our side of the dungeons."

"Won't it be locked?" Shay asked.

Jake shrugged. "It never is whenever I pass through. Where could Dennis and the others go? They can't get through the metal wall. However, the door at the end of the ward is always guarded. It leads to the stairs down to the bottom level, where the generators and portal silo are located," Jake explained.

The woman with Doctor Cleary turned side-on to the camera as she entered the space between two cots and bent to help a patient stand.

Will gasped. "That's my Clare!" He jabbed his finger at the nurse. "It's her! Clare's alive!"

Iona squeezed his arm. "I'm so happy for you, Will!" She turned to Flix and asked, "Are you alright to go on?"

The Lacunae fluttered her wings in the dragon equivalent of a shrug. "I didn't transpose far, and without a passenger, too. I can manage one more transposition." She pointed a claw at the guard onscreen. "I can take him out the same way I overcame the false nun."

Iona grinned and Honoria glowered at them both.

Quintus frowned as though he'd just remembered something and, folding his arms, stared at Honoria. "What have you done with the duke's heirs?"

"They're safe," she answered evasively.

"That's not what I asked. Where are they?"

Honoria looked down, shuffling her feet, and Iona poked her with the gun. "Answer him!"

"They're with Blaine in a hidden bolt-hole inside Lord Peregrine's castle apartments," she answered unwillingly.

Dareesh's newly freed wife, Linessa, suddenly appeared on the stairhead with Royston Hamm, Will's second-in-command. "Karnax reported back to Sister Myriax, and she's here with Prior Fidelmus and Brother Florian. They want an update on the situation," Royston called down.

Shay looked at Quintus. "You'd better go and break the news about the duke's murder. Take her with you," he gestured towards Honoria. "She can *show* you where she hid the boys or face the consequences if she tries to mislead you. Fidelmus should take them to the safety of the priory until all this is over."

Quintus appeared torn, and Shay added, "Royston can take your place here."

The ex-monk nodded, his sense of duty towards the innocent children, his fourth cousins, overriding his reluctance. They used Honoria's habit girdle to tie her hands behind her back, and Quintus wound the rope belt's other end around his fist.

Shay beckoned to Royston and Linessa, who descended the stairs. "We know where the kidnapped villagers are held; those still alive, anyway," he said with a cautionary glance at Royston, whose son and brother had both been taken. "We're going in now to get them out, but we'll need support on standby when they come through the door here; they aren't in the best of health." Having seen Clovis' guests on the camera feed, Shay added, "I'd rather not take any fighters off guard duty. However, not all the duke's guests were his allies. Linessa, free Aylard Quillen, the lawyer, and anyone else he can vouch for. Fidelmus knows who he is. Ensure the helpers remain in the vestibule except for yourself. No one must venture beyond the metal wall; they aren't equipped to deal with the dangers that lie behind it. Go now, with Quintus."

Linessa transferred her gaze from Shay to Dareesh, who stepped forward to take her hands in his. "Go on Lin; I'll be fine. I won't do anything stupid." Linessa arched a doubtful eyebrow but didn't protest. She kissed her husband and turned to Honoria, gripping the false nun's arm to hustle her up the stairs. Quintus trailed her, tether in hand.

Before they entered the dungeons, Jake briefed them on the layout changes not visible on the original floor plans. "They are on four levels. We stand on the top floor corridor, with the metal wall dividing us from the larger prison cell area. A door on the left of that room accesses a short stair flight leading to the landing on the next level. The door to Dennis' lab is on the landing's right, with a blank wall to front and left. Access to the ward is through the lab via a door opposite the outer one. A stairwell at the ward's far end leads down to the next level. It bears left to the tech room, Peterson's lair. It's a long room with windows overlooking the lowest level, a cavern-like space below the hillside, where the big machinery is located. A gantry platform abuts the window-side of the tech room, with stairs down to the cavern floor. Access onto the gantry is directly opposite the tech room's outer door."

Shay entered the empty room behind the wall first, with Jake at his heels, laptop open on a split-screen view of the levels below to give warning of danger ahead.

Iona slipped through the door next, gun held at the ready. Flix and Belonyx squeezed in behind her, only just fitting through the gap. Will followed with Royston, who eyed the laptop askance. Though his comrade had assured him the device didn't employ magic, the ex-miller remained dubious. Still, if it helped them retrieve the missing, then he'd accept its aid and be damned. Dareesh brought up the rear with Calixo, who had to turn sideways and crouch down to clear the entry.

They stood in the holding room where Sir Norris and his men had delivered each consignment of kidnapped villagers. Barred lockups lined the walls, and Peterson's fake alchemy lab stood beyond an archway at the far end. Unlike the lower tiers, this floor relied on torchlight for illumination, necessary for Peterson to maintain the fiction he had spun for Duke Clovis and Sir Norris, who had gone no further than this level.

Squinting through the gloom, Iona spotted the door at left which accessed the stairs downward. With no cameras between this room and the ward, they must tread carefully.

Shay opened the door a fraction and put an eye to the gap. "There are just six steps between this door and Cleary's lab, so we haven't far to go. I'll check out his room before the rest of you descend. Wait for my signal." Shay ghosted down the ill-lit steps and carefully cracked open the unlocked door below. Electric light spilled from the aperture, and Shay blinked as he peered through. He opened the door wider to illuminate the steps and beckoned to the others.

With everyone gathered in the empty room, Jake placed the laptop on a lab bench so they could view the ward beyond the closed door.

"Unless Dennis returns to this room, there's no way to warn him about our intentions, and we can't afford to wait until he does. Flix must take out the guard now, and we'll worry about reassuring the captives afterwards," Shay opined in a low voice.

Flix eyed the monitor and remarked, "The guard is still in the same position by the far door. I must say, this contraption is most useful; we didn't need those tower floor plans, after all!"

"Hmph, the floor plans I almost got killed to obtain!" Iona muttered.

"It was Ennis who nearly got killed," Shay corrected with a wry half-smile. "Flix, the guard's gun is in his scabbard. You must prevent him from drawing it at all costs."

"Holster," Iona said.

"Pardon?"

"It's called a holster, not a scabbard."

Shay gave Iona an old-fashioned look, and she held her hands up in mock apology.

Flix glanced at the screen again and abruptly vanished.

The others crowded around the laptop and witnessed Flix's sudden reappearance *on top* of the guard, her clawed hind legs pinning his arms to his sides as she wrapped her forelimbs around his head. Flix beat at the man with her wings and he sank to the floor beneath her onslaught.

It happened so quickly that the people in the cot beds barely had time to react before Shay burst through the door with Will and Royston at his heels. Flix kept the guard pinned until Shay reached them, swerving past a startled Doctor Cleary, who recognised the priory ranger. Flix's right-hand claws, wrapped in a cage around the guard's gun hand, didn't relax until Shay removed the weapon from its holster.

Will cried, "Clare! Clare!" as he ran towards his wife, and she turned from the astonishing spectacle, her eyes round with disbelief.

"Will?" Clare took a hesitant step towards him. "Will! By the wheel, it *is* you!"

As they met in the aisle's centre in a bone-crushing embrace, a hubbub of voices broke out around them, and Will pulled away long enough to gesture for silence. "Please, please, remain calm. We've breached the metal wall and are here to get you out! You must keep the noise down if we're to rescue you without alerting your captors."

Dareesh jogged past the couple towards Shay and dragged a sheet from atop a cot, muttering an apology to its occupant. He tore it into strips, which they used to bind and gag the hapless guard as Royston went from cot to cot, searching for his son and brother.

Iona hurried up the aisle towards Flix, who huddled near the far door, but paused when a lad in his late teens stumbled past calling, "Pa? Pa!"

Royston whirled around, joy transforming his dour face when he beheld the boy. "Euan, my son!" He closed the distance between them and flung his arms around the lad. "Is Martin here with you?"

Euan hung his head. "No, Pa. Uncle Martin died in the other world."

With a lump in her throat, Iona left them to their shared grief, and continued on past Shay and Doctor Cleary, deep in urgent conversation, until she reached her goal. "Are you alright, Flix?"

"I will be. The *taint* on my earth sense is stronger here, nearer the silo."

"You have done enough and must return to the priory. Calixo sent me to fetch you. He didn't want to obstruct the aisle, so he's waiting with Belonyx in Doctor Cleary's room."

The Lacunae rose to her feet and followed Iona. After all they had suffered, the villagers appeared remarkably unfazed by the dragon, who had subdued their despised guard.

The ward evacuation began immediately, with the stronger villagers helping the weaker up the short flight of steps and through the holding room to the metal wall, where Linessa waited with Brother Florian, who had insisted on lending his aid. They formed a chain with Royston and Doctor Cleary to process the column through the jammed door and up the next stair flight to the vestibule, where the helpers whom Linessa had gathered took over. Will and Clare moved up and down the line behind the metal wall to keep it moving, supporting those who required assistance.

Jake rested the laptop on a cot near the locked door down to the bottom level, and Iona, Shay, and Dareesh gathered around him. The monitor, in split-screen mode, showed the area before the metal wall, and the tech room above the collider. Jake brought up a third view that looked down upon the floor beneath the gantry, and Iona noticed six trikes had joined the original two near the generator system.

"I've tried to keep track of Peterson's armed security guards. One is stationed near the trike port, but I don't know where the other two went. They're still around somewhere as the trikes they came in on haven't moved. Of the three unarmed employees, two appear engaged in maintenance work on the machinery, and the third is in the tech room with Peterson," Jake informed.

He shrunk the new image, which overlay the other two, and they observed Peterson, now clad in a lab coat, speaking to his employee. The woman moved to a PC and clicked on a data file, ignoring a pop-up notification. She scrolled through a subroutine, highlighting a series of numbers that she relayed to Peterson, who entered them into an algorithm on a laptop. When the technician finished, she idly tapped on the notification and sat up straight in alarm.

"Damn! The tech has just accessed the security camera network! We must have triggered an alarm when we destroyed the door controls!" Jake exclaimed, thumping the thin cot mattress.

They watched Peterson peering over the woman's shoulder until a sudden movement on the other feed caught their attention. The door in the metal wall emerged from its slot and, with a shudder, began to slide closed. Only Royston's quick thinking prevented it from shutting entirely. Grabbing the edge with both hands, he strained to push it back.

"They've engaged the emergency backup system to control the door remotely from the tech room. It can also override the sensors that prevent it from closing when someone is in the doorway," Jake explained.

With nearly half the villagers still behind the wall, it seemed unlikely Royston could hold the door open long enough to allow them all to exit. It jerked against his hands as, with gritted teeth and corded neck muscles, he shoved back with all his might.

Shay swore, but before he could rush to Royston's aid, Will appeared on the door's other side and lent his weight to Royston's. The blacksmith, strong as an ox, wrenched it backward, and with both men shouldered against it from each side of the wall, Clare chivvied the villagers through the narrowed gap. The prospect of losing their promised freedom galvanised even the weakest amongst them, and Iona prayed the men's strength would bear up until everyone had escaped.

Peterson turned to gaze at the camera behind him and, curling his lip in a smirk for the rescuers who watched, snapped his fingers dramatically at the technician, and the laptop monitor went blank.

Chapter 31

"The bastard has denied me access to the system," Jake fumed.

"Perhaps we should retreat to the camera blind spot and plan our next move," Iona gestured towards Doctor Cleary's lab where the two remaining dragons waited. "Let's hope Peterson doesn't rewind the footage and spot the Lacunae, otherwise we'll lose the element of surprise."

Before they could move, a barrage of bullets hit the locked door behind them, and they ducked as wood chips flew from the reinforced panels. When the hail of gunfire ceased, presumably while the aggressors reloaded their weapons, Shay and Dareesh pushed the cot bed onto its side, and the now useless laptop fell to the floor. Upturning the next cot in the row against it, mattress-to-mattress, they yanked Iona and Jake behind the improvised barrier.

"I guess that answers the question of where the other two guards went. They must have been stationed outside the tech room door; another blind spot," Jake said; clearly terrified, but knowing he had run out of choices – it was do or die.

Shay turned to face the open door of the doctor's lab and signalled the Lacunae to stay back.

Jake spotted the guardsman's confiscated gun, stuck through Shay's belt. "You'd better learn how to use that quickly. I don't think the door will survive the next round."

"Why don't they just use a key like normal people?" Shay replied, peeking over the barrier.

"I imagine it's because they don't know how we penetrated the metal wall. Even armed, as they are, it's risky to burst through the door without knowing what defences your enemies have at their disposal. Peterson is watching the feeds now, remember? He'll have seen the door guard trussed up like a turkey. They'll shoot from a distance until they know the score."

Shay withdrew the gun from his belt and examined it. "Do *you* know how to use one of these?"

Jake shifted uncomfortably, but admitted, "I won the county-wide, under-twenty-one clay pigeon shooting championship in my youth, but it's a lead-shot rifle sport. The only handgun I've used was a video game controller during a brief stint as a wargames developer in the gaming industry."

"I've no idea what you're talking about. Can you use it?"

Jake sighed. "I guess so."

Shay handed him the weapon, and Iona removed Honoria's small pistol from her waistband. "I've never fired a gun, but if that evil bitch can use one... I'll give it a bloody good try, anyway."

Jake glanced at the pistol in her hand, and his eyes widened. "Iona! The safety catch is off! I'm surprised you haven't accidentally killed someone already!"

He showed her how to work the catch, and then asked Shay to make him a sight hole through the cots, close to the floor. "They'll expect us to fire over the top," he explained, so Shay and Dareesh obliged with their belt knives, slicing through the mattresses between the canvas webbing that formed the cot bases. They settled back to wait.

But not for long – the next fusillade burst the door asunder.

The first gunman approached the shattered remains, staying close to the stairwell wall, and spotting the makeshift barricade, aimed his gun at it through the doorway. But Jake, lying full-length on the floor with his eye to the gap, the gun thrust through it in a two-handed grip supported by the webbing, fired twice at the man's legs, scoring a hit on one knee. The guard staggered, dropping his gun, and losing his balance, fell backward down the stairs.

Silence ensued as they waited for the other gunman to appear... and waited some more.

"What are they *doing*?" Iona fretted; a bag of nerves, the gun butt slick in her palm.

Shay scuttled to the side of the doorway in a crouching run and, peering around the smashed frame, ascertained no one occupied the stairwell's upper half. He snatched up the fallen gun and, moving to the turn in the staircase, put his back to the wall and glanced around it. Iona moaned in anxiety when Shay boldly stepped forward and disappeared around the bend. He reappeared in short order, although it felt like ages to Iona, and hurried back to the barricade carrying two guns.

"The stairwell is narrow and, as far as I can determine, the injured guard swept the other man's legs from under him when he hurtled backwards down the stairs. The other man must have been standing at the bend, and when he, too, fell, his gun discharged and hit his colleague in the neck, killing him. The second man died from a broken neck. Not bad, Jake, not bad; two birds with one stone," Shay complimented with irony. "I guess you were worth saving, after all."

Jake wore a bemused expression. "What incredible luck! Even if it *is* bloody farcical."

Shay handed the second gun to Dareesh, saying, "It looks like we both must learn to use these fast."

Dareesh accepted the gun with distaste. "What horribly unsporting weapons these are! Give me a sword any day to fight my opponents in fair combat."

"Peterson doesn't play fair," Shay replied laconically as he crossed to the trussed guard, buried beneath a mound of broken door fragments, and fished in the man's pockets. He found what he searched for and held up a keyring for the others to see. "The tech room door is locked."

Iona turned at the sound of footsteps and saw Will jogging towards them. "I feared the worst after hearing noises like... distant thunderclaps, one after the other. Was it guns?"

"Yes, but any more such noises will come from us," Shay replied, gesturing to their newly acquired weapons. "Did you get everyone out?"

"We did, and I made Clare and Royston go with them. Linessa and other Zingari gathered metal weapons and armour from the guardroom while one of my men helped me hold the door open. They piled them in the doorway to stop it from closing and trapping us behind."

"Good. Any news on the duke's heirs?" Shay asked.

"Yes, I just heard. Quintus and Fidelmus found them safe and well and made Honoria command Blaine to surrender them. Luckily, the man was armed only with a sword. The boys are on their way to the priory with Fidelmus, and Quintus is arranging transports to transfer the worst afflicted villagers to the infirmary, where Brother Florian and Doctor Cleary can treat them properly."

"Excellent. Alright, Will, you must return to the castle and take charge until the situation here is resolved."

"But... don't you need me to see it through with you?"

"There's four of us with guns, plus two Lacunae. I believe there are just five of them, only one of whom is an armed guard. With Clovis' death, it's important that order is restored at the ducal capitol. Go back to your wife, Will. You've been parted from her long enough," Shay said, clasping Will's shoulder.

When Will departed with some reluctance, Shay gazed at the camera above the lab door. "I dare say I ought to practice using this," and he raised his gun.

He aimed at the camera and pulled the trigger, hitting the hard plastic casing. Having gauged the weapon's reaction, he adjusted his grip, grinned evilly into the lens for Peterson's benefit, and scored a direct hit.

As glass tinkled down, Jake turned to Shay. "You're a natural."

Shay shrugged modestly and beckoned to the two Lacunae, who could now fly the length of the ward to preserve their transposition strength without a spying eye to observe them.

The four humans descended to the tech room door, leaving Calixo and Belonyx hidden behind the turn in the stairwell. Iona stepped gingerly over the two dead guards, trying not to look at them too closely. Jake had less compunction, searching their pockets for more bullets.

As he reloaded Shay's gun, Iona asked, "Now we've evened the odds, won't Peterson simply trike back to our world?"

"Not bloody likely! There's no way he'll leave his precious silo open to sabotage!"

Jake, who stood close to the door, handed the gun back to Shay and held his hand out for Dareesh's weapon. The Zingari chieftain unhooked it from his sword belt just as the door slammed into Jake's shoulder, knocking him to the floor, where he lay stunned.

Iona, back pressed against the wall near the open threshold, stared in shock at the empty trike that protruded through the doorway, the green light on its monitor screen signalling activation. However, Shay and Dareesh, who'd reflexively adopted a fighting stance with their guns extended, stared past it as though nothing blocked the entrance. Iona suddenly remembered the cloaking device, which ensured no one could see the trikes when initialised — except those who'd ridden one and connected with the entanglement at a quantum level.

As she opened her mouth to warn them, large capital letters stuttered across the screen, which faced her. *'I'd keep quiet if I were you. Unless you want me to roll the trike forward and detonate the explosive device that sits above the front wheel arch.'*

Iona's eyes flicked to the front frame and, sure enough, a red light blinked atop a black box.

'Step onto the running board, and hold on tight if you value the lives of your lover and friends.'

Iona glanced down at the metal ledge below the nearside pedal, a feature absent from the trike she had ridden. Though she knew she'd regret it, that blinking red light convinced Iona she had no choice, and she stepped up, one hand on the closest handlebar, the other gripping the saddle.

Shay cried, "Iona!" when she moved away from the wall and vanished, concealed by the trike's masking function.

Jake staggered to his feet in time to witness the trike shoot backwards before the door slammed shut.

The trike halted a short distance beyond the door, and Iona felt relieved it had not transported her farther than the tech room, as she had feared. She quickly stepped down, and the white-coated technician strolled towards her, Peterson at her shoulder. The woman thumbed a switch on a hand-held device, extinguishing the red light on the black box.

"The new remote control performed well," the tech remarked, tucking a strand of hair into her neat chignon.

Peterson gave a humourless smile. "In more ways than one. It certainly fooled the *Eterna*."

When the woman hit another switch, the green monitor light winked out, and Iona felt sick as comprehension dawned. "The so-called bomb is merely a device to move a riderless trike remotely?"

"You've got it in one," Peterson drawled and signalled to the third security guard who stood in the open doorway to the metal gantry. The man climbed onto the trike and, with some effort, the tech lifted a curved windscreen off a worktop and passed it to the guard, who slotted it onto a fairing behind the trike's handlebars.

Spotting Iona's puzzled expression, Peterson explained in a prideful tone. "It's a Lexan bullet-proof shield designed for motorbikes, which I adapted for this new trike-type. Anyway, I think it's time we repaired to the gantry." He grabbed Iona's arm and hauled her onto the platform above the collider arrangement.

"With you as a hostage, hopefully, the other three will come quietly. After all, I'd rather not kill them — yet. I can't think of a better way to begin my regency than to make a public example of the villains who murdered my dear brother-in-law. It is a pity about Jake, but I must ensure the executions fit the crimes."

"But Honoria killed the duke!"

"So? As the saying goes, *history is written by the victors*."

"You're mad!"

"Less of that, my dear, otherwise you will share their fate, rather than quietly *move on* to make way for your successor."

Someone outside wrenched the tech room door outward, remaining concealed behind the wooden panels. Iona strained to see through the open gantry entrance, opposite the tech room door, but the short passage before the stairwell appeared empty, and she guessed the men had crouched on either side of the doorway. Was it her imagination, or did she discern a glint of scales near the staircase bend, there and gone? Had the Lacunae peeked around the corner and *seen* the security guard on the trike? Or at least *felt* the trike's presence through their earth sense? Since Peterson hadn't mentioned them, she guessed he'd been too busy to rewind the camera footage, deeming it more urgent to track the intruders in real-time.

The technician fiddled with the hand-held remote, and the trike inched forward. As it moved closer to the door, the security guard raised his long gun, and Iona suddenly recognised it for what it was — an air rifle tipped with a hypodermic needle, such as zoo vets used to tranquilise large animals. Hadn't Peterson said he wanted to capture the men alive?

Peterson continued to grip Iona's arm, preventing her escape, but she heard Jake's shout of warning just as the trike, invisible to Shay and Dareesh, emerged from the doorway. Someone fired, but the shots bounced harmlessly off the windshield, and the guard raised his rifle.

Despite Iona's doubts, she felt no surprise when Belonyx materialised above the trike and dropped onto the guard. The man toppled sideways from the saddle, and the tranquiliser dart whooshed past Shay's ear, burying itself in the dead body of the broken-necked gunman.

The man fought hard but was no match for the pony-sized dragon. However, this close to the silo, the strain on Belonyx's earth sense affected his physical strength, and he tired quickly. Dareesh took over and finished off the guard with a sword thrust to the heart.

Peterson's grip on Iona's arm tightened painfully. His eyes darted this way and that, mind racing to think of a way to retrieve the situation. He barely noticed when the technician brushed past them and fled down the gantry stairs.

Jake hurried to the wide instrument panel that, with all its sliding knobs, resembled a sound engineer's control board. Realising Jake's intent, Peterson dragged Iona back against the gantry railings and, stepping onto the narrow ledge beneath, hoisted her up as Shay shot through the platform door.

"Tell Jake to step away from the controls, or your lover goes over."

Shay didn't hesitate to obey. "Jake, step away from that board now!" he bellowed.

A surprised Jake looked through the window, and observing the situation, stepped back with alacrity and came to the door, where Dareesh joined him.

Iona glanced over her shoulder and wished she hadn't. It was a long drop to the concrete floor.

"Put down your guns, all of you, and pile them beside the gantry door. Your swords, too," Peterson commanded.

Remembering the pistol tucked into her wide Zingari sash belt, Iona surreptitiously inched a hand towards it, convinced Peterson would chuck her over the railing when he'd dealt with the others. After all, he required her to *move on*.

"Gather on the stairhead," he continued when the men had complied.

Iona's hand grasped the gun butt, but the stock caught in the bunched-up sash fabric, and Peterson felt the movement when she extricated it with a tug. He made a grab for the pistol, unbalancing them both, and it went off in Iona's hand, shooting Peterson in the stomach. Blood blossomed on his lab coat, and he toppled backwards, taking Iona with him.

Shay roared and launched himself towards her, but she was already falling, screaming as she went... and landed with an *oof* of expelled breath on a scaly stomach.

Calixo tightened his forelimbs around her and, flapping his wings, glided to the floor, where he set Iona down gently beside the still figure of Peterson; his skull smashed open like an egg.

Shay raced down the gantry stairs and, lifting Iona against him, pressed his face to hers, their tears mingling. "I thought I'd lost you," Shay murmured, and her arms tightened around him.

A hunched-over Calixo stirred behind them and, releasing Iona, Shay turned to the dragon who'd transposed dangerously close to the silo to save Shay's *ves'tacha*.

"Thank you, Calixo. I'll be forever in your debt."

The Lacunae waved a claw as though it was nothing, but his eyes and scales appeared ominously pale.

"Can you fly?"

"That's probably not a good idea. I think I can manage the stairs with some assistance." Noticing Shay's worried frown, he added, "I'll be fine once I gain distance from that… that thing," he gestured towards the silo.

As Shay and Dareesh helped Calixo up the gantry stairs, Iona trailed behind on trembling legs. She glanced back at the trike port, where the technician and the two maintenance engineers had bunched together. They gazed at their employer's body and, as one, turned away and mounted their trikes. This was Iona's chance to escape back to her world. Five trikes stood unoccupied, but she faced forward and mounted the stairs.

Shay sent the two Lacunae back to the priory – hopefully, they would be strong enough to fly when they exited the tower.

Jake stood before the control panel, studying a manual excerpt he had printed out. "Right, I think I know the correct sequence." He flicked a couple of switches and altered the position of four sliding knobs. Hitting a button, Jake stared expectantly through the window, and the others followed his gaze.

A turret-like structure on the silo-top sank into it and, as though it couldn't wait to be freed, an inky blackness immediately issued from the place where it had stood. It spread like a mushroom cloud and hovered near the ceiling. Iona gasped in shock when the silo *atomised*; the particles sucked into the blackness above. The collider arrangement followed in a swirl of molecules.

"The trikes should be next. I had to turn them off remotely before I could begin the release cycle," Jake informed, not tearing his gaze from the awesome spectacle.

"When? When did you turn them off?" Iona asked, with a feeling of foreboding for Peterson's three employees. She glanced over her shoulder at the 'combat' trike, now visible to all.

"As soon as I knew you were safe, I came back here to ready the system."

The trike shuddered and disintegrated, its particles flowing through the open gantry door to be subsumed into the *blackness*. Feeling the control panel vibrate, Jake stepped back and said, "It's time we scarpered. Anything connected to the network is toast."

He snatched up an electric torch and ran to the stairwell door, the others at his heels. Turning around at the last minute, Jake threw the torch to Iona and hurried to the worktop where Peterson's laptop rested. He unplugged it from the mains just before the windows blew out, and all the electrical systems, including the control panel, vaporised; molecules streaming through the shattered windows.

As they reached the ward, the electric lights extinguished with a crackle, plunging them into darkness. "That's the generators gone," Jake explained, hugging the laptop to his chest.

Iona switched on the torch, grateful for Jake's foresight and, leading the others, dashed down the aisle. On gaining the holding room, they discovered the metal wall gone, though weapons and armour littered the floor. Jake seemed unsurprised. "Peterson linked the door to the tech room backup system. Hurry, let's get out of here before the control room above succumbs."

They staggered out into early morning daylight, surprised to find the night had passed, having lost track of time underground. Will ran towards them, his relief they had survived evident on his face. "Calixo gave me an update before he returned to the priory. He advised me to clear the tower vicinity, which I've done. We transferred the defeated defenders, whom we had under guard, to the castle dungeons, for now, to await judgment. Some were only doing their job, but the Janus Spire *specials* all knew where Norris took the villagers. Is... *it* done?"

Shay nodded. "Yes, we hope so –"

A crashing noise resounded behind them, and they turned to witness the control room windows on the tower's top floor shatter outwards.

"Come on!" Jake cried, running towards the stairs leading up to the curtain wall's southwestern corner and the tower equidistant from the Janus Spire at its southeastern end.

Iona exchanged glances with Shay, and they sprinted after him, Dareesh and Will at their heels. She hoped their vantage point would be far enough from the Spire to escape whatever was about to happen.

As they watched from the parapet, a swathe of the hillside below the Spire erupted in an explosion of earth, stones and vegetation, and the black mass shot from the hole forced by its passage, climbing into the sky, where the atomised control room equipment streamed to synthesise with it. The Spire's top floor caved in with a *whump*, and stone dust swirled as the roiling blackness blocked out the sunlight.

Shivering with fear and awe, Iona gasped when the mass shrunk to the size of a beachball and streaked towards the menhir. The blackness *absorbed* into the megalith on impact, vanishing abruptly.

As a deluge of earth and rocks rained down to fill in the hole, something somersaulted through the air to land at Iona's feet. She peered down at the object lying on its side – Peterson's weird executive toy, the centaur with wheels instead of legs.

Chapter 32

Iona stood on the riverbank, staring across the water at the stream of villagers crossing the bridge to reclaim their lost loved ones from the priory infirmary.

It was the day after the portal had returned to its rightful home. Peterson's personal laptop, a backup he had never connected to the network as a precautionary measure, had proven to contain all the scientific data, algorithms and testing software for the micro black hole. Jake had discovered a pen-like device with a hoop at one end, some kind of mini particle detector, slotted into a plastic case attached to the laptop's lid. He had squatted before the menhir, pointing the hoop at the ancient monument, its thin USB cable connected to the laptop feeding information into a diagnostics program. Back in his room at the priory (the guest room next door to Iona's), Jake had sequenced the results, confirming the portal was active. He had then run the data through a computational modelling program to determine how long it would remain open...

Iona sighed, remembering the Madjia had predicted she would face a situation demanding a decision based on her conscience. She'd believed it fulfilled with her part in the trikes' destruction, which had scuppered her chance of returning home. Now, she wasn't so sure; Jake's revelation had changed everything.

She had made her choice but must still tell Shay.

Iona watched two mounted men emerge from the covered bridge onto the far bank, and take the path past the Zingari encampment – Prior Fidelmus and Quintus, on their way to the castle. By some strange twist of fate, circumstances had placed Quintus in line for the regency of Kentauros. Through a combination of deaths, ill health, age (too young or too old), sex (wrong), or ability, Clovis' council of nobles deemed his closer relatives unsuitable for the role, leaving Quintus and his brother, who had stolen Iseult from him, the main contenders. Quintus had no desire for the honour, but with his brother the alternate choice, he might reconsider. Iona shook her head, *what a tangled web*.

She ruminated on the gossip about Lady Madeleine that Binny had shared. As Lord Peregrine's wife and the duke's lover, that same council had advised her to retire to a nunnery. As a God-worshipper rather than a *Great Wheel* adherent, Madeleine was *most* unsuited to *that* kind of anchorite life. Iona *almost* felt sorry for her. Still, her fate seemed preferable to Honoria's. *She* had murdered the duke before witnesses *(what was the term for that, anyway? Duchycide? Dukicide? No, neither sounded right)*. As the killer of a ruler, Honoria would face the death penalty. As for Vincent, *he* hadn't murdered anyone, though not for want of trying. Still, he had seemed strangely relieved the whole thing was over. Fidelmus had still not decided what to do with him, and the weak creature who had allowed his wife and Peterson to control him remained locked in the priory wine cellar.

Iona started from her reverie when arms encircled her from behind. Shay kissed her on the side of her neck, and she snuggled into his embrace.

However, Shay could read her like a book. "What's troubling you, Iona?"

"Jake says the portal is stabilising. He intends to return through it tomorrow."

"Yes, he told me. He hoped Dennis would go with him, but the doctor said no, he wants to live out his life here. When he 'borrowed' Gavin's trike, he only intended to 'nip back' to the primary world for medicines. Furthermore, Dennis told Jake he wanted to join the order."

Iona smiled. "Binny will be pleased."

"So, what's the problem?" Shay asked again.

"There's something I need to do that you won't like. Hell, I don't like it!" Iona said, and felt Shay stiffen.

"You're going back, aren't you?" he said woodenly.

Iona turned to face him. "Not forever! Jake said the modelling algorithm predicts the portal will remain open for two months to reclaim the stolen time and reset the cycle back to how it was before. The particle thingy can detect the portal's fluctuation strength, which is at the expected level for such a timescale. Although, Jake isn't sure if it will re-open afterwards in thirty years' time per the old cycle, or fifty years to compensate for the twenty years— "

"Iona!" Shay interrupted, his eyes closed and his hands held to his temples. "How accurate is this prediction?"

"Ninety-eight percent. That's almost as good as one-hundred, isn't it?" Iona said in a falsely bright tone.

"No," Shay replied, opening his eyes to gaze at her. "Why take the risk if you've chosen to remain here? Look what happened to Dennis when *he* decided to *nip back*."

"That's not the same, and you know it! Shay, I *have* to do this. *This* is the decision I must make based on my conscience that the Madjia spoke of. I *cannot* leave Skye and Dad to forever wonder what became of me when I've got an opportunity to let them know I'm alive and well. Such selfishness wouldn't be *right* or fair to them! I'll go back with Jake and find a way to explain the situation to them and say my goodbyes properly. While I'm there, I'll set my affairs in order – the flat, the business, my bank accounts and so on. That way, I can return here with a clear conscience and a clean slate. Don't you see? If I don't do this, I'll never find closure, and I don't want regrets to cloud our life together."

Though Shay's stance appeared loose, his hips relaxed, he stood with his hands resting on them and stared at the ground, betraying his inner turmoil. Iona remembered their encounter at this spot after her dance lesson with Eliza. He'd asked her if she would seize the chance to go home if given the chance, even if it harmed Fidelmus' plot. She'd found him insufferable, and mentally compared him with a hot cover model on a romance novel, arrogant and aloof, but she hadn't known him then as she did now. Still, though she *hadn't* put her own interests first, as he had once feared, it would injure no one at this point if she slipped home briefly.

Shay looked up at last, and Iona studied his face. He still resembled a hot cover guy, but now, she saw him as *her* romantic hero, that missing part one could only unite with in dreams in strange, fragmented snatches that resembled peering through a glass darkly at a parallel existence. She must be mad to think of leaving him, if only temporarily.

"You're right. Of course you're right," Shay said, stepping towards Iona and enfolding her in his arms. "I would feel the same. You're giving up a lot for me, and I mustn't make it harder for you. I admit the thought briefly crossed my mind that once you returned, you'd realise how much you missed your old life and decide not to come back. But I know that won't happen. We belong together, and you belong in this world, with or without me. I've always known that even when you didn't."

Iona hugged him tight, lost for words.

"Perhaps I could go with—"

"No, Shay," Iona stopped him. "It's much too risky. You may think you'll be okay since it'll just be for a month or so, but you spent six years there, and who knows how much it's already affected you? Your mum came here *because* you were fading. Besides, what if that two percent is significant? You could become stuck there, and I refuse to have your death on my conscience. If *I* get stuck, at least I'll know you're alive and well on the other side."

"Well, I'll be alive…"

"Don't say that! And you'd better stay alive as I *will* come back, even if I have to wait for thirty years!"

"Ninety-eight percent is excellent odds. You'll return in no time," Shay said with false brightness, attempting to reassure them both.

That afternoon, the four Lacunae set the transposition basket down on the riverbank above Saint Aurigan's Grotto near Glassnesse. Shay climbed out with the hamper and canvas sack Binny had packed and then helped Iona to alight.

Mother Wilfrida, Sister Myriax, and Calixo would return to

Glassnesse Abbey later that week, where they planned to openly celebrate their ties now the crisis had passed. The Tritaurium common folk and those amongst the merchant and noble classes who had not supported Clovis, had hailed the dragons as saviours after Will and Royston had disseminated the story of the villagers' ordeal. Hopefully, in the coming weeks, it would spread throughout Kentauros. However, Karnax, Belonyx, and Flix intended to return to Saint Lexis on the morrow after they had delivered the lovers back to the priory.

When the Lacunae vanished, Iona and Shay descended to the river margin and entered the grotto, where they would spend their last night together before Iona returned through the portal with Jake. They had not spent time alone for a week and wanted to make these last hours memorable in a place special to them.

With the blankets spread on the sandy ground and the candles set out for later, they returned to the shore and sat with their backs to a shallow dune, watching cloud reflections scud over the water, and dragonflies dart in and out of the bulrushes.

Iona breathed in the clean air. Out here, away from human habitation, everything seemed fresh and *new*, unspoilt by the ravages of development and the fumes from car exhausts and heavy industry. She knew it wouldn't last, but hopefully, the people of this world would manage it better than hers had when progress finally caught up with them in the distant future.

The late summer sun shone hot overhead, and Shay pulled off his boots and sword belt. "Fancy a swim? The river is slow-moving here and not too deep."

"Go on then," Iona replied, kicking off her footwear.

Shay shrugged off his shirt, and Iona admired his splendid physique, sheened golden in the sunlight.

They never made it into the water, not then anyway, their need for each other was too great. All Iona's senses felt heightened, and the intensity of their love and desire couldn't be denied……

Later, after a dip in the river, they sat back against the dune, draped in the linen towels from the sack, and watched the sun go down, turning the river molten orange.

When they retired to the grotto, Shay lit the candles and Iona investigated the contents of Binny's hamper, setting the food out on the rock seat. Binny had taken to helping out Dara, since Fidelmus had not yet chosen a new guest master to replace Quintus. Iona wondered who it might be, mentally working her way through the brothers.

Iona sipped at her wine, the candlelight glimmering and refracting off the polished abalone amidst the other shells that decorated the grotto named for Shay's ancestor. "It's strange to think I'll be the last *Living Aurigan* now the trike operation is over. Perhaps that will entitle me to live permanently at the priory and become an illuminator!"

"Or you could marry the ranger. That would give you an unalienable right," Shay said lightly.

"Yes, I could do that," she replied in the same tone.

Shay smiled into his wine, and Iona's heart skipped a beat as she studied his profile. She never tired of looking at him.

"Is that what you want? To live at the priory?" he asked.

"Hmm, perhaps at first. We could travel with the Zingari for a while, or rent an elegant Glassnesse villa, and sit on the docks to watch the ships come in."

"Go where the fancy takes us, you mean? Are you already pining for more adventures? There's nothing to stop us from boarding one of those ships. We could visit Truscaromia, Gallegia, or any other country you fancy, though I think you'd miss your friends if we stayed away too long."

"Yes, I think you're right. But so long as we're together, wherever we are will feel like home."

Shay set down his wine and turned to Iona, slipping his hands beneath the linen towel and pulling her onto his lap.

She gazed into his beautiful brown eyes, soft in the candle glow, and his lips met hers in a sensual kiss……

Much later, Iona asked, "So, what are Zingari weddings like?"

"There's a lot of dancing."

"Mm, sounds perfect!"

Shay grinned. "I thought you'd approve!"

Iona draped a blanket over their cooling bodies and laid her head on Shay's shoulder. "There *is* one place I'd love to return to and stay awhile."

"Let me guess; Saint Lexis Priory. Me, too."

Iona smiled into his shoulder. "I wonder if the Leons are still there? If they are, the Lacunae can give them the good news about Clare when they return home tomorrow. Bertrand will be overjoyed."

In the dimming candlelight, Shay murmured, "I love you, Iona."

"I love you, too, Shay; so very much."

The Lacunae returned early the next morning and transposed Iona and Shay to the priory's library courtyard.

Iona embraced them all in farewell. She wouldn't see them again unless she and Shay made that future journey to Saint Lexis they had discussed.

When Calixo transposed back to the barn, and the other three to Saint Lexis, taking the basket with them, Iona entered her cloister room to prepare for her own return home later that day.

She placed the two box files in a sack, having agreed with Shay they belonged in her world with the new menhir portal Watcher – Jake Halstead. Who else could do it? Besides, Hyraxus had copies of everything. Iona added the folder containing the triker testimonies, including hers. She gazed around the room she had come to love. As the last *Living Aurigan*, would it always remain hers?

Washed, and dressed in the leggings, vest, hoodie, and ankle boots she had worn when Jake trapped her in this world, she picked up the sack. As she passed the table near the door, her eye fell on the executive toy. Iona didn't know why she'd kept it, instead of hurling it from the castle battlements. Hesitating, she placed two fingers on the centaur's back and pushed it back and forth on its wheels before she picked it up and placed it in the sack.

Iona and Jake stood before the menhir.

Mother Wilfrida, Fidelmus, and Binny had come to witness their departure, but after Iona had embraced them all, even the abbess, they kept well back across the road. The megalith emitted a subliminal, invisible deterrent force when active, but the trio maintained a distance to avoid attracting attention.

Iona glanced at the hillside above, noting the disturbed, slightly concave area where the black mass had erupted from beneath. Once the vegetation grew back, it would hardly be noticeable. Looking up farther, she discerned workers erecting wooden scaffolding around the Janus Spire. It was a miracle it hadn't collapsed completely.

She turned towards Shay, who waited beside her, and placing the sack on the ground, threw her arms around him. He hugged her fiercely, and murmured into her ear, "I'll camp right here until you return."

"I know it'll be useless to try and dissuade you, but if you're going to do it, at least camp across the road or on the hillside. I don't like the thought of you so close to the portal's influence."

"He'll be alright," Jake said, shamelessly ear-wigging. "The menhir somehow *grounds* the portal and blocks the kind of leakage Peterson's silo emitted."

Shay frowned at Jake, who got the hint and turned his back to grant them privacy.

Cupping Iona's face in his hand, Shay whispered, "Come back to me soon, my ves'tacha," and put all his love into the kiss he gave her.

When she at last picked up her sack, Jake shoved the laptop beneath his right arm and held out his left hand. Iona gripped it in hers and they faced the menhir.

On trembling legs, they stepped forward.

Chapter 33

Still holding hands, Iona and Jake opened their eyes, which they'd instinctively closed when their bodies touched the menhir.

Blinking, they scanned the wooded copse that surrounded the megalith at their backs, and furtively edged to the treeline, keeping an eye out for guards. The downland beyond the copse stretched away on all sides, fenced around with wire mesh, through which they saw yet more rolling hills.

"Blimey, we're miles from anywhere. How are we going to get back to civilisation? I don't have any cash. What about you?" Jake asked.

Iona shook her head. "No, I've none either. According to the files, we're somewhere in Wiltshire." Looking to their left, she shaded her eyes with her hand. "There's a building in the distance. It must be the old Aurelius manor house Borderland purchased with the land; you know, where Peterson held the villagers."

"There don't appear to be any guards manning the fence up this end. I guess we should check out the house; see if we can find a phone. If anyone challenges us, we can say we're hikers who lost our way," Jake suggested.

"I agree. My *dad* lives in Wiltshire, so it makes sense to go straight to him from the house. I'll need your help to explain what happened," Iona replied, pointing to the laptop. "Where do you live, Jake?"

"Clapham in South London."

"That's not too far from my flat! Dad will help us both get home afterwards."

"Okay, good. I need to take a portal reading from this side first," Jake said, holding up the laptop. "Wait here."

Jake returned to the megalith, and Iona gazed at the horizon, already missing Shay. Even so, she felt a knot of excitement in her stomach at the thought of seeing her dad soon. She rehearsed in her mind what she would say to him, but she knew how crazy it sounded.

"I got the reading, but the laptop is almost out of charge," Jake said behind her, almost making her jump.

"You can recharge it at Dad's. Come on, let's go."

Iona and Jake approached the manor house with caution. Though several cars stood in what appeared to be an old stable block courtyard at the side of the house, they saw no sign of life.

Rather than ring the front doorbell, they tried the back door (locked), and then a side door that accessed the house from the car park.

"We're in luck! This one's unlocked," Jake said and pushed it open partway to peer into the short hallway beyond.

Iona and Jake crept inside as noiselessly as possible, and moving through the ground floor, checked rooms at random. In one office, they detected signs of a hasty exit, with papers strewn on the floor and two PC motherboards smashed to pieces, as though to destroy evidence. The place had an air of abandonment, and judging it deserted, Iona and Jake didn't bother checking the upper floors.

Near the house's rear, they came upon a laboratory and a large room containing complex equipment and scientific instruments. Someone had also taken an axe to the PCs in these rooms. The corridor between them led to an annexe, and Iona gasped when she opened the door.

Five trikes stood along the rear wall, with spaces between that showed where other trikes had once stood. Iona inched closer and saw nameplates on the wall above them – *Professor Bhaskar, Doctor Evans, Ward Security, Aurigan 2,* and *Collette Peterson*, the last trike covered in plastic sheeting. She recognised two names above empty spaces – *Professor Randy Peterson*, and *Honoria Kuiper*.

Jake walked along the line, thinking aloud as he tried to work out how many people might have fled the manor house. "Professor Bhaskar, a physicist, sometimes came to the dungeon ops area, but he was mainly based in the house. If his trike is here, I guess he must have scarpered when he realised something had gone wrong. He would have detected the portal's return to the menhir with his equipment. The empty space next to his trike must be the technician's. I guess she got vaporised with her trike. Doctor Evans, struck off for malpractice, had charge of the villagers at this site. We can assume he fled. Two guards handled the dungeon ward security. When one triked in, the other triked out on the same machine. So, I imagine the off-duty fella got away. Let's see, another five empty spaces next, presumably the three guards who perished and the two maintenance engineers."

"Collette Peterson," Iona read out. "Clovis' dead wife. It looks like Peterson mothballed his sister's trike and allowed no one else to use it."

"Seems that way," Jake agreed. "And then we come to an allocated parking space for the missing *Aurigan One. Aurigan Two* is here, though. I assume it means Peterson kept two trikes in reserve for his great con."

Iona, peering into a packing crate, beckoned to Jake. "This must be *Aurigan one,* dismantled and ready to be shipped off to the latest mug."

Jake sighed. "So, at least three people deserted the sinking ship. The other trike owners are all dead, apart from Honoria, who soon will be."

Iona shivered. "This place gives me the creeps. Let's find a phone and get out of here."

"The only phone I've seen is the landline in the site office near the side door."

They returned to the office, and Iona tried the phone. "Shit, it's dead!" She rummaged through the desk drawers to see if she could find some petty cash, with the idea it might be possible to catch a bus somewhere nearby. Spotting a strip of pre-printed labels, she realised they bore the site address. Iona tore one off the bottom and showed it to Jake, who had noticed a metal key cabinet on the wall. "At least we know *exactly* where we are now. I estimate it's roughly twenty miles from here to my dad's house."

Jake opened the cabinet door and peered at the labels on the keys. He snatched a Land Rover key fob from a hook, and turned to Iona, dangling the key in her face. "T'da! This must be for that Defender parked outside. The back of the fob is marked 'estate vehicle'."

"You're suggesting we steal it?"

"Borrow, steal, whatever!" Jake grinned.

Iona returned his grin. The idea of committing car theft would have horrified her once – but not anymore.

They left the way they had come, and stood in the car park, regarding the vehicles that belonged to people who'd never return to claim them.

"The Aston Martin must be Peterson's. Pity I couldn't find a key for that!" Jake only half-joked.

Iona rolled her eyes. "Pinch the most conspicuous car? Yeah, great thinking!"

They unlocked the Defender, pleased to find the petrol tank full. Iona placed the sack on the back seat and climbed behind the wheel, since she had some familiarity with the local roads. Though the four-by-four didn't have a Satnav, they found a road atlas in the passenger door pocket. After plotting a course, Jake held the map open on his knees and Iona pulled out.

As she drove through the wide-open gate in the wire fence, Jake pointed out the smashed security cameras. "Looks like the three deserters wanted to ensure they wouldn't get caught on camera. It's the first thing the police will look at when someone reports Peterson missing."

"I hate the idea there are three people at large who know about the portal. Apart from us, I mean," Iona said.

"Me too. Hopefully, they'll concentrate on distancing themselves from Borderland in anticipation of the hoo-ha that will erupt when Peterson's disappearance is discovered. The portal will have closed by the time it dies down."

"I wonder if any other portals exist in other parts of the world?"

"I should think the chance is slim. A micro black hole that opens and closes *and* is tied to a specific location on *Earth*, rather than in Space, must be near-unique. I say 'near' because of the portal in Scotland that's linked to the same secondary reality. Some exponents of the parallel worlds theory posit that an infinite number of other universes or realities can be reached through black holes; either slightly different versions of our reality or totally disparate and unconnected, depending on which theory you subscribe to. Me? I believe there's room for both types. They speculate that our consciousness might be subliminally tied to versions of ourselves in parallel realities, or can link to other worlds that are *not* versions of ours under the right conditions."

"As opposed to visiting one physically, as we did?"

Jake shrugged. "It would be a bit difficult to visit a world via a black hole located in Outer Space. However, I can't see how one's various versions can link to a *non-parallel* alternate world lacking a clone of oneself *unless* a version has *physically* gone there."

"I see... I think... So, do you believe the secondary world linked to this one is a sort of... dream world made real? After all, its people cannot survive in ours. Maybe we can exist in theirs because they are *our* dreams?"

"That's an interesting theory. You're saying the Secondary's people are real if they stay *there*, but fade to nothing *here* because they're constructed from dreams?"

"I don't *know* what I'm saying... Maybe our collective dreams created the secondary reality, but once established, it took on a life of its own *apart* from us?"

"It certainly bears thinking about."

When Iona pulled into her dad's driveway, she spotted another car parked beside his. "That's Skye and Dave's Skoda!"

"If they're here, it will save you from having to tell the story twice," Jake remarked.

Clutching the sack and laptop, Iona and Jake stood on the doorstep and, taking a deep breath, Iona rang the doorbell. She heard footsteps in the hallway beyond, and Skye opened the door, her expression of shock turning to joy. She flung her arms around Iona, who dropped the sack to return the embrace.

"Where the hell have you been? We've been worried sick and the police are searching for you nationwide!" Skye scolded through her tears.

Iona's dad appeared over Skye's shoulder, his face a picture of relieved happiness. "Let them through, Skye! Don't keep them standing on the doorstep."

As Skye stepped back to admit them, she gave Jake a suspicious glance, as though he might be responsible for Iona's disappearance.

Iona's dad hugged her tight, and her tears wet his old cardigan. Pulling away at last, Iona wiped her eyes on the back of her hand and gestured to the stranger gripping a laptop. "This is Jake Halstead. Borderland Incorporated kidnapped us both."

"Kidnapped! I'd better call the police!" Iona's dad exclaimed, reaching for his mobile.

"No, don't call them, Dad! Things are not that straightforward. You must listen to what we have to tell you." Iona scooped up the sack and removed the laptop USB cable Jake had pinched from the manor house office. "We have something to show you, but we need to recharge this laptop so you can see it."

Iona's dad looked dubious, but he ushered them into the lounge, where Dave had listened from the doorway, staying out of the way to avoid crowding Iona. Dave hugged his sister-in-law and delegated himself to the role of hot drinks maker. Iona's dad set the laptop down beside his own on a table and plugged it into the mains to charge.

When the coffee arrived, Iona closed her eyes to savour the drink unavailable in the Secondary world, at least the parts she knew about. She put down her mug and glanced at her family's expectant faces. "My— *Our* story," she glanced at Jake, who sat beside her on the couch, "will require you to suspend disbelief, at first. All I ask is that you listen until I've finished and you've seen the evidence before you interrupt or make judgments. Can you do that?"

Her dad and Dave agreed at once, but Skye frowned before she nodded with reluctance.

"It all started for us both with that damn exercise machine we trialled for Borderland……"

When Iona finished narrating her tale, Skye knitted her brows in concern. "Are you sure Borderland isn't some kind of cult that brainwashes people into believing crazy and untrue things?"

Iona shook her head tiredly. "I knew you would react this way. Randy Peterson is... *was* a well-known figure in the world of scientific innovation *and* a bigshot businessman. Look him up online if you don't believe me."

"I've heard of him," Iona's dad said. "There was a big to-do when he fenced off the old Aurelius estate and denied access to walkers."

Iona lifted the box files from the sack. "The Aurelius papers I mentioned are all in these. You can read through them later and decide for yourself. Jake will show you the tech stuff relating to the black hole portal." She nodded at Jake, who stood and moved to the table, where he sat down before the two laptops.

Iona's family hovered over Jake's shoulder as he showed and explained the schematics and data. Dave, a science-fiction enthusiast, appeared a little more convinced than the others, but, as Skye suggested, the whole thing could be an elaborate hoax designed to fool the gullible. However, she could offer no reason Peterson would go to such lengths to construct something this complex just to fool others.

Jake closed the data folders and clicked on a video file. "I filmed this earlier today with the laptop's camera."

Iona's jaw dropped when she saw herself surrounded by the Lacunae in the library courtyard, hugging them in farewell, Shay beside her. Taking the angle into account, she realised Jake must have filmed it from the cloister before their rooms. "I didn't know you did this! Bloody hell, Jake! You could have said!"

Jake just grinned, and Iona turned her attention back to the screen, where the Lacunae popped out of existence. Iona heard Skye's indrawn breath at that, but didn't look at her sister. Her gaze remained glued to Shay, her heart beating faster at the unexpected sight of her beloved. As Shay embraced her, Jake zoomed in cheekily, but panned back when Iona smacked him lightly on the shoulder, embarrassed.

"I take it *that's* Shay? He's a bit of all right, I must admit," Skye remarked, and when Dave raised his eyebrows, she added, "I'm just saying!"

"Before you say *this* is a hoax, it isn't. That's me, I was there."

They observed Brother Kian walk past in the background and stop to pet Thomasine, who wound around his legs. Jake dismissed the video and opened another, a view from the castle battlements when the black mass erupted from the hill. The image, grainy in the swirling dust, jittered when Jake tracked the darkness as it coalesced and zoomed down to the menhir. Iona had to admire his quick thinking; recording the scene with the laptop would never have occurred to her.

"I filmed the Secondary world once before when I was still a triker. Someone set fire to the studio where I left the footage for analysis," Jake informed in an ominous tone. "If you still don't believe us, you could take a trip to the megalith and walk in and out of the portal yourselves."

"Not bloody likely!" Skye exclaimed.

Iona's dad sat down at the table's other side and drew a notebook and pen towards him. "I watched the documentary about Gavin Whyte's disappearance. Can you give me a list of the other names, please?"

"Robina Shelton, known as Binny; Jake Halstead, of course, Doctor Dennis Cleary, and Bethany... hang on, I don't know her surname." Iona fished in the sack for the testimony folder and thumbed to Bethany's account. "Lewis," she informed, placing the folder beside her dad's notebook. "But that's just the ones we know about. The operation started twenty years ago."

Iona's dad pulled his laptop across the table and researched all the names. "It appears they all vanished under mysterious circumstances, according to the news reports."

"Do you believe us now?"

"I'm getting there. I'd like to read what's in the boxes and folder. But what are your intentions? An exposé to claim compensation from Peterson's estate?" Iona's dad asked.

"*Great Wheel*, no! The Secondary world must be protected at all costs! That's Jake's job as the new Watcher."

"I thought not, and I understand why you'd do nothing to jeopardise its integrity and the lives of its people. But it's more than that, isn't it? I saw how you looked at that young man, Shay," her dad said shrewdly.

Iona closed her eyes briefly and bit her lip before taking the plunge. "I only came back to say goodbye. Shay's *the one*, and we intend to marry. He'll die if he returns here, so I must go back for good. It *isn't* a sacrifice, except I'll never see you all again, well not for thirty years, anyway. You see, I *belong* there. It's where I *need* to be."

A furore ensued after her announcement, and in the end, their father took Iona and Skye aside, and said bluntly, "Skye, you have a husband and will soon start a family. With your career to boot, you will not always have time for your sister. You cannot deny her a life of her own, a husband of her choosing."

"But I'm not! I'll be happy if she gets a… *normal* boyfriend and wedding bells result!" Skye retorted.

"As much as I'd like that to happen myself… Look, Skye, you cannot force Iona to do something she might always regret. Your mother was *the one*, and I still miss her terribly. I wouldn't wish Iona to go through what I have."

"But she's only known this guy for a little over a month!"

"I knew your mum was *the one* after our first date," their father said, smiling in remembrance. "But Iona, if you're going to exile yourself so finally, you must make damn sure you're doing the right thing. It's not Australia! You won't be able to call or email! What happens if you fall sick? You won't have access to modern medicines or surgery!"

"There's Doctor Cleary, who has trained the infirmarians in modern methods, and Binny, a former chemist… It could be worse. Highly effective natural remedies grow there, unavailable here," Iona thought of the contraceptive leaves, "and there are no pollutants, cars, or guns. In some ways, it's a safer world than ours."

"We don't have sea serpents!" Skye said with unwilling humour.

"Granted. But if you were in my place and Shay was Dave, what would you do?"

Skye opened her mouth to make a sharp comeback and closed it again, looking down at the floor.

"Even taking Shay out of the equation, the Secondary world feels like… *part of me*. I can't explain it. Having said that, if he could come here and *survive*, I wouldn't leave you and Dad."

They finally reached a compromise. Iona promised not to do anything rash. As her father said, she had almost two months to settle back into modern life and discover if she still felt the same when the time drew near to leave. Iona knew it would make no difference, but she gave her word of honour to placate her family.

Iona knew Skye secretly hoped the portal would prove to be an aberration that might not work when she tried to pass back through. However, when she and Dave read through the papers in the box files, Iona witnessed her sister's growing conviction they were authentic.

Their dad called the family liaison officer appointed to them by the police and informed her that Iona had turned up safe and well. He concocted a story, saying Iona had disappeared off-grid on a wellness retreat. Though she had sent him a postcard to let him know, it must have gone astray in the mail. The police knew about Iona's accident, and it didn't take much to convince the officer Iona had gone away for health reasons, never dreaming it would incite a missing person's hunt.

Iona slept that night in her childhood bedroom, with Jake next door in the spare room. After he'd visited his mum and boyfriend, he intended to come back to Wiltshire to monitor the portal until it closed. Iona's dad had invited him to stay at his home for the duration, and they'd decided it might be wise to leave the laptop and files with him until Jake returned.

The next morning, Dave suggested they dump the Borderland car on their way home to London. After she hugged her dad goodbye and said she'd return as soon as she'd sorted out her affairs, she hopped behind the Defender's wheel and followed Dave and Skye's car to a remote spot ten miles from her dad's house. Leaving the vehicle off-road, she jumped into the back of the other car with Jake.

They stopped for coffee at a motorway service station, and Skye bought her sister milk, bread, and other necessities in the mini supermarket.

When they neared Clapham, Iona asked Jake, "Will you tell your mum the truth?"

He shook his head. "No. I'm not planning to return through the portal like you, so there's no point in telling her all this crazy stuff."

"So, what will you say? You've been missing even longer than me."

"Something involving amnesia. I'm still working on it…"

"And Daniel?"

"I don't know, yet. It depends on whether he's still my boyfriend."

They exchanged mobile numbers before Dave pulled up outside Jake's rented flat. When Dave drove off, heading for Iona's place, Skye asked, "Do you trust Jake? After all, he stole your trike."

"Yes. Yes, I do. He's more than made up for that. If not for him, Peterson would have won."

Skye and Dave came in for a cup of tea, but didn't stay long.

When they'd gone, Iona removed the centaur on wheels from the sack and entered her bare, windowless office, where Peterson's employees had installed the trike. Not sure why she did it, she placed the executive toy on the exact spot where the trike had stood and left the room, closing the door behind her. She would never open it again.

In the days that followed, Iona concentrated on tying up loose ends. She transferred the flat into Skye's name – she didn't have the time it would take to sell it. Iona ebayed anything of value and withdrew all her savings. To her surprise, she discovered Skye had deposited ten thousand pounds into her bank account. When she called her sister, Skye said it was only a fraction of the flat's worth, and she would give her a share of the sale proceeds when (if) she returned for a visit in thirty years. A jeweller friend of their dad's helped Iona purchase diamonds and gold nuggets with all the monies – easy to transport, and sell for cash in the Secondary world, where the rate of inflation mirrored mid-mediaeval England. Her 25k investment would be worth one thousand times more beyond the portal – enough for her and Shay to live comfortably.

Iona didn't contact her friends – it would complicate things too much. Skye would find a way to set their minds at rest after she'd gone, although Iona felt guilty for deflecting the responsibility onto her sister. She had nightmares about the portal closing early, and felt relieved when Jake phoned her from Wiltshire two weeks after visiting his mum and Daniel and told her the fluctuations remained stable. It appeared his erstwhile boyfriend had given him up for dead and moved on. Jake didn't seem *that* upset, acknowledging to Iona his experiences had changed him and made him see he needed a partner who would value his true worth. Iona sent him money to buy her a handcart that wouldn't look anachronistic in her adopted world, and set to gathering the stuff she intended to take back with her.

She filled boxes with practical items – non-prescription medicines for the infirmary, tampons, underwear, elastic, and dental products. A strongbox held the gold and diamonds, and another contained objects that would be her and Shay's secret – three Kindles loaded with enough books to last a lifetime (one each plus a spare), three MP3 players likewise filled with music, and eight two-in-one hand crank and solar charging portable power banks to recharge them with. If the devices failed at some point, then so be it. At least Shay would have experienced the music and literature of his mother's world. Iona added USB cables and several sets of headphones to the box before closing the lid, smiling as she wondered if the music might inspire a new sword dance routine.

Iona sat down at her laptop and downloaded schematics she found online for a flushing toilet, picturing Shay's amusement when she showed him the printout. Okay, it may not be one of the great inventions such as Saint Aurigan had introduced, but it had its place. Iona mused on whether she might become famous as the Thomas Crapper of the Secondary world.

Skye took time off work to spend it with Iona and their dad, and they drove to Wiltshire three weeks before the portal's due closure, the car boot crammed with Iona's supplies.

"What did Dad mean when he said you'd soon start a family, Skye?" Iona asked.

"Can't you guess?" Skye replied without taking her eyes from the road.

Tears pricked Iona's eyes. "You're pregnant."

Skye's lip trembled, and looking into the rearview mirror, she pulled into a layby. The weeping sisters embraced with mixed emotions – happiness at the news, and melancholia that Iona wouldn't be there for the birth.

"I'm so happy for you, but sad I'll never know my niece or nephew," Iona said.

"I know, but at least you came back long enough to discover you'll have one."

A week before the portal's due closure, Iona and Skye shopped in Salisbury for baby clothes, their last sisterly act.

They were stuck in traffic on the way back to their dad's when Jake called Iona on her mobile. "I'm at the megalith. You need to get here fast! The fluctuations have become unexpectedly erratic. I think the portal will close earlier than predicted. I called your dad, and he's loaded the handcart onto his Land Rover trailer. He'll meet you with it here. Don't forget to come via the hole I made in the fence up top; the manor house is swarming with police. I guess someone finally reported Peterson's disappearance."

"Shit! Shit! Shit! How long have I got?"

"Hang on, I'm waiting for the new estimate to load. I'll call you back."

Iona brought Skye up to speed and agitatedly drummed her fingers on her knee.

"Did you load everything onto the handcart?" Skye asked.

"Yes, thank the *wheel*! We don't need to return to the house."

Five minutes later, Jake called back. "The calculation is two hours, tops. You should be OK if you hurry!"

Iona ended the call and moaned, "I should have returned through the portal last week, just in case... It'll take more than an hour to get through this traffic!"

"You delayed for the sake of me and Dad. Don't worry, I'll get you there in time!"

Skye wrenched the wheel and made a U-turn to a chorus of angry car horns, and drove through a one-way street to the blares of more. She made a series of turns into side streets until she emerged on a B road heading north.

Iona stared in awe at her sister – a woman who always kept strictly within the law.

They made it to the road parallelling the wire fence in forty minutes, and Skye pulled up beside their dad's car, parked in a layby at the upper end. Jumping out, they ran to the fence and found someone had extended Jake's hole. The sisters presumed their dad had done it to accommodate the handcart, and they followed the tracks of its wheels towards the wooded copse where the megalith stood.

However, they hadn't gone far when they observed a line of police officers heading towards them from the manor house. They beat the ground with sticks, and Iona murmured, "They must be searching for Peterson's body."

She dragged Skye behind a tussocky hummock, and they crouched down to avoid detection. "What are we going to do?" Iona fretted, anguish consuming her at the real possibility she would become trapped on the wrong side of the portal, a world away from Shay.

"Right, this is what *you* will do," Skye said calmly. "Remember Dave's clipboards and high-vis vests we found in the car boot? Well, you must fetch them. Keep low to the ground until you reach the hole; it isn't far. Put one vest on and brandish a clipboard as though you have every right to be here. Bring a vest and clipboard back for me, and we'll walk openly into that tree copse looking official. Hopefully, the police will ignore us, thinking we're part of the investigation."

"Genius!" Iona murmured as Skye handed her the car keys.

She wriggled through the long grass on her stomach until she reached the hole and made a dash for the car. Shrugging on a vest, Iona folded another into its pocket and reached for two clipboards. She spotted a construction safety helmet and plonked it onto her head for added effect before returning to the hole.

The police searchers, still some way off, glanced up as Iona strode purposefully across the grass and stopped at the hummock, where she pretended to scrawl on her clipboard. Losing interest, they looked back at the ground and Iona dropped the other vest and clipboard at Skye's feet. Suitably attired, Skye crawled away, keeping the mound between her and the police, before she stood and walked back towards Iona, where she mimed comparing notes. They walked slowly towards the tree copse, stopping now and then to scrabble in the soil and write nonsense on their clipboards.

When they at last stood beneath the boughs, they couldn't believe they had got away with it. In an agony of fear, Iona sprinted to the megalith, flinging down the clipboard and throwing off the helmet. Jake and her dad glanced up as she skidded into the clearing, followed by Skye.

Iona stripped off the vest and pulled Skye and their dad into a three-way hug. "Take care of each other. I love you both."

Jake, hopping from foot to foot, called, "Hurry, Iona!"

As she broke away, her dad murmured, "We will, and we'll take care of Jake, too."

Iona beamed at him through her tears and turned to hug Jake quickly before she seized hold of the cart handles. She backed towards the megalith, staring at Skye and her dad, wrapped in one another's arms. "I'll see you in thirty years," she declared. Though her dad would be eighty-five then, she would just have to hope…

She took the final two steps, and when her back touched the ancient stone, she closed her eyes and continued walking backwards, pulling the handcart along with her.

Iona's shoulders bumped into something, and opening her eyes, she beheld the menhir and the castle on the hill above. Letting go of the cart handles, she turned around as the person she'd collided with spun to face her. With a joyous smile, he swept her into his arms.

"Shay!"

Epilogue

In a Mirror Reality

Skye let herself into Iona's flat and stooped to pick up the mail from the doormat, popping it into her bag to sort through later. She wondered if she'd have time to flick a duster around before she drove to the hospital.

She opened the door of Iona's windowless office to air it out and flicked on the light switch. Gazing around at the stacks of cardboard boxes on the desk and floor, Skye's shoulders slumped in despair. Her sister had not even had time to unpack her stuff before she'd collapsed in the hallway of the new flat that she'd only lived in for one day.

The doctors said she'd suffered a ruptured aneurysm, almost certainly connected to the freak accident that befell her a year ago, some kind of delayed reaction.

Skye sighed and decided to go straight to the hospital. About to switch off the light, her eye fell on something in the floor's centre. She walked towards it and recoiled in distaste. It appeared to be a freakish toy, a centaur with wheels instead of legs. Skye had never seen it before and wondered where on earth it came from. It hadn't been here when she visited the flat last week. Had Dave left it as some kind of joke? No, he'd never be so insensitive at a time like this. Skye picked it up and stuck it in an empty box.

Sitting by Iona's hospital bed in the ICU an hour later, Skye stared at her sister's comatose face and reached for her unresponsive hand. *Where have you gone, Iona? Is it some place one can only visit in dreams?*

Skye suddenly remembered the documentary she had watched with Dave, who enjoyed all that science stuff. *What was it now? Quantum Theory?* She had struggled to understand most of it, but one thing stuck in her memory. The boffin had talked about multiple, parallel worlds where the same event in all might lead to different outcomes in each. He'd even theorised that in exceptional circumstances, one's consciousness could connect to their selves in another reality. Perhaps in a parallel world, Iona had avoided the head injury when she had the accident. It comforted Skye to think she had entered a different state of consciousness that allowed her brain to hook up with a healthy, happy version of herself who would live, even if this one died……

She shook her head at her own foolishness and froze when she saw Iona smile. Skye shot to her feet, but before she could react further, Iona called out, "Shay!" in an impossibly strong voice for someone who'd been in a coma for two months.

To the sound of strident beeping and flashing lights, the heart monitor flatlined.

Other books by Helen Huber

A Town Called Epiphany Book 1: Wild Cass Devlin
A Town Called Epiphany Book 2: Havoc and Daiyu

Printed in Great Britain
by Amazon